THE VIOLENT FAE

AN ORDSHAW NOVEL

PHIL WILLIAMS

MMXIX

ISBN-13: 978-0-9931808-9-7

Cover design by P. Williams

Published by Rumian Publishing

Visit **www.phil-williams.co.uk** online for more information and
regular news regarding the writing of Phil Williams.
Join the newsletter to be the first to hear about new projects.

PART 1

1

Letty had a simple plan.

When the physician returned to take her vitals, she'd jam the plastic fork in his eye. Well, *near* the eye, close enough for him to hand over the keys and whatever information she needed. The guard, a young one-eyed guy with a half-melted face, would get it, too. She'd recovered enough energy now. Her chest barely hurt, she was breathing freely. All good, considering the last thing she remembered was getting shot in the chest. There was a bruise, but no bullet hole, no scar.

Her captors had healed her, but it didn't excuse them locking her up in a whitewashed room with no windows and an adjustable bed as comfortable as a pivoting plank. She was going to break their jaws and get out. Then she'd tear through Ordshaw following Lightgate's blood trail. That lunatic Fae needed her face smacked into the ground before she hurt anyone else. And to get her back for that gunshot in the chest. And just because she was a lunatic.

With that done, Letty would break into the Ministry of Environmental Energy's offices and take the Dispenser by force – fuck it – and finally lead her people back underground.

She'd do it all, the second she got her hands on that plastic fork.

The lock clicked and Letty clutched the side of the bed, ready to pounce. But the Fae who strolled in behind the one-eyed guard was someone new: a beanpole in a three-piece suit, slim with little round glasses perched on his nose, holding a big plastic disk. He was young, with the aura of a lofty accountant, and spoke in an educated tone: "Letty, good to see you awake." She'd heard that voice while wrestling through drugged-up sleep. And – yeah – she'd met him, in Broadplain, around the time she realised Lightgate was preparing to screw everyone. "You remember me? Edwing. The Chair of Information for the Fae Transitional City. This is my brother, Flynt. I want you to know you're not a prisoner."

So the one-eyed guard was this beanpole's brother. Slim but ripped with muscle under a tight t-shirt and jeans, Flynt stood at Edwing's shoulder, a revolver holstered low at his hip. His dark hair needed combing, and while an elegant black patch covered one eye, he could've done with covering the rest of that burnt half of his face. Words catching in her dry throat, Letty growled, "A locked fucking door is a prison."

Flynt grinned, showing a damned gold tooth. That smile disappointed Edwing. "You can go, Flynt. We're sending the wrong message."

"All the same, *Edwing*," Flynt said, "I might talk her language better than you."

Still, Edwing indicated the door. "I'll shout if I need you."

Flynt took his time leaving and the suit paced further into the room. Past the room's one decorative feature, a mounted flat-screen. "Sorry there's no view, but –"

"I can improve it," Letty said. "Once I ram your head through that TV."

Edwing faced her dead on. Either too arrogant or too ignorant to be afraid. He held up his big plastic disk and turned it around: a concave, elliptical device with three concentric rings on its curved side, the outer two translucent like tube lighting. "Do you know what this is?"

"Robotic human diaphragm?"

"It's a Clear Glider," Edwing said. "Released this spring. Almost silent, mimics a second wing so well you wouldn't notice the substitution. The system of Svenkin propulsion, I'm told, is the closest we're likely to get to an anti-gravity engine."

Letty had no idea what *Svenkin propulsion* was, but got the point: this thing could replace her severed wing. The ability to fly properly would greatly improve her chances of escape. "What do you want for it?"

"Nothing you don't want yourself," Edwing said, resting the Clear Glider on the foot of the bed. "You remember what you went through? You were unconscious for some time."

"Sure. Lightgate shot me when I tried to stop her killing humans. How'd that go?"

"Not well," Edwing replied. "You, however, were lucky. The strap of your artificial wing stopped the bullet. It left you with a cracked rib and concussion from a nasty fall, but nothing a course of medicinal dust couldn't take care of. You'll soon be fighting fit."

"I'm never not fighting fit," Letty said, stirring. "I could be flopping about on bloody stump legs and still be fighting fit. And you know that, with your 'not a prisoner' bullshit."

Edwing didn't blink. "You're tough, Letty, but it's dangerous outside these walls. Half the Fae call you a hero, the other half a liability. Both hold you culpable."

Letty snorted. "And Lightgate?"

"No one admits to having seen her. I'm afraid you have all the attention. Hence, this room."

"Hence, you're a dick." Letty adopted his stuffy tone. "Tell me you know where she is, at least? Tell me I gave *her* more than a fucking bruise."

Edwing shook his head. "Fortunately, Flynt found you before anyone else did, but she was long gone. Well enough to escape, it seems."

"She's never been well in her batshit life."

"Nevertheless, Governor Valoria's Stabilisers are scouring Ordshaw for *you*."

"Let the fuckers come!" Letty spat aside, a globule of saliva hitting the wall. Edwing stared with more curiosity than distaste. Not taking her seriously. They both knew the significance of the Stabiliser threat. Val's elite soldiers, Fae who hunted other Fae.

"We're at a crossroads," Edwing said. "Valoria is still telling everyone that your human friends are a serious threat to our community – that they're on the brink of invading us, even. She plans to cut the FTC off from the humans entirely. Her people are tracking down other Ordshaw Fae exiles to limit potential leaks."

Letty gave him a level look. "So give me that wing and I'll take her down."

"You don't understand. The FTC is locked down. You are *not* a prisoner, but –"

"I understand well enough."

Bracing one hand against the bed, Letty launched up with an

outstretched kick to Edwing's chest, a glancing blow but enough to send him stumbling. She swept the Clear Glider off the bed and rolled to the floor, down into a crouch, ready when Flynt rushed in with his gun drawn. He was looking Edwing's way as she charged. She drove her shoulder into his gut and burst past into a short corridor, hatches to other levels in the floor and ceiling, another door at the end of the hall – an exit. Running, she rolled the Clear Glider over in her hands, searching for a way to attach it – the back had a couple of pipe holes. Was this some kind of fucking joke?

Not stopping to figure it out, Letty slammed through the door onto a tight metal platform, a balcony with no railing, four Fae storeys up. She skidded to the edge, catching her balance before falling. There was hard concrete below, a metre or more down. Too far to jump. Breathing into her wounds, she realised fresh pain was already spreading across her torso. She spun and saw rungs beside the balcony, sunk into the wall like staples. The most rudimentary Fae fire escape. Opposite this building was another, about a foot away, made up of stacked metal containers, each the size of a human shoebox, welded together from scrap. Beyond that was empty space, the vast floor of a human warehouse with a wall far away. Hell. It was the edge of the Fae Transitional City itself. The place she'd been driven out of so many years ago. And there was a lot of open ground to cover, on foot, if she was to leave again.

"Letty," Edwing said behind her, urgent, "come back!"

"Piss off." Letty held up the Clear Glider like it would protect her. Flynt was next to Edwing, his pistol down at his side, looking more worried than threatening. These whelps weren't stopping her.

Dropping the useless artificial wing, Letty jumped onto the ladder rungs and started down. She descended a storey before the pain in her chest made her pause.

"Letty!" Edwing hissed, leaning over the balcony, fearfully quiet. "It's not safe!" Flynt was scanning the sky above. Between them and the distant ceiling was a whole lot of nothing.

"Movement," a metallic voice called from somewhere unseen, and a glare appeared, high up. Someone with a searchlight. Letty checked the next balcony, a short distance below. She jumped as the light swung from the opposite block towards her. The voice returned, through a loudhailer: "Peripheral citizens are *not* to move beyond the city limits."

"We got a right to be here!" Flynt called up as Letty darted into a doorway. Just in time; the searchlight scanned the balcony, its source getting closer. Bracing herself against the door, Letty found the handle and rolled inside.

"Scout Chief Flynt?" the metallic voice continued.

Letty scrambled into an unlit corridor, kicking the door closed behind her. A light came on, and Edwing appeared halfway down the hall, pulling shut a ceiling hatch behind him. Trapdoors – the Fae answer to stairs.

"The hell is –" Letty started, but Edwing put an anxious finger on his lips for quiet, floating to the floor. Above them, Flynt was talking to someone, a man.

"They want you, Letty," Edwing whispered, "for the same reason we do. You have friends amongst the humans. Ones outside the Ministry. The difference is, *we* want to nurture that."

He said it almost pleadingly. Talking about Pax, wasn't he? The one human Letty could rely on. Hell, the only *person* she'd been able to rely on. Pax risked her neck to get the Dispenser back from the Ministry's Greek Street office, before everything went to shit. Then what? Stopped the Ministry from decimating the FTC after Lightgate unleashed a monster on them, surely. Pax was the only person remotely capable of convincing the Ministry goons to give the Fae a break. But where would she be now? If not wanted by the human government, then another target for the Fae?

Letty gave the exit another look. She'd need that artificial wing, and more of what this clearly harmless suit was offering. *Perhaps* her escape plan had been rash. She turned back to Edwing.

"You got a phone?"

2

Pax held a pair of queens.

The best cards she'd had in an hour. Half a day into the World Poker Tour, she was barely hanging on. The biggest game in town – maybe the biggest in Europe right now – and a win could cover her bills for five years. Could build a career to replace hustling for pennies. Except tournaments required the sort of luck you couldn't wait for, and she'd barely picked up a decent hand all morning.

The kid in early position mumbled a big raise, turtling inside his grey hood; an internet player who would push with nothing, just what she needed. Except Dutch McRory followed, in middle position. "I'll raise." He barely looked up, as casual as ordering an espresso. He scanned his own stack, the pot in the middle, the young guy's stack, running the calculations. "Six thousand."

He'd tripled the kid's bet and created a pot half the size of Pax's modest stack. A roller-coaster drop: if she wanted in, she had to bet everything. And one of these two would certainly see her. McRory was a legendary poker author and three times World Series bracelet winner. Re-raising in middle position, against an early opener, he *had* something. Almost certainly a pocket pair, aces or kings, ace-king at worst. Or did he just have the gall to move against an overeager youngster? With four people still to act? Unlikely.

The action folded to Pax and she gave her queens another look. The third-best starting hand in Texas Hold'em. Against two guys claiming something big, third-best was dubious. Lose now, with a month's rent spare, and she was back to grinding local clubs. Brushing shoulders with men she now knew to be bloody criminals, who she'd rather never see again. Bees, Jones, Monroe – all men who knew *she* knew they were bloody criminals.

She needed these queens to be good. Go All In, triple up against two weaker pocket pairs or an ace that didn't hit? Or lose and put herself firmly in the gutter? Her instincts said walk away. Survive for later. Or was that just fear? Another way to lose, folding away to nothing . . .

In the background, the central hall of Featherback Casino was loud with spectators and table shuffling. The World Poker Tour's first Ordshaw outing had swelled with the city's recent troubles: poker players were nothing if not thrill-seekers, and the crowd was eager to explore dangerous Ordshaw for mutant alligators, since the news had reported subterranean tremors and sewer monsters attacking offices. The reports were a long way from the reality: those monsters and crumbling buildings were connected to forces no one understood. In case she unwittingly revealed she knew that, Pax had been studiously avoiding TV cameras and loudmouths who hounded her on realising she lived here. She was trying to focus, at least for a minute, on improving her life.

As the minute dragged longer, McRory gave her a gentle look. This man had taught her so much through his books, and they had never spoken. Now he was reading her, this daft woman in loose jeans and a tatty hooded sweatshirt, better suited to loitering on street corners than challenging poker millionaires. And she saw, in his expressionless face, that to go All In with the queens would be desperate.

"I want it too much," Pax said, and slid her cards to the dealer.

Two more folds and it went back to the kid, who immediately announced All In himself. McRory called without excitement and the kid flipped over ace-king like he'd already won. McRory showed aces. Bullets that would've cut Pax down. The dealer drew the community cards: a king on the flop, so the kid would've beaten Pax, too. Instead, he mumbled ungracious defeat and stalked away. McRory offered a sad look, this ruddy white-haired American who'd seen off countless hopefuls. He asked Pax, "Queens? Jacks?"

"Queens," Pax admitted. A rake-thin player in a loose red shirt laughed. It was the table's other celebrity, Yannick "YnkSpotX30". An online millionaire who hadn't met a single person's eye since he sat down, and didn't now.

"Thought you were off with the fairies," Yannick joked in a Scandinavian accent, massive Adam's apple bobbing. Pax blanched at the expression. By pure chance, he'd broached the exact subject she was avoiding thinking about.

Part of her *wanted* to lose, to be away with the fairies. Her Fae friend Letty was out there unaccounted for. Sam Ward from the

Ministry of Environmental Energy had failed to make any inroads with the Fae Transitional City; no one knew what the Fae were planning behind their closed doors, nor if they had any idea themselves what had become of Letty. Last located at the scene of a massacre, no doubt caused by Lightgate. No doubt something Letty tried to stop.

What the fuck was Pax doing? Mulling over cards while her friend might be dead –

Yannick continued, "Champion material, she is. Representing for you, girls."

Pax frowned, drawn back into the room. Yannick was addressing his fans, who offered appreciative hoots. The group gathered at the rail comprised spotty, bespectacled guys and glamorous blonds, none much older than twenty. Except one. Catching her eye, Pax half-rose from her seat.

Holly Barton, penned in by younger women, smartly presented with her short bob of hair and ironed blouse, didn't share the mood. She waved with an awkward *not-sure-what-I'm-doing-here* smile. Pax's heart skipped – did Holly bear bad news: another kidnapping, a Fae attack, something worse? She excused herself from the table and pulled Holly aside. "What are you doing here?"

"Joining the zeitgeist, apparently," Holly said, jostling to get free from Yannick's fans. "How long has poker been a spectator sport? I have no idea what everyone's watching – were they impressed that you *lost* a hand?"

Pax almost smirked, but the ill-feeling remained. "Holly, is something up?"

"What? Oh." Holly threw a look back towards the main entrance, the gilded double doors barely visible through the bustle. "Grace wanted to come, but I called and they wouldn't let a teenager in. I told her we'd only be distracting you –"

"Why would Grace want to come?" Pax guided Holly away from the crowds.

"For support, of course," Holly said. "Though Grace shouldn't be walking anyway. Which Diz isn't helping with, jaunting about like his ankle was never broken. Thank you, miracle glowing liquid. And where are *your* family, your friends?"

"The guys I play with would find this game too rich or too public." Thankfully. "But you're not *really* here to cheer me on, are you?" Pax could buy it from Holly's daughter, or the wayward young vagrant Rufaizu, who the Barton family had temporarily taken charge of, but Holly was no cheerleader.

"Well," Holly said, cagily, "you've not answered our calls."

Pax offered a guilty smile; Holly didn't sound entirely serious. In the two days since they'd all escaped the threat of gun-toting fairies, no one could blame Pax for being a little on the quiet side. She had imagined the Bartons, like her, had mostly been sleeping and talking evasively with Ministry agents. Only, where Pax had swindled a ticket to this tournament, they'd had the responsibility of house-training Rufaizu.

"Seeing you here, I'm guessing you're convinced we're safe," Holly continued. "You're not suffering from" – she waved a hand to indicate Pax's body – "you know?"

"Period pains?"

Holly's face shifted incredulously. "What – why would –"

"No." Pax moved closer, lowering her voice. "I've not been suffering from any weird side effects. And we've been out, Sam and me, checking some old locations where Darren saw the blue screens. I didn't feel anything."

Holly's expression was sceptical. The Bartons, like Sam Ward, wanted to believe Ordshaw's Sunken City had given Pax some kind of superpowers. Rufaizu called it the Bright Veins, the universal life energy that Pax had seen glowing under her skin. She *had* felt the force of the blue screens, the two-dimensional creatures responsible for the monsters – responsible for everything – when they manipulated energy. But not since she'd killed the grugulochs, their totem. Her brief trip to underpasses and grim alleys with Sam Ward had confirmed the screens had gone into hiding.

"But the Ministry don't know –" Holly started, conspiratorially.

"They don't know *anything*," Pax said. "Only Sam knows. I'm not giving the Ministry an excuse to dissect me. Being accountable to you guys is scary enough." A cheer rose behind them, distracting Pax. Her chips would be dwindling. Good cards might be passing by. "Holly. What's really bothering you?"

Holly cleared her throat. "Actually, you'll be happy to hear it, I think. We've every intention of lifting some responsibility from your shoulders. Diz and Rufaizu have been getting ideas, about making up for the work they did under the blue screens' trickery. They want a second chance. Down in the tunnels."

"You . . ." Pax trailed off, stunned. And Holly wasn't scathingly brushing the idea aside? She had come for Pax's blessing. "You're not serious?"

"It's not ideal," Holly said, "but we discussed it, at length. And I had a rudimentary chat with Sam. We're all in this now, aren't we? It's our city we're talking about. We can't turn the volume up on the *Bake Off* and pretend it's not happening. My husband coped down there drunk, I expect he can do it sober. With help. You've shown everyone how important a fresh perspective is."

Pax was quiet. Of course, Sam had pestered her about going back underground, so why wouldn't she ask the Bartons, too? "I just wanted to get out alive. Holly –"

"Between you and Sam, we can get some licences to roam or something. I don't see it being a problem. I wanted to see where you stood, though. From here, you look ready to move on."

Pax shook her head. "It's not that, I needed to –"

"That wasn't a judgement. It means it can't be all that bad. Otherwise you'd have felt something, wouldn't you?"

Pax gave her a worried look. Thankful, if she was honest. If the Bartons helped the MEE, she might not have to. If she let these hapless fools risk their lives instead of her . . .

Holly's phone vibrated in a pocket, which she gave an annoyed frown. She frowned deeper as she checked the screen. "Unknown number – could be work. I called in sick."

"Go ahead, I oughta get back, anyway." Pax hurried out a conclusion: "And thanks for coming, Holly – if you think going back down there's a good idea, then, sure. Rather you than me."

Holly nodded and went to answer as Pax turned. The caller spoke so sharply it made her stop: "No time for your shit, Holly, pass me to Pax."

"Excuse me –"

The little, familiar voice gave Pax a light thrill, and when Letty insisted, "Now! Now!" she was ready with her hand out to take the phone.

"You're alive! Where are you?" Pax asked.

"With some fucking nerd. Well, maybe not a *fucking* nerd. We've only got a minute – where are *you*?"

"What? Why only a minute? They said you were at the FTC."

"I still am. Have you seen Lightgate?"

"No – I – I'm in the WPT, but we –"

"Playing *poker*? No, that's good – might convince the Fae you're done. At least as far as the Ministry's concerned. Look, the FTC is on lockdown and I can't leave. They're saying our people are hunting Fae expats to keep things quiet, some serious isolationist shit going on, scared of human corruption."

"What? But the Ministry are trying to reach out to your people – no one's talking."

A pause from Letty. "That's our governor fucking around. But there's Fae who disagree with her. This egghead who I'm with wants to talk –"

"Ten seconds!" another voice said, somewhere behind Letty.

"Fuck." She rushed out the rest. "This egghead thinks we can start talks, but we'll need to figure out how. I'll call back, okay? Keep your head down. Crush that game."

"Letty, if you're –" Pax started, but the call cut off. She found herself breathless with excitement just from hearing the fairy's voice. Alive. But trapped? With Fae everywhere in danger? Didn't matter, she was *alive*.

Holly took the phone back, regarding it like it was soiled. "Why was she calling on *my* phone? How did she get my number?"

"They do that," Pax said, unable to stop smiling. "Guess she wanted to avoid direct contact? Or didn't know I got a new phone – who cares – this is amazing – she's okay. And she has help." Pax checked the room around them. "She knew we were together."

"Indeed," Holly said, looking violated.

"I'm sorry. That was – Christ. I'm doubly happy you came now."

"I'm happy for you, too," Holly murmured, uncertainly. "A little surprising, that's all. The Ministry insisted we were clear of the Fae, they gave us devices to alert us of them. They *said* we were safe."

Pax didn't answer that. The Ministry was anything but infallible. She turned on the spot, taking in the casino anew. Invigorated where before she'd been distracted. Her friend was alive and she would hear from her again soon, *surely*. In the meantime, yeah – she needed to crush this tournament.

3

Sam Ward crept down a spiral stairwell with her Maglite held high, creating little splashes with each step. What liquid collected down here? Did she want to know? At the bottom of the stairs – fifty or a hundred feet below ground? – her torchlight barely penetrated the gloom. No side doors, only a long walk. She resisted the urge to look back. Something might appear if she turned. And her breath was too loud, she hated it.

He'll meet you at the end of the hall. That's what the email said.

London hadn't bothered to mention the hall was a terrifying gauntlet of the imagination. Punishment or a test? Sam Ward, desk jockey – if she's scared down here, how can she manage the Ordshaw Ministry of Environmental Energy?

Sam swallowed. Absolutely she could. In the two days since Deputy Director Mathers' (brutal) death, she'd whipped her staff into a storm of efficiency. You wouldn't know the Ministry's staff numbers had been cut by almost half. Or that their ruling body, the Raleigh Commission, was inert, under investigation for corruption. And Sam had got Pax on board, a woman worth half a dozen, even if they had only taken baby steps towards exploring the Sunken City together.

The light caught the tunnel's end: a riveted door suitable for detaining psychopaths. *The end of the hall* clearly meant *in whatever death-den lay beyond.* The door shrieked open onto a glare of light. It revealed a broad space with brick walls and pillars, with a vaulted ceiling divided by rib-like supports. There was another door in the far wall, and smaller ones to one side. Fluorescent lights buzzed overhead, and at the centre sat a single desk. He was sitting there.

Sam cleared her throat as she approached. He didn't look up, stooped over a mobile phone. "Hello? I'm Sam Ward, Acting Deputy Director."

The phone looked tiny in his hands. The man was built like a golem, square all over and far too big for the desk and chair. He finished typing as Sam considered making a leading statement. *They sent you from London* was ridiculous – as if there was any other possibility.

The man placed the phone aside and sat back. His eyes ran over her, feet to head, his wide mouth open in an expression somewhere between disgust and confusion. His hair was slicked back from an already high hairline, accentuating the size and squareness of his forehead, and his deeply unfashionable wire-frame aviator spectacles added to the overall effect of a human brick. Finally he said, "No."

He kept staring, mouth open – his default expression?

"Excuse me?" Sam said, when it seemed he wasn't going to continue.

"No," he repeated. A low Yorkshire accent. "You are no longer the acting deputy director. I am."

Sam tensed. She'd hoped the choice of location indicated something that needed her attention, not a usurper.

"Wayne Obrington," he said. "Special Agent to them in London. *Your* new chief." He stood and Sam took an involuntary step back. Obrington looked like the worst kind of bouncer; one whose awful glasses invited challengers. Here to obliterate Sam's sensible plans in favour of Management boondoggling. He turned to face the door at the rear. "Come with me."

He marched to the door, opened it and stepped through.

As introductions went, it was an odd one.

Sam hesitantly followed. The dull, off-green glow of old lights revealed another long corridor with an arched ceiling and sweating brickwork. Older and danker than the Sunken City Sam knew.

"It's not the Sunken City," Obrington said, reading her thoughts as he kept walking ahead. "Old post-sorting station, built by a tea shipping company in the 1890s. Been vacant about thirty years. Up to here, anyway." He indicated another door, heavy wood. "*That* is a Sunken City entry point, and it's been making strange noises."

He heaved it open, with effort, and Sam looked around him onto another spiral staircase. They were on the north-west side of the city, while according to the MEE's latest readings the horde of monsters was far south; it should be safe, but the darkness looked decidedly uninviting.

"I was pottering about before you arrived," Obrington said, stepping aside. "Kept hearing a tapping. Thought I'd wait for you to investigate properly." He paused, both of them listening. Nothing. "You armed?"

Sam shook her head. This was *surely* a test, seeing how she performed in the field.

"I've read your reports," Obrington said. "Spreading your limited resources thin, aren't you? Two field agents active at a time, and one of them busy sealing access points?"

"I only *had* –" Sam began to explain, but he didn't let her.

"I get it. A couple days spent closing our least-used doors and we cut future patrols by half, without too much impact on our ability to get underground." There was a sound in the stairwell. Something tapped against the stone. Obrington ignored it. "Except while you do that, places like *this* aren't being guarded."

"We've got sensors," Sam said uncertainly. Support always picked up movement near access points. Had he told them to keep this one quiet, to surprise her?

Something scraped against the stone steps. Then a heavy footfall. Something coming *up* the steps. A pause as whatever it was scented the air. It shrieked, shaking dust from the walls; an avian cry followed by a sudden patter of ascending feet.

"We should –" Sam said, twisting to Obrington, but the stare he gave the shadows stilled her, saying he would not be undermined by some monster. Sam's eyes darted back to the doorway and the charging noise – if it was a test, she was surely safe, shouldn't show fear –

The thing launched out of the darkness with reaching claws, and with a short scream Sam ducked back, hands up. A gunshot made her wince, followed by the loud crash of something big and hard hitting the wall. She looked up again. Melting from the top step into the darkness was the lower body of an animal with thick legs, skin marked by patchy scales, jointed like a horse and finishing in spiky claws. A ravisher: a three-legged, wall-climbing creature with an acidic tongue. The shadows hid its thin-haired head of mandibles and jagged teeth. Obrington prodded it with a shoe, pistol at his side, as its acrid smell invaded Sam's nostrils. She wasn't sure whether to vomit or flee.

Obrington said casually, "You're unarmed, Ward, you oughta have run."

Sam straightened up, heart pounding in her ears. He'd shot it like it was nothing. They should *still* run, lock these doors, call on Support for an explanation and Operations for a clear up. "It shouldn't have been here."

"Likely to be more of them? What is it?"

"Um." Sam struggled for the MEE's exact faux-Latin wording. "*Ultra* – no, *ultro rapientis*. Commonly called a ravisher. They're solitary – only a handful down here." Trivia studied for Ministry exams flooded back to Sam. The ravisher's existence had only been confirmed in 2012. Before then, everyone had believed it to be one of Apothel's inventions. Like the blue screens.

"Good. We'll get someone to clear it up later." Obrington pushed the door closed, jolting the creature's limbs out of the way. He tramped back the way they'd come. Sam stared dumbstruck at the closed door. Heart not quite still. Solitary as the ravisher was, it still belonged near the horde, following the *praelucente*, Ordshaw's great energy parasite, currently on the other side of the city.

"Back in the office, if you please, Ward," Obrington called out, already re-entering the big chamber. That jarred Sam from her concerns.

"*Office*?"

"Complete with plumbing and electricity, all we need."

Sam raced to catch up, throwing one last glance back to the stairwell door and the horror it hid. "Wait. You intend to work down here?"

"Me and everyone else. Exciting, isn't it?"

"But . . ." Sam trailed off. Not only was it far too close to the Sunken City monsters, but there was zero natural light, or air. It couldn't be healthy.

"The word" – Obrington jabbed a blocky thumb upwards, indicating the city – "is we've got rogue Fae and unstable creatures on our hands. This is the safest place in the city. No Fae underground. *Supposedly* no buggers coming this far out of the tunnels." Sam bit her lip. The ravisher had come far enough. But he said, "I've been down here an hour or more and that thing didn't come beyond the door. It *is* secure here. We're circling the waggons, understand?"

Sam said nothing. Pot plants and ergonomic chairs weren't going to make this place comfortable, and she definitely didn't feel secure.

"Sealing off access points is a fine idea," he went on. "Cutting back patrols is *not*. Considering that this grugulochs thing you took down supposedly controlled the *praelucente –*"

"It didn't control it, it *used* the *praelucente*," Sam corrected. "The grugulochs was merely diverting energy from it."

"You make a habit of interrupting people, Ward? No? I'll continue, shall I?"

Sam felt her face flush.

"Considering this thing, now dead, *had an influence* on your monsters, and we had a great beast tear apart your old place of work, the Sunken City warrants clearing out. Yet you're not enacting Protocol 38."

Protocol 38. The plan to purge the Sunken City of its uniquely vile creatures. Particularly the *praelucente* itself. The Ministry had believed it benevolent, so their plan to remove it was entirely theoretical and relied on unproven weapons. Sam had prepared an answer as to why they must wait. Not the truth, which was that she and Pax feared attacking the horde would drive the blue screens into deeper hiding, but something close to it. "I can explain my thinking –"

"Save it for your therapist." Obrington didn't give her a chance. "Hotshot young department head unsettles decades of stability *and* stokes a conflict with the Fae. Doesn't want to make things worse. Sound right?"

"I didn't –"

"You didn't do anything wrong," he said, surprising Sam into silence. He waited for that to sink in, then continued. "But the accepted opinion on Ordshaw is that you leave it well alone. You don't poke it. People itching to poke it, they get moved somewhere that *needs* poking. Mathers should've transferred you two years ago."

"He was effective in his way," Sam replied, only polite now he was dead.

"He was a musty fart with no imagination. But since you *did* start poking, we now need to draw this fiasco to its conclusion. You're scared of following through, which leaves *me* sitting in that chair." Obrington indicated the desk. The chair behind it was a small plastic thing, suitable for a school hall. Did he carry it and the desk down here himself? "You're not an idiot, are you, Ward?"

Sam stalled – trap question? Her hesitation cost her the chance to respond.

"You're gonna be my right hand, because your innovation is bleeding useful. In fact, I'll de facto let you run this show. Give you a chance to prove your mettle. But you're gonna assume I know what's best. Understand?"

Sam replied quickly, "Are you going to –"

"No. See." Obrington drew this out. "I didn't ask for questions, did I? I asked *do you understand*?"

His rocky disposition challenged her to answer carefully. Not voice the nagging thought that poor communication had got them in this mess.

"Yes or no."

"Yes," Sam said, with just a little defiance.

"Yes *what*?" Obrington pressed.

"Yes, *sir*."

"I was going for *yes, I understand*. But that'll do. We'll keep at what you've started, but manoeuvre towards Protocol 38. Once we're better staffed. I'll have more agents here in a few days. Meantime, talk to me about your proposals to use these pesky civilians."

The Bartons, an idea Sam had already relayed to Management. She said, "I'm already working with them. They've been cleared, we can –"

"Some of them have been cleared. Pax Kuranes raises a big question mark."

"We're lucky to have her," Sam rushed out. "Her perspective is refreshing – free from Ministry prejudice."

Obrington's eyes bulged behind those glasses. "You sleeping with her?"

"What?" Sam exclaimed. "No – I'm not *gay* –"

"Try not to sound so offended. We'd *all* do best to avoid prejudice. But nine out of ten potential recruits, it's an agent trying to get in someone's pants."

"That's not true." Sam stopped, flashing on Cano Casaria. The man who'd recruited her certainly made enough awkward passes, culminating in a narrowly avoided violent outburst recently. He'd gone off the rails chasing Pax for the same reason, hadn't he? Obrington's claim might be a little true.

"Pax has connections to the Fae," Obrington said. "Making her suspect. Especially as *you've* not managed to follow up with them since the attacks?"

Sam paused again. This was a bad start. She had been careful about exactly what she'd said to Management about Pax, and her unique senses, aware that her superiors might take rash action against either her or the Sunken City. Obrington's comments were giving her no confidence that she could safely share Pax's full situation with him. Partly to steer the conversation, partly because she had even less confidence that the fairy situation was under control, Sam said, "I hoped London might've heard from the Fae. Management kept such information from me in the past."

Obrington regarded Sam like he'd stepped in crap. "London hasn't heard a thing. This is *your* problem. These fairies took our weapons? All those men dead? And you can bet the Fae aren't sitting idle. Holding off following through there too, aren't we? Haven't you got gasses that could kill a Fae colony?"

"You're not serious? Our priority is diplomacy."

"Purging the Fae would sure make it easier to focus on the Sunken City."

"Absolutely not," Sam said suddenly, and braced herself for a scolding. He glared, waiting. "With respect, the Fae can be talked to. They can *help* us. And enacting Protocol 38 would be reckless considering our current lack of understanding." She gave another look towards the rear door, picturing that errant ravisher. Were there others like it, creatures lurking unchecked?

"We're not performing an academic study," Obrington said. "We're securing this city so I can go home to my tabby in Pelham and *you* can maybe take this chair." He rattled the little plastic thing at the desk. What a reward. "Protocol 38 is the –"

"We've been manipulated," Sam insisted, quickly, before her courage failed her. "We have no idea if our weapons will work on the *praelucente* or just piss it off. But we do know the Fae had a weapon that hurt it, a weapon we ourselves lost, outside their community. We can't move until we properly understand what we're dealing with. If Mathers had listened to me, he might still be alive – if Management listened to me, this city might already be secure."

She stopped to catch her breath, like she'd run a mile. Face impassive, Obrington let out a thoughtful croak. "And you think we can afford to hesitate?"

"Haste is far more dangerous," Sam said, finally sounding confident.

"Well. I'm not gonna be the fool that disdains the woman who dethroned the Raleigh Commission. And I *want* to believe you know what you're doing, so I don't have to *stay* in this bleeding town. So here's this. I'll give you all the rope you need to hang yourself, Ward, but only as much time as it takes to get our pieces in place for 38. Sound fair?"

Sam merely stared for a moment. It almost sounded like a compromise. "As long as it's enough time to revise our novisan scans. Our methods are time-consuming –"

"Ah, the scans," Obrington said. "Here starts a lesson. I can bring in new equipment, and new people, to speed things along, but if I do that, are you gonna accept responsibility for them?"

Ominous and ambiguous. Why shouldn't she? Was it another test? Sam nodded slowly. "That's what I'm here for, isn't it?"

The slightly slanted edge of a smirk on his face warned her it was a mistake. Another part of the test, though, sowing doubts?

"Right you are, Ward. Let's get started."

4

Fresko watched the townhouse opposite, focusing on the wall-mounted air-conditioning unit. The sound of stuff being smashed drifted up from within. It had to be Stabilisers, damaging shit for the sake of it. There wasn't anything in the Fae hideout that'd indicate where Fresko and Mix had gone; the pricks were only sending a message. The pair got the message clear enough from the windowsill opposite, having taken cover after hearing the disturbance.

"Three of them," Mix counted. "We can block the entrance and gun them down."

"You know what happens to people dumb enough to cross Stabilisers?" Fresko said.

"Ain't *they* already crossed us?" Mix grunted. The grizzled veteran looked more grizzled than ever, bruises still visible from the hiding their former chief, Letty, had given him. He'd been itching for another fight ever since, and it was only a matter of time before they got one.

This was their second den the Stabilisers had busted. And from the word on the Fae wire, it wasn't just them. Fae expats all over the city were in for a rough time on account of Letty's mess. If you weren't in the FTC, you didn't belong in Ordshaw, they were saying. Even those that never did a thing to anyone, or those, like Fresko and Mix, that had actively followed Val's orders. After kidnapping a human and trying to cover it up, they were especially high on the Stabiliser shit list.

"Got them!" a voice shouted from above. "Out here!"

Shit – another shape, a dark figure on the gutter of the adjacent roof. One hand to his ear, activating a radio, the other resting a gun against his hip. Mix drew a pistol as Fresko spotted another guy rising from beyond the A/C unit. The shadows inside scrambled for the exit. Fresko pulled Mix back. "Too many, come on!"

The Stabiliser above fired; a sharp crack and the bullet hit brickwork a few inches off. Cursing, Mix twisted to join Fresko in speeding away. Another gunshot zipped past. Fresko called out, "Split up – meet at the bridge!"

Mix peeled away, sticking close to the building fronts, as Fresko dived low, down through a treetop, deftly avoiding branches. A Stabiliser wasn't far behind, radioing sharp reports: "On him – left – through the trees."

Fresko rolled around the trunk, doubling back, and caught a glimpse of his pursuer doing the same. Fast. Human cars passed in the road below. Fresko banked out of cover and flew over a moving van. He turned suddenly, darting alongside the vehicle. The Stabiliser shot overhead. Sensing he'd made a mistake, the guy turned in the air. Fresko pushed himself against the van for support and swung the rifle off his shoulder. He fired and the Stabiliser moved to the side. Missed, but Fresko followed him with the scope while keeping pace with the van, fired another shot as the guy dived behind a bin. Fresko dropped down, under the van's carriage, and watched for a passing car – flew for that one. He caught hold of a metal fixing and hung underneath, bouncing over the road. Checking one way then another. They hadn't seen him, had they?

The car carried him away, turning and continuing up the road. No sign of Fae following. Fresko let himself breathe. There had been a half-dozen of them, at least. Not thugs bullying people out of town, but a bloody death squad.

Another couple of blocks and Fresko ventured out from his cover. He flew up, higher and higher, to get an aerial view of the city. Looked clear. He drifted back towards central Ordshaw, aiming for the river, slow and cautious. Narrowing his eyes, he spotted another Fae converging on his position. Mix had made it. He gave Fresko a brief salute, and Fresko indicated their destination ahead. Midway across the August Bridge he dropped onto a tower, skipping a few steps to regain his balance before checking the sky.

Mix stumbled to an even less graceful stop, a pistol in each hand. "I don't like running."

"You hit?" Fresko asked. His companion's glare said it was insulting to ask.

"We could've taken them," Mix snarled.

"You and what army?" Fresko replied, scoping the central

riverbank with his rifle. Plenty of humans, joggers, suits on phones, delivery boys. You couldn't see Fae at this distance, if there were any. "We'll hit Farling next, if they haven't been there, too. Pick up some shit, make for the suburbs till this blows over."

Mix rubbed his nose with a fist and holstered one pistol. "More running? To the *suburbs*? Might as well ditch Ordshaw completely. We want to take charge, Fresko, for fuck's sake. Trade one of those human bitches to Valoria – the poker player – gotta be worth something."

It was a bad idea; the sort that got them mixed up in all this to start with. But the comment drew Fresko's attention to the north bank, where Featherback Casino sat. A crowd was gathered outside, half styled by wealth, the other half with no style at all.

"Oh no." A voice made them both spin. "The Ministry are sure to be watching *her*."

The newcomer stood unfazed by their guns aimed at her chest. She wasn't a Stabiliser, though. The bloodstains on her slender white suit were offset by her bright, toothy smile, the grand mane of side-swept hair, and the gleaming polish of her holstered pistols. Even the sling holding her left arm looked stylish. Lightgate. Not just well-presented, but capable of reaching them unseen, even with all this empty space in every direction.

"Fuck me." Mix exhaled.

She responded with a slow drawl. "You are too old, too fat, and dress like a biker's charity sale. So no, thanks. But I have a better proposal than whatever *you're* thinking."

Talking to Pax had a surprisingly calming effect on Letty. So much so that she stopped berating the men gathered in her room long enough to enjoy a hit of medicinal dust while they arranged another call. It was the job of a Fae tech, Newbry, a gangly guy with long, rank hair, a big nose, and a shirt and trousers too loose to look presentable. He had a bulky laptop and smelt bad; probably enjoyed unlit rooms and animated porn. But he was evidently Edwing's resident computer whizz, having pinned down Pax via Holly Barton, and arranged a call the Stabilisers couldn't trace. He said he couldn't repeat it right away, though. Something to do with riding their signal on the back of someone else's, careful timing, concerns about Pax being watched.

Whatever – Letty could wait.

While she did, she planned ahead, most of her ideas centring on how to get a longer conversation with Pax. That seemed to be Edwing's plan, too, never mind what they might actually achieve with it. They both knew if they got to Pax without MEE or FTC interference, things would be easier. That meant directing her to another Fae exile. Letty had precious few friends left, though. Palleday?

It was late when Newbry announced he was moderately confident he could put a call directly through to Pax's phone. He had traced her to her apartment, back after her day in the casino, and connected them with Flynt and Edwing watching. As soon as Pax answered, Letty started, "Big day, champ? The website says you're still in, 84 out of 121."

"Yeah," Pax said. "I'm doing what I can. Hard to feel really safe yet. Are *you*?"

Letty tried to hide a smile. This big idiot, worrying for everyone. "Sure, and I've got some Grade A dust that makes the pain go away. Don't worry, when I get out of here we'll sort out your poker game, get rich on it, buy a mansion, booze until the early hours."

She could practically hear Pax smiling, too. "I'm game. How do we get you out?"

"Well, there's the sticker. Sneaking out is next to impossible, they're saying, which leaves dealing with the lockdown itself. Bringing in fucking Lightgate is option one. Securing the Dispenser would be another starter, force Val to act, once she can't deny the weapon's still out there."

"Wait. You don't know the Dispenser's in there?"

Letty froze. "Come again?"

"The Dispenser, your people have it."

"The fuck they do. Val hasn't said shit about it."

"You were there, outside the FTC, when all those Ministry men got gunned down, weren't you? They had it with them – your people grabbed their weapons before the clear-up crew got there."

"By leopard's ghosts," Letty huffed. "How the hell did you stop the Ministry dropping bombs on us?"

"By opening their eyes," Pax said. "The force behind all this had control of the Ministry, had been manipulating them for years. Maybe the blue screens got to your people, too?"

"Hold up," Letty said. "You figured that how? You tracked that

Blue Angel down?"

Pax took a breath. "Shit. We got time for the long story?"

Letty gave Newbry a look and the technician shook his head. "Better keep it short."

"The blue screens themselves were the problem. They absorb novisan – the energy driving the Sunken City, the same being drained from people – to create things, like the liquid glo, or the monsters. One changed the Ministry's documents, pretending to be a guy called Lord Asquith. Your leader might know him. I'm certain your people can bridge gaps in our understanding here. Your Fae dust, for example."

"You want –" Letty started, but a bang above cut them off. Someone hammering on a hatch higher in the building. She frowned at Flynt, and he in turn looked at Newbry.

The technician tapped at his computer with mounting concern. "There's a trace –"

"Oh you shit," Letty hissed. Another bang came with a muffled shout as Flynt ran into the corridor. "Got to go, Pax. You need Fae help, you won't get it from the FTC."

"Move!" Flynt returned, waving hurriedly.

"– your last warning!" a man's voice bellowed above.

"What's going on, Letty?" Pax asked. "We need to talk –"

"Yeah. Go to Palleday," Letty barked. "Sandwich shop on Dresden Street – our people won't touch him – and watch out for Lightgate!"

She hung up and Newbry closed his computer to run for the door.

"Go, Letty!" Edwing urged. "I'll hold them off!"

Something weighty cracked above, the intruders' voices getting louder as they broke in. Flynt opened a floor-hatch, guiding Newbry down as the hatch above rattled against a lock. "Open up in the name of the FTC!"

Letty climbed through the trapdoor as Edwing shouted, "This property belongs to the Informations Department! We have every right to –"

"Break it!" another man shouted. As the hatch slammed behind Letty, she heard the one above being smashed. Flynt pulled her away as men descended on Edwing.

*

"You trust Lightgate?" Mix asked, leaning against an upturned tuna tin littered with empty beer bottles. A table they'd used for years, soon to be discarded forever, once they ransacked the Farling den for ammo and drinks. "Swaggers in out of the blue claiming she can rally exiles? A thousand to one she's as crooked as Valoria."

Fresko didn't bother responding. Lightgate had given them instructions to round up whatever friends they had left in Ordshaw for some kind of rebellion, and Mix hadn't kicked up a stink then. Only now that they were alone, getting ready to do as she asked, did he get bold.

"Us getting our mates together while she does *what* exactly?"

"Drinks herself into a stupor," Fresko said. He knew Lightgate liked to delegate; either to get other people in trouble, or to buy time to lose what little mind she had boozing. She could tick off both the boxes with them. Chasing other Fae allies would put them in the Stabilisers' crosshairs, keeping her safe. But you didn't say no to Lightgate. They'd have to bring her someone or she'd gut them.

Tossing bullets into a bag, Mix complained, "When did we lose our dicks? One bitch after another telling us what to do – Letty, Val, Lightgate. Fucking bitches."

Fresko couldn't deny that. Human bitches, too, if you included the poker player. He paused, looking at his old tea-light candle seat, the wax warmed into just the right shape for a Fae rear. They used to be comfortable here. It was Pax who had taken all this from them, wasn't it?

"The fuck you thinking?" Mix demanded, before dragging heavily on his beer. "Always fucking thinking. Never sharing it. Getting some other genius plan?"

"Regretting where we are, is all," Fresko said.

Mix's fist tightened on his bottle like he wanted to smash it. "Yeah. Well, Ordshaw still beats being halfway round the world drinking fermented rice or some shit."

"Better than never drinking again. I got no desire to take a bullet."

Rather than respond, Mix rummaged in his pockets, searching for what was left of his Fae dust. He snorted some greedily, powdering his face in exhales of hungry breath, then rammed the rest into his beer. Maybe it'd calm him down.

"You done?" Fresko asked. "Got any ideas for who we go to now?"

Mix shook his head, focusing on his high.

"We wanna hedge our bets. Go someplace that looks like we're doing Lightgate a favour without putting our necks on the line. Not somewhere the Stabilisers will be watching, or someone that might actually join up with Lightgate."

"One of the dead gangs? Hooky in New Thornton, he moved on six months ago."

"Too obvious," Fresko said. They needed someone more or less hidden. A forgotten Fae. "What about fucking Palleday?"

5

Cano Casaria exuded nonchalance as he entered 14 Greek Street, the Ministry's drab shared office block and his supposed base of operations. Things had been hectic since the various disasters they'd faced, so he didn't fault Management for failing to call him in; they probably assumed an agent of his calibre would return on his own initiative, anyway. But enough time had passed, while things were likely racing ahead, and his supposed injuries were all but gone. Granted, his toe was never coming back, but it wasn't like it *hurt*. He climbed the stairs to the sixth floor, since the shattered remnants of the lift were hidden behind caution tape, and he put on a smile for them all.

There was no one there to meet him.

An old fax machine sat at the centre of the room, like a shrine to offices past, disconnected and partly dismantled. The device Pax claimed the blue screens had used to control the MEE, with faxes supposedly from Lord Asquith. Now, a husk of ancient electronics, dissected and abandoned.

Everything else was gone, as though it had fled from the taint of this shameful object. Not even the reception desk remained. Unattached cables stuck out of the floor, dents dotted the carpet where desks and chairs had sat, and discoloured squares showed where monitors once hung.

Casaria frowned into the unlit gloom. He wandered towards one of the side offices. Through the partition, he saw it was empty too, but went in anyway. In the middle of her office, Casaria considered simply calling Sam Ward. He had failed to force a chance encounter outside her apartment, most likely because she was working all night, and now he had missed her packing up and leaving. But calling reeked of desperation. It was her place to call him. She knew he was an asset.

Casaria inhaled deeply, searching for inspiration.

He could call someone else. Landon, or the Ministry hotline. Merely ask for the new location. But those lower-level minions would delight in thwarting him. He could hear their remarks: *no one told you the new address?* No, thanks.

Hands back in his pockets, he considered another option. He belonged in the field. That's where he'd find his people.

Buzzing from the drama of Letty's call, and the prospect of tracking down this Palleday, Pax had slept poorly. Then she'd woken up too late to go after the Fae before the WPT resumed. She hated putting it off, but she couldn't throw away her tournament. Her chance at creating a life for when this drama blew over. A mansion for her and Letty? She settled into the game with her chips low and a niggling itch to be elsewhere. The lunch break was already closing in when a chance to make a stand came: she hit bottom two pair on the flop, tens and nines – good enough to throw her meagre chips at. Except the opponent ahead, another odorous online player with buck teeth, bet first.

And then she felt them.

For the first time since encountering the grugulochs, Pax was hit by the movements of the screens. She winced and put a hand to her head, pretending she was struggling with the decision to call the bet. But something throbbed under her skin, a pulse of shifting energy, somewhere far away. Beneath the city. Underground, all together – clustered as one. There could be a handful of them, thirty or a hundred.

South of the city.

But – something else – directly north –

The feeling passed and Pax sat back with relief. She needed to tell Ward, the Bartons, anyone. Buck-teeth goaded, "Don't faint on us, yeah?"

Pax tuned him out, searching for the screens. Ignoring arrogant men of all ages was something she'd mastered years ago. She wasn't so used to picking up on disturbances in the world's energy. It had to be something she could use. A sense, an understanding, that could open a gate to the Fae. If she could tap into this, she could do something *useful*.

But they were gone.

"You got top pair," the man guessed. "Not enough to call, not for your tournament."

Blinking to reality, she quickly reconsidered her cards. They were good enough to push in on a bet, if not to call. Sensing the screens made it tempting to just go with the bad move and get away from here, to figure her mad feelings out. Throw away her shot at a big cash injection.

"Do I need to call the clock on her?" her opponent asked, and Pax shoved her chips in, already half out of her seat. Get this done, go find Letty's friend, call Ward, *something*. Murmurs of interest rushed through the crowd. The internet guy looked disgusted as he turned over top pair himself – with an ace kicker. The other players gave agonised groans or impressed gasps at Pax's hand: good, but at risk. The dealer brought out an ace on the turn. The hotshot laughed like he'd planned that sick luck and the audience's heart broke, but Pax was ready to run. A miracle ten came next. Full House. She'd doubled up.

Buck-teeth jumped up, demanding to know how in hell she could make that call – he could've had trips, a better two pair, anything. Pax stared in disbelief. Twice the chance, now, to win big. She shook herself out of it, and let people congratulate her as she left anyway. The extra chips would buy her time. She needed to move.

In the hall, trying to calm herself, she brought up Sam Ward's number. At the very least she could get a handle on what had just happened. But she stopped dead as a man caught her eye. Walked out of one bad feeling right into a monumentally worse one. *Him? Now?*

Stacey Monroe was flanked by two big guys in American football jerseys. With his shaved head, thick woollen suit and heavy gold rings, he belonged in a garage peddling boxes of contraband. Not here, reminding Pax he'd almost made her witness to a homicide four days ago. Monroe's men had captured and tortured Casaria, a government agent, pursuing an interest in Ordshaw's tunnels. She didn't know exactly what Monroe did, but she knew it was nothing good. His head didn't reach the other men's shoulders, but he was dominating their conversation, rough accent audible from a distance. "Trust me, I'll take care of you."

Monroe and his men weren't on the tournament roster, Pax had checked. But there had always been a chance they'd show up. She had a plan: back slowly, discreetly into the shadows. As she took one step back, he saw her and his round face stretched into a lurid grin. Who was she kidding. He might've come deliberately for her. His hands went up to pat his companions. "Here's a local legend you might get a chance to play with."

He sauntered towards her with the men, square-headed Americans of the most cliched variety. Pax stood rooted to the spot.

"The inimitable Pax Kuranes, one of Ordshaw's finest. Sits on all the best games in town. I heard you made fast friends with Dutch McRory, you planning on bringing him to the Baudelaire Club once you're crowned champ here?"

Pax opened her mouth but no words came out. Just as well, because the words were: *last time I saw you was in a torture chamber*.

"Meet Hugh and Brutus," Monroe continued, like she wasn't frozen in awkwardness. "Brothers outta Houston, you believe that? Flew all the way over for this. I'm reckoning they'll make back some of that airfare in the big game. You *will* be there, won't you, love?"

It didn't sound like a threat, but it wasn't a request either. Monroe's eyes said *we've got unfinished business*. And it stank because if he'd ingratiated himself with brutes like this – one even called Brutus, for crying out loud – then whatever game Monroe was peddling would be worth her while. A clear hustle.

"Sure she'll be there," Monroe decided for her, when she still hadn't spoken. "Make a bloody party of it, won't we."

The Americans were confused by her silence, but she pulled just enough sense together to hold out a hand to shake. "Hope to see you there."

Satisfied, the pair let themselves be dismissed by Monroe and wandered off talking at an unapologetic volume. "A chance to play with Dutch McRory? Are you kidding me?"

Monroe watched with amusement, like he'd just given tourists the wrong directions, before turning to Pax. He said, with no indication that it was a compliment, "Well, don't you look a picture. You know I got a monkey riding on you?"

"What?" Pax replied, a weird image springing to mind. But he meant money. A lot of money.

"Ton on you reaching the final table," he elaborated. "The rest to say you'll cash."

She said, weakly, "*Why?*"

"It's nothing." Monroe patted his chest, like she'd touched his heart somehow. "I got faith in you, darling, that's all. Placed the bet with Lorenzo when you were two above the fold, got great odds. Lorenzo out of Ripton, know him? Didn't believe in you like I do."

"You probably should've listened to him."

"Bollocks." Monroe jabbed an authoritative finger towards her, "There's only two of our own left in the field, you know? Yourself and Wonky Gunry, and we both know Gunry used up all his luck standing out of bed this morning. You're going all the way, my girl. Make Ordshaw proud."

"And if I don't?" Pax heard the question before she'd thought it.

"You will," Monroe shrugged. "No question."

Pax gave him a conceding smile. Why not add the prospect of being accountable to a criminal's losing bet to her worries. Desperately wanting to get away, or at least change the subject, she searched the hall for inspiration. At least there was no sign of Bees or Jones, his hired goons. Last seen trying to stab Cano Casaria. She said, "Your men weren't interested in playing?"

"Ah," Monroe said. "Those boys chewed my ear off for a month about sponsoring them. But we know where the smart money's at, don't we? Come by the Baudelaire Club this evening, there's gonna be stacks on the table, substantial buy-in. Bring McRory and I'll stake you. Gratis."

It gave Pax pause. This was all wrong. He should've been angry at her for upsetting his stabby plans. Paranoid about her snitching on him, at least. But he was cheery, offering her a place at a game worth a small fortune. If he wanted to lure the world-class players, they'd be looking at five-figure buy-ins. Four-figure *hands*. "You're serious?"

"As a nun's drawers, you've earned it." Monroe put his hand on his heart again, making Pax frown. "Least I can do. And it's good business, besides."

"Mr Monroe," Pax said, carefully. Again, the words didn't come: *shouldn't we talk about what happened? You vicious bastard.*

"Apologies my dear," he said. "I'm distracting you from the tourney. Don't worry, alright? We're good, Pax. Two locals shooting at the moon, rolling over foreigners come to take advantage of our town. Kind of noble, I reckon."

Pax merely nodded, sure this was a not-so-subtle reference to his business dispute with Jamaican gangs coming into Ordshaw. Monroe, she had learnt, was patriotic in a murderous way.

He finished, like a proud uncle. "That's my girl. You're gonna play some great cards, aren't you? In there, at the Baudelaire. What do you say?"

Fuck, is what Pax thought. Already preparing to face psycho fairies and ethereal screens, now she had to weigh the patronage of a gangster against a good business opportunity. Would he even let her say no? Her eyes picked out a brass-rimmed clock above the reception counter, the second hand ticking away all the time she had for these huge problems.

"Pax." Monroe brought her attention back to him. "You know the sort of figures I'm talking, right? Your stake in this. Don't that sound good to you?"

She frowned again. Was this something else? His way of buying her silence, or even *apologising*? Hell. She could work with that. "Sure, Mr Monroe. I'll be at your game."

6

Sam marvelled at how the new Ministry chamber had come to life. Though she couldn't quite call it an office yet. Removal men and technicians had swept in overnight, and desks, computers and monitors now lined the underground lair. Tall pot plants *had* added colour, and a ventilation system somehow kept the air moving. Everyone was in early, along with a couple of tough-looking men in dark suits: Obrington's new hires, who were being briefed on something by their resident tech expert, Dr Galler. Sam also had the very promising prospect of taking Darren Barton into the Sunken City today, to expand her surveying – which Obrington showed little interest in observing: "Your people, your problem."

In general, Obrington ignored everything to lean against his desk, thumbing through his phone and making calls. That suited Sam fine; he genuinely didn't look like he intended to stay. She might yet get the chief's chair for herself. The Support team were already turning to her for leadership, things were running smoothly. Mid-morning, there was a flurry of excited activity when the *praelucente* created a surge in novisan. The team checked for fluctuations across the city, to be sure the energy wasn't being transferred, and settled into a congratulatory atmosphere, concluding the surge was localised.

When Sam's phone rang and Pax's name came up, it felt like the cherry on the morning's cake. Besides their rather abortive visit to a handful of reported blue screen locations, during which Pax had been notably quiet, they'd had less contact than Sam hoped. But with time and space, Pax would surely come around to throw herself into the Ministry's work. Sam answered cheerily, "Pax, how's the tournament going?"

"Yeah fine," Pax replied a little shortly, sounding rushed. "About a half-hour ago, maybe more, was there a surge?"

"Yes!" Sam said. Too enthusiastic. She tried to contain the excitement, lowering her voice. "You felt it?" Overcompensated, sounding like a posh gentleman. "I mean – gosh – so it's working?"

"My magic power?" Pax said. "Did you just say *gosh*?"

Sam fumbled her phone to adopt a casual posture, even if Pax couldn't see it. "It was south of the river, between Broadplain and Tupsom, is that where you felt it?"

"I don't know exactly but they were all in one place. And they did something. You caught that? Right in the opposite direction."

"What? No." Sam scanned her colleagues, relaxed at their screens, obliviously continuing their tasks. "Our scan goes citywide now, showing the fluctuation was localised."

"Okay. Except it wasn't."

A moment of dread swept over Sam. She picked out Obrington, breathing through his mouth with an expression like his phone was insulting him. He wouldn't want to hear that their expanded surveys might be flawed. No one would want to hear that. And how could she tell him, short of subjecting Pax to a hefty Ministry investigation? But even without having proved Pax's esoteric abilities, Sam trusted there was *something* in it. She asked, "Where was it? This other . . . thing?"

"I don't know."

"But – are you tracking it now?"

"No. I'm in the middle of something else."

Not the poker; she would've said if it was that. "What sort of something?"

"I'll tell you about it later, best you not get involved yet. Look, all I know is those screens were together with the minotaur when it fed, all of them." The minotaur, her word for the *praelucente*, borrowed from the long-dead civilian, Apothel. "That's a good thing – we can round them up if we can catch it feeding. But they *used* that energy, and that's bad. At best, they've still got a screen roving separately. There's plenty worse options, though."

"But you can't pinpoint it . . ."

"North. I was in the casino, it was north of that, I can't say for sure." Pax gave it a moment's thought. "Relative to the surge? I'd guess roughly the same distance in the opposite direction. Roughly."

"I can work with that." Sam waved at a Support tech. "Pax, I'd like you to come in –"

"Not now. Not today."

"Why? At least tell me what you're doing?"

"Hanging up." And the line went dead.

Sam cursed, but put it aside, with the tech already waiting for orders. She instructed him to recheck the novisan scans to the north, then crossed the office to Obrington. Those scans wouldn't show anything; they needed to get someone out there. Obrington lowered his phone, pushed off from the desk and stared at her to ask the question: *what?*

"Could we spare a couple of agents to investigate an anomaly?" Sam asked, keeping her voice quiet so the rest of the staff wouldn't hear her meek request.

"You tell me," Obrington answered, as loud as she was soft. "We've got Vinton and Bolton sealing doors in Farling, and Marks and Lungen getting ready to hit Nothicker. Or there's your civilians, you want them investigating *anomalies*? Your initiative, your choice."

He made it sound condescending, but it *was* her call. "I think the –"

"Wrong answer."

"But you don't know –"

"Ward," he said, "that creature manipulated your office for a long time. There's gonna be plenty of anomalies. Want to hear one I discovered? Some bright spark had your pulse pistols set to the wrong frequency. Deadly, but *not* the quietest shot. Presumably based on faulty advice from your faxes. Why do you suppose that would be?"

Sam considered it. "To make us less effective culling the creatures?"

Obrington shook his head. "Guess again."

Unable to answer him correctly, Sam merely went quiet. Another Management figure appearing to know everything. If you'd care to share with the rest of us, instead of using information to puff up your own chest, perhaps we could make progress?

"What's that?" He raised an eyebrow and Sam froze.

Did she say that out loud? She shook her head to indicate she hadn't spoken.

"*My* guess," Obrington said, "is it made you *visible*. Your master manipulator was using faxes to communicate, right? It didn't have access to our computers. Didn't necessarily see all that was going on. But it could've picked up on specific signals, like the right energy gun frequencies, to watch your men at work. What do you think?"

That suggested the blue screens sensed energy in a different way to them. Beyond their understanding. About par for the course. Sam said, "Well. We're doing a full review to avoid mistakes like that. But it's not enough."

"No. Good thing I'm here, isn't it? Come with me, there's someone we've got to meet –"

"Can it wait a moment, sir?" Sam blurted out. "This anomaly, it's a *specific* hunch. Related to the recent surge. It's time-sensitive."

Obrington gave her his usual open-mouthed glare, inviting an explanation. She wasn't sure what to say. Without revealing Pax's connection to the screens, and risking more interference, how could she explain why they needed to search an area their equipment showed to be inactive? Her eyes wandered to the office's rear door. That was it. "That ravisher didn't show on our scanners," Sam said. "I'm concerned we might have similar strays, and want to do a sweep to be sure the surge didn't unsettle anything we're not seeing."

"Search the whole city for something we haven't detected?"

"Just an area fitting previous patterns of energy transferral."

Looking entirely unconvinced, Obrington shrugged his big shoulders and said, "Your initiative, Ward. Your choice. You understand, though, that you go chasing enough wild geese and it'll become harder to fill this seat I want to vacate."

"Not if I catch them," Sam said. Which she thought was rather bold and clever. His sneering face suggested it wasn't.

"Do what you have to," Obrington said. "Then join me upstairs. In a matter of minutes." He padded away without room for discussion, and Sam wasted only a moment watching him go. She hurried back to the Support tech, who was already frowning.

"What is it?"

"There's only two access points in that area," the man said. "Not a historically busy zone." He wavered, worriedly. "It's the warehouse district. The closest tunnels to the Fae Transitional City."

"Ah." Not good at all. They couldn't send agents that close to the FTC, not this soon, without communication from the Fae. But that couldn't be a coincidence. Were the screens advancing on the Fae themselves? Somehow planning to use or abuse them? One way or another, they were looking to cause trouble. Sam said, "Message the FTC, saying we're investigating unusual activity in the area. And get hold of Darren Barton, I want him to meet me there."

"But there *isn't* any unusual activity –" the tech protested.

"Just do it!" Sam ordered, drawing a few nearby looks. She didn't meet their eyes, racing after Obrington.

They walked a block away, around the corner to a row of brown office buildings, Sam itching to get away to whatever was happening near the FTC. A man was standing by a car in a parking bay, halfway down the road. Sam trotted to catch up to Obrington, and he said, "I called in a favour. This chap should've been kicked to the curb when he left the Ministry, frankly, but he has some uses."

"Left the Ministry?" Sam echoed. They approached the man too quickly for more.

"Agent Obrington?" He was shabbily suited, wearing a tweed jacket and brown corduroys, and his short mop of curly hair needed cutting. He smiled unhappily as he held out a hand. "Simon Parris."

Obrington shook with a grip that made Parris wince. "This is Sam Ward, *Acting Assistant Director*. Glad you could make it."

Sam held off questioning the title Obrington had previously denied her, as Parris maintained his unsettled smile. She shook his hand too. Clammy. "Anything for the Ministry," Parris said. "This is about the recent troubles, right?"

"It's about you paying your due," Obrington answered bluntly. "What've you got?"

"You know it's risky?" Parris said, his anxiety drawing Sam out of her Sunken City concerns to the fresh worry of what was going on here. "I've said in the past – it's not like we're unwilling to share, but if this gets noticed –"

"Save the patter," Obrington told him. "Ward takes full responsibility, don't you?"

There was that word again. What was he getting her into? She had to play along to see where this was going. "I need to see it first . . ." Whatever *it* was.

Parris nodded obediently and moved to the back of his car, an ugly cube of a Nissan. He opened the boot, looking about in case they were being watched. Obrington's bulk blocked Sam's view of whatever was inside.

"Three of them?"

"All I could get," Parris said. "And I need them back by tomorrow."

"You'll have them back when we're done with them."

Obrington stepped aside so Sam could see. Lying on a rumpled blanket was a set of long, matte black tools vaguely resembling rifles. Each sleek metal barrel split into prongs at the end, like a massive tuning fork, and there was a tablet panel near the back, above the handle and a distinct chrome badge. The logo was immediately recognisable; a D designed to resemble the tip of a speeding train. Or a bullet. Duvcorp. One of the most powerful companies in the world. The owners of Ordshaw's tallest building, comprising a trio of staggered towers that dominated the Central skyline. Duvcorp had made their mark in the American automobile industry before segueing into mainstream electronics and beyond. How had they crossed into MEE territory?

"What's happened?" Parris asked. "The Sunken City –"

"Is something you shouldn't ever mention, isn't it?" Obrington said.

Parris paused, suitably scolded. "Of course. But my bosses will want to know –"

"These things easy to use?" Obrington interrupted again.

Parris gave Sam a look for support, but she was impassive, waiting for this to play out. He answered, "Yes. That button activates, and when the light goes green, that one starts the test. The display" – he tilted one device – "gives you the SURE reading. Expect around a 23 for humans; electromagnetic field manipulations go as high as 50. Atmospheric readings usually even out around 10. Anything below that is strange."

"Fantastic." Obrington turned to Sam: "Think you can handle that?"

"What's happening?" Parris asked. "There were big SURE fluctuations surrounding those quakes last week – we've even got our COO in town asking questions."

"Want to tell your bosses anything," Obrington replied, "say we're testing new equipment and want to check benchmarks. But it'd be better if this co-operation was kept quiet, wouldn't it?"

Parris didn't press the point, starting to wrap the scanners. Obrington bid him a cold farewell, then hefted the weapons up against one shoulder and moved off towards the office. Sam gave one final look to the dishevelled Duvcorp man, now silent, merely waiting for this to be over. She hurried back to Obrington's side and asked in a hushed whisper, "What's going on? How much do they know?"

"*He* knows a lot," Obrington said. "Including that *we* know how to bury people. He's never shared our secrets with Duvcorp, but nor has he shared theirs with us. That company gives us a run for our money in the shady factor."

"And you wanted me to take responsibility to shield yourself?" Sam demanded.

"Obviously," Obrington said as though it wasn't cowardice or betrayal. "You think I'm planning on visiting from London every other weekend to handle the fallout from this? The consequences are on you."

"Jesus." Sam exhaled. "You people can't ever just be straight with me?"

"How's that not straight? You wanted new equipment, fast, I got you some. Return the scanners without drawing attention to ourselves and that's that. *Should* Duvcorp happen to come calling, you'll have a chance to prove you're Management material."

"Without knowing their angle? What do these things even measure?"

"SURE," Obrington said. "Their take on novisan. Special Unexplained Residual Energy, they call it. Special because URE is bleeding awkward to say. They don't know about your Sunken City because, strange as it might sound, Ordshaw's energy levels are curiously *normal* compared to most big cities. But they know a thing or two about novisan in general."

"And the MEE allows this research? Surely they'll –"

"Don't overestimate our influence, Ward," Obrington said. "Our work gets bent by committees and budgets, and the good of society; they are more efficient, better funded and ruthless. We've kept our secrets from them, they've kept some from us, neither of us wants a fight over it."

Sam ran this through her head, thinking of the Ministry's technology. To the best of her knowledge, they had nothing that directly measured novisan, only complicated systems of deduction. The implications were clear. "They could've uncovered things paralleling what we've found in the Sunken City?"

Obrington scoffed, though she couldn't tell whether he was dismissing the idea as silly, or aggravated that it might be true. "Best keep your eye on the goal right now. With these scanners, you'll be properly informed, for once. Perfect your monitoring equipment, test your Protocol 38 weapons, make some bloody progress."

Sam held off from replying. A long way from at ease. But there was something in it. Better equipped, she might make sense of what was going on. Starting with Pax's concerns in the warehouse district.

7

Pax parked her spluttering moped on Dresden Street, thankful that the elusive Dr Rimes had lent it to her, *more use to you than me*. It would've taken an hour to reach Ordshaw's under-served Nothicker on public transport; instead she'd arrived in twenty minutes. She scanned the grimy neighbourhood, walls soiled by the detritus of time, then double-checked the electronic device the Ministry had given her to track Fae. The little black box resembled a metronome, and Sam Ward had insisted it would alert the MEE if any Fae targeted her. She had turned it off, so the Ministry wouldn't blunder in and upset things when she found Palleday. Which they definitely would, given the chance. Ward couldn't have sounded happier to hear from Pax. An echo of Cano Casaria, exposing her to their work with dreams of signing her up. One of us, one of us. Pax's special sense for the blue screens made that all the more uncomfortable: it would be better if she had imagined that latest surge. If it wasn't the blue screens potentially spawning new and more terrible monsters only she could sense.

Putting that cheerful thought out of her mind, Pax approached the shop, *The Sandwitch*. Its barred windows were plastered with faded newspapers, the sign weathered like driftwood. Did local children think the store haunted? No, children living in Nothicker had bigger problems than ghosts. She punched the shop's buzzer, and it produced a fierce buzzsaw sound. The intercom crackled to life. A hoarse, older man's voice said, "You got ten seconds to get clear of my property."

Pax looked up, through the frosted glass of the window, no sign of someone inside.

"You hear me, I said ten seconds! Must've been eight by now."

"Palleday?" Pax said.

The speaker cut out for a moment, then came back. "I'm counting from five. Four."

"You know Letty? She sent me – she's a friend."

"Three."

"We need –"

"Two – one!" He rushed the last numbers and Pax jumped aside. The intercom hissed, something spraying out of it, barely missing Pax. She crouched, a hand over her face, coughing. The gas stung without making contact, burning her eyes, her nostrils.

"There's more, you hang around!"

"You prick!" Pax shouted. "What's – what was that?" She wheezed, spitting burning phlegm on the pavement. Her head spun, ears popped – was it some foul Fae technology, an airborne chemical weapon? Pax staggered against the wall and took deep, gasping breaths.

When the man spoke again, his voice sounded uncertain. "I warned you . . ."

Pax slowed her breathing, the burning slowly starting to pass. She blinked bleary eyes and swallowed to clear her ears. "Jesus fuck, I came to you for help."

"I got no help for a Fae-eating monster." His voice wavered. "Walk away. Please."

"Now that you've . . ." Pax breathed deeper into her recovery. It wasn't mystical, or deadly. "You *pepper-sprayed* me? All I've been through, now I get maced trying to knock on a goddamned door for *help*?"

The man didn't respond. He had to be Palleday, or a friend, knowing the rumour that she'd eaten a fairy. Pax said, "Letty trusted you! She's trapped, and I need you to help me help her." And then *we* can save this whole damned city, can't we?

"Ain't no human helping her," the voice crackled through the speaker. "Ain't no *one*."

"You know where she is? What's going on?"

The speaker crackled off.

Pax took another breath, and the pepper had a minor resurgence at the back of her throat, making her gag. She hit the buzzer again, and shouted, "Give me a glass of water at least, fuck! A tissue!"

"I told you to leave –"

"I'm streaming! Streaked with snot. What's wrong with you? Palleday!" She raised her voice. "Palleday, you bastard, open up!"

He hissed panic through the speaker and the intercom beeped a different pitch at last. The door clicked. "Inside, quick – stop using my name!"

Pax entered onto the stench of wet mould. Clamping a hand

over her mouth, she continued past a crusty sandwich counter. With barely any light seeping through the papered window, she squinted through turning dust to the choice of steep stairs or a doorway to an ominously black back room. She called up the stairs, "You here?"

Climbing the creaking steps took her above the smell, and she inhaled an approximation of fresh air. Two closed doors sat ahead, with a small rectangular window to one side, open a crack, casting dim light on the stained red carpet. In the centre of the corridor sat a roll of toilet paper. He must've moved fast to leave it for her.

"Quite a place you've got," Pax muttered, scooping up the roll and tearing off sheets to dab her eyes. She blew her nose loudly.

"I got no water, not for a human," Palleday said from up near the window. Apology in his gravelly voice. He was hidden by the window's glare. "Say your piece, before I do you worse."

"Like feed me a sandwich?" Pax sniffed, pocketing more paper for later. "I'm not the enemy. A lunatic called Lightgate tried to use me to spark war between the Ministry and the FTC. Letty tried to stop her and got trapped in the FTC. She said you were a friend."

Palleday's continued hesitation gave her hope. Pepper-spray or not, he hadn't threatened her life in the usual way of the Fae. He said, "The news pinned it all on Letty. Say she was working with crazy humans. But Letty, she's got a good heart. Lightgate . . .a pox on whoever brought her back." He spat. "But there's no help here. You know my name, and I guess that's all."

"Yeah," Pax said. "So fill me in. Can I see you?"

"I ain't giving you a chance to snatch me, human."

"It's *Pax*, not *human*. And do I look like the snatching type?" Pax spread her arms wide. "I've got the reflexes of a sloth."

"And the trickery of a fox," Palleday said. "You're such good friends with Letty, tell me why you came here and didn't go to her crew?"

Pax recalled the Fae who had kidnapped Grace and tried to kill them all. "We fell out."

"When you ate young Gambay?"

"No," Pax answered seriously, no idea who that was but fairly certain she hadn't eaten him. "I don't know what ideas they got about me, but they weren't working with Letty in the end. We had the weapon to kill the minotaur, they tried to kill us to get it back.

Now it's fuck-knows-where and we're grasping about in the dark. Only I *know* your people can help us finish this."

"Because we're special," Palleday said, defensively. "That sounds like eating talk to me."

"What –"

"Think you'll gain our *powers*. Who knows what ideas you have."

"Your powers? I can be coarse, antisocial and violent without resorting to cannibalism."

"Cannibalism," he said, "is reserved for equals."

"Can we park this? I didn't *eat* anyone and I'm not going to. Bottom line is, Letty sent me to you – you're not in the Fae city, I need a go-between."

"Fat chance," Palleday snorted. "I live out here because I got no love for the FTC, but I got less love for humans. You could do a lot of harm. They just wouldn't let me build no more. They leave me alone, I leave them alone." That brought reflective sadness. "Now. Once, men fought wars over my towers."

"And women knew better?" Pax offered.

He paused. "It's a joke to you, is it?"

"No," Pax said. "I just don't know what you're talking about. What towers, why would they stop you from building?"

"Because it wasn't *right*, not for their kind of living. They said." He made a snuffling sound. Torn between paranoia and wanting to share. "You want to see them?"

"Sure. If they're, say, less than two minutes away?"

"Open that door. The one ahead of you."

Pax looked from the frail door back up to the shadows. She crossed the corridor and opened it. The room beyond was dark, barely lit by one small window obscured by clouded glass. It made the contents unsettling: column after column of organic shapes, each as tall as her, pitted with warped openings, like the mouths of tortured souls.

"Jesus Christ," Pax said. Something moved near her head, making her sidestep.

"Yes." Palleday hovered by the doorway, rubbing his little hands together as he looked upon his work. He was as small as Letty, no more than two inches, but had grand, lacy wings, and a long mane of mucky grey hair, thinning up top. He wore a patchy boiler suit and his long, bony limbs gave him a more insectile appearance than other Fae. The slightly manic look on his face conjured the impression that he hid in the shadows of these massive anthills, waiting for rodents to walk by.

"You built these things?" Pax asked quietly.

"And more, so much more." Palleday hovered a little closer, enraptured by his own achievements. "Wonders of Fae civilisation, forgotten, no longer deserved." With him distracted, Pax realised, she could actually grab him out of the air now. For a laugh. Palleday turned to face her and shot back with surprise. Sensing her intention to prank? "What are you doing?"

"This stuff." Pax ignored the question. "Was this how the Fae cities used to be? The sort Letty told me about, under the city, before the monsters."

Palleday's expression softened. "She spoke about that? What do you know?"

"Not enough."

He made a low, curious noise and flew into the shady room. A moment later, the overhead light blinked on, an old yellow bulb that stretched the openings of the many structures in pained shadows. Palleday resurfaced in the middle of the room. "See it for yourself, human."

Pax placed a hand on the doorframe and said, "I can see well enough from here."

He made a sound of disapproval as he emerged from between the structures, flying with a halting action, his old wings unfit. He perched on a ledge at the top of the nearest tower, eye-level. "One of these fit a family, long ago. A pillar of faith in ourselves. Not *possible* in the new way, they said. Small, mobile, that was all they wanted. Even as – even if –" He floated off the ledge again, pointing a shaking hand across the room. There was something beyond the structures, tucked in a corner; a frame of some sort, pipes and poles with taut wires running between them, arching over the top into a system of pulleys, with wheels at its base. "I gave them options, they wouldn't listen!"

Pax looked from the elaborate machine back to the towers, whose organic, drooping style made them look half-fused to the floor. If he was suggesting he could move these towers with that thing, she could sympathise with the Fae who doubted him.

"I am redundant," he continued, grimly. "A relic. Sculpting alone. A sideshow for a human."

"Letty understood, didn't she?" Pax said. "She wants to restore what you had before."

"She's a dreamer. And you must be, too. Think there's any hope we can live side-by-side? Our own people can't even get along. No. The best, only thing I can do is this."

"Your people had the Sunken City once, it could happen again."

"You seen the things down there?" Palleday scoffed. "The light – the electric arms. Paws, claws, teeth; all coming faster than you can scream. Drove us up here, where *your* people chase us with fire and gas. Again and again, moving. Every time abandoning my creations, watching them crumble to dust."

"I'm sorry," Pax mumbled, aware of the futility of saying it. She couldn't imagine all that had been lost with each forced migration. But it raised another thought. She'd seen it herself, when the Sunken City horde swarmed towards her. The fairies had drawn them her way. She'd felt it, too, riding the tube with Letty. The monsters hunted the Fae. Wanted to feed on them more than anything. "What *is* so special about your people? Why are the creatures drawn to you?"

Palleday gave her a miserable look. "You oughta be able to answer that."

Pax shook her head, but an idea was forming. Even without understanding why, she could imagine how that unique Fae energy might draw the monsters and the screens all together. Then the Ministry could have their purge. If they could get a handle on Fae energy. If they could get the Dispenser back. If she could rescue Letty. A lot of ifs, all requiring the co-operation of more reasonable Fae. Pax said, "Is there anyone in the FTC that actually likes humans?"

"What do you think?" Palleday said. "Even the soft young bloods must be reeling at you, since the return of this Apothel Five and Fae getting" – Pax gave a warning look – "Fae getting *hurt*."

"Someone's with Letty, inside the FTC. Helped her talk to me. Could you get them a message? Find a way we can properly connect?"

"I look like someone with contacts?"

He really didn't, but she said, "Letty thought so. You think of a way, and I'll clear out the Sunken City. You'd have space for your towers. Protection. Maybe people to live in them."

Palleday was quiet. Imagining it. He said, "You know all that's down there."

"Not *all* of it."

"Lot of Fae won't want to return. Most Fae are too young to remember, but I saw things. Troubling things."

"Yeah, me too. But we can explore all that once it's safe to, can't we?"

Palleday's eyes were glazed over in memory.

Pax continued, "I'll be at a card game this evening, at the Baudelaire Club. A good excuse to keep the Ministry from watching. You send someone my way, anyone that can help, I'll be waiting."

Palleday regarded her for a moment. "Don't hold your breath. But I'll see what I can do." After another moment's thought, he added, to remove Pax's smile, "As long as you realise there's plenty more people want you dead than alive, right now."

Once the human was gone, strolling self-satisfied away, Fresko and Mix drifted through the pillars of Palleday's building graveyard. Mix said, "We could've done her here. Like we should've before."

They settled on the ledge next to Palleday as he watched them. A battleaxe of an old Fae, long past his prime. He said, "She seemed genuine."

"Yeah?" Fresko replied. "The human promising impossible things seemed genuine?"

"Says the man under Lightgate's thumb?"

Fresko let him have that; he trusted Lightgate even less than he did the human. But Lightgate was at least a Fae. And much more likely to make them pay for crossing her.

"We can *still* get her," Mix said. "The Ministry aren't watching."

"And they won't be later," Fresko said. "She gave us a time and place. We bring the meeting to Lightgate, it might get her off our back."

"You heard the girl, didn't you?" Palleday said. "Letty's been set up by her that sent you. What you oughta bring Lightgate is a stick up the arse."

Fresko said nothing. If Letty wasn't responsible for the

Ministry deaths, more fool her. And if this girl *was* genuine, didn't that just make her another dangerous woman? Why not put her together with Lightgate, see what sparks flew. He caught Palleday reading his face and said, "That human caused us all sorts of shit."

"I'll say it again – you heard her. She's not what you think."

"You want to help her, that it?"

"I see no reason not to reach out to the FTC."

"To fucking Val?" Mix demanded, but the architect was already shaking his head.

"Take me for an idiot? I got people I can talk to, hell. Might even get word to Letty herself."

Mix gave Fresko a look telling him this was his call. Fresko kept staring at the old man; a legend of the Fae world, the sort you left alone. Smarter than most, for sure. Then, it didn't take a genius to know the less you had to do with Lightgate the better. Fresko said, "Alright. We'll hold off. See where this meeting goes and make a decision then."

"Knock yourself out," Mix said. "I'm ready for a fucking drink."

8

When Apothel's Miscellany was couriered to the Bartons by a man in black, Holly had started studying it keenly. The leather-bound tome looked like it belonged in a university library, to be handled with microfibre gloves. She warned Darren off touching it with his greasy fingers, likewise Grace. She especially turned Rufaizu away, though the book technically belonged to him; she had seen him make the dishes dirtier when he washed them.

In the book, partly translated by Pax, Holly discovered fantastic creatures she knew to exist under their feet. Among Apothel's sketches was a plant he called a *seeping sour flower*, resembling a foul thing she'd seen herself. Imagine experiencing such things – widely unknown, radically different – without the looming threat of death. She understood how the place had enchanted her husband. Or ensnared? Regardless, when the call came, Sam Ward giving Darren an okay to access the Sunken City, Holly had to be there.

At the edge of the desolate warehouse district, they found Ward in an empty gravel car park, waiting by a big metal door with an object whose long barrel split into multiple prongs. It vaguely resembled a weed-whacker. Ward regarded Holly with surprise. "Mrs Barton – I'm not sure you should be –"

"It's fine, Grace has Netflix to look after her," Holly said, nodding for her to get on with things. Ward looked uncomfortable, but Darren shook his head to warn her not to argue. She didn't question Rufaizu's presence, either. The bright-eyed vagrant was grinning, washed and groomed and newly clothed, though he'd refused to give up his ever-present tatty turquoise trench coat.

"Well," Ward said, "I appreciate your help. Revising our surveys is a complex task. And this is particularly sensitive, as we're not hugely far off the Fae city. I hoped your presence would make this investigation appear more neutral than if we'd brought our own agents."

"The Fae have little love for me," Darren said, in his typical gruff manner.

"You've never actively attacked them," Ward reminded him.

"Why are we here?" Holly asked. "What've the fairies done?"

"Nothing we're aware of," Ward said. "It's the – something to do with the screens. Our scans don't show anything in this area – the horde hasn't been near here in weeks – but Pax sensed something. We've got a new piece of equipment." She held up the odd device. "An energy scanner. And I brought this." She pulled back her suit jacket, revealing a shoulder holster holding a chunky pistol. "Darren, you might take it, while I –"

His blank look stopped her. "I never needed one before." In his striped polo shirt, with a crutch and one foot in a cast, he certainly didn't look like a gun-toting assassin.

"And hopefully you won't today," Ward said. "But it's an MEE energy weapon –"

"Allow me," Rufaizu offered, reaching towards it, but Ward stepped back. She looked from the young man to Darren, clearly imagining he was the only responsible gun-wielder in the group. He didn't budge, and she let the jacket fall back over it.

"We shouldn't need it. Holly, perhaps you could take notes." Ward took out a phone. "Tap here, and the GPS will record the location." She pressed a button on the big scanner and aimed it into the car park. Various numbers increased on its digital screen before decreasing again, settling on averages. A series of green lights came on, one after another, and the screen lit up: LEVEL 12. NORMAL.

Ward nodded to Holly and she pressed the phone, typed in 12. Ward grinned proudly. "Well done."

Holly shared a despairing look with Darren. Did the woman work with imbeciles?

"Let's go, shall we?" Ward opened the door behind her, revealing steps descending into darkness. Holly's heart suddenly beat faster. They were really doing it. Those things she'd read about, seen before . . .

"Your equipment pick up raptors?" Darren commented, following Ward inside. "They're small."

"Or ripple worms," Rufaizu suggested. "Buckets of them, sometimes, isn't there?"

"Yes, our motion detectors would've spotted those," Ward said.

Holly came warily behind them, unsure what raptors or ripple worms were, and thinking she might do better to spend more time reading about such things than actively seeking them out. Noting her hesitation, Darren let Rufaizu pass him on the steps and said to her, quietly, "You okay? You don't have to do this."

She tightened her hand on Ward's phone. "I hardly think we can trust you to do it alone."

At the base of the stairs, the endless possibilities of the tunnels stretched ahead, lit by sparsely spaced tube lighting. The corridor of concrete walls was interrupted by occasional branching passages and smelt like chalk.

"It's clean," Darren said. "No weeds, no cracks." He ran a hand over the wall. "Used to be no lights down here, we carried three torches each, to be sure. There were plants, too. Creepers. Some of them glowed, for a bit of light."

"We clear the worst of the weeds away, to limit creatures spreading," Ward said, moving ahead with the scanner held up. "Electric weed, as you called it, for instance? Glogockles thrive on it."

Rufaizu whistled. "Been so long, so long. Buda be damned, it's good to be back."

"Why would anyone damn Buddha?" Holly said.

"No! The Buda Labyrinth, what once held Dracula!"

"Of course," Holly said. "Let's bring Dracula into this."

"Ah, it's nothing – for tourists now. Staryn took me, says, here's your tunnels. See there's nothing to see. What do you need Ordshaw for? For the *minotaur*, I told him. That's the fight." He skipped about, beaming idiotically. "I was ready then, I've *been* ready."

Darren slowed to study the base of the wall. Scratch marks surrounded by murky brown patches. Holly asked, "What is it?"

"Trail of a tuckle," Darren said. "They squeeze down the tunnels." He followed the scratches as they passed the first break in the tunnel, a passageway Ward was nearing. "Hold up." Darren took the lead with quick taps of his crutch. He leant around the opening while Ward took an energy reading. "See that?"

Holly joined them. The passage was another identical corridor, this one ending in a T-junction a dozen metres away. A dangling weed hung in the intersection.

"Sickvine," Rufaizu said with wonder.

"Best not go that way," Barton said. "Usually indicates ankle raptors. Little packs of them wait for something to touch the vine."

"But your people said it was clear?" Holly asked Ward.

Ward frowned. "It must be an old vine." She stepped into the tunnel, raised the scanner and took another reading. "Thirty-four. We'll continue the other way."

As she continued, distractedly, Rufaizu resumed his wandering thoughts. "I always had to come back. The other tunnels, other places, they're *lost*. Gardossa and those in the Alps, we never saw it."

Ward gave him a questioning look. She had already listened, with the rest of them, to the young man's stories of old understandings of novisan and the things that preyed on it. A Bohemian city called Gardossa, an Antler King in the French Alps and an ancient hunter named Theo Murhaimer. Though perhaps steeped in nonsense, the stories paralleled Ordshaw's: Murhaimer carved messages in walls, gone by morning. Gardossan legends of an unseen beast. The Antler King's influence spread through caves.

"Have you connected that history to Apothel's book, yet?" Ward asked. The tone of her voice suggested she'd welcome a distraction from whatever was worrying her.

"No, but I'm curious about the Gardossans," Holly offered. "The Sect of Fore, have you heard of them? Not the number four, but *fore*, from the idea of *forward-thinking*. Supposedly they received messages in the catacombs."

"Prophecies!" Rufaizu interjected, and excitedly took over. "They were guided against the *beast* and warned of disaster."

"Apparently not very successfully," Holly added, "as they all died and the city was destroyed."

About to ask something more, Ward stopped suddenly, and they all almost collided. Rufaizu opened his mouth to question it, but Holly hissed for quiet. They all listened. A sound was coming from a distant tunnel. A rush of air.

"Fans?" Holly asked hopefully.

Ward shook her head and continued. The sound was escalating, like a broken gas pipe. Darren growled, "That's a dreadhorn."

"What?"

Darren hobbled quickly towards another gap in the tunnel.

"What's a dreadhorn?" Holly asked.

Darren didn't answer, adjusting his grip to hold the crutch like a spear. The sound was building, blowing up a gale, and a rush of air passed over them. He stumbled to a halt at the tunnel edge, and his grim look spurred Ward into action, dropping her scanner and clawing at her pistol. Rufaizu ran to Darren's side and Holly followed. As she drew alongside him, spying a heavy-breathing critter squatting in the branching corridor, the gusting wind pulled her hair across her face. The silhouette sat in an unlit stretch of tunnel, jagged knees pointed so far out they almost touched the walls. Its head was crested with spikes, as though wearing a homemade mantle, and its torso expanded as it inhaled, the rush of air drawing towards it.

"Get back!" Ward instructed, hopping towards them with her pistol caught in its holster.

The creature's knees bunched awkwardly in as it rotated towards them. The faint light from their tunnel caught the edges of mandibles, and the glint of soulless green eyes. They narrowed, focusing on the group, as its head stretched and chest inflated with the immense inhalation. Holly patted her hair back and steadied herself.

"Cover your ears – its scream will burst them!" Darren shouted, limping forwards.

Ward finally got her gun loose, but Rufaizu ran into the way. "I got it, I got it!"

He sprang through the air as the dreadhorn reared up, its shadow blocking the tunnel. Rufaizu made a shout of attack as he punched at it, and the creature crumpled to the side, cutting off the huge rush of air. It clattered back with crab-like motions as Rufaizu's momentum took him to the floor. It wheezed, mandibles working in and out.

"Yeah, have some!" Rufaizu laughed.

Holly watched aghast as Ward aimed the gun uselessly, blocked by the two men. The dreadhorn was regrouping, backing into the light of the far tunnel, continuing to breathe in and expand. Darren raced past Rufaizu. Visible in bright highlights, the creature's leathery skin stretched over bones as it ballooned with every second. Darren stumbled against the wall and cried out. Rufaizu overtook him again, snatching the crutch.

"In the mouth!" Darren ordered, and Rufaizu jammed the crutch forwards, just as the monster turned to them – caught it right between the mandibles. The dreadhorn deflated with a huge outward gasp, shrinking inwardly. Rufaizu backed off, hands held aloft like he didn't mean to break it. Darren let out his own deep breath of relief and turned slowly back. Ward lowered the gun.

"Done." Rufaizu hopped over the dreadhorn's final death shudder. "Is it done?"

"It's done," Darren said, pushing off the wall.

"How – how dangerous was that?" Holly stuttered. Ward gave her a backwards glance: best not to ask. "What would happen if these things got *out*?"

"That's the point," Darren said, limping back. He eyed Ward accusingly. "Your sensors said there was nothing here?"

Ward bit her lip with clear concern, then passed Darren to approach the monster's body. She leant around the tunnel's end, checking up and down, saying, "This isn't right. Our motion sensors *should* have told us that was here. And the energy levels are much higher than I'd expect –"

"You have no idea what's going on down here," Darren said.

Holly huffed in irritation. "But Pax knew? What's that tell us?"

"For one, we can trust her senses," Ward answered quietly.

"It tells us we still *can't* trust the Ministry," Darren said.

That worried Ward more than everything else. "No – we're fixing this. That's the point! But it's not your place to be here. We should leave."

"Leave?" Rufaizu exclaimed. "You want to *leave*? When it's getting interesting?"

"He's right," Holly said. It was clear enough that between Apothel's book and this government ministry's studies, there were big gaps in any academic understanding of these monsters. The reality was that no one would get a damn thing done without certain intrepid people braving the tunnels themselves. However daunting the place was. "If we leave now, we're no closer to explaining what's wrong. Seeing as your fancy equipment can't be relied on. No, I think it's best we continue."

9

Light spilled into Letty's fresh hovel as the door opened. Fresh was being generous: this box made the white room look big. Just enough space for a dense sponge bed, an old TV and a pile of boxes. Someone's forgotten storage chest. She stood from the sponge as Flynt entered. He'd adopted the same sort of disguise they'd rustled up for her: a dark green plastic poncho, hood up, glasses and a smog-bandanna, like a bookish crossing guard. The disguise didn't hide the concern on his face.

"We're good," Flynt said, pulling down the bandanna. "Edwing convinced Val's people he's been trying to draw outsiders back into the FTC, peacefully."

"But . . ."

Flynt bit his lip, too nervous to say.

Letty regarded him critically. The Scout Chief. Responsible for the Fae's scavengers, youthful, smooth-skinned where he wasn't burnt, and *nervous*. She said, "Hell's biscuits, before the scouts were run by a guy whose voice could've rusted plastic. How'd a whelp like you take over?"

Flynt put a hand on his hip, drawing attention to his pistol bulge beneath the poncho. "Got you back here, didn't I?"

"Got me *stuck* back here."

"With Lightgate still prowling out there."

"Spin on it. What's *happening*?"

He paused, still reluctant. "There's rumours going about. Emergency broadcasts on the big screen. Val's recalling my scouts, saying only Stabilisers are allowed out."

"Because they caught us making a call?"

"Because the Ministry have been spotted nearby. Teaming up with the Apothel Five. Like, ten blocks away."

"Pax?"

Flynt's blank face said he didn't know.

"Fuck this." Letty pushed past him to the door and he reached for her arm; she snatched his hand, twisted him round, lightning-fast, to press his face against the wall. "I ain't sitting around waiting for whispers, not with shit like that happening! You're at least gonna show me what's happening out there."

"Put on the TV –"

"Screw the TV," she hissed in his ear. "I want to *see* it."

She released him, stepping back, and he dropped his arm, more ashamed than annoyed. Defeated, he sullenly nodded and led the way. Out onto the warehouse floor, in the shadows of the towers. Flynt craned upwards, then whispered, "Okay, it's clear."

His wings took him silently across the path, to another building where he twisted back and watched for Letty to follow. He waved a hand and she lifted off, too. The Clear Glider worked. It had taken some painful jabbing and manoeuvring to connect it, but it was worth it. She flew with a graceful spin. Effortless, and a sign her injuries were basically healed. Hell, this would give her the edge once she tracked down Lightgate.

Flynt directed her around a corner, across another empty space to a major thoroughfare. One of the big avenues of the Fae city; nothing at ground level, but walls of homes and businesses looming over them. Having earlier escaped through shadows and alleys, Letty was finally able to see the city proper, and it wasn't pretty. Lit partly by skylights high above, partly from the many-coloured lamps and signs outside Fae dwellings, everything looked so *clean*. The stacked homes, variously coloured structures the size of human shoeboxes, were neatly painted and aligned. The air traffic, with Fae gliding from one opening to another, was eerily well-ordered, gravitating towards the centre and the broadcast Flynt had mentioned.

Floating high above it all was a great screen with drone propellers, broadcasting a news channel for the whole damn city to see. Even from this distance, the image was clear. Footage of that mousy MEE agent alongside Barton, his wife and Apothel's boy. All of them hustling into a tunnel entrance. A headline said: *APOTHEL FIVE WITH MEE ON FTC PERIMETER.*

The image cut to Valoria, the pompous governor. Bulkier than any Fae had a right to be, chains around her neck, hair in loose braids, wearing a velvet dress like a medieval queen. Standing at a podium looking Deathly Serious. Letty's skin crawled with the urge to pummel her glutinous face.

"This is clear provocation from the humans," Valoria

announced, her big voice echoing past the buildings. "So soon after their brazen attack, returning to our territory."

"Our territory?" Letty said. "They were going into the Sunken City, how do we know it's anything to do with us?"

"With no word of warning from the Ministry," Valoria continued, "we can only assume the worst. But I have personally been preparing a response to the human hostilities. The Council will meet tomorrow afternoon for a vote to move forward with it."

"Where's Edwing in this?" Letty turned on Flynt.

"Talking to others sympathetic to our cause. There are dissenters, he might be able to delay whatever she's planning, sway this vote –"

"Votes, delays," Letty said. "She's gearing up for a shitshow and you're talking fucking politics? We need to act. Wherever your boy is, we're here now and we know, at least, that she's hiding the fucking Dispenser. You know where?"

Flynt hesitated. "Only place completely secure is the vats."

"Too right, the fucking vats. So we bust down the door and stick it to her where it hurts. You and me, right this minute."

"What?" Flynt squeaked. "There's –"

A shadow passed over them and he ducked against the wall, pulling Letty with him. She shoved him off and leant out. Whoever had flown over was gone. She scoffed, "You ever actually *been* in a fight? How'd you lose the eye, coffee pot explode on you? What are you, twelve?"

He stood taller, trying to show he was a big, grown-up Fae. Hell, him and Edwing both, they were fully mature, but Fae reached maturity quickly, that could've meant anywhere between ten and thirty years old. "I've done things –"

"Screw it, come on." Letty pulled him out into the open. He stumbled after her before regaining his footing. She squinted up, searching for the black armour of Stabilisers, and spotted a couple watching the screen. Letty flew up, sticking to a wall, all the way to a nearby roof. A better vantage point, out of their view but revealing half the city.

Flynt landed alongside her, panicked. "You can't be out here –"

"Look at those mugs." She pointed. "They're all rapt with this fucking broadcast. You need a lesson, Cyclops: everyone here got comfortable, no one expects a beating. Like you. Strike hard and fast, they'll be too surprised to react. Where are the vats?"

"Hell, you can't – come back down, let me call Edwing –"

"Why'd you rescue me at all? You got no idea who I am? How I work?"

Flynt firmed up with a new trace of defiance. "Of course I do. Our old Scout Chief, Bevans, he flew with you, told us all the stories. Syphoned oil from a Warlowe Ltd truck? Ransomed a kid in West Farling? Edwing, he says, *she knows we're meant for better things.* When they said a human *ate* you, I said bullshit. Not Letty. We believe in you, alright. That's why I gotta keep you alive."

Letty took in a breath and let it out. His innocent tirade almost made her feel bad. Almost. "You know me so well, you think I need *your* protection? You know what I see, looking at you? A guy keen on action who's never seen it. Let Edwing do his thinking, he's not *here.* We go in quietly, get proof Val's got the Dispenser, that she's a lying bitch. Give your brother something to talk about."

Flynt hesitated. Long enough to say he was game. "Let me call Newbry."

Letty folded her arms as he made the call with quick, quiet commands. Asking for door codes, camera scrambling, hacker spy shit. While he talked, Letty gave the city another look. There was so much openness. Floor-to-ceiling windows, wide terraces; fragile structures that you couldn't easily move. She squinted at the stacked buildings: the securing clips were still there, these stacks *could* be detached, but this FTC was no longer mobile.

Her roving eyes picked out a familiar word, above a wholly unfamiliar leisure unit. The sign read *Rullion,* the name of the clubhouse the city's best scouts used to frequent. But the building had a pillared facade and a swimming pool visible through the big windows. "What in holy rat rot . . ."

"The Rullion?" Flynt caught her staring, ending his call. "Yeah. Mostly the Council and Stabilisers use it now. But we've got our place, too. The Bloodtooth Bar –"

"Don't, just don't." Letty shut her eyes against the madness. "Are we on or what?"

"Yeah. But we'll need to cut the fence."

"Got my knife." Letty patted her thigh where the sheathed blade lived. "That'll do."

He gave her a sceptical look. "Okay." He flew past her and

down, gesturing that she follow him. "Careful – stick to cover."

Letty kept pace with her own concerns. "Why's everyone dressed like mundane humans? Where's the shouting or gunfire or blaring music? This place is fucking *quiet*."

Flynt shrugged, leading her through gaps between homes. He pointed out the bigger landmarks she didn't recognise. "There's the Council Chambers" – ornately carved rotundas, mimicking classical architecture – "and Ducker's Exchange, biggest marketplace in town." A wide-open shopping centre, lined with shelves like a damn human supermarket.

"Oughta correct the first letter," Letty said. At floor level, a couple of slumped, shuddering Fae in rags caught her eye. "What's that? All this opulence, and junkies can't get good human drugs?"

Flynt glanced at the men. "That's dust withdrawal."

Letty followed Flynt until they were one tower removed from the dust vats. Landing on a lookout ledge, Letty considered the dust economy uncomfortably. She'd experienced medicinal grade dust that could heal. Were they also churning out the polar opposite?

The site responsible sat on the edge of the FTC complex, separate from all the other buildings and notably more horizontal; like four overturned bathtubs, connected at various heights by dull pipes, accessible through a foot-wide circular bulkhead in the roof of the farthest one, or via a set of double doors at the base of the nearest. Armed guards loitered around both, and wire fencing encircled the lot like a net. The fencing had one entrance, another foot-wide gate on electric rollers. No one outside Val's inner circle of workers ever got in. As long as the dust kept flowing, everyone was happy with that.

"Over there." Flynt pointed, checking against something on his phone. Newbry had come through quickly. "There's a blind spot. Through that fence, we can get to the walls, then it's the ID checkpoint. See, up there, the guards are turning the corner."

Letty watched the patrolmen drifting out of view, around one of the vat buildings. Both looking over towards the broadcast screen. She darted down to the fence, across the open ground, as Flynt raced to keep up. She drew her knife and slid it through the links; a quick slice and they fell away. Flynt watched in awe at the blade's sharpness, but she gave him a dismissive look. Who'd want a knife that couldn't cut metal?

Letty pulled a gap open for Flynt and they continued to the main gates, where he keyed a code into a number pad. Newbry had pulled his weight there, too. And presumably he'd neutralised the cameras? A surprisingly useful gaggle of nerds, these boys.

Slipping through the door into a small antechamber, Letty spotted a desk behind a glass panel. A single Fae sat watching TV. As Letty's shadow passed over him he looked up, mouth open, and she knocked him to the floor. Jumped on him, spun him around, too quick for him to see her. She hissed at Flynt, on her heels, to find something to tie him with. Together, they bound the guy into his chair with tape, then Letty checked the desk's monitors: familiar outdoor scenes – perimeters like the ones they'd shot across – patrols flying oblivious. Good. Then interior shots. The vats themselves, big cauldrons with pipes running in and out, a couple of walkways over them. Production lines with conveyors, grinders and robot arms processing sludge into dust and pills. One shot of a packaging area. Very few workers, most of the operation automated.

None of it seemed out of the ordinary. What they'd come to find wasn't on camera. Letty checked the screens against a map on the desk, showing the four buildings divided into sectors. The monitors had corresponding labels: Silo 1, Sector B. Packaging North. She said, "What's not being watched?"

Flynt checked. "Packaging West?"

True. No sign of the name on the monitors. Letty snatched the guard's keycard and paused to look at the TV. The broadcast was still going. A sallow-faced Fae in a suit had taken Val's place to talk about the dangers of interacting with humans. Fucker.

Letty ran at a half-crouch from the entrance into one of the silo rooms – a massive chamber, thick with the rumble of machinery and the hum of electricity. It stank like iron and earth. Pipes ran from the base of the enormous vat into the ground. At least a Fae's width thick, riveted shut except at a couple of small viewing panels. Whatever was inside glowed, faintly. It gave Letty a chill.

"What is it?" Flynt asked.

She wasn't sure herself. Pax came to mind. Saying dust sounded like the humans' glo. And here was shit glowing in the pipes. Junkies on new strains of dust getting high somehow. High-grade medicinal dust . . .

Shaking the thoughts clear, Letty dashed down a short corridor to an adjoining building, then skirted a production line to reach the doors to Packaging West, labelled with a big sign. Locked. The guard's keycard produced a red light. Cursing, Letty gave Flynt a look. He shook his head – no solution. In the gap between the double doors, there were at least three bolts holding them together. No way of forcing this one. But with that kind of security, they must be in the right place.

"There," Flynt whispered, pointing at a guy in grey overalls strolling onto a walkway above. Letty shot up between poles and pipes and dropped behind him. As he turned, she got a hand over his mouth and shoved him into the rail. She dug her pistol into his gut.

"Not a sound. You're gonna open the door down there." His eyes were terrified but he shook his head quickly. She dug the pistol deeper. "We can do it quick and easy or slow and painful."

He mumbled a frightened response, eyes desperate, and she released her hand just enough to hear it. "I don't have access! No one gets in from here! Please! *Please.* I know you – I've got a kid –"

"To hell with your kid. Who *does* go in?"

"Stabilisers," he said. "And Nimm. But he's not *vats* staff –"

"You got the Dispenser in there?" Letty said, storing that name for later.

"What? I don't know! But – there's a ventilation shaft – not big enough to go through, only to see – but I'm begging you –"

"Move."

Letty shoved him into flight, and the engineer took her to where a metal shaft entered the wall. He opened a panel and she wriggled her head and shoulders into it, keeping one hand clamped on his neck. There was a small grate looking into Packaging West. And there was her goal. The brass and glass casing of the cylinder was unmistakable.

"Satan's mule," Letty said. "That's my fucking Dispenser."

But it wasn't all that was there. A handful of Stabilisers were gathered around a stack of crates with Cyrillic lettering, and behind them sat a pile of earthen waste. A big pile, clumps of mud and tangled roots running through it. Bits of it glowed softly blue. Letty ducked out, glaring at the engineer. "What the fuck are you doing in here?"

He squeezed his eyes shut in fear. She got no chance to quiz him further, as Flynt called a warning: "Got people coming, time to go!"

10

Pax was almost breathless when she made it back to her seat at the casino. Fifteen minutes late; not bad considering she'd been right across town and met with a crotchety fairy. Only a few chips gone. She muttered apologies to the players eyeing her like she must be mad to miss a single second of the game. It was worth it. Palleday had hinted at a way forward, and that was all she needed. Some Fae, somewhere, would help. Now, she could play.

In theory. With one eye on the game, her mind wandered as she bet and folded her way through hands. Palleday's words drifted into her consciousness.

More people want you dead than alive right now.

And a lot of those people thought she was a Fae-eating monster. Trying to consume their powers for herself, he said. A relevant fear, considering something in their energy made the minotaur desperate to consume them. Did they understand it themselves, well enough that they might use it to fight back?

She picked up a king and queen, and everyone folded to her. Three people to go, and she once again had a dwindling stack. To hell with it, she would figure something out later; now she had to get back in the game. She pushed her chips in.

The next player called immediately, to two more folds, and showed a pair of kings.

Oh.

Pax stared with little feeling as the dealer drew the five community cards, whispers of upset as her march towards success was cut brutally down. The kings held up. She was out of the tournament. Her chips were callously swept away. Disbelief for a moment. She nodded to the vague sounds of people's condolences. Pax stood, forcing an uncomfortable smile, and ran a hand through her hair. Oh well. Oh well. It was just an opportunity to get rich. Just a matter of getting her life secure.

"Congratulations," a voice said at her ear, the tournament director, come to lead her away. "You did excellent, Pax."

An announcement penetrated her numbness. "– Kuranes, placed 68. Ordshaw's own, everyone please, give her a hand."

Two tables over, Dutch McRory was standing, joining in the applause. He gave her a kindly nod and she smiled back. Placed 68. In the money. Stacey Monroe would get paid. A camera crew were hustling through the crowd, waving for attention. She hadn't done much, but she was a woman, local. A Story. Bowing her head, Pax turned away. "I've got to go."

Avoiding well-wishers and the disappointed camera crew, Pax hurried into the lobby with the tournament director close behind, chatting about her winnings. Couldn't face this, needed a distraction. She took out her phone and he backed off, no stranger to the odd behaviour of an eliminated player.

It took a few rings before Ward answered this time. Good for her.

"Pax, how's it going?"

"Yeah," Pax said. "It's gone."

"Huh?"

"Never mind. Where are you?"

"Underground. Scraping the surface of exactly how corrupt our reporting systems might be. You were right, Pax, there *was* something – the true novisan patterns were hidden from us, our calculations misaligned somehow. But we've got new equipment –"

"As long as you're straightening things out."

"That's an overstatement. Pax, we've got creatures a long way from the *praelucente*. Near the FTC, even – it's rare for them to come this way. You were *right*, the blue screens did something."

"The FTC," Pax echoed. She saw a big screen over the main desk, the rankings for the tournament updating. Her name right at the bottom: PLACED 68. What was that worth, a couple of grand? A long way from a house, or retirement, or anything more than scratching about to live. The gains she might've got with a bit more focus – no, stop thinking of it. She had worthy distractions. "What are you saying? There's monsters coming for the Fae?"

"I don't know exactly, yet," Ward said. "And it's only getting stranger. Our new equipment, it comes from a private source. Duvcorp – I had no idea of their research. Christ, I'd really like your read on *that*. When can you come in? Are you still playing?"

Pax dragged a hand over her face, seeing kings and queens and fucking failure. Forget that: monsters were moving towards the Fae. Had the blue screens used their energy to spring an attack?

After all these years keeping themselves to themselves? It was a *good thing* she'd gone bust, wasn't it? Not answering Ward's questions, Pax said, "What do you know about Fae energy?"

"What do you mean? They tap into our electric grid, but it's so minimal we –"

"No, their physical energy." The camera crew entered the hall, and Pax hid behind a pillar. "What makes them Fae? How do they impact novisan?"

"Um. I'm not aware of the Fae affecting novisan any differently to how we would expect people to on that scale. We trace them using their heat-signature and sound. Their wings create a pattern unique in nature – that's what guides our shock guns."

"The blue screens kept us apart for a reason," Pax said. "The horde goes mad on their account. These things are controlling, and Fae energy makes them lose control."

"You do have something, don't you? Where were you before?"

Pax paused. *Before*, she had a chance at financial independence. Now, where was she? Twisting in the confusion of monsters.

Dutch McRory came around the pillar and Pax yelped.

"Jesus fuck – sorry, hell –" Pax put a hand over her mouth at the older man's gentle amusement. Great move, cursing heaven before a poker legend. "Mr McRory, I didn't mean to –"

"My bad, I wasn't looking to intrude. I only wanted to say…" Dutch held up a business card. "It'd be good to share some hands again, before I leave town."

Pax looked at the card with alarm, fingers barely daring to touch it. The words come automatically, "Actually. There is a game – this evening."

"Send me the details." He smiled and moved away with a light remark, "Back to work!"

"Pax, was that someone –" Ward started.

"Poker, Sam," Pax replied quietly. Had that really just happened? It seemed less real than the monsters. Was 68 maybe not that bad – she still had a future? Monroe's game would be big. And the Fae . . . there might be Fae there. Yes. She said, "Listen, I've got another game that I need to be rested for. Might lead somewhere good for both of us. We'll discuss everything tomorrow. Deal?"

"What?" Ward asked. "Wait, what is it –"

"I'm out of the tournament," Pax said, to an apologetic sound from Ward. "I need this." Not just for money. Pax stared at McRory's departing back. Connections, security, Fae meetings. This evening would have it all. "It's important. And these aren't the sort of people that'd take kindly to government interference, understand?"

Ward hesitated. "I'd really like you to come in, Pax."

"I will. Tomorrow. Right now you've got to trust me."

"I do, of course I do . . ."

Pax almost cringed at how desperate Ward was for an ally. Pax *wanted* to help, after her own problems were managed. Was there some little way to show that? "You're underground now? Near the FTC?"

"Kind of. We've been moving away, checking the tunnels –"

"Move *further* away. At least until I get a better idea of what's going on. Don't do anything to provoke the Fae, don't go near them."

"The creatures might threaten them, we could *help* –"

"The Fae aren't going to see it as help, Sam. Get out of there. I'll take care of it."

After surveying the Bartons' tidy lawn, Casaria knocked. He turned to watch the house opposite. Casual, hiding his desperation in coming here after he'd found no one from the Ministry at three separate Sunken City entrances, and seen Pax wasn't home. Anyway, there were months' worth of debriefs to be done with this family, so it wasn't unreasonable to drop by.

"Hi, can I –" a teenager's chirpy voice said behind the opening door. "Oh, it's you." Grace, the inexplicably perfect daughter, made cheap ripped jeans and a loose t-shirt look fashionable. Her feet were bandaged and a pair of crutches was propped by the wall.

"Young lady." Casaria showed his teeth in a grin. "Your parents in?"

With no smile of her own, Grace shifted a foot. "You don't know where they are? I thought you might be with them."

Casaria kept the smile. So his instincts were right, and the MEE were in touch with the Bartons and not him. "Of course I know. I thought they were due back, though?"

She looked uncertain, but said, "Do you want to come in? I was making a drink."

It wouldn't do to be found alone in this house with this young lady, but it was all he had. Casaria nodded and she used the crutches to swing down the hall. He followed, finally losing the smile as he watched the strain in her movement.

This is why we do what we do, he told himself. A delicate flower like this needs so much protection. Let them think badly of him for coming here, for all he did in the course of his work. His work was necessary.

"This way." Grace continued to the kitchen. Music played softly from a low-grade speaker. A trashy pop tune, matching the sound system. She added milk to a pan already steaming on the hob, and put a second mug alongside one on the counter. "They said they'd be back by dinner, but I've got some macaroni cheese in the fridge anyway, and enough episodes of *Culture Snap* to last me like a week."

"They haven't been in touch?" Casaria asked. "Not said how they're getting on?"

"Mum messaged an hour ago, actually," Grace said, pouring hot milk into the mugs. "To remind me about my medicine. But they're not telling *me* things. I mean, if I'm really careful Mum might let me look at that" – she pointed at a book – "but I'm supposed to keep out, otherwise. It's okay. Rufe will fill me in. Do you like Rufe?"

Casaria wasn't listening, eyes on the book. The big leather-bound tome of Apothel's Miscellany, the collected thoughts of a madman. Entrusted into these banal civilians' hands. And they were off with the Ministry? Had the world turned upside down?

The girl was suddenly in front of him, smiling, with a mug held out. It gave a rich waft of chocolate. He took the drink stiffly. He hadn't asked for it – likely to give him spots – but her face was insistent. Disarmingly encouraging. He took a sip as she watched, and he offered the slightest nod, which somehow lit her face up with delight. She twirled back to the counter, towards her own drink, using a crutch like a vaulter's pole.

"You probably don't have real chocolate at work," Grace said. "Dad complains about his office; *they* have a choice between sugar water and *shit* wa –" She froze, a hand over her mouth, giving Casaria a secretive, cheeky look. "Sorry, Mr Casaria. I wasn't thinking."

He mumbled a response behind another sip of the drink as Grace took her own. This young beauty, joking with him, knew his name? He certainly shouldn't be here. Did she even understand flirting?

"Do you want to know what I think?" Grace asked. "Rufe's *fun*, but he needs to separate the stories from the reality. His dad might have been the same."

"Is *he* here?" Casaria asked. Surely they hadn't enlisted that bum Rufaizu, too?

"No, he went with them. *I'm* the only one too young. Old enough to get kidnapped by fairies, though."

Was anyone but him not involved in this? "Who did they go with exactly? Where to?"

Grace's eyes focused in realisation. Casaria forced his smile, but wasn't feeling it. Her face didn't shift. Was she going to scream?

"They left you out, too, Mr Casaria?" Grace spoke softly. He gave a dismissive snort, but had no immediate rebuttal. "They keep asking me if I'm okay. Like, do I have bad dreams or something? I told them it was nothing. My dad lived through this stuff over and over, I just had a few bad days. And I was *fine*. This" – she held up a bandaged foot – "wasn't even an *injury*. Too much walking, that's all. I mean, yes, it was scary, but I'm not gonna *stay* scared, am I? I'd rather get over it."

Casaria said nothing for a moment. Was she making a point? He had a bad foot, too. She'd got over her fears, he should too? But he didn't *have* fears. "Is that what they think? I'm not fit for work?"

Grace studied him for a confused moment. "I wasn't . . ." Then her face became very serious and she put her mug down. "Mr Casaria, is this to do with Ms Ward? I think they *are* with her. But listen, there's this guy in my class, Luke Merrick, he spent months talking to everyone *but* Claudia Newman, and when they finally got together, it wasn't even worth it. They split up like three weeks later. You like her but are worried because she's your boss? I'd just get it out there, if I were you."

Casaria's eyes were wide with . . . something. Shock? Anger? The cheek of this brat – the presumption – the same nonsense Pax had spouted. He lowered his drink to admonish her. But hesitated. What if Sam Ward was keeping him at bay out of similarly misguided awkwardness? Perhaps the girl was right.

11

"Stinks to heaven and hell," Letty told Edwing, pacing what little floor space her dark hideout permitted while Flynt watched with his arms folded. "The Dispenser's one thing, but that weed? Your new strains of dust? The glowing shit going into *pipes* – Pax was onto something, wasn't she? There's more behind Val's tricks than keeping us under lock and key. Connections to the Sunken City she's hiding."

"All the more reason to approach this diplomatically," Edwing said. Letty had expected a berating for their little break-in, but he'd come with quiet concern rather than anger. He'd spoken softly to Flynt, worried he might've been hurt. It was all good. They'd gone more or less unseen; the first guard wouldn't identify them, the engineer was too cowardly to raise a storm. And Edwing was looking forward rather than back. "If there's a connection between dust production and those tunnels, bringing it brashly into question could see us connected to the humans as a threat to our society. Raising treasonous suggestions. We can't risk undermining Valoria until we know what the connection is."

"You need to undermine the fuck out of her right away," Letty said. "She'll destroy the Dispenser – the only drastic thing you could do would be *not* storm in and secure it. Drum up a mob and pitchfork your way through!"

Edwing looked to Flynt and the scout said, "I could get a couple dozen guys –"

"All we'd do is expose ourselves," Edwing said. "She could say she was testing it in private, ensuring it was genuine, or safe. She would hide anything truly implicating her before we got in."

"You were there," Letty said to Flynt. "You get the need to act, don't you?"

"I get it," Flynt replied, looking to his brother. "But we've gotta act *smart*, don't we?"

Letty took that in unhappily; an echo of the comments she made to her own boys. They might've simply broken into the FTC and settled here under the radar, if she hadn't always been trying to do things *right*. That's what this kid wanted. She shook her head. "Maybe fast beats smart, right now."

"Short-sighted as ever, Letty," a low voice said, as a man entered. Edwing stayed Flynt's hand going to his pistol, as Letty recognised their guest, from long ago. Smark, pear-shaped and bald with swollen facial features; his loose suit was greasy in patches, perfectly fitting to his yellowing skin and an array of jewellery hanging from his left ear, chosen for size rather than elegance.

"Welcome, Smark," Edwing said. "Letty, this is the Waste Chief, I invited him."

"Chief now?" Letty said. He had been around before she was exiled, a neighbourhood junker back then. With ready access to human amenities, few public industries really mattered to the Fae: dust production and trade, entertainment, health and education were high up there. A few rungs down were the junkers: people responsible for sanitation and, more importantly, for removing all traceable evidence of the Fae. Letty commented, "For someone who's gone up in the world, you look worse than I remember."

"Feeling's mutual," Smark replied.

Behind him came a tall, greying woman with a dark suit and the flitting eyes of the perpetually nervous. Edwing said, "And this is Deidre, councilwoman for housing in the bottom third." An even lower role, really: anyone could manage static living spaces. "Deidre, Letty."

"The troublemaker," Smark surmised. Letty's grin told him to sit on a rusty spike.

"Letty and Flynt entered the vats. They've confirmed Valoria has the Dispenser."

"Entered the vats?" Smark responded incredulously, while Deidre offered hushed surprise: "That's good, no?"

"It's not good," Letty said, "because Val won't use the fucking weapon."

"Is that news?" Smark said. "Why should the Sunken City interest us when we've got humans on our borders?"

"Val obviously cares enough to avoid the place, you pile of bile," Letty snapped, then asked Edwing, "What are these pricks here for? This mug used to spend Saturdays hosing down vomit."

"Letty, please," Edwing intervened, holding up his hands. "We need to approach this from the top, where we can effect wider change. We need the Council – it can't just be my voice. Deidre's district contains our broadcasting equipment, she keeps us concealed while we spread our message, and between Flynt and Smark they have a network of traders. Supply routes, safe passage for our people – none of us can do as much alone as we can do together."

"Our networks have almost zero movement," Smark said, "now that her friends have everyone scared."

"Screw your network," Letty said. "I could put that weapon in the hands of someone that would actually use it, *alone*. We give people a place to go, Val's FTC loses all its clout. And from there we can figure out what else she's hiding."

"Put our weapon in the hands of a human?" Smark countered with disgust.

"One worth a hundred of you," Letty said. "If Pax doesn't already have answers, she'll have people we can talk to. Ways to show humans and Fae can figure this out together. Then Val has to put up or shut up."

"Or history repeats itself," Smark said. "Not the first time Letty had a plan involving a human, is it? Last time they miraculously stole from us."

"*That* human wasn't working with me when he took the weapon," Letty said through gritted teeth. "Because he didn't trust the Fae to use it."

"No, I agree with Letty," Edwing said, carefully. "Building goodwill with the humans, that's where a better future lies, for all Fae. And I have news of my own, in that regard. Now we're all here." From the way he watched Letty, she could tell it was something she wouldn't like; a reason, now, that he wasn't so mad at them breaking into the vats. "I have an opening. I received a hailing from Palleday, the revered –"

"Palleday!" Letty said. "She actually met that dinosaur? Found a way to connect? While we're yakking like arseholes?"

"Pax spoke to him, yes," Edwing admitted, slowly. "She proposed a meeting. But what Smark says is no exaggeration. Valoria has the city scared. We have no idea what the humans were up to in the nearby tunnels, and I very much doubt it was hostile, but the fear has been stoked. The FTC holds its breath. Even the scouts are grounded. The drain tunnels, the crawl webs, are all alarmed. If there was ever any doubt the Stabilisers knew the secret entrances to the FTC, not any more. Yet *I* can go, alone. I've got enough influence, yet, to leave the FTC on legitimate –"

"Like hell you're going without me!" Letty flared up, stepping so close Flynt moved to shield Edwing. The one-eyed Fae looked more worried than threatening, determined to hold her off nevertheless. His courage made her look unstable. She forced herself to act calmly. "She's my human. I need to see her."

"I wish you could," Edwing said, earnestly. "But the borders are sealed. And after a break-in at the vats, it'll surely get worse. But Valoria accepts that some neutral, *important* Fae, like Palleday, may be persuaded to move on without coercion. Under the guise of seeing him, I can go to Pax. While you two," Edwing told Smark and Deidre, "start a public conversation. Raise the questions our people need to hear. How can we truly justify exclusion from the humans?"

Deidre deferred to Smark, and he gave Letty a stony look, not happy even having her in the room. He said, "If it means sticking it to Governor Magnus, I'll do it."

"A true hero," Letty said. "Reluctantly standing up for what's best for everyone."

"Anyone would think you *want* a fight," Smark sneered.

"Yes I fucking do, isn't that why you need me?" Letty turned to Edwing. "And while you're making friends, we're supposed to wait and leave Val with the Dispenser?"

"The Council meets tomorrow afternoon," Edwing said. "Give me until then. I beg your patience – don't rock the boat, and I promise you we'll be ready to act."

Letty wanted to say fuck that. To hell with subtle plans and talking and her being trapped here. But she caught Flynt's eye again. Asking her to stop, to have faith. She huffed. "Tomorrow afternoon. Then, if you don't fuck shit up, I will."

12

One by one, the Bartons climbed out of a manhole in New Thornton, exhausted. Barton was vaguely aware that he should've stopped a few hours ago, when his ankle started aching, but the draw of the Sunken City was hard to ignore. When the women asked, he said he was fine. The place kept him awake. Rufaizu's enthusiasm even brought a smile to his face. The boy hopped about recounting adventures that never really happened, reminding Barton of Apothel, the cheery loon who'd drawn him into this world. It disarmed Holly and Ward, too. Their walk through the tunnels stretched into hours as Ward's worries faded, taking them away from the warehouse district into New Thornton. There were signs of creatures, but not recently. Claw marks left from sickles, scorch marks from helluvian hounds. Just like old times, with the added beeping confusion of the Ministry's scanner informing them things were unstable.

They ran into no more errant beasts, but Ward's analysis, and occasional calls back to her office (*her* phone worked down there), suggested other problems. Her people were reassessing everything they thought they understood of the underground lair. Same as Barton. Hard to believe he'd been so naïve, believing what those blue screens told him . . .

Out on the street, Holly called Grace while they waited for someone from Ward's office to ferry them home. Rufaizu slumped a few paces away. Finally spent. Barton heaved the manhole cover into place as Ward double-checked her readings.

"How messed up is it?" Barton asked.

"Well," Ward said, "the bulk of the horde has evidently stuck together, which is both good and bad. It's not a widespread problem, but it suggests the screens can direct strays to targeted locations. A dreadhorn might've done a lot of damage, unchecked."

"The way we had it," Barton said, "nothing *controlled* those creatures. The screens needed us to report their whereabouts.

Needed *you* to do the same. We were their eyes and ears, weren't we?"

"That's the theory. But if we're looking at them manipulating energy, who's to say what control that gave them. Even if they couldn't necessarily track the creatures themselves, perhaps they still had some ability to influence their movements. It might be peripheral, uncontrolled."

"Like a lucky dip. They drop a defence and we see what slips out."

Ward hummed uncomfortably to say it was perfectly possible. "Not to worry; we'll start pinpointing the problem areas very soon."

"The problem is clear enough already," Barton said. "This novisan energy is more complicated than any of us thought. The tunnels themselves could be pooling it or something – if the screens can manipulate where the monsters travel. Makes me wonder if drinking glo hid stuff from us – what are the effects of just being down there?"

"You feel any effects now?" Ward replied. Checking over his body, he wasn't sure. Mostly he felt tired. She continued, "No, if we absorbed any of what's down there, it was too minimal to affect us much. But your glo, our novisan scans, they *were* blinkers. The blue screens didn't want us to understand anything fully."

Barton heard his own instinctive growl. Those bloody screens, with their broken English and cryptic messages. "If I could just get my hands on one . . ." He'd what? Punch a wall? Rufaizu caught his eye with a tired but encouraging look.

"Never met a foe the Citizen couldn't beat," the young man said. "But might not meet them again. Might never see them."

"We'll keep at it," Barton insisted. "We'll find them."

"I'll have more agents in tomorrow," Ward said. "You can take a break."

Barton watched Holly, across the road, with her back to them. Having overcome her initial reservations, she'd want to keep at it, the same as him. "It's fine. We're ready for more."

Holly briskly returned, sighting on Ward like a hawk. "Where's this pick-up?"

"Something wrong?" Barton asked.

"Indeed. Not that I don't appreciate your people's help, but I'd rather Grace *not* be left alone with any of you. Least of all Mr Casaria."

"What?" Ward and Barton voiced alarm together. Ward added, "Is he there now?"

"A fleeting visit, apparently," Holly said, icily. "But not a good start, is it?"

"I'll handle it!" Ward insisted, marching aside to make a call of her own. Barton met Holly's fuming eyes. What were they thinking, leaving Grace alone so soon after what she'd been through?

"Where are you?" Ward barked into the phone, equally incensed. "You've got no damn right, Cano. How dare you?" Her assault stalled with whatever he said. "That's because you're suspended, we're not *hiding* –" She stopped again. Swallowed it. "I'll send you the address. Come in at once. You're on your last warning. Understand?"

She hung up and offered an apologetic, worried look.

"If he touched –" Barton started.

"He wouldn't," Ward said. "I'm sure in his head he was doing something right. I'll take care of it – this shouldn't have happened."

Holly was staring at Barton, imploring him to do more. He didn't know what. He could throttle that smarmy agent. He couldn't shout at Ward, though; she looked as troubled as them. He said, "You . . . you'll handle it. We need to go home to our daughter?" It came out as a question, directed at Holly.

She held her indignation high, but said no more.

The Baudelaire Club sat in an upper-floor suite of an old converted bank, south of the River Gader. Its pillars and triangular pediment recalled a grandiose government building, the clubrooms harking back to colonial times, interiors framed in dark, expensive wood interrupted by deep green wallpaper and ornate carpeting. The furniture was big, heavy and sculpted, and every hint of metal was polished to a brass shine. Cigar boxes sat between crystal decanters, and the terrace looked down on a private park.

Pax had been once before, for a game out of her league. Being a token female player was good for opening most doors once, but it took real work to get invited back to the Baudelaire Club. Its members had old money and old values, expecting their women to show flesh, not intelligence. Pax had earned modest winnings on a hefty buy-in, but offended a member who offered her his number to arrange a dress fitting for her next visit. She'd suggested he didn't have the figure for it.

It wasn't something she regretted. But now she'd been invited back, with the many trials the last week had dumped on her, she came in wary of burning more bridges. Her single all-purpose dress wasn't classy enough for the Baudelaire, so she'd opted for a pair of black trousers and the sweater she'd acquired while on the run, striped and inoffensively slim. She'd also tied her hair back in a short ponytail, going for discreet over any attempt to make it look *classy*. She didn't expect to turn heads, but she could avoid turned-up noses. Quite aside from a chance at money and security, it was important, after all, that she stayed long enough to meet any lingering Fae.

A doorman in a burgundy suit led her to the game, past suits sipping cocktails. The poker room held eight men, the locals in their finery, the foreigners notable for their lack of it. The big Americans were near the balcony terrace, as was the pro Yannick (had Monroe approached him after seeing him at Pax's tournament table?). And there by the bar was Monroe, talking to a tall, slim gentleman in a tuxedo. There was something familiar about him. His angular features and narrow, judging eyes exuded power, definitely a few stations above most people. Even his jet-black hair, barely a centimetre long, likely cost a fortune to cut.

Monroe waved Pax over. About to say hello, Pax looked past the two men into the beaming face of the barman. Monroe's big henchman, Howling Jowls Jones, was polishing a glass, dressed in shirtsleeves and braces. A large square block of a man with the chiselled jaw and curly blond locks of a model, offset by a wonky smile and Pax's memories of him stabbing Casaria. Out of character, he said nothing, leaving the introductions to Monroe.

"Pax, our local champion," Monroe said merrily, lightly tapping her arm to break the look of uncomfortable recognition she gave Jones. "You know the most eminent Mr Tycho Duvalier?"

Recognising the name with surprise, Pax took in Monroe's companion again. This game was even bigger than she'd anticipated, and a response slipped out to alienate herself from it:

"No, Mr Monroe, playing cards in dark alleys and above Chinese restaurants doesn't often bring me into contact with the 1%."

"You're a pro?" Tycho asked politely, as he held out a hand. His enunciation was so crisp she wouldn't have been able to place the accent if she didn't already know he was American. Pax shook his hand – *ridiculously* smooth skin – and wondered if her peasant fingers just rubbed off thousands of pounds' worth of manicure treatment.

"Yeah, I'm a pro in the loosest sense of the word," Pax said, part of her screaming to stop talking before she ruined everything. Tycho was heir to the monstrous fortune of Duvcorp, richer than a Byzantine emperor. Ward had name-dropped the company earlier, she recalled with a flash of unease. Pax tried to push the feeling away with humour. "I sometimes make enough to buy a takeaway."

"Modest *and* charming," Monroe said. *Charming*, about as glowing as *homely*. He was putting on an act for Tycho, reining in his broad Farling accent. "Pax did Ordshaw proud today, didn't she? Queen of the World Poker Tour. Plenty of pros out of Vegas didn't come close to her."

"They'll write history books about it, the 68th Place Champion," Pax said.

Monroe laughed. "Did better than Dave 'the Cave' Spencer, didn't you?"

"Did I?" Spencer was a two-times WPT champion. Between scheming over how best to stretch out her £4,238 win and her anxieties over the Fae and underground monsters, Pax had paid little attention to who was still in or out.

"And she's bringing us Dutch McRory," Monroe continued. "Legend, ask anyone."

"I know the name," Tycho said, then asked Pax, "He's a friend of yours?"

"About as deep as my friendships go." Pax smiled. True enough.

"Oh for sure," Monroe said. "I'm surprised you didn't come together."

She kept her smile, holding his gaze. Of course, her stake here depended not just on her winning personality but that pro's presence, too. She'd texted McRory the address; seeing the clientele, she wondered if it was even necessary. "I'm sure he'll be here."

Monroe betrayed no aggravation, and said, "Drinks, then, Pax. You're a Scotch girl, aren't you? Jones, whip her up something special."

Something special, Pax saw without looking closely, was a whisky that would've been locked in a safe in most places she drank. It would help ease her nerves. She might even enjoy this. A mediocre prize in a tournament, a seat at the Baudelaire, making herself difficult in front of the world's richest men. A quiet hope of seeing an anonymous Fae. However uneasy she felt, things were on track.

13

Following the club's activity through the floor-to-ceiling windows that looked out onto the terrace, Fresko wished he could see the players' cards. It was obvious who was in charge of each hand – he could pick out the winners from the losers without fail – but it was dull as hell. He shouldn't have let Mix off, even if the man was a drunk liability. Some company would've been nice, waiting in a tree, trying to decide exactly how to handle this situation with Lightgate.

The Baudelaire Club brought back memories. Three years back they'd plotted a raid here. Bigwigs swilled brandies you could trade for cars; even their tiepins were worth a fortune. And they insisted on privacy that kept even the Ministry at bay. Letty's gang had sneaked in, taking trinkets for about a month until it got noticed and was pinned on three long-standing members of the staff. A concierge with decades of spotless service took the main blame. They'd laughed like hell about it, and it still made Fresko smile. But watching the building, waiting for the lummox to step out of the game, he got grim again. Was he gonna chat with the woman who'd torn their gang apart, or what? She was enjoying herself at this big poker table, drinking, chatting with some slick prick, now introducing some old fart who everyone seemed eager to suck off. Her granddad?

"Dutch McRory," a voice said. "He wrote the book on human poker."

Fresko's heart jumped but he didn't flinch, calmly looking up from his rifle scope to find Lightgate had crept up on him. She could've just arrived or could've been there an hour, for the calm way she sat on the branch beside him. How the fuck did she find him?

Keeping his voice neutral, like he'd been expecting her, Fresko said, "The girl doesn't belong in there. Not her class of people *at all*."

"I have decided," Lightgate said, with tired deliberation, "not to underestimate her. Notice anything strange about this place? It's . . ." She trailed off, eyes narrowing, scanning up and down. She sniffed, too. There was a good hundred metres of unlit grass and trees between them and the building. No way this woman could see nor smell anything of note.

"Wanna borrow the rifle?" Fresko suggested.

Lightgate shook her head, and put a hand into her sling. Rather than produce her own scope, she pulled out a hip flask and took a sip. The fumes burnt Fresko's nostrils.

"What is that shit?"

She held it towards him, silently studying the building.

From the way she'd settled into position, he guessed he wasn't in her shit-book. She must've figured he was scouting out an opportunity. There was no way she could know the plan; she hadn't followed them to Palleday's, had she? To appear helpful, Fresko said, "You wanted a chat with her, this could work. Assuming you don't just wanna put one in her from here. Wait till someone steps outside, with the door open, it'll look like an aneurysm."

"You probably don't remember working with me before," Lightgate said, taking another swig. He gave her a disbelieving look. How could anyone forget the ill-advised times they'd flown together? "I remember you guys. You were supposed to be the smart one. I don't want her dead. You moron." She said it so blandly it took a moment for Fresko to take offence. "We'll take our time. See what opportunities arise."

He frowned, dreading whatever plans she might concoct. She definitely hadn't been following them earlier, though, or she'd already know Pax was expecting a meeting.

Pax considered how far she could push Tycho Duvalier. He was a tight player, only getting involved when he had the best hands. And right now, her read said he *thought* he had a good hand, but not the best. A bet before the flop, barely big enough to drive everyone else out. A bigger bet when an ace came with a seven and a three. Then a hesitant call when she raised him.

It was just the two of them going into the turn, when a king came. Perfect. Tycho mulled it over before betting again. A dutiful one, less than a third of the pot. Pax had drunk just enough whisky not to overthink this; she called and let the river come. A nine. No straights or flushes available. Tycho made one last stabbing bet and Pax pushed in big without hesitation. Doubling the pot. He stared at the chips and she knew she had him. Absolutely. It didn't matter that she held Shit All. Or that there was close to three grand sitting there. Almost as much as she'd made after two days grafting in a tournament she'd waited her whole life for.

Well, she couldn't *quite* ignore that. It was a fucklot of money.

But this was her work. Waiting, needling, studying people and picking her moments with craft, unlike the tournament that forced panicking, blundering heroics. This felt *right*.

The room was silent. The only people remotely relaxed were McRory and Yannick, who likely read the hand exactly as Pax did. Monroe greedily salivated by the bar; the bigger the pot, the bigger his rake, as host.

Pax had Tycho's measure after only an hour at the table. Moneyed types usually bullied their way through pots – three grand was nothing to them – but Tycho valued being seen to make the right decisions. His family didn't become billionaires by throwing money away; that was written all over him.

"You put me in a difficult position," Tycho said.

"That's the idea," Pax replied, desperately waiting for him to make the right move. He had to believe she had his ace-queen beat. For sure, those were his cards: good when opening the hand, but not good enough to go mad with. Worried by that king, reminding him of at least one obviously *better* possibility. His thin eyes ran over the cards and chips multiple times. He had to fold, Pax must have ace-king at worst. Possibly a set.

Her eyes rested on the money again.

That three grand might be Pax's only big pot of the night. Yannick and McRory had been taking most of the hands, with her bowing to their more confident styles. This was her moment, and she silently begged Tycho to fold. If he called, she would be close to walking away empty-handed; a big blow to Monroe's generous stake for McRory's arrival.

"You've got something," Tycho concluded. She gave him a sweet smile. More confusing than a blank poker face. But Ward's comment about Duvcorp flashed up and her smile faltered, paranoid for a second – *what's he doing here?* Had he come for her? Was she drawing too much attention to herself?

Silly. He was the COO of a truly enormous company, for crying out loud.

He sighed. "I've enough on my plate already without adding this uncertainty. Well done." Tycho pushed his cards to the dealer.

The other Americans celebrated with loud congratulatory comments. One of them demanded, brashly, "So what'd you have?"

"A gentleman shouldn't ask," Tycho admonished the man politely.

"What I *have*," Pax answered, masking massive relief to drag in the winnings, "is enough money to avoid stealing soap from public toilets this month."

It got a few smiles, icy enough to suggest this wasn't the place. Tycho took it well, though, saying, "We supply sanitary products across Europe, I could get you a deal." It was hard to tell if that was a joke or a genuine offer, given Duvcorp's ubiquitous interests. Then he was standing. "Gentlemen. It's been a pleasure, but my father would disown me to see I was knowingly playing at a disadvantage. That's been made clear. Somewhere in the world, it's daylight, and I have work to do."

He folded his coat over his forearm and waited by the door for Monroe to cash him out. The next hand was dealt and the other players made comments about Pax driving away their most interesting guest. She tried to focus back on the cards. Thankful for the dual reliefs of winning big *and* banishing her sneaking suspicions of Duvcorp.

Then Tycho called over, "Care to walk me out, Ms Kuranes?"

Not good. Either an indecent proposal or Sunken City complications? In both cases, saying the wrong word to a man of his stature might open up doors she'd rather leave closed. God knows she'd done enough of that for one lifetime.

"Won more than you bargained for?" Yannick sniggered.

Struggling not to let the worry show, Pax forced another smile. She excused herself quietly – not quietly, she tripped on the chair – before exiting ahead of Tycho. The hallway was empty, and it swayed as Pax realised she was a little light-headed. The price of her whisky courage, mounting tiredness and high-stakes giddiness.

"I won't keep you," Tycho said, closing the door and lowering his voice to a whisper. "Only, I *can't* simply leave."

Here it was. Come to my hotel, or worse? *We've been watching you.*

"Did I make the right move?" he said.

Pax paused. He'd brought her out here for that? Rather than show crass curiosity in front of everyone? She said, "Ordinarily, I'd say the time to pay for that information has passed."

Tycho's eyes watched hers like a retinal scanner. Deciding whether or not she was inviting a bribe. He chose correctly. "I'm at the mercy of your charity."

"You had ace-queen," Pax told him, and he raised an eyebrow in surprise. Said nothing, waiting for more. She didn't give it to him. That she'd figured out what his cards were should've told him he was beat, one way or another.

"I was right to fold," he admitted. "I should not have been playing."

Correct. Pax smiled to herself. A little more at ease in this territory. Then it just came out. "Can I ask *you* something? Are you in town because Ordshaw's falling apart?"

Tycho's turn to pause. "With the animal attack and the train accident?"

"And the collapsing buildings, yeah. You've got that shiny tower to protect, after all." She heard herself but could not stop. "Why else would you be here?"

"A hundred reasons," Tycho said, amused by her forthrightness. "*Tonight*, I shall be briefing a management team overseeing our plants in China. Likely they need replacing by morning or we're down a few million."

"Must be an expensive garden," Pax said. He stared. "Plants. Like . . ."

"Ah," he said. "No, I meant factories, making computers."

"Got it," Pax said. There'd be no fairy tale wedding to this wealthy prince.

"But I'm curious. Why would your city's problems gravitate towards *us*, exactly?"

"Evil lurking under the city targets the government," Pax shrugged, "maybe it'll target other powerful institutions in the area."

The analytic eyes were back. "An interesting perspective."

Yeah, she didn't like piquing that interest. Really should not have spoken. "I'm babbling, aren't I? Look, I'm bursting for a piss, so I'll just –"

"But you're right," Tycho said. "That's the funny thing. My father *was* concerned by Ordshaw's news. Not through any fear for Duvcorp, mind. For more . . . esoteric interests. I'm humouring him, coming here, otherwise he would have sent someone less discreet. But that is an interesting thought. The UK government was *targeted*, wasn't it."

Pax quickly shook her head. Christ, he hadn't given a shit until she opened her stupid mouth. "I've had too much whisky, it's just –"

"Pax." He said her name like they were old friends, moving closer. "Let me confide. My father entertains ghost stories that strain relationships and drain funds. Mostly it's nonsense. Yet, as the whole world knows, he sometimes strikes gold."

Great: exactly the strange sort of turn she wanted to avoid. Still, she had to ask, now they were here. "What sort of gold would involve us, here?"

Tycho's smile revealed too-straight teeth, as he seemed to remember where they were. "That's a game *you* should not be playing. Thank you for this evening. I trust you'll use the winnings responsibly."

And with that, he walked away.

Pax watched him disappear around a corner. He had unwittingly imparted some curious details she wasn't quite able to unpack, while she might've set him on a dangerous path. And she had told one of the world's most powerful men that she was bursting for a piss, to get out of it.

Really. Great.

Fresko watched Lightgate with complete uncertainty. The woman had been sitting staring into the shadows for minutes, seeming to scent the air, ever since some unseen occurrence had drawn her interest. It had happened when Pax left the table, making excuses, following that rich prick out. Lightgate had been suggesting following her when she instead stopped abruptly, entering this weird attentive state. Fresko didn't dare interrupt. If it meant not causing a bloodbath, he could live with sitting still.

Finally, Lightgate held the hip flask out in front of her, arm straight, tracing something in the air. Fresko followed the gesture through the rifle scope. He couldn't see anything. She explained, "We are not alone. *Very* interesting."

There were no humans, clearly, and if she meant Fae, how in hell could she see?

"Tonight, we observe, my dim-witted friend," Lightgate said. "I've got a good feeling about this."

14

Returning to the Ministry's new chambers, Sam was greeted by her young analyst, Ryan, frantic to tell her something. She wanted to brush him off, to draft a report that would slow Obrington's purge down, but Ryan insisted with waves to his desk.

"It's strange. Maybe nothing?" He brought up the Ministry's map of the Sunken City on his computer screen – a three-tier plan of tunnels. It was overlaid by shades of colour, from yellow through to red. "We've been going over *everything*, rebooting the motion sensors, physically going down there. Meantime, I revised our historical markers. This heatmap shows the horde's movements over a five-year period. All the creatures. An even distribution, right?"

"Yes."

"But look here. And here." He pointed from one spot to another. Then tapped the monitor in a dozen more places. "All these spots."

Sam didn't follow. He pointed at a gap between the outer edges of orange colouration. "There's nothing there."

"Exactly," Ryan said. "Nothing in any of these spots. Sixteen of them."

"There's a lot of tunnel space," Sam said. "Some spots are bound to go untouched."

"But *nothing* has been in them. Crusads and bunch spiders, they get all over the place, and look, this one, the horde passed right by this room. Nothing slipped inside?"

Sam's first thought was that the Ministry had been monitoring these tunnels for years; if such a pattern was relevant, someone would have spotted it. But by that logic, they should've spotted the novisan transfers Pax uncovered. The areas were mapped, so the Ministry had been to these locations, but perhaps only once, ever, without movement there. Maybe he had something.

"Prepare a list of co-ordinates," Sam suggested. "Check them against novisan scans and see what's above them."

Just what she needed: a new problem. Thankfully, as she moved to her own desk, Obrington didn't wave her over, too engrossed in his phone to say hello. At least all these additional confusions would build a case for delaying Protocol 38. Sam just needed to get the report written before Casaria arrived, as he would make it next to impossible to complete it with a clear head. It was her own fault, she shouldn't have left him in the wind. Damn, it was a minor miracle the Bartons hadn't gone ballistic.

Casaria swept into the office before Sam had written an introduction to her report. He was clad in a pressed suit and starched shirt, not a hair out of place. Obrington gave Sam a look, directing the problem her way. She opened her mouth to invite his input, but he was already texting again.

Steeling herself, Sam sat up straight. Casaria limped over, examining the vaulted chamber, his toothpaste grin a little uncertain. He indicated the plastic "guest" chair Sam had on the other side of the desk. "You mind?"

"A little," Sam said. "But go ahead."

"Surprised to see you here." Casaria gestured from her desk, on the outer perimeter of their open-plan workspace, to Obrington's central position. "Shouldn't you be there?"

"Shouldn't *you* have stayed home?" Sam hissed, refusing to let him mock her.

"According to you." Casaria sat down and stretched out his injured leg, wearing his usual arrogant smile. The cut running across his eye was almost healed. His skin, somewhat concealed by foundation, looked its usual tan-tone, with only a few scrapes showing. Besides the limp, there was nothing visibly wrong with his leg; no cast or bandages like Darren or Grace Barton had, though he'd lost a toe. Sam knew he was a mess inside, though, even if his appearance hid it. Casaria had risked his life for Pax and the city, but had shoved Sam, and might've done worse if he hadn't been interrupted.

She raised her chin. "Yes, according to me. Your superior. You want to get fired? What the hell were you thinking, going to the Bartons' home?"

"Relax," he said, cautiously. "I only went because I didn't know where any of *you* were. It's no secret you need staff, how could I sit idle?"

"Casaria, for the shit you've done, you could be *hanged*," Sam said, as firm as she dared without raising her voice. To hell with it, it was time to put him in his place – but his face clouded over with an unfamiliar emotion. Some sort of . . . shame?

He answered quietly, "I waited by your place."

Sam's eyes shot open. He had gone to her bungalow? Her oasis, where the streets were unlit after 10pm because it was *safe?*

"I didn't go in," Casaria continued, some consolation. "I could've, your neighbours aren't exactly vigilant."

Sam was about to question him, but caught herself. How would her neighbours let him in? Then the realisation hit her. They'd shared rides when they patrolled together. Three years ago. He didn't know she'd moved out of her West Farling apartment building. She said, "You should have called."

"*You* didn't. And I don't like doing things over the phone," Casaria confessed. "Not ones that matter." He sat forward, then back, unable to pick a pose. "Pax is okay?"

"You didn't sit outside her apartment, too?" Sam replied. Casaria covered his hurt look with another smile. His demeanour was off, nervous.

"I'm a professional," he said. "Worrying about the people of this city is my job. And I didn't *sleep* with her, before you ask." Said like it should reassure Sam. "Look. I didn't scare the Barton girl. Good *someone* checked in on her, if you ask me."

"How can –"

"I was trying to find *you*," Casaria quickly continued. "I've been thinking – a lot – and it's not good. Before – in Greek Street, when I came for – you know –"

Sam raised an eyebrow. Had the possibility that he might have seriously hurt her stuck in his mind, too?

"I lost a lot of blood," he said. "I'd spent two nights without a bed. I wasn't myself. I didn't want to scare you. I would *never* hurt you."

A derisive snort escaped Sam's nose. She covered her face. "Sorry. Cano. Do you really believe everyone is stupid, or is it just that you keep convincing yourself of your own lies? You're suspended because you can't be trusted. You're unstable and definitely *wanted* to get in Pax's pants." She wasn't proud the last bit came out. But it was true.

Casaria was speechless. Some of the glow was gone from his blue eyes. Yet he would come out with some offensive or dismissive comment. Damned if she would let him.

Sam said, "You see Obrington over there? Your fate's in *his* hands. But I'm pretty sure I can predict what he'll say once I tell him you couldn't lay low."

"Please don't," Casaria said, a shimmer of fear finally on his face. "You're right, okay? Pax spun me out. Talking to her –"

"We're gonna go in circles," Sam huffed, but he hurried on.

"*She* said the same things. Not just her. I've *really* been thinking. In that church, I was there to protect her, but it was me on the floor, her firing the gun. If I wasn't good for that, then what?" He continued with a mad smile, almost laughing. "I don't *know* what I've been doing, and I'm pretty sure she hates me and thinks I'm useless, like you – but I found her, at least, didn't I? She told you about her sensing things, the . . ." Casaria held up his own hands, fingers spread, as if that explained something. "I made mistakes, but it was on her behalf. And I don't want anything more from her – or those civilians – I just want to keep doing a good job. Don't take that from me."

"You want to prove you're professional, wait for us to contact you," Sam said, trying to remain firm. Panic crossed his eyes, like an opportunity was slipping away.

"But you know me," he said. "And this isn't over, is it? You need those tunnels secured, and the Fae –"

"Casaria." Sam held her mouth closed.

He paused and seemed to suddenly sense his own pitiful display. His grin came back, utterly empty, and he stood. "Right. No, I'm sure you're hard at work. Always at it, aren't you?" He straightened his jacket. "I'll go. I didn't mean harm – you know someone should've been checking on that girl anyway." He paused again. Then rushed out a final idea, almost as one word: "Maybe I could get you dinner when you're done here?" Only the briefest pause for Sam to take it in. "You know, to apologise. If I need to? I don't know how upset you are?"

No words came to Sam. Her face was stuck fast, wide-eyed, as she realised this wasn't about his job. Not entirely. This self-pity and apologetic routine, his nerves – was he psyching himself up to ask her out? Sam feared the slightest movement might make her gag.

Casaria's eyes slowly tracked up to read her stricken face. Then he muttered under his breath. "Of course. Stupid idea." He turned to leave and Obrington finally intervened.

"You two having a good meeting?" he boomed, pacing across the room. Sam gave him a cringing look, not wanting to stretch this out. Had he been waiting to make sure the conversation reached its awkward zenith before joining them?

"I'm going," Casaria said.

"Oh, but we haven't had the pleasure." Obrington made it sound like an order, positioning himself in Casaria's way. Sam hadn't quite recovered enough to know where she wanted this to go. She simply wanted it gone. "Wayne Obrington, your new chief, in case that wasn't obvious. Ward, I take it you're reconsidering sidelining this man? Might be as well – when my next set of steel-dicked agents with fingers on the triggers get here, I've got a mind to –"

They were saved from hearing his plan by a loud beeping, a flashing red light drawing their attention to a Support computer. Ryan raced to check the details, calling out, "Proximity alert – human – maybe a blip."

"You can tell that from the pitch of a beep, can you?" Obrington said, sarcastically, as Casaria gave Sam a knowing look. One that said, *see, this place is falling apart.*

"There's been a couple today while we reset the sensors," Ryan explained, frantically deactivating the alarm. "It's BGb-67, up on the –"

"St Alphege's," Casaria said. "The closest access point's the Victorian sewer, off Meer Street. There's about two blocks between that and BGb-67, no way someone gets that far without setting off another sensor."

The flashing light and the beeping stopped. Sam stood carefully as Ryan's hands went up, denying responsibility.

"Sometimes the myriad creatures trigger the human sensors," he said. "Cloth frogs, maybe."

"This how you usually deal with blips?" Obrington said. "Reason your way out of it with whatever daft idea pops to mind? On a day when we've seen *repeated* evidence of things not being where they're supposed to?" He turned to Sam. "Anyone nearby?"

Sam shook her head, aware that Landon was starting a shift in East Farling and Obrington's new men would be finishing up in Nothicker. "We're closer ourselves, by far."

"How fortuitous," Obrington said. "Guess you recalled him at the right time. Agent Casaria, are you up for some redemptive casual reconnaissance?" His eyes stayed on Sam, weighing her up. "Assuming that's what this is? A rallying of the troops?"

Sam stared back. Definitely not what this was. But she had to get her report written, and this potential confusion certainly needed investigating. Casaria looked hopeful, to the point of restraining himself from speaking. He *did* know his job, despite his faults. And it would keep him away from her. Sam said, "Yes. Let him go. Just for this."

Casaria's grin returned. "I'll be back before you know it."

"No weapons, no heroics," Obrington ordered. "Get eyes on it, that's all. I don't want any extra crap hanging over us tomorrow."

Casaria was already halfway across the room, eager to prove himself, limp conspicuously gone. Obrington turned back to Sam. "I appreciate you being proactive, we might need him for Protocol 38. But you've got a screw loose if you were flirting with that one."

Sam could have screamed, but chose not to. Casaria was out the door. Everyone would be going home soon, tomorrow was a new day. Best, she calmly told herself, to complete this report.

15

Pax leant on the marble counter of the sink unit, staring in the mirror. A little more exhaustion and she'd be wearing panda eyes. She splashed icy water from a gold tap over her face. Her brain warned her it wouldn't *actually* help her stay awake. She groaned, piss off brain. She was having fun, making money in a place where, with these opulent toilets, they literally threw their money down the shitter. The potential danger of Tycho Duvalier had wandered into the night and even if Monroe took back half Pax's earnings it would be a profitable evening.

But wasn't there something else?

"Excuse me, please don't be alarmed," a polite voice said, and Pax turned to search for its source. She was vaguely aware that this was a unisex toilet, but it had definitely been empty. And the timbre of that voice, well-spoken as it was, carried a quiet pitch that she'd been getting used to. She lowered her eyes.

Oh yes. There was something else.

A tiny man stood next to the faucet, hands clasped genially across his waist, lacy wings up over his shoulders. Holding onto the counter, Pax bent to bring her face down to his level, a little too quick in her slightly inebriated state. He took a step back, but just one.

"Sorry," she muttered. "Hey. Are you wearing glasses?"

She gripped the counter tighter to resist the temptation to poke him. He offered an uncertain smile. A businessman of a fairy, he would've fit in at the club.

"Is that a real tie?" Pax squinted. "That knot must be *tiny*."

"Yes." The fairy adjusted the tie. "I understand you proposed a little talk."

"Well, it'll have to be, won't it?" Pax's hand was up near him, then, thumb and index finger held apart in an estimation of his size. "Little, I mean."

The fairy looked from her fingers back up to her face. Hearing her own words confirmed again that the whisky had been a bad idea. Her attempt at an encouraging smile didn't seem to help, so she tried to shake herself out of inebriation, only making him retreat from the flailing hair that came loose from her ponytail. Pax backed off, centring herself, before trying again. "Palleday got a message to you? Wait – where's Letty?"

"Yes – I'm afraid until our political situation changes, she is stuck in the FTC."

"So you've brought me a plan to bust her out?"

"I have a plan to bring *change*. My name is Edwing, I'm a member of the Fae Council. I don't know how much Letty shared with you, but our governor, Valoria, has institutionalised a fear and hatred of humans, promoting *peace* as zero human contact. You said –"

"*Peace*?" Pax said. "She tried to kill me!"

"She's spun many lies. But I believe in the sort of connection you formed with Letty. In an openness that can benefit us all. *I* believe human and Fae can work together." He finished with a proud, upturned head.

"And" – Pax couldn't help it – "you said you're called Ed*wing*?"

He hesitated. "Yes. My parents were patriots."

Pax offered silence to that. Fuck, she really shouldn't have had that whisky. Or spent all day playing poker or delegated anything to Sam Ward – this was the important stuff, *fuck*. "We need to get clear of here for a proper chat. Let me make an exit, we –"

The door creaked on its hinges. Too late.

Without thinking, Pax spun to shield the counter and threw her hand back, closing it over the tiny man. Just in time, as a newcomer strode into the washroom and paused. Jones, hulking in with his shit-eating grin. Acting like she was turning off the tap, Pax moved her hand from the sink to her trouser pocket, Edwing rigid in her loose fist, not struggling. She held him there, keeping her wide eyes on Jones.

"Thought I heard you talking?" he said, brightly.

"What if I was?" Pax answered.

He scanned the room, as if to say: *there's no one else around.* She let her eyes talk, too: *figure it out for yourself.* With no explanation forthcoming, Jones took a big step closer. His lopsided grin, she saw now, was uneven from cuts and bruises, concealed with makeup. He said, "I don't mean to intrude, you know, it's technically not even a ladies', this place. Not sure they *have* a ladies'. I read it wasn't until the '90s that Baudelaire first let a woman through the doors. I swear."

"So who cleared up after them before? Black folk?"

Jones laughed, in a measured way, not his usual whoop. "Stinks, don't it? I said to the boss, he wants to hook us up with this room and swanky company, we oughta take extra for our efforts, right? Bet some of them decanters are worth a boatload."

"Except the *game* is legal," Pax said. She shifted, trying to relax the hand in her pocket without drawing attention to it. Edwing wasn't moving. Hopefully out of caution, not because she'd hurt him.

"Those guys in there," Jones said, "you think they made their fortunes paying taxes? You, schmoozing with Tycho fucking Duvalier? Heir to that corrupt throne? What'd *he* want with you?"

"A goodnight kiss, what do you think?"

"You entertained him? Billionaires on the backs of paupers, Pax, you want to talk criminals, give me strength."

"I don't especially want to talk at all, to be honest," Pax said, meaning *with you*.

"Yeah, you see..." Jones sidled closer, approaching the counter, and Pax took a step back. He was bigger than ever in this space, an impassable obstacle between her and the door. "I thought there might be bad blood between us. The boss, he says don't bother Pax, for the sake of the game and all. But we need to clear the air, don't we, you and me? How am I gonna serve drinks smiling like a prat with you thinking I'm some kind of asshole?"

"Shit, Jones." Pax sidestepped, an eye on the door. "That never bothered you before."

"Ouch!" Jones whooped. "See, I don't want to lose that! You are special, Pax, you're one of *us*."

That rooted her to the spot. She'd imagined threats, mild intimidation or knowing remarks. Not camaraderie. She didn't want that, and was shaking her head to say so. But Jones nodded more vigorously.

"Come on, by now we must be practically family. We work *well* together, don't we? Holy *fuck*, we torture a guy and you get us off the hook?"

Pax felt Edwing shift. "That wasn't me."

"Alright, look." Jones held up big, calloused hands. "I get it.

You're cautious and that's good. And the boss, he's super cautious too, so he says, leave Pax be, I do it. This conversation never happened. But I gotta speak, and you know Bees would say the damn same. I'm giving you space, right." Jones moved towards the door. Hands still up. "But I'll give it to you straight, too. Come in, you get compensated good. Real good. You already earned it."

"I don't need space," Pax said. "It's already a no."

"It's already a *go*." Jones winked. "Just a question of you getting paid or not."

Her face twisted in confusion. He wasn't talking about what they'd already been through, but something new. Together with how well-meaning Monroe had been, with his hand-on-his-heart shit, this didn't sit right. "This game *is* legal, isn't it?"

"Hell yes." Jones dropped his hands, suddenly serious. "Fuck, don't even joke on that, we're on a serious earner tonight. And here's me not rocking the boat, right? But be in touch. I feel rotten the way we left things, don't I? You know Bees does, too."

The mention of Bees only made her more uneasy. "Where *is* he?"

Jones stared for a second, then his goofy grin was back and he ran two fingers over his mouth to imitate a zip closing. He continued talking anyway. "You know me, I care about careless talk. Enjoy the evening, Pax. I'm rooting for you."

Pax took a step after him as he made an exit, wanting to know more but remembering the rather more pressing concern of the fairy in her hand. As the door swung shut, something light brushed the back of her hair. Her spare hand was halfway up to swiping at it when she felt a pinprick of pressure at the top of her neck and a harsh male voice snarled, "You let him go right now."

Ah shit, another one. And what, a gun to her head?

Holding up her free hand, Pax slowly drew Edwing out of her pocket, lifting him as gently as she could. "I was trying to protect him."

"A human, protect him?" the man snapped. Young, edgy. "Don't *ever* touch him."

Pax uncurled her hand and Edwing stood out of it. He straightened his jacket and trousers. Then his tie, and finally his glasses. Unhurried, if a little nervous.

"You okay?" his unseen companion asked.

"It's fine, Flynt," Edwing said. "She meant well. Didn't know any better."

He beat his wings, lifting gracefully to float back from Pax. The pressure was relieved from the back of her head, a little breeze hinting the other one had taken off. Pax half-twisted but didn't see him. She said, "Sorry. I *do* know better. You guys can hide like magic, can't you? With that dust of yours –"

"Most humans don't notice us," Edwing agreed. "There *are* exceptions. So thank you for trying. I apologise for my brother's enthusiasm."

"I'm used to it. Last time I touched Letty I got pistol-whipped." She indicated the tiny cut above her eyebrow. "Deservedly so."

"Well. Where were we?"

"Not somewhere good," Pax replied, Jones' words hanging over her. "You've got somewhere else we can meet? I'll go straight there."

Edwing considered their options. "I'd like only a small concession from you today, to take back to my people. You told Letty the Ministry sought peace with us. Valoria Magnus claims otherwise, that there is no safety in trusting them. They've even been spotted near us, unannounced. Can you see a way forward?"

"Absolutely." Pax nodded. "I'm sure they *were* announced, your people must've hidden that. The Ministry are trying to get their act together and them being in your area was nothing to do with you. Talk to them – I can call them now."

"I'm our Chair of Information," Edwing said, "and I cannot guarantee the security of our electronic communications. But if you could arrange a meeting in person, then I can take that to my people, for sure. You have someone that you trust, from the Ministry? We could meet tomorrow – would midday give you enough time to arrange this?"

"It's a date. The Ministry want it, too." Pax paused. It meant another half day of waiting for answers – surely she could get something now? How to quickly explain the blue screens situation? Or that Pax wanted to know everything about the Fae. The whisky helped. "You know what makes your energy special? The Sunken City and you all, the Fae, there's something going on there."

Edwing gave it a moment's quiet thought. "We have much to discuss. Tomorrow. Come to the Tupsom lido."

*

Fresko watched Lightgate's face as the toilet meeting drew to a close. The white-suited fairy kept drinking from her noxious flask and betrayed no clue as to what she was thinking. There were a couple of bombshells in there: this young suit was undermining Val, and Letty was working with him. With Pax and Edwing going their separate ways, Fresko asked, "Our turn?"

"Next time," Lightgate said. "Wouldn't want to get in the way of this."

"Think that square can make a difference?"

"I told him —" Lightgate choked mid-sentence. She turned away, covering her mouth, and shook her head at her inability to talk. She finished, "I gave him ideas. Ways we might screw with the FTC. With these disruptive humans. We'll see what he comes up with. How close to *revolution* he can take us."

The way she said it, Fresko knew she had a different idea to what Edwing was planning. He was only a disruptive councillor; this woman thirsted for something Edwing had never dreamed of. It was all getting too much; no clear lines in this sand, and Fresko only wished someone would've simply asked him to shoot the human.

16

It took all Letty's nerve to sit doing nothing. They were out there talking to Pax, making plans, and Valoria was scheming, pulling apart the weapon she'd worked so long to find. A city on edge, and people like Lightgate taking advantage on mad whims. But Edwing was right – this was complicated and breaking into the vats had been reckless. On the slightest excuse, Valoria might start randomly executing people.

No, Letty couldn't interfere. But she couldn't stay put.

Pushing aside their warnings, she donned the poncho disguise and slipped out between shadows, off to find Flynt's Bloodtooth Bar. It had a big neon fang flashing on one side, no windows, and inside were grimy, mottled metal walls hung with faded bottle-caps. Heavy metal music played quietly from a jukebox, with scarcely a dozen Fae there, divided between old overweight bruisers and young posers too clean to have ever done anything of worth. A long way from the debauched chambers of FTC revelry Letty used to promise the boys. Euphoric dancing, fistfights at midnight, they used to have that at the Rullion. Now the whole city was stuffy as a fart in a box.

At least the whisky was fine; incredibly smooth. Fae culture wasn't a total bust. She chased that with a mug of mead and slipped into a corner booth, hood up, no one looking her way. She listened in on three old boys grumbling about a lottery of locations permitted for scouting. *If* they reopened the gates. When they lamented not having won the storage facility ticket, the nearest active human building, Letty couldn't hold back. "Are you fucking crying about getting permission to scavenge?"

"What's this?" the one doing most of the talking said. He had long wiry hair and a big old mole on his cheek. "Cocky young blood, thinks she knows better?"

"You might have longer teeth than me," Letty said, "but you ain't got half the experience. We're Fae, we take what we need; you don't get told where not to go."

"We're *Layer* Fae, not Rostov madmen. We work within the guidelines."

"Like fucking cowards," Letty scoffed.

"Who you calling a coward?" The man moved to stand but didn't actually rise.

Letty did, hood falling back. "You, you geriatric wart."

The room got two shades quieter, all eyes on Letty.

"You want to – you want to watch it," the old boy said, hands up off the table, away from the gun at his hip. Showing her with his body he didn't want trouble, even if he said otherwise.

"Yeah?" Letty swept her eyes across the room. "You can all have a go." No one moved. A guy near the bar had a bottle half-raised to his mouth, mid-tilt. "What's happened to this place? You still call it a night out going home without a black eye?"

"Some say it," a single confident voice replied. Coming from the shade of the entrance. Letty narrowed her eyes at Smark, the bald bastard plodding in with two burly Fae at his shoulders. His minions weren't dressed in ragged junker getup, but in thick, familiar armour. The bar got impossibly quieter. Letty hadn't sensed she was being followed. Seeing the pair of Stabilisers explained why.

"You all recognise her?" Smark said, moving into the room. Letty's hand drifted towards her pistol as the Stabilisers fanned out to the sides. The two men had the utterly impassive expressions of career killers. Smark pointed. "That's Letty. The troublemaker." He looked at each Stabiliser for confirmation. Then met the eyes of others in the bar. "Very much alive, and very much still a believer that the Fae can work for something better."

Unsure if it was her mistake coming here or Edwing's for trusting this bastard, Letty figured it didn't matter either way. She told the room, defiantly, "Yeah, it's me. What are you gonna do about it?"

Men exchanged glances, hands hesitantly hovering over guns. One of the Stabilisers drew something like a cattle prod, a stick that suddenly crackled with electricity.

"How many here think someone like Letty should be cut down?" Smark asked.

No one dared answer as Letty's eyes bored into the crowd.

"You're all scouts," Smark continued. "You've seen something of the human world. Or want to. How many of you think we're where we belong? That our doors should be locked?"

Again, there was silence. His eyes fell on the closest scout, a young guy, staring at the crackling electric baton, unsure how Smark wanted him to answer. Letty wasn't sure, either.

"I got word from Edwing," Smark told Letty. "I gather the meeting pleased him. Confident we'll find human allies."

"And you?" Letty asked.

Smark indicated the Stabilisers, to let them answer for him. One of them said, loudly, "My uncle died out in the warehouse plains. Because Valoria wasn't prepared. You gonna stop that happening again?"

Letty met his eyes.

So this was Smark making peace. Coming to protect her? And this whole bar better damned well like it. She said, "Too right I am. Are you gonna drink to it?"

Dutch McRory caught up to Pax as she started down the stairs, hands in pockets along with £2,300 in cash. Monroe, high on the success of his game, said the profit was all hers. Put that together with the four grand from the tournament and she was on her way. Bills covered for half a year, if she was careful. She could buy proper salmon in Sainsbury's instead of mangled trimmings. When was the last time she had so much at the same time? Three, four years ago? No more waiting until Christmas for socks . . .

"Not tempted to push your advantage?" Dutch asked with his genial smile.

"Not tonight," Pax told him, trying to look equally pleasant. Lying, because she was desperately tempted to try busting these moneyed bastards. But paranoid with Jones lurking and Fae in the air. "Be careful yourself, Mr McRory."

"Dutch, please," he said. "And *careful* is how I made my career. We'll have another game tomorrow, hope to see you there."

"I . . ." Pax stalled. Definitely have other commitments. Don't trust coming near Monroe again, for sure. Don't trust not blowing this money as quick as it came. But would *so* like to recreate the joy of seeing Tycho pay out. Ugh. She said, "I'll see."

"Do. You've got potential. You play in London?"

"Not often."

"Vegas?"

"It's on my list."

"You come out there," McRory said, "you've got my number.

Out there, someone like you, your wings'll spread wider."

"Someone like me?" A smile tugged at the corners of Pax's mouth.

McRory nodded without explanation, patting her arm and bidding her farewell. "Take care, Pax. I look forward to seeing you again."

Pax didn't dare say more.

The warmth of the conversation lasted half an hour, until her taxi crept into her neighbourhood of Hanton. She passed a house party with students spilling onto the street, shouting into each other's faces as they waved bottles above their heads. Three blocks from home, the taxi stopped at a red light, the driver cursing. A young man was retching into the drain. Another pair pointed and laughed from a wall.

Without the affluence of a taxi, Pax would be out soaking up such antics. As far from Tycho Duvalier's incongruous accent and Dutch McRory's promises of overseas potential as you got. No responsibilities, like the midweek vomiter there. Fuck it, she told the driver she could walk from here. A voice in her head warned her it was this kind of thing that got her drawn into the Sunken City in the first place. But that voice could spin on it. Pax jumped out and breathed in the night air.

"You looking for the party?" a student called out from the wall.

The house was alive with flashing lights and throbbing bass, so Pax gave the banal question the raised eyebrows.

The young man hopped off the wall. "I got beers in the fridge – Peroni, the good stuff?" He was reasonably lucid for a drunk, only his untamed volume giving him away. A slim, dark-skinned guy with a round face and gentle eyes, talking fast and friendly. "What music are you into?" Citing classic hits, Sinatra, Lee Hazlewood, to prove he was deeper than the pop coming from the party. Then from music to films, as Pax silently searched her own feelings. Watching the building. Her warm well-being quietly faded. Her fingers tingled, not unlike the sensation the blue screens gave her.

Something here, close.

Shit.

Not the screens. Something else. In that building? It wasn't bad, was it? *Good* energy? Was this what novisan felt like when people partied? Bringing out the best in each other? Pax allowed it. It didn't have to make sense. It was enough to feel like she wasn't up against the whole world. Only part of it.

The student's chatter demanded her attention. "What do you think of it? I bet you've seen it, you have to have."

"Huh?" Pax frowned. No idea where his private conversation had taken him.

"*Devilfist Noon*. I must've watched it twelve times now."

The odd title caught Pax's attention. "Devil *what*?"

"Easily Rik Greivous' best. And that's saying something, all he touched was gold."

Those comments jarred Pax. The beat in the house cut out and another tune came on, more muted, to a few groans inside. With that shift, the energy Pax was on the cusp of feeling was gone. Pax stared numbly at the young man. "Come again?"

"Greivous? You're a fan? Oh come on, he was the master."

"The film-maker?" Pax ventured, uneasy at hearing this recently-familiar name. Rik Greivous, Apothel and Barton's friend, had disappeared a long time ago. The name brought the same fears Jones' hints gave her. Something going on she wasn't aware of.

"I could lend you a copy?" her new friend offered.

Pax turned to leave. "I've gotta go."

"Hey no, wait! You didn't see the graffiti wall?" The student pointed back towards the party hopefully, not following. Pax pulled her jacket tighter, to feel for the cash and the little comfort it brought. Her life, back on track, soon –

Another student mocked his friend. "Mate, a woman like that would've eaten you *alive*."

Pax froze. Echoes of McRory: someone like you. A woman like that. Palleday afraid she was a monster. She felt the blood turning in her veins. Stirred by the energy of the party, the uncertainty over Duvcorp, the complications of whatever Jones was up to, the monsters wandering the city, the blue screens busy – she felt it *in her veins*, and fought down a despairing sound. She was the centre, not the screens, not the minotaur or the Fae. She and her unnatural bloody senses. Unable to flee to Vegas leaving Sam Ward and everyone else holding the ball. Unable to be unassuming, unattached, Pax of the shadows.

She had to own this. Master it, understand it, before shedding it.

She had to *be* something.

But at least she didn't have to do it alone. Continuing home, Pax wrote Ward a message: *Tell your boss we'll meet in the morning.*

*

The problem with women, Cano Casaria decided, trekking through the St Alphege's sewers with only a torch for company, was that they had *many* problems. Sam Ward, for example, was both arrogant to the point of being above an apology dinner and yet craven enough to roll over for the first boss-figure to come along after she'd usurped control. At once fiercely ambitious and cowardly. Rolling a panel of heavy wooden slats back from a hole in the brickwork, Casaria considered how she revelled in theory but not in action. She probably described imagined dates in her diary rather than ever actually talking to anyone.

Dates – Casaria admonished himself for the word. He ducked into a tunnel, a small unlit cave, taking care to squat low so his shoulders didn't brush the ceiling. That's what she thought he was doing, wasn't it, asking her on a date. That's what Pax would say, laughing. Not even considering that he might honestly be remorseful for his actions.

Fuck the pair of them. And fuck that Barton child for putting such ideas in his head, that he should be clear and straight with any of these women.

Ward should have been thankful for the offer. It would've been punching way above her weight. Or was that it? Was she intimidated? Not from any perceived threat – he had apologised for that, after all – but because she didn't feel worthy? He smirked. When she went home to scribble about it in her diary, would it make her a little excited?

The narrow dugout opened onto a wider tunnel, which Casaria scanned with the torch. No lighting here, either; the passages at the edges of town, stretching north and west into St Alphege's and West Quay, were broadly neglected. Likewise the ones south-west through Nothicker. The *praelucente* and its horde rarely came to these areas, most likely because the energy above wasn't a worthy draw. So, in turn, the Ministry left light bulbs unchanged and power lines untended.

Continuing down a long hallway, Casaria noted a similarity to the Ministry's new office. Older brick tunnels and archways, damp and smelly, fitting to the bloated ogre that had instructed they move. Most likely they had been afraid to give Casaria the new address, knowing he'd disapprove.

He'd have words with them, alright. When his search reminded everyone how much they needed him. Sam Ward would recall he was a good team player. Hell, she was courting Pax herself, she had to appreciate what he'd done for her . . .

BGb-57, Casaria was aware, wasn't much of a place at all. An intersection of a couple of tunnels. He'd reach it soon, see there was nothing, check the batteries on the motion sensor and report back. Quick and simple. Those new agents would probably quake coming down here. Spend all night checking shadows for spiders.

Sam Ward certainly wouldn't venture this far alone. She'd been apprehensive even in his company. He sighed. He'd gone about it wrong, hadn't he, offering himself as supplicant? She needed a guiding hand. He could try again tomorrow. Not ask, but tell her: we'll go to dinner. For my apology. You'll enjoy it.

Women liked that, didn't they? Being told what –

Casaria stopped, torchlight hitting a shape where two tunnels crossed ahead. It was big – not quite person-sized but bulging with muscle. Cracked flesh dark all over, the shade of a *scorpio mites*. A territorial creature that warranted shooting on sight. And Casaria had no gun on him. Only his fists. There were stories that Darren Barton got into fistfights with them, but Casaria had never had the opportunity himself. The Ministry had regulations to prevent that; forms you'd have to fill in. But with the leeway they'd given Barton, they might turn a blind eye for him, too.

He edged closer, turning his rear foot, ready for action. The creature wasn't moving. It was slumped against the wall. There was no glow between its muscles. Casaria traced the torchlight up the wall. A dark splatter.

He approached quickly, then, and checked both directions down the adjoining tunnels. No sign of any other creature. There'd been no reports from Support of any activity here – what did this?

Casaria lit up the creature's grotesque face. Just above its crescent eyes, that was where the wound was. There were a handful of creatures in the horde that might make a hole like that. The needle-nose of the *corno cattus* might – but that speared animals at waist-height. And it wouldn't leave a corpse untouched. The more logical explanation opened a world of darker possibilities.

A gunshot wound.

If a human handgun killed this creature, the Sunken City had been compromised.

PART 2

1

The FTC was stirring.

The secret was out, after the revelry that left Letty, in the morning, with a headache and red knuckles, and her poncho torn on the floor. Fine by her, she had never been one to hide; she felt better in her short shorts, sheath knife and pistol on show. Between that and the marks from last night, the sight of her gave Edwing and Flynt a start. Edwing was halfway to arranging medical aid when she explained she'd only been drinking. Instead, he called up Newbry to see how much exposure she'd had.

The story had reached the Fae media. They took enthusiastic bar patrons' accounts out of context to say Letty had emerged looking for a fight. Defying her exile and their peaceful ways. Smark spoke into cameras saying he didn't know her whereabouts or plans, but that she was welcome in the East Eight blocks. That focused the Stabilisers' search, at least. Meanwhile the news anchors questioned his loyalty to Fae security.

Once Edwing was done taking in Newbry's report, an index finger tapping his chin, he said, "I intended for Smark to approach this subtly. He shouldn't have encouraged you. I have my own message, one that doesn't involve fighting."

"It was a bar brawl," Letty said, sitting on her sponge bed while Flynt watched from the door. "It's in our blood. Isn't it?"

"An outdated concept," Edwing said.

"You're a bloody outdated concept," Letty said wearily. "No one from that bar's ratting me out, Edwing. This morning, some bruised punk with a couple teeth missing woke up thankful he ran into me."

"Meanwhile the patrols are doubling and they'll be aware exactly who broke into the vats," Edwing said. "And any statement I make about the humans will be connected –"

"To *me*?" Letty snapped. "Sorry, your majesty, does my name sully yours, when I deliver such things as a healthy contact with a human?"

Edwing gave her a wary look. "I appreciate it, deeply. I have faith in Pax, and if what she says is true about the Ministry, then there's hope for everyone. But you *have* to go to ground until we get there."

"I'm not running," Letty said. "And I wasn't just boozing. This news is working for us. Smark's got Stabilisers chasing their tails in the wrong part of the city, while *others* are willing to help us out. They can get Val's science prick Nimm's address. A key to his place, even. While you do your thing, I can do mine."

"It has to wait!" Edwing was in danger of showing emotion. "I will make Valoria account for the hiding of the Dispenser, and her false claims about communications with the humans. But targeting her dust facilities and people gives her an opportunity to deflect from those issues. You've done *plenty*, isn't it our turn to do something for you?"

"I don't need anyone to do nothing for me. Never have. Never will." Letty looked away from them, nothing to fix on but stains. Never needed anyone and where did it get her. Hiding while these morons were talking to Pax? The thought gave her pause. She asked, "How was she?"

Flynt answered, "I'm not convinced."

"We didn't meet her at the best time," Edwing explained. "But I trust she is exactly who we need."

"She's safe? Any mention of what the Ministry are doing? Lightgate?"

Edwing shook his head. "From her situation, she seemed at ease."

"I've never been that close to a human," Flynt said. "I can . . ." His nose curled in distaste. " . . . still smell her. Took a lot of restraint not to hurt her." Letty's smile faded. "I don't get it. What makes you so sure she's not like the rest of them? She could've killed him."

"Nonsense," Edwing replied plainly. "She demonstrated quick-thinking."

"What happened?" Letty demanded.

"A man interrupted us," Flynt said, "and she threw Edwing in her pocket. I had to pull a –" He stopped, rather than talk over Letty's laughter.

Pocketing a Fae councillor? The girl didn't give a shit. Wiping a tear from her eye, Letty read Flynt's humourless glower, noting his fear. "Pax is harmless. She's just a bit handsy."

"And you did *not* need to draw a gun on her," Edwing admonished. "Clearly she's given a lot of thought to our people. She asked about our specific energy."

This idea again. "Any insights?"

"I thought it best to leave such discussion for a more formal setting. But I look forward to our next meeting."

"Questions about our *energy* clearly intersects with the Dispenser and Val's glowing crap in the vats. We could be talking to this Nimm chump already. I can be subtle."

Edwing eyed Letty. Surely thinking she was going to do it anyway, wondering how he could prevent a disaster. "I intend to leave Flynt with you. He knows how the city works, how to stay hidden."

"While you head into Ordshaw alone?" Flynt said. "No chance."

"I'm not the one being hunted," Edwing said. "The trouble is here, in the FTC, where you're best able to protect Letty. I'll be fine."

"The hell you will!" Flynt flared. "That human –"

"Will not hurt me," Edwing replied calmly. "I want you two safe and ready, for when I return. Letty, if you can only wait –"

"Like Val will wait?" Letty said. "She'll be covering shit up, smearing her trail, silencing leads. While I wank in a corner?"

"Things will change," Edwing answered calmly, quietly. "Today. I will release a statement, saying I am working with you, and know Pax Kuranes and the MEE intend to vanquish the creatures of the Sunken City. When we address the Council, the FTC will have to act."

Unmoved, Letty replied, "You actually going to use that word, *vanquish*?"

"Yes," Edwing told her seriously. "This *is* a righteous struggle."

She went quiet at the gravity of his conviction. Deny it as she might, she couldn't suppress the hope he exuded. For once, maybe she wasn't alone. Meaning she'd better listen.

2

Pax took in the coffee shop, relieved that they were meeting somewhere welcomingly normal, rather than the tunnel where, according to Sam Ward, the MEE was now based. Apparently that now meant members of the public, or bigwigs out of the government, were greeted in plastic-coated booths over a battered sausage and a milkshake, before the Ministry disappeared back underground like mole people. The waiting staff wore chequered uniforms in the fashion of tea towels, and their customer base comprised paint-splattered labourers whose main criteria for food was maximising calories.

Strangely, Sam Ward and Wayne Obrington fit in perfectly, as though obvious spooks were the other natural inhabitant of a greasy café. Alongside them and the labourers (on a Sunday morning?), Pax alone stood out in her ordinariness, dressed in her least-stained jeans, a green hoodie and her second-best coat. The suits were huddled together on one side of a booth, waiting for her; this bull of a man could've used a bench to himself, and struggled to get around the table to stand and shake her hand. Ward was grinning at Pax, and had probably lost sleep over what they might discuss.

Obrington introduced himself with a smile, gesturing for Pax to take a seat. "You'll eat something?" he suggested, squeezing back into place. Ward gave a quiet hello, with a little wave. Obrington passed the menu over. He already had a large plate overflowing with sausages, eggs and beans. "Forgive my appetite."

Pax gave the menu the quickest glance, aware of the sort of fare available. If they had salmon, it was better that they keep it. A middle-aged waitress joined them, inviting Pax to order with a cocked eye, and Pax asked for a black coffee and eggs on toast. Ward, she noticed, only had a glass of water. Probably ate a salad before starting work, what, eight hours ago?

"I've read the reports," Obrington said, cutting mercilessly into a sausage, "including Ward's weighty new edition. So I'm not gonna insult anyone's intelligence, or time – let's agree the Sunken City doesn't add up and the fairies might be important. That it *might* be prudent to take our time before enacting Protocol 38. And you, for reasons currently beyond me, have some keen insights into that. Correct?"

"It's my natural curiosity," Pax said. "I couldn't do your work with all the questions your lot have left unanswered."

Obrington looked to Ward, inviting her response. She cleared her throat, and Pax picked up an uneasy edge in her voice. "Management tend to believe we can do our jobs without overextending ourselves. Understanding is not an absolute requirement for keeping order."

Pax didn't let her look away, trying to weigh up the conviction in the assessment. Then said, "Management have royally fucked us all for a fair while, haven't they?"

Obrington snorted through a mouthful of food, seeming to approve, and waved his fork for Ward to continue, flicking brown sauce onto the table. Ward waited as the waitress returned with septic-smelling coffee, then said, quietly, "We're starting to uncover the full breadth of the grugulochs' influence. How much we don't know. The truth is, without your . . . curiosity . . . we might never have recognised the fox in our own henhouse."

Pax watched Obrington, as Ward was clearly saying it for his benefit. He shovelled more food into his mouth and worked his bovine way through it, offering no input.

"Okay," Pax said. "I can contribute more, but I want to be careful about how we involve the Ministry. I'd like to borrow Sam, but otherwise have no one else nearby. And I'd like you to press pause on provoking the Sunken City creatures. Definitely don't go near the FTC again."

Obrington stopped eating. "Funny, I thought you came to help, not make demands."

"I *am* helping."

"You're aware the creatures have been moving erratically? Approaching some very compromising positions?"

"Yeah, and I'm concerned that simply killing them might make that worse."

Obrington looked sideways at Ward, and she fumbled for a compromise. "Perhaps if we knew where –"

"I think I can work with the Fae," Pax said. "But not their leaders."

Obrington sat back. "You've experienced their lunacy. They're a bloody nuisance."

"They're more than that," Pax insisted. "The horde go after the Fae with more passion than anything, but the blue – the *grugulochs* never sought them out, not since they were driven above ground. Your leaders were corrupted a long time ago but only took action against the Fae last week. Only now have you seen a creature venture towards them, right? The grugulochs was scared of them."

"They developed weapons dangerous to it." Obrington shrugged. "So have we. Only difference is we had no inclination to use them before."

"The bigger difference is you've no idea if *yours* work, do you? You're finding your existing tools aren't all you thought them to be. Understanding the Fae is the only sure way to get a complete picture here."

"Alright." Obrington put his fork down, like this detail was enough to cost him his appetite. "Say you're right. Say you're not just, for example, buying time to get your little fairy mate back? The one accused of killing our people? Let's say –"

"Oh, piss off," Pax cut in. "She did *not* do that. I'm doing this because you've no idea the damage you might do messing with powers you don't understand."

Ward averted her gaze. Hiding a smile? Unfazed, Obrington said, "Implying you *do* understand. Why would that be?"

"I'm smarter than you? Then, it doesn't take a genius to see co-operation with an otherworldly race with miniature technology might benefit us."

He clicked his tongue in thought, then deferred again to Ward. She said, "I've always promoted a better working relationship with the Fae. I don't see the harm in exercising caution."

"You think it's *cautious* to work with the people that gunned down eight agents?" Obrington said.

"We're looking for the fairy Lightgate," Ward said. "That's –"

"Don't care. You keep this up, I'm stuck lurking in this backwater. Wasn't I clear about that? I don't like to lurk anywhere longer than necessary. Least of all places where you're exciting a dormant force of evil or two that we'd rather *stay* dormant."

"It has been for decades," Pax said. "You can afford a few extra days."

"I also don't like having a civilian presume to tell me my business," Obrington said. "This is really how you do things?" Ward straightened up, not meeting his eyes but steeling herself to defy him. As she took a breath to speak, he continued, "Don't know why I'm even pretending this is my rodeo. Whatever, you take Ward. Get yourselves murdered. Anything else you need, seeing as you got all dressed up to meet us?"

"Yeah." Pax ignored his attempt to wrong-foot her. "I want to know where your Management stand on genuinely offering the Fae something."

"Something like asylum? Some part of these tunnels we'll shortly be clearing out?"

"Something like that."

"It's an option," Obrington said, plainly. "London are open to it, considering the mess our system of miscommunication created. Couple of backbenchers in Parliament might push Fae rights into a carefully hidden reality. Protected under UK law. Without revealing them, of course."

Both Pax and Ward gave him open-mouthed responses. Where had this man come from? Pax said, "You're serious?"

"Theoretically. But it's a big ask, for a very unclear reward, besides general harmony. We're talking about legitimising terrorists. Based on the whim of a pretty young lady with a hunch? I've merely been exploring options. Only seems sensible in case our people *were* gunned down by one rogue agent. But Ward, Ordshaw's your screwy town. You've gotta live with it, I'm just here to put a lid on the bleeding chaos. When that's done, you can make those screwy calls yourselves."

It took Ward another moment to recover, unable to believe her luck. "Of course. I want to do whatever we can to open channels to the Fae –"

"Fine." Obrington waved a finger in the air, calling over the waitress, and eyed Pax again. "But I'm not done with you. Before you two get yourselves killed by insects, you can at least pay lip service to our primary goal. We're tripping over mysteries left and right."

"Like the black spots?" Ward suggested, brightly. Obrington eyed her in a way that said that wasn't necessarily what he had in mind, but that it warranted consideration. She explained to Pax, "We've found pockets of unreported activity, or unreported inactivity, more accurately. Places where energy *isn't* manipulated. But we don't have the manpower to check all this out – the Bartons are ready to help out, and I'll be meeting with them once we're done, but we can't throw them into this without at least some initial exploration ourselves."

"And here we're all sitting not pulling our weight," Obrington said. An idea had started ticking in his mind, a way to lean on Pax and make a nuisance of himself. "We'll take a look ourselves, shall we? Investigate one of Ward's curiosities and give me an idea that you really are in this to help, all in one."

Pax bristled at the sudden demand. Obrington's magnified eyes tested her resolve. His new venture was not optional. And Ward wasn't much better, eagerness trumping concern as she was getting every treat under the tree all at once. Pax in the tunnels *and* a potential meeting with the Fae, what a day.

"Can I eat my eggs, at least?"

Footsteps stirred Casaria. Not from sleeping, he told himself, only rest.

He scrambled up, fumbling at his torch. The switch didn't work; batteries dead after so long waiting. He pocketed it and used his phone. Stopped and listened. Yes, the tap, tap of footsteps, people approaching. At least two; talking in low voices.

Holding his hand over the phone screen to hide the light, Casaria checked the time. Hell, it was morning, no wonder he'd dozed. Should have returned to the office and called for backup or proper surveillance. But those idiots would've sent someone like Landon to scare off intruders by breathing too loud.

Casaria, on the other hand, would catch them red-handed. He'd haul them into the office by the scruffs of their necks. See what Sam Ward thought of him them.

As the footsteps got closer, he made out what was being said, the voices rolling around the tunnel. "– not a bloody gorilla, I keep telling you."

"*Like* a gorilla, I said. That covers a lot."

"It doesn't cover this, see. It's some Big Foot level shit."

Casaria recognised the voice. It had sifted in and out of his mind while he'd been tied to a chair, waiting for injury. One of Pax's uncultured, violent associates. Low and slow and continually churning out ridiculous ideas.

"Things mutate living underground, don't they? It's true what they say about alligators in New York. And pigs under London – monstrous things."

Casaria edged along the wall, hand going back to his torch. Heavy enough to knock a man down; and he'd knocked this particular man down before. But he'd also been knocked down by him. Beaten, a toe severed . . .

"– taken to speculating," the second voice said, a nasal tone, higher-pitched, someone small and disagreeable. "Take a blood sample and prove it's just something escaped from a zoo. You're tired, eyes not adjusted down here."

"I know the difference between sleep-induced psychosis and seeing something unnatural, Vulcher. Would've saved us all time and effort if that were taken as given."

The footsteps tramped past as Casaria tensed. Moving in a parallel tunnel, close but then gone, echoing around a corner. They were looping to the intersection. Casaria pressed himself back into an alcove, a foot or so deep.

They pattered on. Turning, getting louder again.

"You sure this is the right way?" the whiny one, Vulcher, asked.

"I've got a keen sense of direction," the bigger one answered. His voice came through clearer, along with the heavy footsteps, as he drew into the same tunnel as Casaria. Torchlight bobbed past. "Twelve lefts and three rights. Didn't I tell you it was about a twenty-two-minute walk? How long's it been?" Which thug was he? The ashen, ugly one or the infuriatingly blond one? Casaria wasn't sure which face he'd rather rearrange.

"Twelve lefts?" Vulcher echoed. "In that order? *One* wrong turn and –"

"I know what I'm doing," the thug said. They finally passed the alcove, and Casaria froze. The ashen one, with his ugly, stony face and threadbare denim dungarees, filled the tunnel, stooped. A smaller figure followed, a scampering silhouette in the bounced-back torchlight.

The thug mumbled something about trust as they passed, and Casaria braced himself to go after them. A quick step behind the little one, clock him with the torch, a sharp punch to the thug's jaw. That'd do it. Only he'd lose the element of surprise on the small one.

Their footsteps were retreating and Casaria hadn't moved.

He'd race up behind them, a knee to the little one's back, carry the momentum forward and bowl the bigger one down. They'd grapple, but he'd knock the man senseless.

The talking got quieter as it became more distant.

They'd hear him now, hear his approach. He couldn't run after them.

He couldn't.

Casaria realised his heart was beating fast. What in hell. He'd waited all night, and they were getting away. They had got away.

He closed his eyes. What was going on.

3

Pax watched Obrington on his phone through most of the journey underground, tapping away like an addicted teen trying to beat a high score. Hell, maybe that's what he was doing. He led them to an unlit stairway that must've gone down fifty steps at least, and they followed his phone light onto another corridor. Pax was glad he was distracted, because with the tension in this place she had no desire to talk.

Finally, Obrington replaced the phone with a small torch, barely the length of his palm but startlingly bright. A handful of doorways sporadically lined the brick hallway.

"That one?" Obrington asked, and Ward checked against a map on her phone. She looked as anxious as Pax felt, watching the walls like she was looking for something. But this was safe, Pax told herself. The "anomaly" was a place where nothing went. A vacant lot in a system otherwise populated by fiends. And she had the company of the Ministry's finest.

Obrington pushed their chosen door and it didn't move. From the look of it, it had been closed for a very long time. He leant his shoulder into it, using all his weight. It cracked open and Ward flinched, a little cloud of dust puffing back over them. Obrington entered into darkness and summarised: "Huh."

Pax looked in herself, trying to see around him. The cold stillness was oddly noticeable, considering it was already so still and cool in the corridor. Obrington took a step further and Pax followed, feeling the sensation that had made him say *huh*. It was like taking a sharp intake of breath.

His torch lit up a large space. A hole in the rock of the earth, unadorned, without the brick or concrete that lined much of the Sunken City. The chamber was roughly spherical, though jagged around the edges, like someone had extracted a giant round boulder, and the doorway entered onto a ledge about halfway up, over a drop of some ten feet.

Obrington waved the torchlight back and forth. Nothing there but this vast, empty sphere. Ward crept around Pax to see for herself.

"Never seen your Sunken City described as cave-like," Obrington commented. "Tunnels, man-made, that's what they say. Any other parts tap into caves?"

"I don't think so," Ward said.

Pax stayed near the door. The ledge was barely a foot wide, and she wasn't sure she'd be able to climb back out if she fell. But that wasn't her main concern. The place felt weird. There was an emptiness to it. A painful emptiness.

Ward said, "There's no other break in the walls."

"Like whoever was digging down here found an air pocket," Obrington said.

"I don't think . . ." Ward went quiet, as if short of breath. She held a hand up in front of her, into the room, to feel something more.

"Dying to hear your take." Obrington turned to Pax, having waited what must have been an acceptable time for Pax to draw Serious Conclusions. About twenty seconds. Pax wasn't sure what to tell him. Ward's face expected something, too. The dug-out space served no apparent purpose, but she could, deep in her body, sense something wrong with it. It was colder than the surrounding tunnels by degrees, and – it was like looking at a flat lake. Eerily calm, with hidden depth. Capable of great change with the slightest touch. Pax sensed something in its silence, too. Or was it the absence of sound? The expectation that she should hear something?

She let out an uncertain comment, just to say something: "Meditation chamber?"

"For monsters?" Obrington said.

"Why not."

"Right." Obrington moved back out into the hallway. "There's something off with it, I think we can all agree on that."

"Yeah." Pax left quickly, now he'd set precedent, with Ward just behind her. Obrington closed the door and Pax tried to ignore his expectant look, to focus her senses. It was suddenly hard to reimagine the feeling from seconds before. "Did it feel cold to you?"

Shrugging his big shoulders, Obrington took his phone out again. Back to work or whatever addictive app he had. "Not especially. Notice anything else? Let's hear you deliver the same insights that cut down the Raleigh Commission and the grugulochs."

The big texting goon said it deadpan, disinterested. Pax replied, more firmly than necessary, "I felt nothing."

Obrington looked up. "Nothing?"

"Literally," Pax said. "An absence. Emptiness. Didn't you feel it too?"

"Uh-huh." He slapped his beefy free hand into the wall before concentrating back on his phone. "As opposed to out here. You feel something different?"

"We never claimed Pax was *psychic*," Ward intervened with an awkward laugh. Essentially informing Obrington that they were hiding something. He didn't look up again, pausing in his typing to read something. Pax was curious herself, despite his manner. Wondering if she *did* feel something beyond general disquiet.

Carefully, she placed her palm against the moist brickwork, and inhaled, drawing in. Ordinary, lifeless brick. Pax concentrated harder. It wasn't lifeless. There was something there, moving. She could imagine it, like worms in the ground. The same way she felt the blue screens when they were active, only less clear.

"It's different," Pax said. Able to draw that conclusion at least. "That room was different to out here. Lacking something."

"Huh," Obrington said, finally sounding interested. Pax was about to elaborate, if she could, when he explained his surprise. "There's been an alert. I have to go. We can pick this up later."

"Go?" Ward exclaimed. "We're just –"

"Turns out there *is* someone in the tunnels," Obrington said. "Casaria's called for backup, and we're closest. Did you know he was still down there?"

Ward's stunned look said she didn't.

"Guess he spent the night." Obrington straightened up, getting into action mode. Ward had her own phone out then. "Probably just a bum got in because we're spread so thin – I'll sort it out. Meantime, Ward, this place seemed harmless enough, your civilians might as well throw themselves into the others."

"I've got an alert, too," Ward said, distracted by her phone. "But it's about the horde. Changing direction. Maybe they got unsettled by the intruder?"

"If your equipment tells us anything useful at all," Obrington scoffed. Pax merely eyed the pair of them; only one useful conclusion worth drawing here. She should leave.

"We're really meeting the Fae?" Ward asked, trying to regain her enthusiasm as they paced towards their respective vehicles. Her unassuming but immaculate Honda, Pax's very assuming rusty moped.

"That's the plan," Pax said, checking the time with growing unease. Was this her default feeling now, everything *uneasy*? Or was there something in the tunnels that caused it? Casaria waiting it out. The horde shifting direction, oh, around the same time Pax had been pondering underground. And it was almost midday – where had the morning gone?

"Who is it? Where are we meeting?" Ward asked. "I can drive, no sense us going separately. If I can just get Barton set up first."

"We're kind of against the clock."

"It won't take long," Ward said. "There's another black spot, near here, accessed via a New Thornton entrance. I only need to unlock the door and give Barton a scanner. Maybe point him in the right direction. With Obrington racing towards Protocol 38, the more we can learn about the Sunken City, quicker, the better."

"It's fine," Pax said. "I'll go on ahead, you catch me up."

Ward slowed down. "You're sure? I don't want to turn up late –"

"It's casual," Pax insisted, thinking if anything this might be good. Give her a chance to chat with Edwing before Ward brought her enthusiasm. "Just get to the Tupsom lido when you can."

Ward squinted, committing the location to memory. As they drew up to the two vehicles, her focus further intensified, as if she was trying to think of how to word something just right.

"Take a breath," Pax said, "before you have a heart attack."

"Okay." Ward actually did take a deep, centring breath and released it, like she had had training. "The Fae – this is a big step for us, that's all. I can't thank you enough."

"Don't thank me yet," Pax said. "Like your mouth-breathing boss said, it might end up getting us killed."

Ward shook her head. "That's typical Ministry prejudice." She paused, considering that. "He is a bit difficult. Was there anything you wanted to say? Away from him?"

"No. I would've asked him to his face what the hell he's keeping back from us, but it didn't seem the time," Pax said, strapping on the bike helmet. "But that black spot shit *was* weird. Gives me the same uncomfortable feeling as the Fae."

"Keeping something back, like, about novisan and the tunnels? Barton suggested the system itself might pool energy, which our equipment is starting to confirm. And – we haven't even discussed this business with Duvcorp. If there's unchecked *people* in the tunnels" – Ward gasped in sudden realisation – "what if it's *them*?"

Pax paused, considering Tycho's nonchalance at the Baudelaire Club, the way he'd been, at least initially, dismissive of Ordshaw's problems. Paired with her blundering comments that might have got him interested. "As it happens . . . I ran into someone from Duvcorp last night" – Pax hurried on as Ward's face showed horror – "and I might've got them a bit curious, that's my bad. But he said they were sceptical about Ordshaw's weirdness."

"But – they came after *you*?"

"Pure coincidence," Pax insisted. "This was just talk at a poker table, no way they know anything about me – *I* brought it up. Look, it could be nothing – your boss didn't seem too bothered about this intrusion."

"No," Ward said, taking care not to sound worried. "No . . . homeless people and kids creep in occasionally. Even when we're fully staffed, it happens. But Casaria shouldn't have been calling for backup for homeless people and kids." Ward went quiet. Still trying to convince herself, she said, "Cano was unarmed, probably tired, if he was there all night."

"Yeah? I'm surprised he's back at work at all."

"It's fine," Ward said, though clearly it wasn't. Ah, Casaria, the foil for her happiness. "I can handle him. Half of success in any career is navigating other people's idiosyncrasies. That's *all* it is. And we need all the help we can get." She emphasised that for Pax's benefit.

"I'm doing what I can, aren't I?" Pax replied.

Ward's silence suggested she wanted more. She said, "All of this is in the air. Just when I thought we were resolving our scanning equipment, we get more unchecked activity. And those black spots?" She took a breath. "I'll get the Bartons started, but we could look at a few locations later ourselves, today. Couldn't we?"

"We'll see how this goes," Pax said, cautious of the snowflakes of responsibility that could soon form an avalanche. "Assuming the tunnels haven't been overrun by something else by then. See you at the lido, okay?"

4

Biting back frustration that, of all people, Wayne Obrington had arrived as backup, Casaria led the overweight vulgarian through the St Alphege's sewer. The man sported a superiority complex while wearing an off-the-shelf suit. His tapered head of hair had an awful, slick style that his expensive barber should have advised against. Everything he said seemed to come out snide, even his weighted comment that another agent was on the way to join them, someone to watch the exits. Like Casaria needed help.

Obrington barely fit through the access point, and bore no consideration for quiet as he plodded ahead with his torch. "I'll give you marks for not wading in like a dunderhead, but I wouldn't punish a *little* initiative."

"I'm up for review," Casaria replied, "for showing initiative."

"You know that's not the reason, don't you?"

Casaria had accounted for himself to Sam Ward, he didn't have to repeat it for this oaf. He pointed. "Down there. There was a body."

"The *scorpio* you say was shot."

"It was," Casaria said, struggling to be cordial. Everything the man said sounded like an accusation. "I take it you're armed?"

From a shoulder holster under his jacket, Obrington drew a small revolver, the sort carried by a '70s TV detective on budget cuts. Casaria gave it the look it deserved.

"It's the man that holds it, makes a difference," Obrington told him. "Shall we?"

Casaria continued, leading him past the spot where the body had lain. There was now a blood trail. Obrington hesitated over the mess. Got your attention now? The criminals wouldn't be far; he'd listened as they heaved the thing back through the tunnels, commenting about setting up in a bigger chamber.

"As far as your review's concerned," Obrington said, volume making Casaria cringe, "I don't question your initiative. And I'll defer to Ward for your character. You clearly have a way with the women." Compared to this wart, Casaria supposed he did. "What *I* question is your integrity."

Casaria stopped and Obrington almost bumped into him. "My integrity? I've done everything with honour."

"Except for lying about how you lost your toe," Obrington said. Sounding unhealthily sure of himself. "And your treatment of this Kuranes girl situation. Or, my biggest question, worth everything: how exactly a fellow agent died on your watch."

Casaria didn't flinch, showing the man he had nothing to hide. There was no way he could be held accountable for the massacre outside the Fae city, nor the deaths in Greek Street.

"Gant, wasn't it?"

That stilled him. Landon's partner? The amateur who'd risked getting them both killed? Why ask about that? They'd been alone – and he had no choice –

"Always an awkward thing," Obrington said, "to lose someone in places like this, no cameras, no easy answers, just a stressed man's word over what happened."

Casaria looked from the pistol up to his face, the oaf's eyes questioning. This bastard might be the sort that would do such a thing on purpose. *Accidentally* hurt a fellow agent. Was he threatening him? "Did you come here for these criminals, or to accuse me of something?"

Obrington answered, "You know who these people are, don't you?"

"What? No – I *saw* them –"

The big man put a finger to his lips. "Hey. Let's keep it quiet."

Somewhere in his blank face was the hint of a smile. Enjoying this? Casaria forced himself not to lash out as Obrington continued, walking lighter now. He followed silently.

The blood came in occasional smears, grit on the ground streaked from the weight of the dragged body. It led to a short set of steps that ascended to a doorway filled with the white light of an electric lantern. Obrington slowed down as they crept closer. There was no sound ahead, no talking or movement. Casaria checked back the way they'd come, a long empty hallway, and he started as Obrington's phone lit up. The boss whispered, "Warning Landon to be ready."

Landon? That was their other backup? That fool, *again*?

Obrington pocketed the phone and lumbered on. Up the steps,

into a wider room. Casaria crept after him, trying to see over his shoulder. It was another vaulted brick chamber, like a wine cellar. And it appeared empty, besides the big floor lamp and the carcass of the *scorpio mites*. Obrington strode in as Casaria followed. He turned quickly – too late.

The big thug stepped out of the shadow of a pillar, pistol aimed at his head, a block of grey menace with his stubbly chin and dusty clothes. The shorter one, a weaselly man in mechanic's overalls, came from the other direction, a stubby shotgun trained on Obrington.

"Gun on the floor," the big one said. Bees, that was his name, wasn't it?

Obrington held up his hands, turning lazily towards him. Casaria tensed, fists clenched. He should've killed the thugs when he first ran into them outside Pax's apartment; men lingering around with guns, unchecked. And they'd just walked in on them, damn this oaf.

"Gentlemen," Obrington started, unconcerned. "You're aware you're trespassing on government property? And threatening, I might add, Her Majesty's agents."

"We're pretty well aware. As, I expect, you're aware that Her Majesty's agents bleed, and disappear, the same as anyone else."

"Not these ones," Obrington said. "Our men are tracking us. The exits to this tunnel system are covered. I suggest you come quietly."

"Awful sure of yourself, aren't you?" Bees said, moving around the room, keeping his distance. No way Casaria could jump him without taking a shot. But he might turn into it, take the bullet in a shoulder, how much damage could that do? Obrington might be killed, but that was his problem. "Serious business you've got here. With your secrets and your . . . infrastructure. What exactly *is* that thing?"

Obrington gave the monster's body a bored glance. "*Scorpio mites*, looks like. Native to Ordshaw. You the mug that shot it? Lucky it was alone. Typically move in groups, isn't that right, Agent Casaria?"

Casaria's eyes were fixed on Bees. He'd pounce with a hair-trigger, the second that the brute took his eyes off –

"*Casaria*," Obrington said. "Your thoughts on how this one got here alone?"

Casaria snapped out of it, glancing at the monster, while Bees' eyes found him, genuinely curious. The criminal said, "You're telling us there's packs of them?"

"Of course," Obrington replied. Why was he humouring these men? "We tend to cull wandering loners, but we've been understaffed the past few days –"

The shotgun went off. The sound tore through the room as brickwork burst from a far wall, the shorter thug folding over Obrington's hefty shoe in his crotch, a kick out of nowhere. The same time, Obrington crouched, revolver firing at Bees. The criminal ducked aside, barely avoiding a bullet that sparked off the wall. Casaria dropped to the floor as the two men exchanged reckless gunfire. Each shot compounded the deafening echo.

Casaria scrambled for a pillar, and as he rolled around it a bullet struck the brick behind him, the criminal taking a potshot. He leant around the other side, finding Obrington taking cover behind a pillar of his own, as Vulcher wheezed on the floor.

The two men's guns clicked empty at the same shot, both testing their triggers a few times for good measure. With a guttural roar, Bees tore out of cover and pounded towards Obrington. The latter, reloading the revolver, stood just before Bees struck. The revolver flew from his hand as the criminal caught him around the waist and slammed their combined weights into the wall. Vulcher scrambled towards the exit.

Casaria ran after him, and unthinkingly put his weight on his injured foot. Pain screamed through his leg, bringing him down. Damned hell it was supposed to be healed! The little criminal was away, feet pattering down the tunnel. On a knee, Casaria tried to push himself up, Obrington and Bees' sloppy fight sounding in dull thumps and thuds. He lurched forward and supported himself on another pillar.

Bees had Obrington from behind, on the ground, his great arm squeezing the agent's neck, turning his face purple. Casaria sprang towards them but stumbled again – useless fucking foot not carrying him. Obrington gargled, feet kicking, not going to make it. His hand grasped to the side.

The revolver was in the middle of the room. Casaria flung himself towards it and his fingers pushed it further away. The gun skidded towards Obrington as Bees squeezed harder, whispering into his ear, "It's done, mate. It's done."

Brushing the metal of the revolver with his finger, Obrington made a final strained stretch. He caught the weapon and turned it up. It went off and the back of Bees' head splattered over the wall beside them. His grip releasing, Obrington sat up, gasping for air. He shunted off the criminal, aiming the pistol back for good measure.

Casaria half-stood, looking from the thug's body to the doorway, Vulcher long gone. Obrington lowered the gun, rapidly inhaling, and checked his glasses with his spare hand. Impossibly, they'd escaped damage. Without ceremony, he lumbered to his feet and stared at his adversary's body.

Casaria breathed heavily, too, wanting to kick the slow, mouthy bastard who'd taken his toe. Lifeless now, a chunk of head missing. Animal bastard, ingrate, uncul –

Obrington patted him on the arm, hoarsely saying, "You can tell me how you know these prats while we round up that other tyke."

Meeting the Bartons and Rufaizu at a site designated AGb-13, with an access point disguised as a transformer box behind a Tesco Express car park, Sam tried not to rush. Pax would wait, and she owed it to everyone to manage the current situation properly. The trio looked rested, even if Barton's limp seemed to be bothering him more than before. It would be lighter work today, anyway. The entire point was visiting untouched locations, a long way from the horde; it should be safe for them to split up with two Duvcorp scanners.

Sam took them into the tunnel and asked Barton if he knew of the black spots they were investigating, but he said it was news to him. Rufaizu offered, "Empty pockets. Places no one and nothing wants to go. Should be sealed off, the Sect had some ideas about that. No good could come from them."

"This Sect of Fore?" Sam said.

"The MEE of their day, I imagine," Holly said. "Off in mythical Bohemia."

"So you heard of something like this?" Sam pressed Rufaizu. "Untouched rooms?"

Rufaizu gave her a smiling look that suggested he did, but he slowly shook his head.

"He does that," Holly said. "Can your Ministry substantiate any of his claims? This Gardossa city, for instance? I have *so many* questions."

"I've got Support looking through the details," Sam said. She had the same questions, and so far the answer was no. The Ministry had no evidence to support the young man's anecdotes. Beyond the blue screens there was so much more to know. It started down here, with them, collecting data. She couldn't wait to finally meet the Fae, but they needed to see the first black spot together, at least. To be sure it was safe. It would be quick – she'd be just behind Pax.

Her phone buzzed in her pocket. Sam took it out, hoping to see a message from Obrington informing her everything was under control. It was the office. Barton asked, "How does your phone work down here? We always had trouble with electronics."

"Special issue," Sam explained in a whisper, as their secretary, Tori, spoke.

"Ms Ward? I don't like to bother you but this sounded serious –"

"They found the people in the tunnels?"

"Huh?"

"Obrington, Casaria."

"Oh that – I don't know, it's not that. I got a call. Someone from *Duvcorp*. They wanted to speak to you, directly – to put you through to Tycho Duvalier."

Sam was too dumbstruck, thankfully, to say, "*The* Tycho Duvalier?" As if there could be two.

"Ms Ward?"

"You have him on the line?"

"Not right now, I have a number –"

Sam's mouth hung open without words. Duvalier, an international *tycoon*, chasing her for stolen property? Damn Obrington – damn all of this. She covered her phone to address the Bartons, worriedly recalling the scanners in their hands. "Wait here a minute, I've gotta make a call. Tori? Get them back."

5

"At a time when Fae doubts Fae," Edwing said, "I declare *no more*. I have spoken with the exile, Letty. Within our very city. We're told she orchestrated the theft of the Dispenser. The slaughter of many humans. The sharing of Fae secrets. The same Letty who strove for nine years to reclaim the Dispenser – not to clear her name, but to complete the very task we've all forgotten? Her intention in contacting the human Apothel. Her intention in contacting the human Kuranes. She *still* believes. *I* do. Don't you?"

He paused to give space for an answer, minutely correcting his posture. "The Waste Chief Smark came forward in Letty's favour, for he recognises what we must all understand. Letty offers change. Hope for something beyond the Transitional City. Hope so many of us lost long ago. Hope that we *can* get along with the humans. Change is frightening. Risky. But it is necessary. We have seen the true worth of our position here, have we not? The city almost fell last Tuesday."

Edwing paused again, using an adjustment of his glasses to let that sink in. "Governor Valoria Magnus warns us the humans are on our perimeter. She tells us they will not negotiate, that we cannot abide communication with them. She keeps them at bay. As your Chair of Information, I tell you it is not the human Ministry putting these barriers before us. Perhaps they won't negotiate – with her. But Letty and her human connected with them – *their* diplomacy stopped the attack.

"Pax Kuranes, some of you know as a monster. I have spoken with her myself, and I tell you this conscientious human wants peace. She is the bridge we have always lacked. She protected Letty. She protected the Dispenser, and she has not exposed us. Even after *our* people tried to hurt her. She has opened a door which the governor claims does not – cannot – exist.

"This will be painful to hear. You may ask why I trust Pax Kuranes. You have been told that the humans will inevitably betray us. I do not expect to change your beliefs in an instant, but I ask you to give me a chance. I will meet with the Ministry myself to learn exactly what the humans can offer us. What we can offer them. Give me that chance. Give Letty a chance. Give humanity a chance."

He lowered his head, affecting solemn reflection. When he raised his eyes again, his tone shifted, graver. "Many are angry for what happened to our city. Afraid. I do not fault the governor's responses. But one of our own did the damage – one called Lightgate. To my shame, I met with *her*, too. Before it began. And as I go to speak with the humans, it is not their species I fear, but our own. Please – consider our future, as you seek vengeance and security. I appeal to Governor Valoria to address these issues publicly. We all deserve this opportunity for co-operation. The real monsters are those that would prevent it."

The broadcast cut back to a newsroom where the glamorous anchor, behind her TV smile, was thrown by the speech. Squatting on a box watching, Letty commented, "He knows how to switch it on, doesn't he?"

"Yeah." Flynt leant near the door. He hadn't come all the way in, watching the airways outside. "You hear shouts? It's gonna get everyone riled up . . ."

"About time." Letty stood.

"You don't think he should've waited?" Flynt asked. "We could have riots."

"He's the brains, you said. Guess he figured this would make it harder for someone to assassinate him. They do it now, Val's culpable."

Flynt frowned, distracted. "Think I heard someone ask *where is he*."

"He's got his plan." Letty patted his arm, encouragingly. "And we should be figuring out ours. It's time we got Smark and his lads to serve up Nimm."

"We can't –" Flynt started with surprise.

"We'll wait on Edwing, okay?" Letty said. "But we'll be ready. Mark my words, Flynt, you win fights by acting, not by fucking thinking about it."

Fresko found Mix with one arm hanging over a doll's armchair. Dropping onto the matching sofa, Fresko kicked his companion's knee. Mix jumped up, grabbing at the nearest weapon, a second from tossing a bottle into Fresko's face when he saw who it was. Grumbling complaints, Mix sat back, dark rings under his eyes.

"Figured I'd find you here," Fresko said. "Trying to get yourself caught?"

It was actually the third place he'd looked, after their water tower and the summerhouse in a Ripton garden. This den, in the eaves above a betting shop in West Farling, was a favourite, adorned with takings from the rich locals – a likely spot for the Stabilisers to search.

Mix croaked, "No one's looking for us now. You didn't see the reports?"

Fresko narrowed his eyes. Mix stared back blearily, not about to explain. Fresko took out his phone and brought up the latest Fae news. The headlines about Edwing, that prick who'd met with Pax, giving a speech. Fresko had looked him up: the youngest member of the Council. Supported by forward-thinking Fae, known to question Val's decisions. Bunch of do-gooders.

"FTC's gone soft, hasn't it?" Mix sneered. "Peace and love shit."

"Yeah," Fresko said. He could've predicted this. *Did* predict it. Edwing was saying they shouldn't hurt one another. Lightgate wasn't gonna like that. "The human and this guy, they've got a meeting happening in Tupsom. Like, right now. Lightgate's gonna be there."

"To do what? Ice the pair of them?"

It might've been a joke, but Mix was probably right. All this chatter and confusion, now this young one was promoting productive dialogue, open up the FTC. How was that gonna play with Lightgate watching?

"Pass me another bottle," Mix groaned.

"You want a coffee," Fresko told him. "You want a hit of dust and a clear fucking head, because once this meeting goes down things are gonna move fast."

"Things," Mix grumbled back. "Ain't we had enough *things* for a lifetime?"

"You don't want in, that's your problem. But I'm not sitting back waiting for this to wash over us. I'm done living like a fucking degenerate, letting other people dick us around. Sit here and drown in puke – I'm heading to Tupsom."

"What's in Tupsom?"

Fresko strode to the exit, but a jangling of empty bottles and Mix's huffing attempt to stand stalled him. "Wait, wait. Tell me. What's in Tupsom?" He swayed uneasily and his foot caught a bottle, which rolled and almost toppled him. He cursed and kicked another bottle into the wall, putting on a whole show of standing. Finally, he straightened his belt and checked his hip-holster. Empty. He scanned the room.

"I told you," Fresko said. "They're meeting there. Lightgate and all."

Mix snorted. "Fine. Pass me my gun. Might as well see first-hand how we're gonna get fucked this time."

Edwing arrived at the lido early, confident after a few circles of the open-air pool and its visitor centre that he was the first there. There was an old canteen inside, perfect for their chat; benefiting from natural light but hidden from outsiders. He flew through a broken window and settled on a central table, where he straightened out his suit, corrected his tie and practised a polite but welcoming posture. Now it was merely a matter of saying the right thing.

Welcome, Pax, good to see you again. Thanks for joining me.

I'm so happy to work with you.

Too formal?

How're you doing? Having a good morning? Perhaps one of Flynt's expressions would work best: Bet you killed it at the table last night? You're looking fine? No. Complimenting a human's looks could only be considered disingenuous.

Edwing cleared his throat and tried, "Good morning Pax, did you sleep well?"

"I can't speak for *her*" – a female voice spun him around – "but I was too excited to sleep, myself."

Lightgate was standing on the table behind him. One arm in a sling, but otherwise as perfectly presented as the last time Edwing had seen her. Pressed white suit, great mane of hair, and a youthful cheer that he now better understood as madness. He took a step back.

"Edwing, my friend," she said. "You never called."

"I –" Edwing stuttered. "I haven't heard from you, either."

"Me? I left a calling card at the FTC, didn't I? If *shooting people* wasn't a cry for revolution, I don't know what is. And now fancy this" – she moved closer – "finding you cutting out the middle-woman. Chatting with my humans. Promising things to the FTC."

Edwing took another step back, eyes on her guns. One bulging under her jacket, the other holstered low on her thigh. She listed to one side, swaying like she might fall, but she stayed upright. "Lightgate – I *did* come to visit you. I told Rolarn –"

"He's dead." Lightgate was mere inches away now. Edwing glanced over his shoulder. He could make it to the edge of the table. Fly for the rafters? Even if he had a gun, he wouldn't dare fight. Lightgate ran a slow finger under her throat. "Butchered by your friend, Letty. Fae on Fae crime, can you believe that? A bit ironic, I think you started your speech about something like that."

Edwing straightened himself up. No, there was no running. He would face her with dignity. "I'm sure Letty acted with good reason. You understand why I'm here now? We have an opportunity to combat Valoria. Things are going to change."

"Yes." Lightgate smiled slightly. "You make good with young Pax and the Ministry. Valoria either agrees to negotiations or steps down. Everyone talks happily ever after?"

"It *is* possible," Edwing insisted. "A bloodless revolution."

She studied him with a sad face, shifting closer. Almost chest to chest. Her breath stank like petrol. "Peaceful change? Valoria retires to the hills?"

"She won't go quietly," Edwing answered warily, leaning back. "But she will go – Fae won't die for her, not when they understand our alternative."

"Poor, naive Edwing," Lightgate sighed, her alcoholic exhale stinging his eyes. "Don't you realise you're saying *all* the wrong things?"

"Lightgate. You came to me, you know –"

"I came to you with great ideas. And you give me this *peace* nonsense?"

Edwing opened his mouth to respond, but she moved quicker than he could speak. He didn't even see the blade being drawn from her sling, only felt the fierce bite as it slid into his gut, all the energy shooting out of him. As he slumped forward, blood glugging up his throat, filling his mouth, he locked eyes with Lightgate, pleading, and she dug the knife deeper, leaning her weight into him with a lover's embrace.

"Shh, Councillor. This is just step one."

6

The Tupsom lido was a place Pax had been only vaguely aware of. It was not somewhere anyone outside the neighbourhood of Tupsom was likely to have visited, even when it was open. Flanked on one side by a weed-riddled playing field, it sat behind a concrete wall, a single-storey building cracked by age. Its plaster mouldings, arched windows and doors went halfway to an impressive design, but the plant life, smashed windows and rotten door frames made it hard to imagine it as anything more than a relic.

It was also hard to believe the signs claiming the place was monitored by CCTV, under the threatening protection of LuxSecur. Aside from there being no cameras, Pax doubted that a firm trendy enough to drop the *e* from their name had set foot here in years. Across the courtyard lay the empty beer bottles and crisp packets of people who had ignored the warnings.

Rather than wait on Ward, who might have a skeleton key, Pax scouted the wall looking for the easiest way in: the main gate's bars were too tight to squeeze through, and too tall to shimmy up. The wall itself looked scalable, thanks to occasional barred portholes, but it was topped with razor wire. No way the crisp-eaters took such risks. Further study turned up a gap in the side-wall, visible across the derelict playing field, which was encircled by a chain-link fence. The fence's lattice was its own ladder, no razor wire there. She managed the climb almost gracefully.

Pax crossed the overgrown grass and squeezed through the wall where a hole had been kicked through, hardly concealed by a broken pallet. Inside the lido's grounds, she went to the main building and checked through the grimy windows. The outside had got in, as nature partially reclaimed the metal tables and chairs with snaking weeds. Pax skirted the building to the back, where the lido itself sat; a concrete dipping pool, partly filled with dead leaves, sludge and – yes – a soiled pram.

Ignoring that mystery, Pax continued to the rear doors, where a bottom panel had been smashed, creating a gap for a person to crouch through. Which Pax did.

It was cool inside, holes and cracks making it as airy as outside, minus the sunlight. Pax walked between changing rooms, through to the reception area and finally to the overgrown café. A delightfully haunting meeting place; thanks, Edwing.

Pax searched the shadows in the corners, around the tiled ceiling. Tiles were missing above, exposing dark cavities, and in one spot the ceiling had collapsed into the room. Pax called out, "Edwing, you here?" She toed a broken chair leg out of her way, moving into the room. "You guys have an affinity for the dystopic, don't you?"

With no answer, she continued, and spotted a dark shape at the centre of the room. Something standing in the middle of a table, the size of a fairy. But the posture was wrong. Pax frowned, getting closer. It was stiff – and splayed, four limbs out like a cross. Humanoid, at least . . .

"Holy fuck," Pax gasped, bending to take it in. It took a second for her eyes to process the sight, then she turned away, hand to her mouth. "Fuck, fuck, fuck . . ."

She gave it another look – had to force herself, to be sure.

That was Edwing's face alright. His tiny glasses, lying on the table behind him. His little stretched limbs, bound to – what – bent wire? And those were his guts spilt out of his open torso. Pulled apart like an anatomy experiment.

Pax turned on the spot. Every instinct said to run, get the hell away, but logic told her it was already too late. He'd been murdered, *brutally*, and left for her to find. Worse – for her to be found *with*. She checked the shadows again, searching for the culprit, sensing who it was. Fuck, *fuck*. She called out, "What the hell is wrong with you?"

"Me?" Lightgate's familiar voice came from an adjacent table. Pax clenched her fists as the miniature lunatic addressed her candidly: "*You're* the one that did this."

Fresko and Mix stopped at the window, seeing the human's silhouette inside. Wordlessly, they slipped in through a broken pane, to perch on a jutting spur of window frame. From the human's stance, something was wrong.

"The fuck is that?" Mix grunted, quietly.

Fresko swung the rifle up from over his shoulder and checked through the scope. He lowered the gun and gave Mix a disbelieving look. Pax, looking ready to gag, turned away from the table. Mix took the rifle and checked for himself. "Shit on a stick. Did she –"

Fresko snatched the rifle back, targeting the human himself. With the canteen separating them, she'd never see the shot coming. But she was saying something, edgy.

"Put her down!" Mix hissed. "About time, isn't it? That psycho –"

"Shh!" Fresko snapped, following Pax's gaze to the next table. "Lightgate's there."

"Shoot the human before she gets her too!"

"*Wait.*" Yeah, Pax looked ready to crush Lightgate. But the white-suited fairy was unafraid. The opposite. She was smiling, her good arm out to the side.

Nothing about this was right.

Dead bloody councillor, *gutted*. The giant lummox standing over him like she'd done it for kicks? Out of curiosity? No. He'd seen them talking last night. Chatting lovey-dovey bullshit about all getting along. She'd asked after Letty. Fresko had made bad assumptions before, thinking Pax killed Letty, and look where it got them. Mix rocked on the spot with agitation, so Fresko held a hand up for stillness. "Just fucking listen."

"Someone," Lightgate said, her voice rising, "tipped off Valoria's people as to where poor Edwing was meeting with a human. But where are your Ministry friends? I was expecting more of a mess."

"Fucking . . ." The human wasn't able to string a sentence together.

"It's Lightgate," Fresko said. "She killed him. Set her up."

"With Stabilisers on the way," Mix added, looking out of the window. Fresko followed his gaze. The Stabilisers would take them down, along with the human, given the chance.

"Shoot her now," Mix suggested, "we're heroes again, right?"

"You psycho!" Pax snapped. She was trying to find words to break out of her shock. One fist was raised, as if she'd ever be fast enough to touch Lightgate. "How – why –"

"You're upset," Lightgate said, helpfully. With gentle wingbeats, she rose from the table to Pax's head height. "So I'll give you some advice. Run. Val's people are nasty – *I* certainly don't intend to stick around to greet them. But I had to say *hi* before I left. If you survive, we'll talk again."

"Fresko," Mix urged, both of them sensing that Pax was about to make a move. This was their moment to take control. Fresko's rifle drifted; his crosshairs trained on Lightgate's chest.

"She's the one murdered one of ours," he said.

"The human can take the rap *right now*," Mix snarled.

"You know," Lightgate said, through a stifled yawn, ignoring Pax's fierce look, "that clown is more use this way."

Pax lunged and Lightgate moved too fast for Fresko to track. Pax's snatching hand closed on air, the Fae suddenly a few feet above her, silver pistol drawn. "Oh. So close."

Ignoring the gun, Pax jumped at Lightgate, tripping over a chair as she did. Lightgate effortlessly evaded her, floating towards the ceiling. Fresko picked her out again.

"Do her," Mix said, meaning Pax. "We wait until –"

"Enjoy the party!" Lightgate shot into the shadows. Pax twisted on the spot, her only hope to spring wings and fly herself. Lightgate was gone, and that only left the reality of the situation. Her eyes went back to Edwing, the poor brutalised sod. Then something else caught her attention, at another window. Fresko and Mix saw it too. Three dark shapes converged on a break in the glass. A man said, "In there, she's with the councillor!"

"I didn't –" Pax started, protesting her innocence. But seeing the newcomers swarming to get in, she changed her mind. She ran.

"Out!" one of the Stabilisers shouted. "Cut her off!"

They hadn't seen what'd happened, they didn't care. The mission was to stop her.

"We take her, Val's gotta reward that," Mix said, drawing a pistol. Fresko grabbed his arm. He gave him a meaningful look, not sure how to explain it, but hoping to get the message across. There were two sides to this. The right one might not be easy, but they'd been screwed around too much, for too long. He was done playing these games.

"We go after her," Fresko decided, "it's not for fucking Val."

7

Pax crashed through the gap in the rear door, catching her shoulder on the broken panelling and forcing her way through. Not stopping as the wood shattered around her, coat ripping. She stumbled through the dry pool before vaulting the edge and charging the wall. She slid through the hole feet first, hitting the pallet on the other side, and scrambled along the wall edge, low. A voice shouted, "In the field!"

Rising to a half-crouch, Pax sprinted – they'd be here any second. The fence blocked her path, but she'd run through it if she had to.

A shape dropped in front of her, a man smaller than a tiny bird. Shit shit. Pax turned to open ground, no cover, no hope – but better than standing still.

"Stop or I stop you!" the man shouted, almost as loud as a human. Pax ran, and a gunshot popped like a carton bursting. It took a few steps for Pax to stop, fearing the next shot, arms out to her sides. Her chest burnt, just below her ribs – had she taken a bullet? Breathing heavily, she looked down, no sign of blood. Nothing. A fucking stitch, muscles not used to moving this fast, weak bloody lungs. She looked over her shoulder. Her pursuer was approaching quickly, rifle raised. A gun the size of a matchstick, but bigger than the pistols that had lanced her leg and riddled the Bartons' house with holes.

"Got her," said another voice, drawing her attention to the side. A second man hovering not two metres from her head. Armed with a similar gun, dressed in the same black uniform. The first man moved in front of Pax. They wore helmets with visors like fighter pilots. Two inches tall, miniature militant police.

"I don't –" Pax began, but a shout from the lido cut her off.

"It's him – the Chair of Information! What's left of him!"

Pax cringed, looking to the wall, no sign of the shouter. "I can expl –"

"Good a place as any?" the first gunman said. The second

scanned the playing field. The only overlooking building was a desolate office block, windows darkly empty. Trees loomed over them in other directions, and the road was a distant, empty dream. She'd fall in the long grass, not be spotted for days. Even then she might be ignored, dismissed as a passed-out junkie. The fairy nodded, and the pair raised their guns. Pax looked down the tiny barrels, and tried one more time. "You've got –"

Something whipped past Pax's ear. The first fairy was struck out of the air. He spun down as the second fairy aimed over her shoulder. Pax flinched at another whizzing bullet and the second fairy was propelled back like a rag doll. He spun into the grass with barely a sound.

Pax didn't move, staring at the empty space that had, seconds earlier, contained her death. Lightgate? That chaotic little shit . . . She turned back towards the lido, and heard the shout of her third pursuer: "Regroup, there's –"

"Have it you bastard!" a new voice shouted. The war cry of a hooligan, followed by a series of roared attacks. Pax stared at the wall, no sign of what was happening, just the huffs of two men brawling with the impacts too quiet to hear. It was over in seconds, before another yell, "Any more? Bring it on!"

She recognised him. Even furiously engaged as he was. One of the men who'd chased her from the Bartons' house. The fairies who'd tried to kill her before. Fuck. Pax took a deep breath and ran for the fence. She crossed the field in seconds and slammed into the chains, vaulting up and over. She ran the second her feet hit the ground, up the road, back towards her moped. Before she got close she saw the wheels – sunk as though melted, punctured beyond repair. *Shit.* She kept going, sprinting towards a bus stop, out across the road without looking, no cars here anyway. No people. The shelter ahead had three walls of Perspex, solid from adverts and torn events posters; she grabbed the edge and used her momentum to swing into the cover of the corner, where she slid to the ground.

Hidden from the outside world, at least partially, Pax shakily took out her phone and raised Ward's number. It pinged, engaged, through to voicemail. Pressing herself better into hiding, Pax hissed at the beep, "I need some fucking help right now. Fae on me." She hung up. She dug into another pocket for the faeometer the MEE had given her and switched it on. It'd send an alert back to their base. As if anyone could get here in time.

When she flipped the switch it beeped. Then again.

Again, and again, getting faster. Faster. Pax stood, eyes wide, as the device panicked: Fae almost on top of her. She looked up the road. Barely a couple of parked cars for cover, and why the hell wasn't Sam Ward here already? The faeometer beeped so rapidly it reached a whine.

"Trying to give yourself away?" yet another male voice said. A higher pitch than the last one. He'd been there, too, on the Bartons' street. Shooting at her.

Pax flipped the faeometer switch, silencing it, as the fairy floated down from above the bus stop. Sharply dressed in trousers and a white shirt, with suspenders and a tie. His wings beat gently, and he held a rifle across his waist that had to be taller than him. Like this tiny man had taken a gun from a toy of a different scale. Was that the weapon that had knocked those two soldiers out of the sky?

"You let her fuck your bike?" the fairy asked sharply, as if it were Pax's fault a fairy slashed her tyres.

She replied with a question of her own, "You're not with Lightgate?"

He looked back down the road, still deciding. His face twitched uncomfortably, and when his eyes rested on Pax he only seemed more troubled. "She's probably watching."

"Got her, Fresko?" the other man asked, the thug, appearing alongside him. He was broader than the others, all denims and leather belts, square head and white hair. Face darkened by something – blood? "What now?"

"We're gonna have a dozen more Stabilisers on the way," the white shirt, Fresko, said. "Twenty minutes at best, out of the FTC, but likely already closer than that. See where Lightgate went?"

The thug laughed with elated bravado from his fight. "If I had, I would've done for her, too!"

Fresko scowled. "Hang around, you'll get your wish."

Great, Pax reflected, at least three separate sets of murderous fairies fighting over her. But these ones had defended her for now, at least. They were Letty's friends once, weren't they? She said, "You guys want to help me, maybe I can get somewhere safer . . . ?"

The pair stared at her like spectators at a car crash.

"Guess she's our responsibility," Fresko said. "But how do you protect a thing like this from *us*?"

"Same trick she pulled before?" the thug grunted. "Toss her down a manhole, back with the fucking critters."

Not the best start. Fleeing into the Sunken City had proved more terrifying than the Fae, last time. Pax leant out from the bus stop again, checking the road. The pair flew higher, keeping their distance.

"There is an entrance," Fresko said. He added harshly, "Lady, you listening?" Pax met his eyes. "About two hundred metres up the road. An underpass with a maintenance hatch, that'll get you in. You'll wanna move quick."

"Yeah," Pax said. "I never *want* to move quick."

The pair exchanged another uncertain look, then the thug said, "You realise you should've fucking died back there?"

"Yeah." Pax moved out of cover. They darted to the sides to avoid her as she looked up the desolate street, in the direction Fresko indicated. "My day's not about to get much better, is it?"

"Ms Ward." Tycho Duvalier's smooth voice finally broke off the incessant chime of a tune that had held Sam waiting. She jumped, anxious to end this call quickly. "I understand that you're in charge of the Ordshaw Ministry of Environmental Energy, correct?"

"Mr Duvalier?" Sam replied pointlessly. Voice too high. "How can I help you?"

"You can start by explaining how you came across our SURE scanners. Imagine my surprise when our inventory showed one of our own was tricked into sharing them with you."

"Tricked?" Sam echoed. Of course, Obrington as much as told Parris to pin it on her. And it was dumb luck they'd noticed at all. Pax's blunder? Sam cleared her throat. It didn't matter. Obrington had insisted she had to own it, and she'd already got in mind what to say. "There was no deceit involved, we requisitioned them for government business of the highest priority."

"I wasn't aware you had such mandates," Tycho replied. "Naturally, we're always willing to help out our friends in the government, but that is *sensitive* equipment and its use indicates rather specific, perhaps unusual interests on your behalf."

Sam was quiet. What else had Obrington said about their research? Likely dealing with things the MEE weren't aware of themselves. Duvalier had to suspect something extreme, and she had to avoid confirming it. She considered their typical excuses. Faulty gas mains, mobile or electrical interference . . . but another option struck her. Complete dismissal. Channelling Obrington's arrogance, making herself *Management material*, she said, "You'll have the scanners back as soon as we're done with them. I can only apologise if it's caused any inconvenience."

"No inconvenience at all. Inconvenient would be getting legal teams involved. Checking the authenticity of that mandate of yours. We're not going *there*, are we?"

Despite the pause, that threat didn't warrant an answer.

"You'll meet me this afternoon," Tycho decided. "I'll come to your office. Shall we say 3pm?"

"Now is not a good –"

"We're talking, Ms Ward, that's all. Two organisations sharing the burden. Let's not make it any more than that, shall we?"

Sam gritted her teeth. Would the world fall apart if she told him to piss off? She didn't choose fast enough.

"Very well," he finished. "I'll have my people call yours. Until three."

And he was gone. Sam closed her eyes. Hell. Forget telling *him* to piss off, she should go back to the office and kick Obrington in the balls. It suddenly felt like a blessing that Mathers had left her out of these sorts of entanglements. But Obrington wasn't *in* the office, he was dealing with his own problem. Which, by the sounds of Tycho's probing, was not of Duvcorp's making. And Sam had other issues, too, missing the Fae meeting. Seeing the time on her phone, she cursed under her breath. She paced back to the tunnel entrance, drawing up a to-do list in her mind.

Set up the Bartons, super fast.

High-tail to Tupsom, solve Fae-human relations.

Speed back to the MEE office, delegate Duvcorp back to Obrington.

Finish the day without any more undue drama.

Simple.

8

The smaller criminal, Vulcher, whimpered like a beaten dog. The sort of coward that creased up at a slap against nearby brickwork. Not that Obrington stopped there, shoving the man into walls, getting in his face. Obrington, Casaria had decided, was unhinged. He'd approached these criminals intending to provoke a conflict, and was now throwing his considerable weight into someone half his size, who was already ready to talk.

When they'd caught up to Vulcher, he was down, hands cuffed behind his back, Landon watching him with a pistol drawn. That piece of human beige explained he'd checked the nearby tunnels, too; found a crate of *powdered narcotics* in a nook. Landon lacked the imagination or experience to say if it were cocaine, heroin or aspirin.

Obrington hauled Vulcher up by his overalls and tossed him across the room. The slight man skittered into the wall, not quick enough to get his hands up to protect himself. He went down, near tears. Landon looked displeased. Had he ever handled a suspect like this?

Casaria had, of course. But only when necessary. Some of them drove you to it. This one hadn't. Obrington was sweating, jacket off, shirtsleeves up, flat mouth letting out occasional wheezes as he relieved the tension left from his brawl with Bees.

That was it, wasn't it? The man could've died. He was processing that. Though Casaria sensed some of this was also for his benefit. He'd told Obrington he only knew the deceased man from Pax's flat, and it hadn't satisfied him.

The oaf thumped over to Vulcher with fists clenched, and finally stopped. "What do you lads think? The boy's ready to talk?"

Landon held his tongue, but Casaria was less shy: "He was ready to talk before we got here."

"That's what you think?" Obrington replied blandly.

"Yes!" Vulcher gasped. "I'll tell you everything – whatever

you want! We were hoping to store some things down here, that's all! Just me and Bees, happened upon the place by chance and –"

There was a crack as his head snapped sideways, jaw taking the brunt of Obrington's shoe. Vulcher fell to his knees crying curses through blood. Landon cringed.

"See," Obrington said. "Still needed some tenderising after all." He grabbed Vulcher's chin, drawing his tear-drenched face up. "Who are you working for and how in hell did you disable our sensors?"

"He'll kill me," Vulcher uttered.

That earned a back-handed cuff. Obrington kept hold of him with his other hand and drew him back to his face. "Name."

"M – Monroe," Vulcher spluttered. "Stacey Monroe."

Obrington raised an eyebrow to Casaria, who nodded. Yes, it was familiar.

"And the sensors?" Obrington demanded.

"Anonymous tip," Vulcher said, trying to speak faster, arms up. "I swear – it's what they called *me* along for and I told them I wasn't handling that shit. Obviously government or high-end security, those sensors – no one with any sense would've –"

"So you got blessed by a guardian angel," Obrington said, giving Casaria a look.

"Boss got a note," Vulcher said. "Someone who knew how to get in. Didn't ask for nothing, just gave us instructions – scrambled the signal. I don't know who, it was Monroe's business."

"Anonymous notes." Obrington walked the short distance to Landon, addressing him now. "Lot of disruptive writing going around, huh?"

"When did you get these messages?" Casaria asked.

"Yesterday," Vulcher answered hurriedly. "Morning, I think."

"After your grugulochs died," Obrington said. He put his hands in his pockets and hummed. "Could be a Ministry agent upset at his job, farming out his knowledge?"

Casaria shifted. "I didn't tell them a damn thing."

Obrington turned square to him. "Come again?"

"Yes, these were the bastards that jumped me. Who hurt me. On account of our run-in at Pax's. But I got free, exactly as I reported, and I never said a word to them. I don't even know what the hell they'd want with these tunnels."

Obrington stared silently. Landon, behind him, looked deeply uncomfortable. Obrington said, "You didn't think it might be worth us following up on people who abducted a Ministry agent?"

"We had big enough problems outside Ordshaw's answer to the mafia, yeah," Casaria said. Like hell he was going to apologise. "Management were screwing us on behalf of a *monster*, so I handled these people on my own. There was nothing to follow up."

"Just let them cut off your toe and be done with it?"

"I gave as good as I got."

"He escalated things at the girl's apartment," Landon clarified. "They were there for her things. It's not unreasonable to think it got personal."

"Uh-huh." Obrington gave Vulcher another look, rocking on his heels. "No. You're a liability and a lunatic, Casaria, but I don't think you're a traitor. At least, you're not the first person I'd suspect, not when we've got a girl no one knows from Adam, secretly best mates with gangsters, asking me to keep our people away."

"Pax?" Casaria exclaimed. This lot were Pax's friends, true. She'd talked them down from killing him. But she'd been trying to keep clear of them, hadn't she?

"We'll bring her in," Obrington said. "And get Support to double-check all the sensors in a mile radius. With *luck*, these mugs are responsible for all our complications." He moved past Landon, who stepped aside.

"And him?" Casaria indicated Vulcher. Obrington looked back like he'd forgotten their captive existed.

"How do you usually dispose of them round here? Feed the beasts? Tree-grinder?"

"What?" Vulcher's panic doubled. "You can't –"

"We encourage them to leave town," Landon said warily. Obrington snatched the pistol from his holster and aimed it at the small criminal, whose hands shot up.

"How many more people know?" Obrington demanded loudly, as if talking to someone who couldn't quite hear.

"No one!" Vulcher sobbed. "It was me and him, bringing –"

"You and him's no one, with Mr Stacey Monroe pulling *no one's* strings?"

The criminal reconsidered, squeezing his eyes closed, shaking with fear. "Don't shoot me, please don't shoot me."

Obrington fired, the sound filling the room. The wall cracked over Vulcher's shoulder. "Next one's between your eyes."

"Monroe, yes! Me, Bees – Jones too. Maybe a few other boys in the warehouse, I don't know – it was a big find, but everyone's been busy with the poker game. Monroe didn't want the distraction, not with all that money on the table. So Bees came here alone, seeing how far the tunnels went, and he found that *thing*, but we didn't believe it – I came this morning, to check – Jones would've joined us later –"

"Blow me, what a mess," Obrington huffed. Aiming again towards Vulcher's forehead, he turned a glance back to Casaria, as though asking for approval. Casaria made an effort not to move, to show no trace of feeling at the threat. Landon was less stoic, grunting to say this was wrong. Obrington lowered the gun. "We'll need to make other arrangements; the cancer's already spread too far to disappear with one or two bodies."

Pax reached the underpass out of breath again, after her short dash down a road empy besides occasional old cars. Scanning the sky for anything birdlike coming to shoot her. Mind racing: not just at the disaster of being marked for assassination *again*, but hell, plunging back into the labyrinth? It had shaken off the Fae last time, but she'd barely survived. And the trip down with Ward hadn't made her feel better about it, knowing even the empty rooms were disturbing. Every new thing she encountered in the Sunken City made life worse.

A grim set of steps led to a maintenance panel, exactly as the little shirted man promised, with big screws at each corner, rusted in place. After making sure she was alone, not even the two gunmen for company, Pax reached towards the first screw.

Her phone rang.

Pax prayed for Sam Ward's name – but Unknown Number glowed big and bold. Letty? She answered hopefully, "Yeah?"

"It's me," Casaria said. She winced. Of all the lifelines. "Are you alone?"

"I am," Pax said. "And kind of mixed up in something."

"Whatever it is, this is more important."

"I doubt that."

"Your gangster friends found a way into the Sunken City.

Someone *helped* them get past our sensors. The new bastard in charge at the Ministry wants you for it."

"Fuck – hell – whatever. If you can get the bloody Fae off my back, I'll come. Casaria, I'm about to break into the Sunken City myself, otherwise I'm toast."

"What? No – don't go near an entrance. Don't even breathe on it."

His tone made Pax freeze, eyes on the panel. "Three fairies came shooting at me, and more are on the way. So unless you've got some kind of Fae-proof shield you can wire me through the phone –"

"You touch that entrance, the alarms will go off and our people will scramble to you. Aren't you listening, we had a Sunken City breach. The *boss*" – he spat the word – "just killed one of your friends."

Killed her friend? Pax's heart jumped in her throat. Had this hit the Bartons? "Which – what friend? Tell me you're not talking about –"

"Are you listening? I'm calling to *warn* you: he's out to get you."

Pax backed away from the maintenance panel. Her reckless escape plan was shot. Her tenuous alliance with the only people who could protect her was shot. "Who got hurt?"

"One of the thugs – and they're claiming you played a game of poker with his boss, just last night. What am I supposed to say?"

Not the Bartons – something to do with Monroe. And the MEE knew she was with him? "Do they know I met a Fae there, too?"

Casaria paused. "What've you been doing, Pax? Criminals, those vermin –"

"Seriously?" Pax answered with acid. "Considering the nature of this call, you fucking blame me?" She checked the entrance to the subway. No indication if there was a threat far away or just around the corner. "Help me out. Turn off the sensors so I can lie low in these tunnels – at least long enough to give the fairies the slip."

"Sensor interference is exactly what they're after you for. Where are you?"

Far away, was the answer. A taxi would take as long as a bus, out here. What could she do? Wait for Sam Ward, who might already have orders to snag her? Run for the nearest tributary to the River Gader and swim underwater to avoid detection? Could fairies swim? Bloody hell, what kind of idea was that, she could barely swim herself. Pax said, "Is there anywhere else the Fae can't go?"

"Only places we protect." A loud voice spoke in the background of the call: Obrington, returning to Casaria. Casaria covered the mouthpiece and replied, "She's coming in, voluntarily." Obrington responded with something unfriendly, and Casaria placated him with obedient responses before unmuffling the call. "They saw your faeometer alert, Pax. There's already a car on its way."

"No," Pax squeaked.

"Stay put," Casaria said, his tone suggesting she needed to do the opposite. He hung up as Obrington started again.

"Serves you right for trusting those Ministry bastards," the miniature thug in denim said, drawing her attention upwards. He was perched on the tip of a caged light beneath the underpass, something sticking out the side of his mouth. A little waft of smoke came out, distracting Pax for a brief moment of wonder. He was smoking? Fresko was sitting next to him, leaning on the large rifle upright between his legs, watching her carefully.

"I can't go in there," Pax told them, pointing at the maintenance panel.

"Nah," Fresko said. "But you've drawn those Ministry pricks out here. Stabilisers won't mess with them. You'll only have to deal with one side or the other, depending on who gets here first."

"Unless Lightgate's still around," the other one added.

Though her eyes rested on them, Pax could no longer focus. Even if the Fae and MEE shot one another, and Lightgate, they'd only add bodies to the pile without setting her in any way free.

"Of course," Fresko said, "there's always that car we passed."

"Oh sure," the other added. "Old model, no electric key shit there. Shame if someone took it."

Pax glared. "You'd better be able to hotwire a car, because I sure as shit can't."

Sam stood alongside Holly gazing into an empty chamber, soaking up its queer atmosphere. A cube hollowed out of the surrounding stone, so perfectly square as to appear unnatural. The stillness was palpable, at the same time unsettling and impossible to resist. With it came a weird serenity, pushing away fears of Duvcorp and anxiety over Sam's lateness in meeting the Fae. Here, she could be at peace.

Until her ringtone shattered the atmosphere. Both women nearly jumped out of their skins, retreating and slamming the door as though the noise might offend the room.

Sam gave Holly an apologetic look as she answered. Obrington barked, "Finally, Ward. Wherever in bleeding hell you got to, grab that woman, *now*."

"Um, you –"

"Grab Kuranes! We've got a situation, in St Alphege's. Drag her here by her teeth if you have to."

"I'm not *with* her, sir –"

"You're what?" It was almost possible to hear him steaming down the line. "You went off following her cock and bull story and you let her out of your sight?"

"I had to brief our volunteers in –"

"That was an hour ago!" Obrington exploded. "Call her. Tell her we want to talk."

"What's happened, sir?"

"I'm being led to think your judgement's been way off, that's what."

"I don't –"

"Are you anywhere near her, at least?"

"I'm in New Thornton, I could catch up to her in about twenty minutes."

"Bleeding Christ and damnation. Forget it, leave it to the professionals. Come straight here."

"Where –" Sam tried, but he ended the call. She held the phone away from her ear in disbelief. The pendulum had swung back to where the Ministry wanted to capture Pax? Why? And she'd been here *an hour*? She hadn't been on hold to Tycho Duvalier that long – what had they been doing? Was there something hypnotising about these black spots? She caught Holly watching with shock, having heard the call.

"It sounds like that man is *not* on our side," Holly said, cautiously.

"Must be a misunderstanding," Sam said. "I'll clear it up." She brought up Pax's number. Damn, this had to have compromised the Fae meeting. But she could get Pax to come in to the Ministry office and sort things out from there. Thinking out loud, she said, "We should probably all go in together."

"Like hell," Holly said.

"What . . ." Sam ventured, then paused. "We don't know what the situation is, and it's best to co-operate, to avoid confusion."

"In my experience," Holly said, "your organisation's idea of co-operation is a one-way street. I think it's best you go alone. I'll find out what hellish trouble Pax has got herself into myself, thank you."

"Without –"

"Diz!" Holly shouted down the hall. "Get over here, we're leaving!"

Sam tried to think fast. Obrington sounded mad and she had to get moving fast. Not to the lido, it was too late. And she'd seen enough unhinged Ministry retaliation in the last week, she couldn't let that happen again.

Holly took her own phone out as Sam held her gaze. This was a moment, Sam sensed, that was going to define their relationship moving forward. She couldn't very well force them to come with her, definitely not with Darren Barton bearing down on her. And if Pax had any resistance to coming in, she might be more likely to answer the Bartons' call than Sam's. Sam lowered her eyes. "I'm not part of the problem. If she won't hear it from me, you tell Pax that. You can find your own way up?"

9

Letty was hunched over some cards on a wine cork table, failing to learn a game Flynt called cuttle, when the knock came. Three sharp raps, and Letty jumped up, hoping to see Edwing so they could finally get to work. Flynt went to the door with his hand on his pistol, less optimistic.

"It's me," Smark announced.

"About fucking time!" Letty said. "We're ready to bust some heads."

"Oh," Smark answered apprehensively. "You've heard, then?"

Letty and Flynt exchanged a concerned look. Letty waved a hand, let him in, and Flynt stepped aside, peering out for trouble. Smark entered sullenly, and reading their postures decided no, they had not heard. He gestured towards the TV. "It's on the news, story broke as I was on the way over."

As Flynt closed the door, Letty said, "Val's responded?"

Smark gave her an uneasy look. He turned on the television himself. "It's hell. I'm sorry." He addressed Flynt: "So sorry."

The channel was broadcasting a speech from Valoria Magnus, in all her resplendent glory. Talking over a podium again. "– put his trust in beliefs that experience has taught us to doubt. We did our best to find the councilman, but he was determined to go alone. An admirable thinker, and a friend –"

Flynt gave Letty a sideways glance. "What's going on?"

Smark grunted, reluctant to say it. "It's unclear – all we've got is her word."

"The young amongst you," Valoria continued, "may not remember the coup. We've moved beyond those violent days. Edwing, certainly, had moved beyond that. But without a crusade to fight, some still seek trouble. And, of course, the influence of that monstrous human cannot be understated. It's a great loss."

"They showed photos," Smark said. "It wasn't pretty. The Stabilisers claim they tracked him down, to protect him, but what they found – they were too late."

On screen, Valoria continued, "She knew exactly how to isolate him. Playing on his hopes. Now, I appeal for calm and understanding – do not blame our dear colleague for his folly, nor his family, nor friends. One Fae alone is responsible. Her and the humans."

A headline scrolled at the base of the screen. *Chair of Information, Edwing, Murdered By Human.* No. Fuck. That righteous idiot got himself killed? What about Pax?

"Who? How?" Flynt said, horrified. "You said he was safe – Val wouldn't –"

"The truth," Valoria said, "is that Letty has been looking for ways to draw the FTC and humanity into a war for decades, even before she left us."

"I fought for *you*!" Letty shouted. She spun on the other two, Smark edging towards the door. "You know this is bullshit, right? She'll do anything to spite the humans!"

Smark was about to answer, but Flynt's anguished look gave him pause.

"Letty *will* be punished," Valoria continued. "The human will be punished. All that is left is for me to appeal to Edwing's people – those of you that believed in him. Hear me. I am as dedicated to resolving our differences with the humans as he was. I feel his loss as deeply as you. I only ask that you work with us. Help me deliver justice for this tragedy. Smark – our Waste Chief – Flynt, our Chief of Scouts, his *dear* brother – if you are listening, *please* be careful. Letty has fooled many in the past."

Flynt's eye shifted to Letty.

"This," Smark said carefully, "is a time to step back. I don't believe it, but if –"

"Pax would *never* have hurt him," Letty spat. "I know her –"

"She grabbed him," Flynt said. "Tossed him in a pocket like a toy."

"You murder your toys? She grabbed *me*, it doesn't mean a thing."

Smark took another step, into the doorway. "Letty, you see how it looks. What if –"

"Fuck you for suggesting it," Letty flared back.

"Anyone," Valoria continued, "with *any* information about Letty's whereabouts…"

"We need to lay low," Smark said. "If I come forward – say I was mistaken –"

"You bloody idiot! Let her win? She's probably flicking herself silly at her luck; no Edwing, no opposition. I warned him this would get dirty."

"Did you get my brother killed?" Flynt asked, quietly.

Letty froze, looking at him sideways. He didn't move.

"I'm leaving," Smark decided.

"Don't you fucking –" Letty twisted towards him, and Flynt shot into action. He shoved her, hard, both hands on her chest, hitting her bruise with enough force that she stumbled. Then he sprang at her. Letty's body took over: she deflected the attack and ducked to the side. He flew up, gaining the advantage of height as she rolled under him. She took one blow to a forearm before grabbing his wrist. She twisted it around and leapt up at the same time, hooking his arm into the crook of her elbow as she rammed her forehead into his nose. With a crack and a cry, Flynt fell, but Letty held him up by the arm, swinging her other fist in. Her arm was caught and she was twisted into a bearlike grip. Smark's face was terrified and apologetic, one hand on her wrist, the other arm around her waist.

"That's enough!" he shouted, fearfully. "He lost his brother for crying out loud!"

Letty shoved free of him but released Flynt, breathing deep. He collapsed at her feet, sobbing and cursing. Letty told him, regretfully, "You've got balls and no fucking brains. I didn't hurt Edwing, I didn't set him up, and Pax sure as shit didn't either."

Smark said, "You're – I can't stay –"

"Fuck off then," she snapped, "but give me what you promised."

Smark shook his head, forgetting himself entirely. Letty glared until he remembered. With hurried nods, he searched his pockets and took out a security card. He tossed it over with a hushed address: "Penthouse 8. And my guy, he hasn't been involved, but some Stabilisers, they've been up to something. Something else. For – for what it's worth."

With that, he hurried out. Flynt lifted his bloody face to Letty, single eye filled with hate, the eyepatch askew and showing a twisted, scarred hole. He spat blood. "Edwing . . . he . . ."

Letty gave him a sympathetic look. Not the first time a good man got beat, nor died. She held out her hand. He took it, limply, and she pulled him to his feet. Pulled him further, into an embrace, and he let it out. Slumping into her arms. Sobbing into her shoulder. He tried to form words, slowly, painfully. "What – what – what are we going to do?"

Lips set in firm defiance, Letty patted his back and didn't answer. Didn't need to, seeing as it was obvious. He already had the right idea, he'd just chosen the wrong target. We're going to fucking well fight back.

10

Pax's nerves were tightening by the second – murder, attempted murder, framing and fleeing were bad enough. Trying to remember how to work a clutch was salt in the wounds. The car moved in starts, something scraping in its pipes every time she changed speed. Christ, did cars have pipes? How the hell did you even describe this mess. All with two fairies giving mad instructions mostly formed of curses. Enjoying it.

"Double shift, for fuck's sake!" the denim one roared from his spot on the mirror.

"Pissing double shift yourself!" Pax shot back, whatever that meant. They jolted onto a long, straight road where Pax could finally relax after what seemed like an eternity of snaking little lanes. She glanced at Fresko, mulling over her phone on the passenger seat. She'd missed a call from Holly Barton, and she didn't dare stop to call back, but the fairy was making little progress doing it for her. Part of her wanted to toss the phone, in case it was being traced, but a bigger part wanted reassurance that the Bartons were safe. Pax said, "There's like three numbers on there, what's taking you so long?"

"I got it, I got it," Fresko grumbled, slapping the touchscreen. It did nothing.

"Turn right, dullard!" the denim one shouted, and Pax hit the brakes. The phone flew into the footwell, fairy with it. When Pax gunned the accelerator again the car shuddered to a stop and went quiet. She stared wide-eyed ahead, thankful that the nearest other car was a long way off.

"Sort it out, Mix, for fuck's sake," Fresko snarled, flying back up to the seat carrying a phone that dwarfed him.

The denim one, Mix, flew down past Pax, complaining, "Amateur."

As he played with the wires to restart the engine, Pax tried to slow her heart.

"You want the clutch totally disengaged when you're moving

that stick," Fresko said, almost without malice.

As the engine coughed back to life, Pax said, "How do you guys know this? You've got cars like ours?"

"Ha, hear that, Fresko?" Mix flew back up to the mirror. Unless barking angry commands, he had a hard time addressing her directly. "Thinks we're driving about in toys or some shit?"

"We've got wings, lady," Fresko told her, deliberately obvious. "Just pays to know your big tools."

Slowly moving the car on again, Pax recalled exactly who she was dealing with. This pair of maniacs had kidnapped Grace using a car, hadn't they? She had no idea how, but it didn't surprise her that they were capable of it. "So has one of you bright sparks got a plan?"

They looked to each other, and Mix said, "Seeing as this genius here got us shooting fucking Stabilisers, how about I give it a go? The only place to hide from your Ministry is with the Fae, only place to hide from the Fae is with your Ministry. Failing hiding, you gotta keep moving. Hence the ring road."

Coming up on it now, she could see the sign. Shit, there was going to be a slip road. Pax's knuckles whitened on the wheel as she picked up speed. She twisted quickly, searching every corner of window-space for blind spots. A truck whizzed past and she braked, jolting forward. Then she was there. On a highway stretching into the distance.

It was a straight line, near enough. Other cars shot past her, but she could stay in this lane, without having to steer, without having to change gears. This was good.

"Okay. Okay, we're safe. We can circle the city forever." She gave Mix a look. "You can syphon petrol from moving vehicles, fly in food, and we never have to leave the A564." She could sleep in stolen seconds, a motorway hermit swung around by the centrifugal force of Ordshaw's chaotic heart.

The electric ring of the speakerphone drew her back from that fantasy, Fresko announcing, "Got it."

Holly answered her phone. "At last. I'm not sure if you're aware, Pax, but the Ministry are after you. I can only imagine my family are in danger again."

"No, this is on me," Pax told her quickly. "Tell them it's nothing to do with you."

"*What* doesn't? Where are you?"

"Moving, for now, while I think of something. I've been set up."

"Of course you have," Holly said. "How can we help?"

"Stay out of it," Pax insisted. "I'll sort it out."

"Oh rot! I don't know how people do things where you come from, except clearly *not very well*, but I'm going to –"

"Watch that lorry!" Mix cried out, and Pax swerved with a screech from the car. They banked, but kept going, and she threw a terrified glance at the mirrors to see she was nowhere near hitting the massive vehicle they had passed. The fairy was laughing.

"You little shit," Pax hissed.

"See her face? Dumb fucking humans."

"Not the time," Fresko said, flying up to the rear-view mirror to join him. He sounded amused, despite the warning.

Pax said, "You're *both* shits."

"Who are you with . . ." Holly asked, worriedly. She recognised the voices. How could she not, when these little fiends had driven them into the sewer at gunpoint? "Pax . . ."

"It's complicated," Pax told her. "But I'm safe, okay?" Notwithstanding hurtling along at high speeds in a metal box of death. "Listen, Holly, if the Ministry *do* come at you, ask for Casaria. He's on our side. In his own weird way. As long as you tell him I said so."

"*He* came knocking at our house unannounced."

"He's there now?"

"No – I mean – never mind. What about Sam?"

Pax was quiet. Good bloody question: why wasn't Sam at the lido? "Is she with you?"

"She had a call from her people. She insisted she's on our side, Pax, but she answered their call, didn't she?"

"Uh-huh." That was a dilemma Pax could scarcely unpack. However amiable Sam had been, she was a company girl, wasn't she?

"We're heading home," Holly carried on. "Go there, we'll figure something out."

Pax wanted, deep down, to take up the offer, but couldn't. "I'll get back to you. Take care, Holly."

She ended the call, passing the turning for Hanton, towards New Thornton and, in its vicinity, the warehouse district. The harbour of criminals and fairies. This reckless escape was taking her *closer* to the threats. The Fae might spot her hurtling past on the raised highway, all of them coming after her in a swarm. Shooting at her from the sky. She asked her small companions, "Is there any way to avoid a shoot-first-ask-questions-later policy with your people?"

Mix gave a belly laugh. Fresko scoffed, more disdainful, and answered, "What for? Who's gonna believe the word of a human?"

"*You* know I didn't kill Edwing," Pax said. "Don't you have some kind of judicial system?" She recalled the way Letty had scolded her whenever she questioned Fae society. They had a university, working computers. "How do you hold trials back in the FTC?"

"Simple," Fresko said. "Hang a criminal someplace public, give everyone a chance to make judgements in passing. Good or bad."

"You hang them *before* a trial?"

"In a cage, dumbass," Mix replied. "You think a Fae ever got executed at the end of a rope? We can *fly*."

"It's a trial by the public," Fresko said. "Everyone's welcome to have a go."

"Leading to some kind of judgement?" Pax said.

"Usually a consensus gets reached, sure. Either, *go on let him out then*, or, you know, the other way. Sometimes in hours, days. Sometimes longer."

"Bana swung in his cage for eight years, the wretched shit," Mix recalled. "No one could decide that one. Did he kill his mistress, didn't he?"

"Wasn't so much no one could decide," Fresko said. "No one cared. Bana and the woman weren't well-liked. Usually those closest to the situation make the call. Doesn't work so well when you're dealing with loners."

"It's some kind of due process," Pax said. "A chance to be heard." She slowed down, making the Fae look around. There was an exit coming up, a sign for Brimlane. The warehouse district.

"The fuck are you doing?" Mix said. "Looking for the worst place to lie low?"

"That's the point, isn't it?" Pax said. "I'm supposed to lie low. We're all supposed to be fighting, blaming one another – no one talking. I'm being blamed for people I know getting into the Sunken City and we're all too busy getting chased to ask exactly what happened. Dial Sam Ward for me."

Fresko and Mix exchanged a look, then had a quick, muttered argument, pushing each other to decide who was going to follow orders this time.

"I'd suggest you, white shirt, seeing as you know what you're doing!" Pax took charge. Fresko gave up; with a snort, he flew to the phone.

Pax steered off the ring road and turned into a quieter street. Pulling up behind some parked cars, she held on to the steering wheel to calm herself. Fresko struggled with the touchscreen, looking like he was playing a game of Twister, so Pax reached for it herself. He scrambled out of the way with a hand shooting to the rifle slung across his back. "You fucking try –"

She ignored him, finding he'd somehow brought up a weather app. Rain all day tomorrow. She dialled the number.

"Sam Ward speaking," Ward answered, anxiety masked by her impossibly polite phone-answering instinct.

"Sam, it's me."

"I know – Pax, what's going on? If it's some kind of misunderstanding, you –"

"MEE policy would be to arrange a meeting and make sure I don't talk, I'm sure."

Ward paused. "Certainly not *my* policy." But that implied Pax wasn't wrong.

"That happens, or I run, and we fall into the same pattern," Pax told her plainly. "I didn't do whatever you think I did. I didn't do what the Fae think I did, either. I don't know if it's the same person set me up twice, but I do know *not knowing* is the problem."

"So . . ."

"Where are you?"

"Hanton, heading to St Alphege's. Where Obrington is."

"Casaria says your boss killed someone I know. You weren't there?"

"Absolutely not. But the intruders – is it – maybe you told them about the tunnels by mistake?"

"I haven't talked to –" Pax paused. She hadn't stopped to think about it. Monroe, Bees, Jones. They knew the tunnels existed.

They'd dropped the subject when she convinced them it wasn't safe underground. Or because they didn't need her to get in? Jones and Monroe had given her those cryptic comments, suggesting she had helped them out – somehow given them access? Pax slammed a hand into the steering wheel. "Bastards! This is Lightgate again – she saw me with them, she knew they knew me."

"Good," Ward said. "We can do something about that."

"No, not good, because Monroe thinks I helped him. Your people go to him, they'll believe the same. Shit. We need to get there first – figure out how she got to him, *show* it wasn't me. Sam. Do you trust me?"

There was hesitation, but it was short. "I do."

"Can I trust you?"

"Definitely."

"Buy me some time. Send your people *anywhere* but after me."

"I can't, Pax, I have to meet –"

"I'm going to the warehouse district. I'd appreciate it if you'd join me. Only you. So at least someone'll know if it goes tits up."

Ward was quiet for a moment. "I'll come." Another pause. "But Pax. The Fae? I heard your message . . ."

"One catastrophe at a time, Sam. Please."

Barton clambered up the stairs back into daylight at a pace that was wearing his ankle back to breaking point. By his side hovered Rufaizu, ready to catch him at any moment, face full of concern. He swatted him away, leaning against a wall instead, squinting into the sunlight to see Holly finishing on the phone.

"Anything?" Barton asked.

"I spoke to Pax," Holly said. "Then I got an address. The MEE switchboard told me where I could return Sam's scanners. So we can at least go *there* and do what we can. Assuming Pax survives the fairies, anyway. I heard them, Diz, on the phone with her – the ones that kidnapped Grace – and –"

Barton heard the crack of the wall before he felt the pain in his knuckles, as he realised he'd punched brickwork. His chest heaved, shoulders rolling, those bloody Fae – he should've killed them before –

Holly's face told him to stop. "Can you engage your brain instead of your testicles?"

Barton shook bits of chipped wall off his hand, cowed.

Rufaizu said, "Where is the bar fly? Can we fly to her?"

"I don't know," Holly said. "But whatever she thinks, I doubt we're safe from this."

"I'm not running," Barton said firmly. "They've been fucking with this city for far too long – the blue screens, the Ministry. I'll go to their office and make them see sense."

From the way Holly stared at his clenched fist, his wife remained unimpressed, but she didn't scold him this time. No better ideas of her own.

"You go," Barton continued. "Take Rufaizu back to Grace. I'll –"

Holly folded her arms. "I think you'll find I can handle these people better than you."

11

When Sam caught up to Obrington, she found the Ministry had created a crime scene out of a white van. Yellow police tape and bollards sectioned off the road, courtesy of one uniformed officer and a patrol car, and beyond that stood Obrington and Casaria, slightly apart from the vehicle, which was being searched by Landon and their tech-head, Dr Galler. Sam ducked under the tape and approached Obrington as he said, "Ah Ward, so *good* of you to join us."

"Apologies, sir, the traffic was –"

"Don't care." Obrington gestured towards the van. "What do you know about this? Exactly how pervasive a system of lies have we got here in Ordshaw?"

"Lies?" Sam looked from the van to Casaria, who slouched like a grounded teenager. "I haven't had a chance to –"

"Drug dealers in the Sunken City," Obrington announced, "who conveniently got access right around the time their good friend Pax tells us to back off, distracting us with stories of the Fae. Arranging things at conveniently unmonitored card games."

Sam's mouth was open, unbelieving. "Drug dealers?"

"It's the same van," Landon said, approaching from behind. Sam gave him the slightest smile of a hello, good to see his familiar face, but his expression warned her worse was to come. "These people were outside Casaria's, remember?"

The issue they'd never fully resolved, his abduction, which he'd claimed was unrelated to the men at Pax's apartment.

"Like I said," Casaria said, "I never got a good look. It could've been them. All I know is they wanted to leave me for dead in a rival gang's territory."

"Yet somehow over the course of this home invasion and abduction," Obrington said, "we get them happening upon a Sunken City entrance, and the means to deactivate our sensors. The same gentlemen who *happened* to burglarise Pax Kuranes' flat?"

"That's how it seems." Casaria wasn't even trying to sound convincing.

"You're effectively Management now, Ward." Obrington let his gaze rest on her. "What do you do in this situation?"

Sam paused, trying to appear in thoughtful control, rather than internally panicking. Casaria had proven himself unreliable, but Pax? Could she have orchestrated anything like this? Why would either of them help criminals?

"I'll make it easier on you," Obrington said. "Start with Mr Casaria. Who you seemed ready to forgive. Suspension, investigation, let him off?"

The *mister* was an insult that made Casaria twitch. Sam gave him an assaying look. Blame him and they'd limit the growing complications of this situation. It would get Pax off the hook, at least. But words came out at odds with that grave chain of thought: "I'd keep him closer, sir. If he's trustworthy, he's an asset; if he's not, he needs monitoring."

"An asset?" Obrington sounded surprised.

"Unless proven guilty, he's one of us," Sam said. "Trained, capable."

Mouth open again, her superior looked down his nose at her, not what he wanted to hear. "Respectfully, I'd say his trustworthiness is well in doubt. I wouldn't permit him to fart in the wind without a full account of his dealings this past week. But we shouldn't let him out of our sight, certainly." Before Sam could respond, he added, "Now where's Kuranes?"

"I honestly don't see her involvement in this," Sam said defensively. "Is it not possible these men, who intruded on her apartment, might have discovered this place without her knowing it?"

Obrington fired back at once, "*Are* you a dyke, Ms Ward?"

Sam tensed in shock. "That's the second time, sir, and I –"

"You seem awfully rosy thinking about Kuranes." Obrington turned to confide this to Landon. "Had them together this morning, can't say I didn't notice a few sparks. Thought I was imagining it, but here, this is a funny old place to be, with a fugitive –"

"You're out of line," Sam interrupted.

Obrington looked amused. "Touched a nerve?"

"Once was ignorant. Twice, it's insulting. To me, to her and to your office." Seeing Obrington's stirring anger, Sam puffed herself up rather than back down, chest high, shoulders back. "How are we supposed to trust your judgement when you say things like that? Do you think it's acceptable just because I'm a woman? Or that I *must* be driven by sex? That'd make it half the population you don't understand."

Obrington's open-mouthed grimace of disbelief was back, and Casaria had rediscovered his own grin. Landon made a noise of discomfort. If words failed Obrington long enough, Sam wondered, would he simply smack her face? His bear paws would flatten her. His goggling eyes vibrated, looking her up and down, until he settled on his best response. "Mathers really kept you in a box, didn't he?"

Sam glowered straight back, tight-lipped. No way she was going to let him dismiss this so blithely. "I respect Pax Kuranes. I believe the Ministry owes her a debt. Whatever you think you have against her, I suggest questioning it."

Obrington narrowed his eyes. "Why?"

"Because she's got a connection to the monsters that we don't, you fat fuck," Casaria blurted out, and it was Sam's turn to stand shocked. Obrington didn't turn to him at once, which was good because Casaria was grinning like he had no idea how else to wear his face. He hadn't meant to say it; Sam's outburst had drawn it out.

With perfect timing, Dr Galler appeared, lightly saying, "Yup, definitely Fae shots."

Obrington's broiling rage subsided in an instant. "What the bleeding hell does *that* mean?"

"The van. You said check for everything – there's bullets in the door. One in the wing mirror. Looks like your average scratch but that's what this baby's for." Galler proudly held up what looked like a microscope from a children's playset.

"You're telling me these mugs had a shootout with the Fae?" Obrington scowled.

"Well, their van did."

Obrington rounded on Casaria. "And you wouldn't know anything about that?"

The answer was clear on Casaria's face. Fully unprepared. He knew exactly who the criminals were and how they'd come to be shot at by fairies. Sam gave him a weak look. For all she'd said,

Pax and Casaria *had* kept a lot back. Were her instincts wrong?

"Care to revise your assessment?" Obrington asked her, considering the same.

Sam shook her head but said nothing.

Obrington's pocket buzzed and he drew out his phone. He frowned at the Caller ID and held up the index finger of his free hand. "Getting more interesting by the second." He answered. "Governor Valoria, I assume? Now is not –" The Fae governor interrupted, talking deeply but not loud enough for everyone to hear. Obrington's brow folded. "Huh. That so." He listened as the Fae railed on, then said, "You understand we're willing to co-operate." More listening. "It's come to our attention, too." He looked unhappy at the next comments. "That might be best for all of us. Good day."

Putting his phone away, Obrington looked at Sam. He adjusted his jacket, and said calmly, "Seems I owe you an apology, Ward."

Definitely a trap.

"I was wrong about one thing. Ms Kuranes wasn't spinning a yarn about her Fae connections. And it has got her in all sorts of fresh trouble. They're connecting her to some kind of political assassination. And you weren't with her at the time?"

Sam's doubts mounted. They'd planned to go to Tupsom together – but Pax had been keen to go on ahead, hadn't she? Hell, why *were* there Fae bullets in this van? And these people knew how to get into the Sunken City – was it possible –

"Know what we do with her now?" Obrington said, self-satisfied. "Besides marvelling at how big a cocking mess she's producing."

The best Sam could do was stare back.

"No?" Obrington said. "The Fae want us to hand her over, or otherwise *handle* her. They're not above capital punishment, yes? Frankly, I'm not in Ordshaw to tango with gangsters and this kind of bloody politics. Remove Kuranes from the equation and it seems to me we've got a much clearer shot at the end goal, don't we?"

Sam shook her head, but still no words came.

"Sounds settled to me. You two" – Obringinton indicated Casaria and Sam – "need a few lessons taught hard, but I can see you've been caught up beyond your station. Here's a shot at redemption. Help make all this go away, *including* Kuranes, and you get to keep your jobs, and your freedom, how's that? But we'll leave hunting her to the boys, shall we, to make sure a proper job's done, Meantime, how about all of us find this bloody Stacey Monroe, whoever he is, and see what he has to say about your star civilian. Casaria, you're with me" – Obrington clicked his fingers at Landon – "and you'll kindly follow on with Ms Ward. Get us a home address. Assuming none of you have any problem with that?"

12

Letty barged through a sleek entrance hall into an open-plan living area. Nimm was at a kitchen counter, startled from chopping vegetables, a gleaming knife in his hand. Pistol drawn, Letty sprang over the sofa then the counter with a quick wingbeat and the hum of the Clear Glider. She knocked the knife away and pushed Nimm into a stainless steel fridge, then jammed the barrel of her gun under his nose before checking the room.

A black leather three-piece suite, polished tile kitchen, resembling the worst, coldest human styles. Right down to a shrieking hussy in an open silk robe, scrambling out of an armchair trying to cover herself up. Flynt pushed her back down, waving his gun shakily. "Not a sound, not one fucking movement."

He looked at Letty, scarred face unsettling with its dried blood and the raw, trembling emotion in his eye. He was straining to hold back. But he was in control. Just. Letty bore into Nimm. "We're gonna have a chat and you're gonna want it to go well, because my mate's looking to work through some emotions."

There was no question Nimm had power: despite the big nose, skin patterned by liver spots, and hair coming out of his ears, he owned a pad like this, waited on by this pretty escort. Letty dragged him around the kitchen counter and kicked him onto the sofa. He scrambled back, hands up.

"There's no need," he squeaked, "the compound is gone!"

Letty paused. "Compound? Of what?"

Nimm's face mirrored her confusion. "You're not here about the septjad?"

"What fucking septjad?"

Nimm looked from one intruder to the other, worry mounting as he reassessed the situation. His eyes rested on Flynt, with a gasp. "No – they're preparing it now, in response – you don't think I had something to do with Edwing . . ."

Flynt's face hardened. "There a reason we should?"

"Shit." Letty stepped between them. This was supposed to be the safer, subtler option, going for the guy knee-deep in the *why* without losing their cool chasing murderers. To Nimm, she said, "We're not here for your fucking *compound* and we don't think you killed anyone. You're gonna take us to the Dispenser, your other fucking sins can wait."

"What do you mean? There's no –"

"'There's no question I'll do exactly as you ask, Letty, it's wonderful?'" Letty's fist was raised, making Nimm push himself deep into the sofa.

"But why? The Dispenser is secure –"

"Not as long as Val's got a hand in it, it's not! Tell me you're not trying to sabotage the thing? Make like it never worked?"

"Of course not, why *would* we?" He genuinely didn't follow.

Letty explained, slowly, "Because Val doesn't want us to retake the Sunken City." It only softened Nimm's features, the threat diminishing as he grasped the nature of the misunderstanding.

"But disabling the Dispenser has nothing to do with that."

Letty cocked her head to one side. He was almost smiling as he saw she didn't have the first clue what Val and her people were up to, even regarding the Dispenser. She met Flynt's eye again, and could see the same concern caught him. He needed clear, cold retaliation – what the hell was this?

"Explain," Letty said, holstering her pistol.

"You're Letty, aren't you? I –" Nimm cut off his attempt to get friendly as she unsheathed her big old hunting knife.

"Explain *well*," she advised.

He swallowed. "Valoria sought to conceal the Dispenser, yes, but only to avoid public concern. There's no need to risk disabling it, it could be easily recreated, and" – he hurried on, past Letty's startled reaction – "anyway no Fae would use it, or *could* use it, safely. The energy it sends out – surely you understand, the interplay with dust production, with electric weed as a fuel – it could kill us."

"What the fuck are you talking about? What's electric weed got to do with dust?"

"They're the same genus," Nimm said, surprised at her not knowing. "There's similar energy stored in dust fungus. Different strains, but similar enough to make the weapon's discharge dangerous. It could create a chain reaction – essentially drawing on that same energy in *us*."

"You . . ." Letty focused on the edge of the knife, trying to keep calm. "You already understand it. You understood it before?"

The scientist twisted in the seat, appealing to Flynt for reason. "Yes, well. The issue with the Dispenser was never that we couldn't rebuild it. We can neutralise Sunken City energy in controlled conditions, with the right materials. The *unknown* is what comes next."

Letty dragged a hand over her face. Of fucking course. She shouldn't be surprised, after Val's betrayal, with all this about the Fae settling into their transitional culture. They weren't ever waiting on her for salvation, the one person that could find the Dispenser. It was *always* replaceable and they let her believe otherwise. For nine years. Nine fucking years. She threw her knife with a snarl – half the blade sank into a wall, the impact making Nimm jump out of his seat. She said, "You fucking . . ."

Flynt moved past her, quickly. In front of Nimm.

"How many people know about this?" he demanded. "How many people know we already had the means to fight the creatures down there?"

"Plenty!" Nimm blurted out, frightened eyes on Letty. "It's not a well-kept secret. Half the workers in the vats must have an idea of it – knowing where dust comes from –"

"What the fuck's that mean," Letty snapped, "where dust comes from?"

"We cultivate a – a particular type of energy." Nimm's voice wavered. "The similarities in the Sunken City creatures are obvious. Likewise, how we might neutralise it –"

"So what's your damn *unknown*?" Letty said.

Nimm stared gravely. "Many tools were tested, before Valoria took power. The Dispenser was merely the last of them. They worked, of course they worked, but the berserker never *stayed* neutralised."

"Didn't . . ." Letty trailed off. They'd actually tested it – attacked the berserker before, that amorphous minotaur, the Ministry's protected *praelucente*. The heart of it all. They had *hurt* it? "This is bullshit. Why not keep trying until it was gone?"

"Because it's next to impossible for Fae to get close unharmed!

All for the possibility of removing a force of energy that's likely to *come back*?"

"But the humans can –"

"Work with humans? For what? We have the resources to expand our dust production here, what more does the Sunken City offer, worth that risk?"

"A home!" Letty shouted. "It's our fucking home! It *belongs* to us!"

Nimm looked at her like she was mad. "But you can't honestly believe it? Those tunnels weren't made for the Fae – I would say quite the opposite."

Letty glared hard, unsure exactly where to direct her anger. Valoria, the lying snake. This whole society, implicitly following her abandonment of the place Letty always aimed to return them to. How many scores of people were simply ignoring that option? She turned to the pretty escort in the armchair, sat in terrified silence, and said, "You know about this?"

The woman shook her head quickly, lost in fear.

"Reckon there's ordinary Fae that would like to know? Might kick up a fuss?"

The woman nodded desperately, agreeing with whatever Letty might say. Flynt came in, speaking low: "Of course they would. Else it wouldn't be secret. Else they wouldn't have killed my brother."

Nimm swallowed uncomfortably. "That is *not* my area. Your brother – Valoria would *not* have dared. She didn't think it necessary. And the things that have been said about *you*" – he gave Letty a look – "it is politics. All she wants is *security*."

Letty frowned. None of it was anything to do with him, from his perspective. "You thought we were here for something else. What's this compound?"

Nimm went quiet again.

"Speak," Letty said, leaning closer to him again, "or I'll cut your fingers off."

He croaked, "The Stabilisers are distributing the septjad compound across Ordshaw, as an insurance, to be ready for when the Council meet this afternoon. With the humans moving in the tunnels nearby, and now Edwing's death, it's our answer – but only as a *threat* – I thought you came to make it a reality."

"I asked what the fuck it is."

"Uh. A poison, water soluble, virtually untraceable. Cultured in Russia. Perfectly harmless in its current state, but placed in a water supply it becomes deadly. A way to disable high-profile humans."

Letty glowered. A poison from fucking Russia. A chemical weapon. The boxes that had been in the room with the Dispenser, all covered in Cyrillic. A gift from the Rostov Fae? Their closest neighbouring Fae community were a collective of unscrupulous psychos who experimented in vile, vicious technology. Perfect examples of what happened when Fae gave up on being civilised. Which was actually most Fae, most places. If anyone knew effective ways to kill humans, Rostov would. While Letty was itching to get back a weapon that was apparently never special, Val's people were preparing something that clearly was. "Val's going to threaten Ordshaw? Poison the humans?"

"She's planning..." Nimm averted his eyes, scared to repeat the governor's spin. "It's merely for the purposes of *negotiation*."

"Fuck's sake. Where the hell do we find it?"

"Why?" Nimm asked. "After what they did to Edwing, surely you want –"

"The humans didn't do that!" Letty told him viciously. "If anything, Val planned this shit herself. How the fuck do we stop it?"

"You're too late," Nimm said. "By now, it's already in position across the city."

Near Monroe's derelict lair, waiting on word from Sam Ward, Pax leant against the stolen car and reflected on her terrible choices. The car in itself was bad; the second time she'd committed grand theft auto in a week. Now she was wanted for murder, too, alongside suspicions for associating with dangerous criminals. Before this, the worst crimes she'd committed involved recreational drugs and drinking underage.

"About a half-mile walk to the FTC from here," Fresko mused from the car roof.

"Trying to make me feel better?" Pax said. He shrugged, not bothered how she felt. Mix was even less interested, standing further away, puffing on another Fae cigar.

"Never knew these guys were here, that's all," Fresko said. "Big city, isn't it?"

"Yeah," Pax said. "But then a pint of beer would be big for you."

"Listen." Fresko took a breath. Something on his mind. "Before you go get yourself killed, I gotta say. Things got out of hand before. Mistakes were made. Things happened. Okay?"

It *almost* sounded like an apology. Pax said, "One of you shot me in the leg."

Fresko looked her up and down. "You're walking, aren't you?"

"Yeah." What was the use. They'd saved her now. "I guess I'm glad you had a change of heart."

"For today," Mix told her. "Or until someone makes us a better offer."

As Pax regarded him warily, Fresko said, "Ignore him. It obviously wasn't Letty, or you, that screwed us. They weren't ever letting us back in the FTC."

Pax folded her arms over her chest, watching the road. "Yeah, we're all victims. Look, you'd better clear off. Seeing as you don't play nice with the Ministry."

"Uh-huh," Fresko said. "But if they don't kill you outright, come find us. I'm interested in what happens next."

"Find you where?"

"Palleday's. Couldn't say your Ministry won't track you, but the Stabilisers should steer clear, considering him neutral, near as I know."

The casual suggestion said they knew she'd already been there. How long had they been following her? When the Ministry was supposed to have her back . . .

Fresko shouldered his rifle and signalled to Mix it was time to go. The pair lifted off. Pax watched them flying with birdlike grace, becoming dark shapes against the cloud. How many times had people seen such sights, assuming delicate birds or big insects, when it was in fact a sweary little man with an attitude? There was something to be said for how far she'd come, and all she'd learnt, no matter where she'd ended up.

Checking the road again, she had another thought. How often did people survive learning these truths? And as if on cue, something throbbed in her. Her fingers tingled, something happening, movement, somewhere far off. The minotaur was feeding again. Drawing energy. It barely felt surprising now, tapping into whatever they were up to. She closed her eyes and focused.

Out east, moving north. The horde was getting closer. The screens were still together. Surrounding their minotaur and drawing energy like limpets. But they were reaching out, probing with tiny transfers. Interacting with their tunnel networks, or their monsters? It was too faint to tell, and faded as fast as it came.

Pax opened her eyes to the road again. Much calmer this time than before. Had she somehow triggered that feeling herself? A little casual probing. Ward would be here soon, and they could figure that out together. Once they overcame the Monroe mess. One step at a time. Provided Ward wasn't coming to shoot her.

13

"You said she had a connection to the monsters. What'd you mean by that?"

Casaria avoided looking at Obrington as they drove to the address Ward's Support team had found for them. If he concentrated on the oaf's face for more than a few seconds he was going to punch him. "I don't know."

"You don't know?" Obrington echoed. "Slipped your memory between hurling insults liable to get you hurt?"

The prick. Casaria saved his life, didn't he? That two-bit thug would've choked him, and where was the thanks? Somewhere behind vague threats of losing his job or violence. Like this overweight buffoon could match him in a brawl. Casaria would break his knees.

"I wasn't thinking." It was true, he hadn't meant to say it. Obviously he wasn't going to share Pax's secret, not if Pax and Sam Ward had kept it hidden. "I meant these criminals. She understands them."

Obrington hummed a sceptical noise.

On the radio, they were discussing the city's news. Someone commented, "It's Ordshaw, Steve – they don't exactly have the same building standards there, do they? Don't they say, those that can, do; those that can't move to Ordshaw."

Seeing Casaria's glower, Obrington said, "Funny because it's true, no?"

"Funny," Casaria replied with venom, "is the thought that people don't even realise how special this city is. You've no idea how important it is, what we do."

Obrington gave him a cock-eyed look. "You think what you do is important, but undermine it by being an insubordinate ass? How about that."

Casaria didn't deign to respond.

They were entering the outskirts of West Farling, and the affluent neighbourhood reminded him it wasn't monsters they were regulating, here, but people. Casaria thought of Pax and that unassuming teenager, Grace. Obrington had shot a man in the face, in the tunnels. He might've killed the small one, too, if there weren't so many loose ends. What Casaria did *was* important, because he kept the Sunken City in order without ruining the lives above. He didn't beat up defenceless people, or resort so quickly to murder.

He decided he did have a response, after all: "It's become clear we need to question Management's decisions if we're to do our work properly."

"Is that so," Obrington replied. "There's assuming you know how to do your job properly. Where'd we get to, before, when we were interrupted? Think I was asking, *how exactly was it that the only agent to die in the Sunken City in six years did so on Casaria's watch?*"

He clearly had an axe to grind over Gant's death. "If you're looking to crucify me, I'm sure you'll find an excuse. Your type usually do."

"You're not shy, are you. Whatever *my type* is, Casaria, you've plainly got a lot to account for. You didn't get on with the young lad, did you?"

"Did he file a report?"

"After he got killed?" Obrington made Casaria face him. The big man was staring, ignoring the road for longer than was safe. Casaria broke eye contact first. "You *believe* you're a good agent, don't you?"

They were passing ever-bigger houses, some of Ordshaw's grander mansions. Typical of a man like Monroe, living amongst the elite. It'd be good blowing off some steam here. Casaria said, "I put myself on the line, every day, to keep this city safe. I do that well, on my own, because I understand those tunnels and those monsters. I only have problems" – he directed this at Obrington – "when other people bring them to me."

For a moment, he couldn't tell if the wide-mouthed goon was going to keep pushing. Obrington focused on the road, and said curiously, "You'd lay down your life for this city, would you?"

"Any day of the week," Casaria said. Hadn't he already proved that, saving Pax and the civilians? Ready to take their secrets to the grave, toe severed while tied to a dentist's chair? A knife in his gut? A shield for Pax when she faced the grugulochs?

Obrington was quiet. Hopefully thinking the same.

A short distance down a hill, they pulled up next to a red-brick mansion, square and tasteless, the grass and bushes of its large open driveway trimmed so neatly it could've all been artificial. "This is it, isn't it?"

The car rocked as Obrington heaved his weight out the door. Casaria exited the other side, pulling his jacket closed over his gun. He studied the road, quiet. Obrington looked unimpressed. "Where's the others got to, then?"

"Sam Ward is very strict on the rules of the road," Casaria suggested, checking the car in Monroe's driveway. A gleaming black Porsche, most likely belonging to a trophy wife half built of plastic.

Obrington had his phone out, dialling. No answer after a long wait. He grunted and tried another number, with no answer there, either. With the third call, he said, "Tori, anything from Ward or Landon?"

"I thought they were with you, sir?" the receptionist chimed back.

"Evidently not."

"So you're not calling about the Bartons?"

Obrington mouthed a disapproving curse to Casaria. "Why would I?"

"They arrived a few minutes ago – insisting that –"

"Arrived in our office?" Obrington said.

"Yes. I thought –"

"For crying out loud, who's running that place?"

There was a muffled disagreement on the other end of the line, and Tori urgently came back. "Sorry, sir, would you mind speaking to her?"

"To who? This is a bleeding –"

"Mr Obrington." Holly Barton announced her presence sharply. "I'll have you know that there are problems under Ordshaw that you are clearly too short-sighted to understand. You know that Ms Ward enlisted our help for a good reason, don't you? Thanks in no small part to Pax's involvement."

Obrington paused at her brusqueness. "Mrs Barton. I'm not sure *you* fully understand the situation with Kuranes."

"*Whatever* it is, it's a damned sight better situation than you were in a week ago," Holly said. "Have you even asked *why* Pax might keep things from you? Perhaps because your blundering management have already screwed this city so successfully for so long? Touch a hair on that woman's head and you'll have a city to answer to."

From the set of Obrington's shoulders, he was not happy about being undermined yet again. Casaria twisted away, to give himself space to smile. "Mrs Barton," Obrington said. "It's not a question of what Kuranes has kept from us, so much as what she's *done*. Though perhaps you'd like to share exactly what you think I should be upset about?"

"Is Sam with you now? Frankly, it's time she explained it to you herself."

Obrington looked at Casaria, then Monroe's mansion, and finally the car, his mouth open in thought. He was piecing together the deception. Pax's connection to the monster, everyone lying to him. Sam Ward not here now. He drew a slow conclusion, and said, simply, "Huh."

Sam was not aware of making a conscience choice to subvert the chain of command, but the moment Obrington's car had turned out of view she advised Landon that they would not be going to Monroe's family home. Landon watched Sam with many questions in his eyes, unhappy about changing course for the warehouse district without telling their colleagues. He asked only, "We planning on arresting her or helping her?"

Sam said she wasn't sure, and he segued into comments about his new Ministry-issued car, to change the subject. A Mercedes. He was pleased about its MPG, engine size and various electronics. Aware that Sam didn't care, but trying to demonstrate two things: he appreciated that Sam had once shown an interest in upgrading his car, and he appreciated that she didn't want to talk about their current situation.

In truth, she was terrified that meeting Pax would mean coming head to head with the very criminal Obrington expected to confront in West Farling. But she was even more frightened about the very shaky ground regarding Pax. She shifted in the passenger seat. Her instincts, her gut, said trust the woman. It was too crazy and dangerous for her to have orchestrated such a mess, with herself at the centre. But doubt crept in from all angles. Casaria's kidnapping and the way he had been swayed further against the

Ministry. These illicit meetings with the Fae . . . what *had* Pax been getting up to? What were they walking into now? Pax wanted her alone, might she be planning something heinous?

What was Sam even doing out here, she belonged in the office – telling others where to go, analysing data. Even if Pax was to be trusted, they had field agents to follow up on it.

"You're not carrying a gun," Landon said, his mind in a similar place.

She gave him a wan smile. Of course she wasn't carrying a gun. Having an energy weapon in the Sunken City hardly helped. It had been years since she last used the Ministry's firing range.

"There's a spare in the glove compartment. You've had basic training?"

Sam let her eyes answer the question. Yes, she could shoot. No, she didn't want to.

"I'll take the lead," Landon said. "It's just in case."

14

Letty expected to find Edwing's war room empty. Newbry should've jumped ship the same as Smark, but Flynt insisted it was the place to go. If they were to have any hope of thwarting Val's citywide disaster, they needed help. He barely said anything else, retreating into his misery once the destination was established, with no discussion over exactly what use an abandoned comms station would be. The basement dwelling wasn't abandoned, though. Newbry was there, sitting amid a heap of wires and computer monitors, and he wasn't alone: in the little remaining space were Deidre and one of the Stabilisers from the Bloodtooth Bar.

"The fuck are you all doing here?" Letty asked, surprise coming out hostile. "The man's gone, shouldn't you be, too?"

"It's because –" Deidre started anxiously, higher than she intended. She tried again: "It's *because* we've lost Edwing that we're here. Flynt . . . I can't imagine." She half-raised a hand in consolation, but didn't come closer. Flynt nodded quiet appreciation.

Letty asked, "Do we know how it happened? How it *really* happened?"

The Stabiliser offered his input. "Near as I can tell they've reported the truth – our people weren't the first on the scene. They're hiding the fact we lost men, too, though."

"What?" Letty said. "How?"

"Only heard rumours," he replied. "Stabilisers got an anonymous tip to be there, but the first ones on the scene got taken down – three of ours. I don't see a human pulling that off, unless it was the Ministry, but why would Valoria hide that?"

She wouldn't, but she might downplay Fae involvement to keep the focus on Pax. Letty worked through that. Pax had other Fae friends? Who would intervene to help her? She asked Flynt, "Your people?"

Flynt shook his head. His scouts had been locked down with

everyone else. No, it was stranger than that. If they set this up, the Stabilisers should've been prepared for trouble. If there was another Fae involved . . . Suddenly it hit Letty. "Fuck, it's her again, isn't it?"

Deidre asked, "Who?"

"Lightgate," Letty said. "Why the hell wouldn't it be? I knew I shouldn't have waited on Edwing's war of words and this shit – and you lot" – she pointed at the Stabiliser – "don't have the first clue about stopping her, do they?"

"Lightgate?" he replied. "We couldn't find –"

"I'm telling you it's her. She saw him vying for peace and that's the worst thing in the world to a psycho like her. Val didn't need to kill him, she could've connived around it, but Lightgate revels in this kind of brutality, *fuck*. Give me your armour. I'll get out, go –"

"No," Flynt cut in.

"What? You listening to me, your brother –"

"Can *wait*." He closed his eye at the pain of having to say this. "Whether Valoria pulled that trigger or not, she's taking advantage of it. She meets the Council in under an hour. We have to stop her using this to do even more harm."

"How's that?" Letty said. "Storm the Council, put one in her head? The FTC doesn't matter."

"No," Flynt repeated, determinedly, "with the vote she'll be pushing retaliation, segregation. It's more important than ever we stand up for what Edwing believed in. Lightgate wants us to fight; we need to be voices of reason."

"Edwing wanted human support," Deidre said. "Without that we have nothing."

"We know what she's doing," Flynt said. "Planning to force her demands through by threatening the humans."

The Stabiliser said, "They've been moving something, Val's closest men."

"We know," Letty huffed. "It's a poison."

"I can tell Valoria *no*," Flynt said. "Make the Council see sense." Emotion bubbled into his voice. Desperate to do this. "It's what Edwing would've done. Stayed the course."

"I . . ." Deidre struggled. "What would we say? I don't know –"

"*I'll* do it," Flynt said. "I got a right, don't I? As a community leader – as his brother. I'll say what he would've. It's not right,

Val's way forward."

Deidre joined the rest of the room in looking to Letty for a decision.

"What? Why ask me? You think you can actually make a difference?"

"I can argue for peace," Flynt said. "For calm, measured justice."

"And we can record it," Newbry said. "I'm set up. Even if the Council votes in Val's favour, we can expose the details to the FTC."

Letty tried to picture it. A Council meeting where they managed to make a lot of angry Fae question Val's corruption. Throw in the message about her disregarding the Sunken City and the Dispenser, they might have something. At least delay what she had going on. Flynt wasn't the orator his brother had been, but it was better than busting heads. Letty asked, "You're up to this?"

He nodded, with the determination of a kid about to jump in water for the first time.

"Alright. But it's not enough. This one's right" – Letty indicated Deidre – "we *need* that human element. Can you get me another outside line?"

Newbry turned to a second computer. "Already on it."

At the ring of her phone, Pax felt a pang of stupid guilt. She still hadn't tossed it, inviting trouble. A tracking device in her pocket. Come get me, lock me up, shoot my knees off, whatever. And now another Unknown Number. She answered, "Yeah?"

"You sound down. Been wrongfully accused of murder or some shit?"

"Letty!" Pax jumped to attention. "Thank fuck! How –"

"You're in the shit," Letty cut in. "We are, too, for what it's worth. An hour or so and Valoria's gonna make contact like this completely impossible. So we gotta talk quick. First, some good news: our weapons *can* get rid of the berserker – your fucking minotaur."

"Great. Can they take out Lightgate, too?"

"Shut up and listen – this thing's still a clusterfuck and we need your help. Specifically, *you*, because you're always finding answers to questions no one's asking. I'm hoping for an answer to stop our people kicking the world in the balls. Point one, the

Dispenser wasn't never some unique, mystical weapon. Like you fucking thought, our energy's all connected, and my people already *know* that. They baulked at it because the buck doesn't stop at the berserker. The Dispenser *worked*, but the berserker came back."

"Came back . . ."

"That's their excuse for giving up and going with whatever the hell Val wants. Our Council's meeting in an hour and Val wants to draw a line we won't come back from. She'll threaten your people with some fucking poison. But if you can give us a solution – if we can resolve the Sunken City, put serious faith in humanity – then we avoid disaster."

Pax said nothing. Not panicking, or creasing up at the responsibility. Calm, strangely, like it made sense. For once, she wanted to be needed. "I'll do it. I'll be there."

"At the meeting? No, that's –"

"I mean I'll figure something out. If I'm not dead by then."

"Get your Ministry mates to earn their keep, they can hold off a few Fae."

An engine grew louder as a shining black car pulled into the road. The sleek heartless vehicle of government spooks, not Sam Ward's Honda. Tracking the phone call?

"Yeah, about that," Pax said quietly.

"What *about that*? Pax –"

"Let's both of us just try and stay alive. Speak soon, okay?"

She hung up as the car got nearer. Through the windscreen, she saw Ward, giving her a wave, but she wasn't alone. Behind the wheel was the older, overweight agent she'd crossed a few times now. Landon. Pax didn't run. It was what it was.

They pulled up and got out, Landon checking the sky, Ward holding back, watching Pax. Dreading the answer, Pax asked, "What's he doing here?"

"Whatever I tell him to," Ward said, with forced confidence. Having satisfied himself with their surroundings, Landon turned to her for instructions. There was a dark look on her face. "Obrington wants your blood. And the FTC got in touch."

"Saying I killed someone and you should hand me over, I guess?" Pax said. "Did they suggest I single-handedly took out the Fae hunting me, too?"

"I don't know." Ward hesitated. "The others are on their way to

Monroe's house, thinking we're behind them. It's just us here."

"They'll trace us before long," Landon added. Prompting a decision. Pax gave him an uneasy look; thinning dark hair dusted with grey, badly dressed and an overall picture of lazy tiredness. She could see why it was this one, in particular, Ward was able to control.

Ward held Pax's gaze, looking like she wanted to ask something, anything, that would make everything clear and easy. Rather than speak, Pax spread her hands openly. She had invited them there, trusted them this far; it was on them now. Ward took a deep breath and shook her head, going with a feeling that her logic was raging against. She said, "We might not have much time. What are we going to do?"

"Alright." Pax fought down a relieved smile, and raced quickly on. "Monroe and his boys, they *think* I'm their mate. They'll give me the time of day – I want to talk to them. Figure out how Lightgate got to them, maybe see a way I can prove it wasn't me. At least to satisfy you. But these are career criminals. If things get ugly . . ."

"We'll have your back," Ward said.

"I've got the impression," Landon said, "these men don't much respect the authorities."

That raised another question. Pax asked, "What happened in the tunnels?"

Landon checked with Ward. She nodded and he said, "They were looking to move contraband under the city. Prepared to kill over it, it seemed."

"And they had help," Ward elaborated, "disabling our alarms. Their interference probably caused our more widespread problems, letting some of the creatures through our sensors. It was pure luck they missed one."

"Lightgate could've got that info," Pax said. Pinning this on the fairy would mean the blue screens weren't conspiring as actively as they feared. To convince herself, she continued, "She has connections. She saw me with these guys, knew we were . . ."

Friends? Bees and Jones had almost killed Casaria, after she'd shared years of banter at the poker table with them. Bees, with his rambling trivia, as close to a friend as Pax had. She asked, "The men down there? Big guys?"

"One big one small," Landon said. "The grey-haired one was at your apartment. He got shot."

"He . . ." Pax averted her gaze. Shot meant dead. Just like that. Bees. She didn't know what to say. This whole damned affair. That little maniac fairy. Well, if Lightgate was here, they would trace a path back to her. Create a gap between the lies and deceits to see a way through. She said. "Come with me, but stay out of sight."

15

In the dim mid-afternoon, Stacey Monroe's dentistry office was lit from the inside, with at least one light on in the opposite warehouse, where his men did their work. Pax had taken grotty alleyways to the back of the small building, rather than risk the direct route, but she might be noticed walking between the buildings anyway. Fine, just as long as there was no sign of Ward and Landon.

She knocked at Monroe's door and waited. There were voices inside, the low chatter of two men. No response to her knock, so she tried the bell. It didn't ring. Pax opened the door, unlocked, and crept in. Through the reception hall, listening for conversation.

"Not what I agreed to, was it?" Monroe said, chewing someone out. "2009 was a good year. The best. Snobs in glass towers write poems about it. 2007 was a year you could wipe your arse with. Understand? I ask for a Jag I don't want to see bloody Peugeot on the bonnet, do I?"

The scolded person mumbled a response.

"You got something to say, say it, but it better be fucking good."

"Sorry, boss. Won't happen again – I promise." A man used to servitude.

"Can't happen again, can it? There's no one else offering eight fucking crates of 2009 Pomerol. The question is how you're gonna make up the difference."

"Two journeys in October," a woman's voice answered, decisively.

"Love, when I'm talking to you, you'll bloody know it."

"Two journeys in October," she repeated, "double your take, that'll cover the loss. If you take the truck off us, we can't earn you a thing."

"The truck? Take the fucking truck? Think your truck's worth that much?"

Christ, enough. Pax couldn't let Monroe get murderous punishing smugglers, not before she'd even begun. She knocked on the doorframe and cleared her throat. "Mr Monroe, you got a minute?"

Monroe froze mid-threat. Opposite him was a tall trucker, slim with facial features all out of proportion; big lips, long ears, bushy eyebrows. At his side was a short woman, wide and stern. Both had peaked denim baseball caps and desperate eyes. Monroe hid his surprise to address the pair: "Saved by the bell, Lucky. Get the fuck out of here and await my call."

The pair looked at him like it was a trick.

"Now!" he barked, and they scrambled to the door. Pax stepped out of the way. "And you'd fucking better run two trips, October. Back on the road by tomorrow!"

"This evening, boss, I swear!" the tall guy promised, not slowing down. The woman gave Pax a passing nod. When the door slammed, Monroe's face flicked like a switch to warm and welcoming.

"I'm blessed, got you making visits now, have we?" Whatever trouble he had with the truckers, he clearly hadn't heard about Bees in the Sunken City. They were alone now, no sound of anyone nearby. He indicated the kitchenette. "Cuppa?"

"Best not," Pax said.

"If it's the game this evening, you could've just called," he said, approaching the counter anyway. "This is no place for a lady. Got your own stake, we're happy to have you."

The game. It felt like she'd left that world a decade ago, even as the WPT was still in swing today. She wondered who was winning. "I'm not here about the game. It's our . . . other business."

Monroe stopped. He put his thumb to his chin, in thought. Really pressed it in, like this was some special technique he had for problem-solving. "Something more you gotta offer me, or something you want for yourself? Be very careful with the latter, I've given you a *lot*, sweetheart."

Pax bit her lip. "It's neither. It's something I heard. Bees was in the tunnels. The ones I warned you to steer clear of. I'm guessing that's why he wasn't at the game last night."

"You heard all that." Monroe's voice was strained. Not liking this. Friendly and reasonable as all hell when it'd work for him, less so faced with a problem. "And, what, you thought these rumours were worth something more than your current compensation?"

Pax shook her head. "I'm only asking. About the how of it. I mean – how you –"

"How, how," Monroe said. "We got a bloody Indian in here?" He opened a drawer. *Please don't pull a knife, please don't pull a knife.* He took out a folded piece of paper, walked to the middle of the room and placed it on the coffee table between them. "How we fared with the advice we were given?"

It was futile to answer not knowing what was on the paper. Hedging her bets, Pax said, "After my warnings, I hoped you might consult with me before . . . you know."

"Between that and this," he said, flicking his hand at the paper, "you're sending me very mixed messages, darling. Haven't I done right by you?"

So the note had supposedly come from her. Tightly wound already, he was unlikely to appreciate the idea that someone had tricked him. She gestured. "Can I just check that?"

"I asked you a fucking question."

"There might be more –" she tried, hoping to explain.

"Ah, there we go." Monroe gave her a faint, fuck-you kind of smile. He took a little phone from his jacket, a two-decade-old plastic lump, and he pressed two buttons. Holding it to his ear, he said, "It's been a long morning, love. We were all up late." Someone answered. "Jones, get down here." As Jones replied, Monroe suddenly yelled, "I don't give a shit about your nails, get your lazy fucking arrogant arse down here this second!"

He hung up and placed the phone calmly back in a pocket, using his free hand to pat a bit of sweat from his brow, face red. Pax was frozen stiff. Damn Lucky and his trucker girlfriend, they'd sowed the seeds of a very angry little man. He didn't even know what Pax wanted and he was furious. He said, "Sorry. I've got staff obviously can't take care of their own business today, haven't I? Now. You want to tell me how it is you see I *haven't* done right by you already?"

Pax held his gaze, not particularly wanting to tell him anything. The wrong word could make him explode. But that paper was her clue towards the real culprit. "You have done right by me, Mr Monroe. I'd only like to double-check the note you received."

"Oh, you're leading me up the garden path now," Monroe said. "Thinks she's fucking" – he drilled an index finger into his temple – "*smart*. Let's have out with it, shall we? Tell me what it is you're after to give me an idea of how big a moron you are."

Pax shook her head, taking a step back. He grabbed the piece of paper and thrust it her way, barely reaching her with its weightless flight. "Go on and tell me, love, what it is you can add, and what it's worth, above what I already done for you?"

The paper flopped open. Pax couldn't make out what it said at this distance, but she recognised the handwriting. There were numbers, a couple of paragraphs of instructions. All in *her* writing. "Fuck . . ."

The door burst open behind her and Pax jumped. Howling Jowls Jones filled the exit, his usual cheery face fixed with concern, hair swept sideways from the run. "What's the beef –" he started, before spotting Pax. "Boss?"

"Pax is back, as you can see," Monroe said.

"As I can see," Jones answered carefully, picking up on the room's tense mood.

"Says Bees has been down those tunnels of hers. Wants to consider a few details about how it is we came to know about that business. Seems sore about it."

Jones kept quiet.

"I think it's about time," Monroe said, "that you took her for a ride. Far enough to, I don't know, have a conversation about manners, coming to my place of work, talking about what people owe one another. You know?"

"I didn't come looking for a handout!" Pax stepped towards him before she realised she'd moved. "I came because I *didn't* write that note – and whoever did got Bees killed!"

The temperature dropped by degrees. Jones shifted, looking from Pax to Monroe and back again, hands opening and closing like he didn't know what to do with them. Monroe didn't blink. He said, "Second thoughts, she oughta take a seat."

"I'm not taking a seat," Pax said, eyes running back to the note. If the Ministry proper were on their way, that was exactly the incriminating evidence she'd feared. Worse than she feared: with *her* handwriting, perfectly recreated, it pointed to the blue screens. How could she convince Obrington of *that*? "I just want to take –"

Monroe snapped ferociously, "Come in here talking about Bees killed and then you're talking about fucking taking? Jones. Help her out."

"Wait, you're –"

"Not another fucking word, you're doing my head in. *Jones*."

Jones' face was a regretful, horrible grimace. Pax stepped back, into the wall. There was the barest slither of space between Jones and the door – the outside world, freedom. Shit, there was a torture chamber somewhere here. She ran, hard and low, driving her shoulder towards Jones' crotch. He moved deftly, a big hand slapping her off balance. The other lifted her deftly off the ground, making her spin as she kicked and cried out.

"Let her go," came a voice from the door.

Pax kept kicking as Jones went still, his grip like steel. She connected her heel with his gut and he wheezed, hands releasing. She darted out of his range, and found he hadn't moved. The massive man steadied himself with a recovery breath, staring past her, with Monroe motionless beyond him, equally still. Landon was standing in the doorway, Ward watching over his shoulder. His legs were spread, arms up, both hands clamped on a pistol.

"Don't know what your game is, my man," Monroe said, voice thickly aggressive, "but you are trespassing."

"Mr Stacey Monroe, we can get onto who's breaking whose rules," Landon said, "right after you both step away from this young lady."

"Bollocks," Monroe answered. "You're not going to shoot a couple of upstanding citizens in their own place of work."

"I'd prefer you didn't make me."

"Fucking desk jockey, isn't he?" Jones said. "Security guards playing at being spooks, I swear."

"I told you about the Ministry!" Pax said hurriedly. "There's still a –"

She jumped as Monroe's phone rang. He lifted it as Landon warned, "Don't move!"

"Relax," Monroe said. "Unlike some people, I believe in good manners. Someone calls, you answer." Unchecked by Landon, he pressed a button, "Monroe." A pause. "Yeah, we do have company in fact. Glad you bloody noticed. What the fuck you think I want you to do?" He hung up. Eyes fixed fiercely on Landon.

With failing conviction, Landon instructed, "I'm going to ask you to both back off. Through there, come on with you –"

"You think we're alone here, you daft bastard?"

Landon said nothing, giving a sideways glance to Pax. Yeah. This was escalating.

"You got a tool?" Monroe said, eyes still on Landon.

"Yeah, I got a tool," Jones replied, one arm moving slowly towards his waistline.

"I said don't move!" Landon raised his voice.

"That you did, mate." Jones put on his wide, white grin. It looked psychotic now. "But there's something I *got* to show you –"

Landon fired.

16

Outside, Pax took cover behind a low wall, hands on her ears as gunfire punctured the sky. Each explosive sound made her flinch. It was a miracle she'd made it out, she wasn't even sure how it happened; in her short darting sprint she must have dodged one or two bullets.

Now there were at least three criminals shooting, and with Ward having produced a pistol there were two shooting back. Pax had no idea exactly where any of them were, save some enterprising lunatic who kept popping up in the upstairs windows of the warehouse, spitting bullets into the street. Landon had rushed inside as Monroe fled, roaring orders. Ward had sprinted to skirt the big building, looking for another way in. And here was Pax, crouched, under fire, jumping at every sound.

The gunmen shouted the nonsensical shrieks of men fuelled by adrenaline. Howling Jowls Jones, back in the dentist's office, bleated, "My leg! My fucking leg! You fucking fuck!"

Pax searched for a way out. Across the road, there was a dumpster, good cover before getting into an alleyway, out of sight. But it was a ten-metre dash, at least. Up the road, there was a pick-up truck, another ten-metre dash. It had already sunk on a rear wheel that had been shot out. Taken bullets without anyone near it.

Then there was back the way she'd come. The dentist's office, with that bit of paper lying somewhere on the floor. With luck maybe Jones would drag himself over it and soak it in blood.

A bullet hit the road near Pax, chipping tarmac with a spark. Beyond that – a manhole cover. She'd never open it in time.

"You're fucking dead!" someone screamed from a high window, followed by another volley of gunfire that scattered around Pax's wall. Holy hell, that was directed at her – why did that frenetic bastard want to kill her?

"Get me a fucking medic!" Jones yelled, close to hysterics.

Pax fought her nerves, the instinct to stay put, not move, not make a sound. She shouted, from her gut, "Jones! Tell them to stop and I'll help!"

"Shove it!" Jones replied at full volume. "Right up your fucking arse!"

Rude.

He kept going, stringing out insults until they degenerated into blubbering, and finally an odd stream of consciousness. " . . . Cottage on Whistler, fucking A . . . never had it . . . small, handy size!"

The maniac inside opened fire again, half a dozen shots tearing through the side of the pick-up truck, shattering a window. He was no more in control than Jones, lashing out madly. Had Monroe simply armed a couple of madmen with instructions to raise hell if anyone started trouble around here?

Pax watched the sky. Where were Fresko and Mix? They'd saved her from one shootout, why not now? Letty would've made short work of this mess . . .

Far on the other side of the warehouse, another gun fired. Lighter, one of the pistols? Small rifle fire (presumably) answered it. Another pistol shot, from off to the right – that sounded like two people advancing on one? A pincer movement, both Landon and Ward still alive? Christ, hopefully.

The madman aiming at Pax had taken a break, and Jones had gone quiet, leaving the road in silence as the wispy mist of gunsmoke rolled over it. Keeping her head down, Pax reassessed her escape routes, left and right. A man dashed across the road, the heavy woollen suit of Monroe. He had the ungainly run of someone who'd heard how to do it from a mate down the pub. But he was getting away, trotting between another pair of buildings.

Bloody hell.

He was getting away to what? Call more boys to finish them off? Send men to watch her home? She had enough unknowns hanging over her.

More gunfire erupted, way off, and a strangled shout said the madman had moved, opening fire at the other side of the building. She was clear. Maybe. Just her and Monroe out here, now. Hell. She had to see where he was going, at least.

Rising to a crouching run, Pax raced after him. She cringed as she went, arms cocked high at her sides as if she might deflect bullets, expecting a shot at any second. But she made it across the road, around the corner, with no one shooting. Another pistol sounded in the distance. Pax picked up speed, breathing hard, and saw the flap of Monroe's jacket disappearing into an alley. She ran after him, and slowed at the alley entrance. He'd slowed too, up ahead. His laboured breath came with curses, phone up at his ear. "Insolent fucks. Reggie? Reggie, I'm gonna cut your balls off when you hear this. I got a job for you."

Pax pushed down her concerns. Any job he wanted to organise at this minute could piss off. She charged down the alley after him, bracing herself, and he turned at the sound of her approach. She jumped, taking no chances, and hit him with all her body. He fell like he weighed nothing, landing heavily on his back to cushion her. Pax bounced, air knocked out of her, but held on, hands on his arms. He tried to buck, snarling and snapping, spit spraying her face, so she dropped her weight onto him, a knee either side of his gut, pinning him down.

"Get off me you fat bitch, I'll cut your throat out!" he snarled, but she held fast, riding him like a bronco. In any other position he might've had the strength to throw her off, but he couldn't lift her weight off his belly, not with her squeezing his arms in – in his thrashing, he snapped himself back into the ground and hit his head. The fight went out of him with a grunt, and he was suddenly limp. His head lolled to the side, a trickle of blood on the concrete behind it. Pax sat back slightly.

Fuck, she'd broken him.

He groaned again, blinking in dazed pain. Hurriedly, while he was stunned, Pax repositioned, hiking her knees over his arms, freeing her hands. She grabbed his jaw and turned his face towards her, his eyes rolling back in his head.

"You done?" Pax asked, breathlessly.

"You fat bitch," he wheezed back.

"Yeah, you're done."

He hawked up phlegm, but before he could spit she pushed his head away and the spit sprayed up over his own nose. He spluttered on it with increasingly severe curses.

"Some gentleman," she said, breathing deep. Running down this alley, she'd sealed a particularly shitty fate for herself. He had friends who would burn down her house or cut off her fingers. But right now she was sitting on him and this was a victory. She patted his face, vaguely aware of the sound of a car braking nearby.

"Come on . . . apologise and I'll let you up. You can walk away, no hard feelings." She even smiled. The Ministry wouldn't let him walk away, would they? "What was your plan here? Disappear government agents? Police must be on the way."

"Out here?" Monroe snorted. It was a point. She'd seen his men at work with torture, wandering around in bloodstained overalls. Now, firing rifles across the road. The area was abandoned. Maybe even because of the Ministry, steering the population clear of the Fae.

"Just you and me, then," Pax said. "But you know what? I've killed bigger monsters than you, this past week."

His weary eyes said he didn't believe it.

"Yeah." The gunfire, the panic, or something else, stirred the memories in her, all this shit she'd endured. "Want to count? Hairless creature with pincers and jaws like" – she gnashed her teeth – "which I took its head and *rammed* it till it popped. Like nothing. And the great – this big bastard tentacled turtle thing with skull heads – I helped drop it down a lift shaft. Then the grugulochs, the simple-minded bloody grugulochs – I put a *bullet*' – Monroe gave it another go, bucking under her, and she shifted her weight, shoving him firmer into the ground – "I put a bullet in its fucking head! You hear me? I'm not scared of you – I'm not scared – and I'm not letting *your cock up* get me killed."

Regaining some of his breath, he snarled, "You're crazy."

Seeing the look in his eyes, she could believe it herself. Beyond frustration and anger: he was genuinely frightened by her. And how else did she get here, if she wasn't mad? Pax said, almost to herself, "I need to be, don't I?"

"You oughta thank her," a man's voice said, and she shot a look to the side. The entrance to the alley was filled by the imposing form of Wayne Obrington. "Now she's gone and caught you, we don't get to say you died trying to escape."

Pax sat motionless. The big man had a pistol out, down at his side. There was no getting past him and she'd used up all her energy for running. She said, "Can we talk?"

Obrington stared at her impassively for what seemed like an age, then reached a conclusion. "You're gonna do a lot more than that. Monster whisperer."

PART 3

1

The FTC Council met in a chamber bigger than most Fae homes, with a massive table encircled by tiered rings of desks. Flags hung from near the ceiling; an FTC coat of arms, the wing badges of the Stabilisers, the colours of old families. It could've fit a hundred Fae, but there were only eleven stuffy suits gathered around that central table, and a half-dozen less-presentable people scattered through the peripheral desks, with Stabilisers at the perimeter. A big projector screen took up one wall, presenting a list of proposed laws. Number One said *Unauthorised Contact is a Capital Crime*.

Valoria had given them a dry intro with references to Edwing's tragic death. Her condolences went out to Flynt, who was doing all he could to keep still at an outer desk. "He had so much to offer us, and shall be remembered. The measures we propose today honour his spirit."

She ran through various forms of rhetoric to explain how great it would be for the Fae, and the FTC. A new era, combining solidarity and security, backed by firm, decisive measures arranged by her people, which need never burden the public. Regrettable events had led them to this point, but the outcome would be historic.

And so it went, softening up a Council that were already hers.

Did she just enjoy hearing her own voice?

Newbry's camera showed the room from up high, a cleverly placed bit of kit. Letty squinted at the screen to read the projection of laws that demonstrated Val's end goal: from punishing contact with humans down to ID and visa laws, regulating Fae movement across Ordshaw. It was probably laced with clauses ensuring Val never lost her title and the FTC never relocated, to boot.

"It's not subtle," Letty said, more to herself than Newbry. "Talking and talking without actually saying anything, all the while hanging this bullshit behind her that basically says we're locking our doors. Can't Flynt just say *look at what the hell you're doing* and be done with it? They got no sense at all, how crazy this sounds?"

"And it'll be with this Council's blessing," concluded Val, "that we address the Ministry of Environmental Energy. I am honoured that you entrust the delivery of this message, and the necessary means to secure it, to myself and the Stabilisers."

The councillors obligingly shuffled papers, all having access to more written down that hadn't been said. Deidre and Smark were there, unhappily reading what was in front of them. Flynt craned forward; no one had printed a copy for him.

"It's a drop in the bucket," Valoria said, looking his way, "but justice for Councilman Edwing is at the very top of my considerations. Followed by an impartial investigation into Tuesday's attack and the Ministry's more immediate movements."

One of her sycophants took the chair for a minute, praising her efforts, saying these terms would benefit the Fae for generations to come. A thin, older Fae Newbry named as Mullon. Not someone Letty recognised, except maybe from the broadcasts, meaning he'd been a nobody before these days where talking was enough to make people important. Finally, he gushed, their children could sleep easy. Letty watched Deidre for a reaction, the councilwoman frowning as she read. She looked like she wanted to speak, but didn't.

Smark, for his part, was statue-still, playing the penitent now.

"As we know," Valoria told the room, "the Ministry plainly have plans of their own, and the sooner we establish new boundaries the better. If I can put it to a show of hands –"

"You're not going to discuss it?" Flynt said. Councillors twisted to face him.

Valoria put on a patient smile, which Letty could've kicked off her face. "We welcome your views, Flynt."

"Seems," Flynt continued, voice high and anxious, "something we should discuss. You've got the means to secure this –" He gestured weakly towards the demands. "But we don't need to discuss how else we might do it?" What?

"Of all people," Valoria said, "I thought you'd approve of this show of strength. For Edwing."

"You can't say it's for him," Flynt said, going for defiant but coming off petulant. He looked ready to stand, unsure if he should. "It's not right – you've got – what about moving?"

The Council wore pitying expressions. He was fumbling.

"This isn't peace," Flynt offered. Every extra word made him seem more uncertain. All the ammunition he had, the fact that Val was provoking humanity with the worst weapons, keeping the Dispenser from her people, that the notion of *hiding* was mad – he wasn't saying a thing. And Deidre kept her head down, too shy to help. Flynt said, "Edwing, he didn't want – wouldn't want *threats.*"

"And we all appreciated Edwing's eloquent dissent," Mullon responded, "but this is a matter for the Council, young man, and perhaps not the place for your concerns."

"Young man?" Flynt replied angrily. "What's my age got to do with it?"

"Apologies," Mullon continued, bordering on sarcastic. "It is rather your grief."

"You puffed-up old bean –"

Newbry cringed, and Letty felt the same. This wasn't what they'd discussed, and she really shouldn't have been surprised.

"Can we stay on track?" another crusty councilman said, this one wearing a waistcoat and a toupee like a soiled mop. "Madam Governor, I think I speak on behalf of all the members of the room, when I say we trust your wisdom."

"You don't speak for me," Flynt said. "I see this better than you – it's a cage we're talking about! Not peace, imprisoning us – and using poison to do it –"

"Perhaps," a woman councillor said through her nose, "the Scout Chief should take leave –"

"Balls!" Flynt stood. "You're flying on an ugly wing! Edwing believed in that human! She was gonna help us, she still *can*, but you're not even discussing it."

"That human that killed him?" Mullon boomed suddenly, taking personal offence. "Regardless of your troubles, Flynt, I will not hear such talk in this room!"

"Who says she did it? Some of you must think differently? Smark –"

The Waste Chief kept his eyes down, refusing to get involved.

"We all *know* the humans to be a threat," Mullon said.

"The governor's proposal is sound." Back to Toupee. "With secure borders, we can focus on internal development. We can –"

"Words," Flynt said, "it's bloody words to avoid the point."

"Yes, please," Mullon said, all sympathy gone, "let the young man explain why we shouldn't be talking using words!"

Nods and sniggering followed. In the furore, Deidre tried to help, with easily missed quietness. "Surely there is a case for delaying to investigate?"

This was what the FTC government had become? The language they were using, their trim suits – a perfect mimicry of the humans' vile Parliament. And Valoria at the centre of it, watching smugly, letting them squabble, knowing it made fuck all difference except to ultimately stroke her ego. She *owned* this. As the volume escalated, she finally slammed a fat palm into her lectern, for quiet.

"Your caution is appreciated, Flynt," Valoria said. "Doubly so as we can see your brother's passion lives on, here in this room. It is a passion the FTC sorely needs. But it's time to take action. Can I see raised hands for the Ayes?"

Ten hands shot up, Smark's quicker than most. Deidre eyed the room with concern. She looked like she was going to raise her hand too, just to fit in. But she kept it down, with effort. Val said, "A clear majority, then. If the Council will take a recess, I will make the call."

"No – you can't!" Flynt tried again, standing, panicking. The two closest guards were moving towards him. "Threaten the humans with poison and we destroy any chance we have!"

Most of the councillors regarded him with annoyance, now, but Val's face shifted in a more calculating way. Understanding the specific nature of Flynt's concerns. She said, "It's best we proceed without further interruptions."

The Stabilisers grabbed his arms as Flynt shoved back. They took his pistol and marched him towards the doors, his shouted complaints going unheard. Valoria looked to her right-hand man, Hearlon, and he followed the others. Letty swore under her breath as Val made a final announcement: "Today, our position is secured."

There was nothing in this they could share with the FTC public that would sway anyone. The phone was quiet, no last-minute save from Pax. No way to delay the threats Valoria was about to make or the laws she was ready to ratify. And worse, her people were taking Flynt.

"What a cockspasm of a mess," Letty said. "Can you jam her calls? Mustard gas the room or something?" Newbry's blank face said she was on her own. She straightened out her gun belt. "Fine. Back to Plan A."

2

With the Ministry crawling over the scene, Pax sat wearily on a low wall, waiting for the axe to fall. She was getting used to this sullen feeling that came after a period of intense life-threatening madness. She just wanted to peel back the tarmac and crawl under it to sleep. Instead, she contented herself watching the MEE at work, avoiding thoughts of the trouble she was in by wondering, distantly, about Letty's plight. How was Pax going to help her from a windowless prison? Or a coffin.

Having apparently tracked their phones, there were three black cars in the road now, along with two ambulances and a police car. Landon had returned from his shootout to give uniformed officers and paramedics bland instructions about cordoning off the area and tending to the wounded. His suit jacket was torn at the shoulder where he'd been grazed by a bullet, and he had a profusely bleeding head wound that needed dressing, but Pax heard him dismiss the ferocious drama: "They'd probably never fired a gun before, any of them."

The backup MEE agents were hard-looking men with hunters' glares. Pax wanted nothing to do with them, though she wished they'd been around earlier. Casaria was there, but he shot her only the briefest look before dashing inside. A body bag and two occupied gurneys were rolled to the ambulances before Pax caught sight of Sam Ward. She drifted out like a ghost, dusty, sweat-wrecked hair in strands across her face. After a few words with Obrington, who was grilling Monroe with one of the police officers, Ward wandered across the road to join Pax on the wall. She said nothing, eyes still focused on whatever she'd seen in there. Pax asked, softly, "Good gunfight?"

Ward's thin, humourless smile said it was far too soon. Dark rings had formed under her eyes and she hadn't quite stopped shaking.

They sat together in silence as Obrington chewed Monroe out, gesturing their way as he threatened the crime boss over any future problems. Pax doubted the Ministry could protect her from gangsters. Then, she needed protection from the MEE, too. The police were finally gifted Monroe, and drove him away cuffed with a Ministry car for an escort. He regarded Pax viciously through the window as they passed. She tried to ignore it, while Obrington approached, blocking out daylight.

"One dead, another two in critical condition," Obrington summarised, catching Ward's concerned attention. Was it her or Landon who'd scored the fatal shot? "Three dead if you count the guy who throttled me earlier. And here you two are, like a couple of schoolgirls caught pinching pennies from the tuck shop."

Pax processed that slower than she usually would. It was an oddly flippant remark considering the gravity of the situation. She said, "Is this where you take me behind a dumpster and shoot me? Tell my parents it was a random mugging. They'll claim they saw it coming."

Obrington didn't answer straight away. He looked around, as though he needed to double-check exactly where they'd got to. The first ambulance was leaving, and one of his agents was carrying an armful of guns towards his car. "This has spread beyond something a few disappearances would contain. Now it'd be more trouble than it's worth."

"Seriously?" Pax said, giving Ward a glance. "Not *oh no, the Ministry would never do a thing like that?*"

"We do what's best for the majority," Obrington answered simply. "Mostly that doesn't involve being deeply evil bastards, but not always. Especially *difficult* people can require special consideration. In your case . . ." His eyes lingered on Pax, the sentence unfinished like he wasn't sure himself. "The chap who actually *saw* something down there will need extra attention. Otherwise, it's a case of some gun-running lowlifes being locked away for shooting at government agents. They had serious gall; the gentleman thought he had friends in high places. Fortunately, it doesn't come higher than us. But even so. Ward. How is it we find ourselves in this situation?"

Ward gave him a look that said she was considering that question from afar. Pax said, "She didn't know about them. I thought I could talk them down and I convinced Sam to help. To avoid bloodshed."

"Because you wanted to get hold of this before we did?"

Obrington took the handwritten note from his jacket pocket.

Inwardly wincing, Pax played it honest. "Yeah. I didn't think you'd understand."

"*We* didn't," Ward came in, a tired fact. "How could we tell who to trust, after what happened with the Raleigh Commission?"

Obrington's face was as readable as a rock. "Third time today I've been told people are willingly keeping things from Management. What is it, exactly, you're all so delicately hiding? Not this criminal enterprise."

Ward wasn't ready to elaborate.

He addressed Pax. "Plainly, with half of Ordshaw fawning over you, you are more in control than me. Agent Casaria got his career tied in knots over you. An intensely irritating housewife gave me an earful on your account. This woman here, with aspirations to head a government department, is covering for you. Why?"

"It's not something I asked for," Pax said.

"I didn't ask for your opinion on it, did I? I figure you're smarter than this. Both of you. I figure there's a reason my gut says don't believe *this*" – he indicated the piece of paper – "is what it appears to be. Likewise, I don't like believing the Fae saying you're a murderer. Is my gut right, or is it last night's curry playing up?"

Pax frowned. It wasn't what she expected from him, and her dislike for the man made her reluctant to simply co-operate. But he was giving her a lifeline. She said, "I was set up, when I went to meet the Fae. And I was set up with these guys. Different people behind it, but the same reason. Neither of them want me building bridges."

"And the one we're talking about here," Obrington said, "would that be the sort of person that could pose, say, as a member of the Raleigh Commission?"

"I think so."

"Back from beyond the grugulochs' grave. So if this manipulative force is not really gone, what have you got against us culling the *praelucente*? Is it not, as you claimed, what our enemy uses to draw strength?"

"We don't know what they are, so it's reckless to attack the one thing we know has value to them." Pax let it out with what she realised was relief. Coming clean felt safer when she knew the guy might listen. "These things seem to exist in surfaces, and they warp how things appear, and they can create lifeforms. Beyond that, all we know is they've gone to a lot of trouble to hide their existence. We go on the attack, they hunker deeper down."

The ideas rotated behind Obrington's eyes. "You're talking about the blue screens themselves. A conclusion we reach because?"

"I've felt them," Pax said. "After I touched the minotaur, I picked up a sense for it. When I killed the grugulochs, I knew they were still there. They've abandoned the places Apothel used to meet them, but I *keep* feeling them." It jogged her memory with a moment's clarity. "You had another surge. In the last hour or so. I felt that."

As Ward gave Pax a concerned look, Obrington took out his phone and called to check, eyes on her all the while. The report from the office came back quickly: yes, there was a surge.

"Somewhere in the east," Pax said. "Moving this way?"

Obrington relayed that and got clarification. Whoever was on the line suggested they were hurrying to check if there'd been any wider effects. Obrington put his phone away, staring hard.

"It wasn't just paranoia that we kept this quiet," Ward said in a hushed tone. "I was concerned for Pax. That you'd want her trapped and tested. Or that *they* would target her."

Obrington's eyes widened, deliberately looking towards bullet holes in the nearby truck, across to smashed windows. Landon was talking to one of the new agents, wiping an absent hand over his bloodied face. "That's what this was, huh. Whatever bastard's got its claws in your town, it wanted us to declaw *you*."

Pax's gaze rested on the handwriting on the note in his hand, a perfect imitation of her own. He was right. The blue screens weren't randomly stirring chaos like Lightgate; this was designed to get rid of her, specifically.

"Why?" Ward asked of the world, slumping forward, elbows on her knees and head in her hands. Pax was unsure if she should pat her shoulder, offer a hug, something?

Obrington asked, "What more do you know? They exist on *surfaces*?"

He was taking all this remarkably calmly. Pax nodded. "They communicated through touch, scratches in walls or whatever. When I encountered one, it couldn't tell who I was by sight. But they're linked to each other like a hive mind, I'm sure. They're organised, somehow, able to communicate through some other means."

"As are *you*, evidently," Obrington said. "Making you a little bit psychic."

Pax gave him a warning look, preferring that not to be true, but it was disarming how seriously he made the suggestion. "You guys know something about this? I'm guessing there's more you've got hidden from the rest of us."

"That might be, but I don't know jack about your blue screens and this grugulochs business. Might've been useful to know when I got to Ordshaw that this wasn't yet a clean-up operation. What were you hoping to do next?"

"Study their patterns," Ward softly rejoined. "They expose themselves through novisan. When they feed, when they make things, when they transfer the energy."

"But they're sticking close to the *praelucente*," Pax said. "Maybe so we mistake their novisan fluctuations for its. They'll find new ways to stay hidden, if they're forced out from under its shadow. They infiltrated our government, hid their own existence –"

"I got the picture," Obrington said. "And you wanted to study this on your lonesome until you could be sure they're not listening. Except you can't ever be sure of that because you don't know what they are. And here we are, with them targeting precisely the person thinking she's got one up on them."

"You believe us, though?" Ward said, hopefully.

"Does it make a difference? Beyond believing neither of you would be idiot enough to join these low-rent gangsters, the details aren't important. You're telling me there's something still out there, suckling at your *praelucente's* teat. They're of the same energy, they'll burn just the same when we fry it."

"We'll send out a party invite, then?" Pax said. "*Come to an all-you-can-eat* and lock the doors? We don't even know how they communicate."

Obrington gave her an unsettling look through his magnifying lenses. "You know why Management sent me up here? Me, specifically. Not a bookkeeper like Mathers. I see a thing needs doing and I find a way to do it. I don't prat about overanalysing it."

"It's an otherworldly creature no one understands! How much analysis is too much?"

"Ward's words," Obrington said. "Understanding is *not* an absolute requirement." Hell, he'd accepted their reality, but it was making no difference. "We can still take a pop at damaging these things. Your problem, in a nutshell, is how do we make sure they're in the right place when we pull the trigger?" Pax began to say they couldn't, so he added, "These things targeted you specifically, Kuranes. You."

His glare told her to really consider that. The screens had plotted to attack the Ministry and the Fae using the turnbold situation. And they helped the Fae kill Apothel, years ago. But true enough, this wasn't them taking advantage of an existing situation, today. They knew things about her and her associates. Meaning . . . Pax said, "They sense me in some way, the same as I sense them. Even after this trick with the grugulochs, they know I'm a threat . . ."

There *was* something in that mantra, that understanding was not a requirement. However the blue screens thought, with rationale or reason, the horde swarmed feverishly when it scented energy – might their targeting of her be the same? And if they had a gentle attraction to her, their attraction to the Fae was uncontrollable. She said, "Certain energies inspire them to act stronger than others. With Fae energy, we *can* get them in one place."

"The girl's a genius," Obrington said, flatly. "So we tie a fairy down as bait."

"What?" said Ward, startled. "The Fae are *people*."

"More important than the entire population of this town?" Obrington replied. "Want to wait until next time these things screw us over?"

"We've already provoked the Fae," Ward said. "There's no way we can ask this."

"Wait," Pax said. The image of Edwing came back to her. That poor, small man, torn savagely open. "I have an option."

"Pax –"

"If I can find Lightgate. We *need* to stop her, anyway. She's as bad as those bloody screens. If I can get her, we can trap the creatures that way." She looked away from them, hearing her own voice. That was where she'd got to. Using a living person as bait for monsters? A maniac responsible for a lot of deaths. Yeah.

"Lightgate," Obrington echoed. "The Fae our people were

scouring the city for? Shall we add a few needles in haystacks to our shopping lists, too?"

Pax shook her head. "No. She's crazy but she's . . ." What had Obrington said? Pax had the whole of Ordshaw fawning over her. Lightgate included. "She sees something in me she likes. I can get close to her." And then get killed?

"Alright," Obrington said. "We'll head back to the office, make a –"

"I can't," Pax said, and explained it to Ward rather than him. "She'd have to believe I'm not with you. Between now and me getting in one of those cars, that's the only time I could make a break for it. They might be watching. *She* might be watching."

Obrington pulled back his jacket, revealing a small bulge in his inside pocket which he tapped. "This would tell us, within a hundred metres. Not just Fae presence; if they were running any equipment. There's no –"

"Thanks but your scanners can piss off," Pax told him. "This is how I've got to do it. I get away from you; out on my own, she might believe I'm desperate, looking for other angles. Help from the likes of her."

"Even if she does . . ." Ward said, but let the question go unasked. How was Pax going to ensnare the city's most dangerous fairy? It didn't matter. She had to. Ward's face shifted. Searchingly, trying to understand Pax's bravery. "You'd do that?"

Pax almost laughed. "I have a choice? It's up to you guys now."

She looked to Obrington. He asked, "Got a weapon on you, Ward?"

"I'm unarmed. Now."

"Right. You'll be on your own, Kuranes. See this gun I'm watching so loosely? Be a shame if you took it. And these car keys. Might be something I'm too big and slow to prevent. But you know what happens, this proves to be anything other than what you're saying?"

"I know," Pax said.

"I'm gonna take out some cuffs. To take you in. Understand?"

He had accepted her proposal, setting a scene for escape. Leaving the only complaint at the back of Pax's own head. It was the best way forward, the only clear path. If you ignored the definite risk of her own violent death.

After taking a breath, Pax grabbed his gun.

3

Sam was not quite able to focus. The spark of action with Pax running for the car, Obrington shouting at his men not to shoot – they needed her alive – scarcely enlivened her. Obrington pursued Pax himself, with his most vigilant agent, in what was bound to be a carefully unsuccessful car chase, while another agent escorted Sam back in.

She tried to strategise, but the face of a young Chinese man kept springing to her mind, lifeless eyes staring at the warehouse ceiling. Shot through the chest. At least, she thought he was Chinese, he might've been Japanese, what did she know. Not even that. Only that he was dead because he'd picked up a gun he wasn't trained to use. Or rather, because he wouldn't put it down again. Why was he dead. Not even connected to the Sunken City.

When Sam finally suppressed that image, she imagined a future not much better. Pax murdered by a fairy, or worse. The blue screens could build a monster to tear her apart. While Sam did what? Managed an office. Overanalysed, as Obrington said.

All heads turned to her as she entered the Ministry office. In Greek Street, late afternoon had been about the time they all started zoning out. Down here, the time of day was less obvious. The receptionist asked what was happening and Sam replied automatically, "Get me reports from everyone, and whatever we've got on Protocol 38."

"And your meeting?" Tori whispered it like a secret. "They weren't happy –"

"Meeting?" Sam frowned.

"I directed them to the café you used this morning, I hope that's okay. We're not setting up meetings here, are we?"

It dawned on Sam like the breaking of a wave. Tycho Duvalier. Oh. Hell. It was almost 4pm. An hour after they'd arranged to meet. "Is he still waiting?"

"I got a call ten minutes ago saying so. Seems they just arrived."

Well, at least there was that; Tycho probably turned up deliberately late. Top-floor office power-plays were the last thing she needed. But after that gunfight, she didn't have the energy to be worried, regardless of Obrington's warnings about Duvcorp. "Tell him I'll be there in five."

Before Sam could leave, Holly Barton raced to her side, ahead of her hobbling husband and Rufaizu, having apparently been waiting her turn. "Mrs Ward, where's Pax? I've got a lawyer in the family, and we'll contact Pax's people – her disappearance will *not* go unnoticed."

"What?" Sam blinked, trying to follow. The civilians' presence was almost surreal down here. "Pax hasn't disappeared. She's fine."

"She's not here now, you're –"

"Honestly, Holly," Sam said. "We let her go."

Holly was ready to keep complaining, but something made her stop. Reading Sam's face, she changed tack. "Are you okay? What happened?" Her hand was up, towards Sam's collar; there was a bloodstain. At Holly's shoulder, Barton's expression was equally concerned. He didn't say anything, but his stare begged for answers.

"Not my blood," Sam mumbled. "They gave us no choice."

"If Pax –"

"Holly, what are you doing here? You should go home."

"Where is she?" another voice hissed, Casaria appearing from behind, slinking into the office with Landon in tow. The latter gave Sam an apologetic look. They must've raced back after Sam. "What *was* that, give her thirty seconds then you come shooting?"

"What?" Sam said. "We let her *go*."

"We?" Casaria snorted. "In cahoots with that fucking oaf?"

"*Yes*," Sam said. Everyone was watching, she was aware. Even those pretending to work. Casaria looked ready to hit something. It must've stung him, missing the shootout, and now being excluded from Pax's flight. Sam explained, "Pax has gone to find Lightgate. The fairy that killed our people. She's going to bring her in."

"You're out of your mind!" Casaria said. "How is Pax supposed to take –"

"She's going to bring her in," Sam growled. Not louder than before, but sterner, going by the startled look on Casaria's face.

The rest of the office was absolutely still. "Then we're going to use Lightgate to lure all the worst creatures of the Sunken City together. *Then* we purge them." She turned on the spot everyone staring, finally focusing her – time to take charge. "Revise the terms of Protocol 38. Test our weapons against the new scanners and produce an action plan ready for this evening. I want the current locations of the myriad creatures, optimal choke points to place field agents. I want *everyone* on hand." She turned back to the Bartons. "If you're staying, Holly, I've got reports you can study. Darren, you can liaise with Support, share what you know about combating the horde." Holly looked like she might protest. Sam didn't give her a chance, clapping for movement. "That's it, people, let's go!"

Staff raced in different directions, a rush of comments passing between them. The older analyst, Roper, guided Barton away while Sam diverted Holly, saying, "Your daughter, is she safe?"

"She's not going to open the door to strangers," Holly replied, with a significant look Casaria's way. "What's Protocol 38?"

"It's where we nuke the Sunken City," Casaria said, bitterly.

"It's nothing without the Fae element," Sam said.

Casaria was about to continue, but Landon intervened. "Didn't get a chance to say so back there: you performed admirably under pressure, ma'am."

Sam squinted at him. Was *ma'am* good or bad? Just a distraction, to block Casaria?

"The city owes you a debt," Landon continued, definitely for the others' benefit. "Scumbags like that might've done some real damage."

Sam hesitated. *Thanks* was the easy option. *All I did was shoot an Asiatic man,* was more honest. Did it make her racist? Three white guys got away alive. This wasn't the time. Everyone was rallying around *her*. She looked from Landon to Casaria, one kindly supportive and the other dangerously aggrieved. She made another snap decision, pointing at Casaria. "Something else I need to take care of. You're with me for a second."

Not sure exactly what she was going to say, Sam entered the café with her head high. Like she wasn't ready to collapse with stress. Her determined energy had kept Casaria tensely quiet for their short walk, with only scant instructions: "We enter together, but you take a seat by the door. Say nothing. Do nothing."

"What –" Casaria started.

"Say nothing, do nothing." Zero room for discussion.

Tycho Duvalier had a booth to himself, sitting patiently upright. The waitress behind the counter was shamelessly staring, somewhere between awe and disbelief that this sharply dressed, familiar face was in *her* diner. A group of builders paid him no heed, but another man in a suit, two booths back from Tycho, stood out. Wearing dark glasses, hunched over a menu but patently observing the surroundings. Yes, Casaria's conspicuously shady appearance made a good choice for backup.

Standing, Tycho wore a welcoming smile, but gave Casaria exactly the sort of wary look Sam had hoped for. He began in a genial tone: "I'm not used to being kept waiting, so I hope you're planning to take us to your *actual* office –"

"Here is fine," Sam cut in. "We won't be long." She hadn't thought this through, and didn't intend to. She had a feeling to latch onto, stirred by surviving a shootout, observing Obrington, watching Pax put herself on the line – Sam let it flow. "You are not being shown our office or our work. We had information that you'd developed scanning equipment that we needed. We'll use it until our benchmarks are reliably satisfied, then we'll return it. We won't be studying the equipment itself, and you will not question our activities. Consider it a tax for doing business in our city."

Tycho's smile was gone. "There were proper channels to go through for –"

"No, see," Sam said, invoking Obrington to sound tougher than she felt. "This is a matter of national security. I'm *telling* you, not asking. The only question you should have is if there's anything more you can do."

The man's face was professionally blank; taller than her, more powerful by a thousand degrees, he studied her carefully. Her skin was sheened with sweat, suit marred by dirt, still smelling lightly of gunsmoke. His eyes lingered on her bloodstained collar, but he didn't ask. Finally, he said, "It's not so much the co-operation that concerns me, as the subterfuge. I discovered this situation on a chance hunch, and I remain in the dark as to exactly how *you* came to know what we were working on."

"Let it concern you," Sam told him, "but think carefully before crossing the Ministry. There's no authority higher than us." She didn't indicate Casaria, but Tycho's eyes went there. Who had the more dangerous goon, here?

"If I wanted that kind of trouble," Tycho murmured, "I would have brought lawyers. I wish simply to see where our interests align."

Sam reached into her jacket, not buying the friendly act. Obrington wanted to distance himself from Duvcorp for good reason. She took out a business card. "Prove that with a meeting in *your* offices. Explain your research to me and I'll consider what I can share with you. How's that?"

Tycho looked at the card. Sam's thumb had left a black smear. She needed a shower. But he took it, the billionaire tycoon pocketing her soiled business card. He said, "It's a dangerous game, believing yourselves untouchable."

Out of nowhere, Sam said, "Less than an hour ago, I shot a man dead." She wasn't sure if it was meant to sound threatening, unafraid, or what. Just had to say it. To own that, acknowledging the weight of things getting out of hand. His sly eyes betrayed no surprise. She continued, "Don't test me. It'll be as before; we won't step on your toes, you won't step on ours. I guarantee we won't do any more than use your scanners to take readings. And then, if you truly want to talk, that will depend on *your* openness. Want to start by explaining what Duvcorp has been measuring?"

Tycho's face gave away nothing. He avoided the question, reaching a businesslike decision. "I'll have them send papers. Properly inventorying the scanners' use. Invoiced at a rate we consider fair. With appropriate NDAs and other legal documentation."

He had bowed to her. In his way; there was no doubt that invoice would be steep. But that was Management's problem. Sam gave him a respectful (thankful?) handshake, and turned to leave before she lost her bottle. She marched outside and up the street. Walking strong, aware she was still visible through the café window. Casaria hurried after her and came close to say, "What was that – what's –"

"Not now."

Right around the corner, onto another street, into cover, and there Sam slumped, energy puffing out of her. She continued quietly back to the office, ignoring Casaria's questioning stare. Christ, she'd just stood up to Tycho Duvalier. Did that make her tougher than Obrington? She allowed herself a faint trace of pride, that maybe she could make inroads into Duvcorp relations where Management had presumably failed.

She was up to this. She was in her element.

Except why had Management failed? What were Duvcorp doing, that Tycho would let them use their scanners to avoid the slightest discussion of their own projects? Hell.

When she re-entered the office, Obrington was back, standing dead centre. Her face lifted, ready to tell him what she'd done, but his grim expression warned her off.

"Got another bleeding call from those little Fae menaces." Obrington's voice bounced off the walls. "Making a whole *heap* of demands. Rights, borders, the full gamut."

Sam frowned. "They want to open a dialogue? Isn't that a good –"

"It wasn't a request. They've got a weapon that they, I quote, *are not afraid to use*. Care to tell me what in bleeding hell septjad is, Ward?"

She stared blankly. Not a word she was in any way familiar with.

"You want to do something about it?" Obrington asked.

From one confrontation right into another. And Fae relations, her burgeoning obsession, threatened to dominate her again. But she shook her head, somehow still riding her authoritative high. "Sir, we're preparing to enact Protocol 38, and I'm confident if Pax succeeds then the Fae situation will become a lot less complicated. I'd respectfully ask that you keep them at bay while I prepare the team. I've just pacified Duvcorp myself."

Obrington almost looked impressed. "Did you now? Then I guess I can hold off the little buggers."

Sam had to fight to keep the satisfaction from showing on her face. This was good. This was how you moved on after murdering someone.

Having missed the drama with the criminals, Casaria had hoped to do at least *something* in Ward's shady meeting, but he was just there for show. While *she* put herself forward as the big dog. What an act. It should've been him protecting the city, then and before. Not nervous Ward and plodding bloody Landon. The criminals were gone. The chance for *justice* was gone, with Monroe on his way to jail, and that blond one maybe bleeding out. And back here, with Pax out on her own, Casaria was wasted. They wanted him to demonstrate weapons to the new agents. Dr Galler's job. Casaria watched Ward instructing Holly Barton, instead. Giving another civilian more attention than her own staff.

Darren Barton limped over, two steaming paper cups in hand, making Casaria square off uneasily. What did this lout want? He held out a cup and Casaria regarded it like proffered vomit.

"Too good for filter?" Barton said.

"Generally, yes," Casaria replied. What was it with this family and hot drinks? Barton kept it out, so he took it. It did smell inviting, even if it likely tasted piss-awful.

"We haven't properly spoken, you and me," Barton said.

"I wonder why."

"Another time, I would've given you a concussion for paying a visit to my daughter," Barton stated, idly.

"And I could've erased you from history for all the irresponsible crap you pulled."

"Sure. I owe you one, though. For helping Grace. And Pax."

Casaria was silent. Unsure how best to respond to gratitude from a man he could not respect. He looked at the coffee and realised what this was. A peace offering. He tried again. "I had no intention of calling on your daughter unannounced. I was looking for Sam Ward."

"I know," Barton said. And left it there. No words of advice about chasing the woman, or that she didn't want to talk to him. Barton took a sip of his own drink, breathed in satisfaction, and gestured to Ward and Holly. "I kept the tunnels from her for years. Figured she'd leave me if she knew. Now look at her, more involved than me."

Casaria nodded. He knew that feeling. "I trained Ward. Introduced her to all this. But she was always too good for me." He stopped dead, not knowing where that had come from. He left it too long to correct himself.

"Guess we both had high opinions of ourselves. It's what happens when us foot soldiers think too much. Word of advice?" Barton said. Here it was. "Stock some beer down here."

With that, he limped off back the way he'd come. Casaria wondered if the man even heard what he said. Ward left Holly, heading for the kitchen area, and Casaria sucked it up to follow. He caught up as she reached the coffee machine and he cleared his throat to announce his presence.

"Jesus, don't creep up on me."

"I didn't," Casaria told her, sharply, and got a sharp look back. Quickly moved on. "Are you hurt? From the shooting."

A pause, like she had to consider it, and Casaria's heart skipped. Had one of them –

"No."

"I would've taken them all down," he told her. "In the café, too. In a heartbeat."

"Maybe a good thing it was on me, then," Ward said grimly.

"I mean I wouldn't have let you go through that. It wasn't right. Obrington had –"

"He's doing okay," Ward interrupted. Casaria clamped his mouth shut. Unable to say anything right. She saw his frustration and softened. "What happened, happened. We survived. And for what it's worth, you were right, Cano. Pax *is* an asset to the Ministry."

Casaria went quiet. Did Sam Ward actually just admit he was *right* about something? He resisted deriding her for it. "I should be out there. Tell me where she went, she needs protection. These new bastards from London don't know the city, do they?"

"No."

Casaria smiled. "So you'll tell me where she's gone?"

"No, I mean you can't go after her. And you're not the first to offer."

Ugh. Fuck the others, what could they offer? He'd –

"Cano, stop, okay," Ward said, and he tried to unravel that. He hadn't been speaking, had he? "Can you just try not to think too much? In that café, just now, that was perfect. Follow instructions, don't second-guess, just assume we're doing the right thing, and none of it's personal."

Casaria stared at her, unsure where this was coming from – twice in as many minutes, told not to think. But he sensed it was important to her. Say no, and she'd remember it. Have what she deserved, perhaps, for all the spite she'd shown him. He didn't, though. He nodded. "Whatever you need."

She gave him the faintest smile before turning back to her coffee. Something moved in his throat. Not risking another word, he turned towards the weapons area.

4

The Fae Council building was a whitewashed monument to opulence. A tapering ringed tower decorated by pillars and arches in a neoclassical style. It stood taller than any building in the FTC, topped by a terrace with a low-walled rock garden, lording it over the city. Ambient spotlights highlighted it, soldiers hovered nearby. They didn't matter: Letty had a way in. She streamlined to approach as quickly as she could, down towards the base and a small ledge. A guard stood by a maintenance door, idly watching the sky.

As Letty got closer, he jumped to attention. She came fast, hitting him as he started to raise his gun. The guy went down and his gun slid off the ledge. He scrambled onto his knees as Letty bared her teeth. The soft-faced fool's eyes ballooned in recognition. "Shit –"

Letty rose to pounce, drawing her pistol, but the guard lifted his hands in surrender. A little whiff of something – hell – he'd pissed himself.

"Get up," Letty instructed. "Open the fucking door."

The man sprang to his feet. "Yes – of course –"

What had happened to this place, were they all this lame?

She dragged him inside, finding a row of hatch-tunnel entrances, labelled for different floors. "Where's the meeting?"

"Level eight," the guard told her. "Concourse."

"Good. Now, I need to punch your lights out, or you gonna keep quiet?"

"I won't say anything, I swear –"

"Yeah, whatever." Letty holstered her pistol. It wouldn't matter either way, they'd know where she was soon enough. She could spare a little sympathy for this loser.

Flynt fought his escort every step from the Council chamber, through the circular corridor and up the hatch. He bucked in their grips, snarled at Hearlon, their leader, and shouted about the mistake they were all making. Val was making her move – *had* made it, while he was being taken away. It was too late. The Stabilisers thrust Flynt into an empty room and locked the door. He clawed at the door, the walls, the ceiling, but there was no way out. The bastards had taken his weapons, and it was only a question of if they shot him right here or moved him somewhere more discreet.

Hearlon returned alone, light silhouetting him from behind. Flynt jumped to his feet and backed into the far wall, fists up. "You try me, man –"

"Shut up," Hearlon said. He was larger than most Fae, with a concrete face, head too big for his body. His black armour added extra bulk. The pistol at his hip was nearly the size of his thigh, and his hand hovered over it.

"That's it, is it?" Flynt said. "Edwing out in the wilderness – me right here in the Council building? Think the FTC won't notice –"

"It wasn't us did your brother," Hearlon said, coldly. "But he had it coming. Arrogant little shit. Guess it runs in the family."

Flynt glared back. "You honestly don't care that Val's imprisoning us?"

"*Protecting* us," Hearlon answered simply. "Like always." He drew the pistol.

"You're gonna bury this city," Flynt said, voice wavering.

"Nah. Only you."

Letty's words came to him, *strike hard and fast*, when they weren't expecting it – but there was no element of surprise here. Hearlon raised the gun and called over his shoulder, to the hall, a long way from convincing, "Ah, no, he's going for my –"

A bang shook them from below.

Hearlon looked down as though he could see through the floor. Another bang followed, distinctly a gunshot, and Hearlon's distraction was complete. "What in hell –"

Letty's words exploded in Flynt's mind – *win by acting, not fucking thinking* – and he sprang forward. Hearlon twisted and the gun went off, but Flynt was already past it. He drove a knee into the big guy's crotch, the same time he slammed his forehead into his face and got a hand on the gun. As Flynt pulled away, Hearlon stumbled into the wall, growling like a bear. But Flynt had the pistol. Right in his face. A corner of Hearlon's mouth rose in distaste and he started to speak. Flynt cut in, "I'll shoot, I swear I'll do it."

There was shouting below.

Hearlon didn't move, face bloody. Not his own blood; Flynt blinked a trickle out of his own eye, wounds reopened from his scuffle with Letty. He flicked it away and said, "Open the door. You son of a bitch."

"I want a talk, that's all!" Letty yelled over the shoulder of a Stabiliser a head taller than she, her pistol digging into his temple. The closest man when she had smashed her way in. As the other guards went for weapons, she fired a warning shot into the ceiling. Anyone who hadn't already leapt for cover did so. "You all keep calm, don't do anything stupid!"

"Letty." Valoria took charge, standing from behind the podium where she'd ducked. Her dignity returned with defiance. "You can't possibly expect this to work."

"Where's Flynt?" Letty shouted. She sidestepped along the wall with her hostage as a shield, getting closer to Val. "Get him back here!"

"He was disrupting the meeting," Valoria answered snidely.

"Did I fucking ask? You want to test me?" Letty flicked the gun from her hostage to the governor, and Valoria's arms went rigid at her sides. She was shitting one, even if she knew how to hide it. "You bring him back, and you – all of you! – sit the fuck back down!"

"Letty –"

"Now!" Letty's voice shook the room.

The guards all had their eyes on her, looking for a way through, as she shifted around, keeping her hostage between them. Fuming on the inside, Valoria held up a hand and spoke with acid. "Everyone keep calm. We are a civilised people, are we not?"

"We'll see, won't we?" Letty bit back.

Valoria slowly pressed a button on her collar, activating a radio. "Bring the boy back in here. In case you didn't hear, we have company."

"Good," Letty said. "Now. You lads – bunch closer together, over there. Where I can see you. Everyone else, in your seats. You're gonna listen to me, seeing as you're all incapable of talking sense. Now!"

The councillors hurried to sit back down, hands up, curling and hunching fearfully. Valoria stayed rooted to her spot. Letty said, "We're gonna have a reckoning, you pestilent grub. Tell these people exactly what you've done."

"There are no secrets here," Valoria answered. "The Council backed the actions we've enacted. For the good of the whole FTC. Whatever you hoped to find, it's not here."

"Uh-huh," Letty said. "They know all about the septjad poison, do they? How you'd risk threatening a chemical weapon rather than fucking *negotiate*? And all about the Dispenser? How you killed Apothel for it, but the weapon was never found? Not then, not now? How about the one about the fact that it never *needed* to be found? That we've got engineers that could've made a new one. Tell me, Val, how none of those are secrets *here*."

Valoria glared in furious silence.

The door creaked open and Stabilisers filled the gap. The governor ordered without hesitation, "Hearlon, join us. Let's see how tough she is with a friend on the line."

Letty watched the door, but the trio of guards who entered were unarmed. The two in front had their hands up. The trailing one was Hearlon, ahead of Flynt rather than the other way round. Flynt gave Letty a triumphant smile. Even better was the look on Valoria's face, crushed.

"Time to talk, Val," Letty said. "Time you fucking answered."

5

By the time Pax reached *The Sandwitch*, the sense that she was doing something remarkably stupid was deeply entrenched. It combined with a rumbling in her stomach, as the coming dusk reminded her she hadn't eaten since breakfast. Hopefully passing Palleday's rotten shop floor would stifle her appetite. When he let her in, the scent of mouldy bread did make her stomach churn. Then it rumbled more. Great.

"In here," Palleday called from the room of towers, where the crappy light was on. Pax strolled in, thinking how best to broach the subject of hunting their most hated felon. She found Palleday standing on a ledge with Fresko and Mix sat next to him, legs dangling over the edge, drinking from miniature bottles.

Fresko said, "You survived, then?"

"Apparently. Is that beer?" Pax leant closer. Did the Fae have glass manufacturing plants? What kind of tiny branding did they have?

"Not so close, *please*," Palleday insisted, holding up a hand, cringing.

"Sorry." Pax backed off. She was right by his buildings now, able to see into the nooks of their cave-like hollows. Empty.

"Yes, well, shouldn't expect a human to realise how big they are. How imposing they might be." Palleday distanced himself from the other two, folding his arms. The pair of mercenaries ignored him.

"Want one?" Fresko said, pushing himself up to approach what she saw was a tiny cooler. As he removed a beer, Mix snapped, "The fuck you gonna waste one on her for? Might as well throw it away."

"It's reckless," Palleday agreed. "Sharing that."

Fresko, apparently driven more by drinking etiquette than logic, opened the bottle with a tiny hiss before holding it up to Pax. She was torn: it was definitely a waste, and it would only irritate the other two, but she definitely wanted to try it. After a bad day and a worse week, hadn't she earned a little merit? Taking great care, she took the bottle in thumb and forefinger and poured the contents onto the tip of her tongue. It was hard to judge the taste from what amounted to a drop, but she told herself it was good. Very good.

"Bloody pointless," Mix huffed.

She dwelt on it for a moment, trying to savour it, and as she did she felt something. A refocusing of her eyes, a tingling around her fingers. The very barest trace of what the blue screens' energy manipulation stirred in her. She frowned, focusing back on the fairies, all three of them watching her.

"What's in it?" Pax replied. "This isn't like our beer . . ."

"It *is* your beer," Fresko said. "We rebottle what you lummoxes make. With twists."

"Twists, like . . ." Pax's voice got deeper. The liquid was taking a familiar but unsettling effect. She sensed her glow without looking down. The electric blue under her skin, the one the blue screens' liquid revealed. And the glow around the Fae; each of them a slightly different colour. Fresko was red, Palleday orange, Mix a steely grey. And the building behind them, it pulsed like it was subtly, slowly, breathing. "What did you put in it?"

Fresko answered slower than she could comprehend, lips barely moving. Pax scanned each Fae in turn as they looked at her with expressions shifting, at glacial speed, towards concern. Palleday's arms started to uncurl, Mix was lowering his beer, Fresko's head tilting to one side.

Pax leant in closer. Time had slowed down; she backed off again, raised an uncertain hand, dropped it, all in the time it took them to widen their eyes.

Then it was like someone hit play again, and all three of the Fae leapt backwards, shouting in surprise; Palleday fell over, crawling away, Mix scooted back, grabbing at a pistol, while Fresko jumped half a foot in the air and hovered there.

"The fuck was that!" Mix roared.

"She – bloody hell!" Palleday gasped.

Fresko kept quiet, staring.

With them watching her like she might explode, Pax remained frozen. "What just happened?"

"You moved like a twitching fucking bird," Fresko said, settling back onto the ledge.

"Bird's not that fast," Mix snarled, getting to his feet, slapping off dirt. "Never seen nothing move like that. Specially not some human."

Whatever it was had passed as quickly as it came. Pax's hearing, vision, and movements were all normal again, no more glow, no unsettling feeling. "What's in that beer?"

The fairies exchanged worried looks. To them, it must've been the opposite of what she'd experienced; in the space of time it took them to breathe in and out she'd gone through all those movements, spoken. Warped time?

"It's standard crank brew," Mix said. "Only a fucking beer." Pax let her eyes express the idiocy of what he was saying. He asked Fresko, "Think it's the dust?"

"Of course it's the dust," Palleday said. He, too, turned on Fresko. "What the hell are you thinking? Born yesterday, giving a human that?"

"There was Fae dust in there?" Pax asked.

"Alright, my bad," Fresko grumbled. "Forgive me for being fucking companionable. Figured you'd already crossed that bridge with Letty, seeing as you're such great mates."

Pax *had* discussed human consumption of Fae dust with Letty, and the conclusion, she recalled, was that it had never been done. That they were aware of. And it wasn't the same as glo, but it was similar. She blinked, trying to clear her mind. There was no more glo, but maybe . . .

"You with us?" Fresko asked. "Gonna tell us where your head's at, human?"

She refocused. "Yes. Yeah. That . . . we'll come back to that."

"Want more, you gotta earn it," Mix said. "It's time you told us what *you* are gonna do for *us*."

"Didn't I make that clear? An end to the monsters – the Sunken City, better relations between our people –"

"Letty gave us the same promises, and where'd that end up? Her fucking fist in my face? You don't have the Dispenser, don't have the Sunken City, or any leverage with the bloody Fae Council, don't even have the Ministry on side. What the fuck do you have?"

"Right now," Pax admitted, "I've got you guys. But I can get those other things, with your help. I need Lightgate."

The three Fae were stunned still for a second, then Mix burst into laughter. Fresko shook his head in similarly amused disbelief, but Palleday wore a look of abject horror.

"Hear me out. As long as she's out there, I figure pretty much everyone is at risk," Pax explained. "And I need a Fae I can take up against the minotaur. What you call the berserker."

"You're mad," Fresko told her, frankly. "Got us shooting at the Ministry and civilians. Got the Dispenser in all the wrong hands, got Letty spun out. Now you want to fuck with Lightgate? You're a fucking blight, you are."

"A blight with a plan. We're on the same side, aren't we?"

"Jury's out," Fresko said.

"This isn't just for me. We can help clear Letty, make things right between our people. If I can get hold of Lightgate –"

"You'll do what, tie her up?" Fresko said. "Someone like Lightgate, it's frontier justice or nothing, a fight to the death. You think no one's tried before? Val's Stabilisers gave up long before Lightgate skipped town. She's a nutcase."

"You're all nutcases," Pax pointed out.

"Not like her," Mix said. "Besides which, you got no chance of finding her. *She* comes to *you*, and you better believe that'll be on her terms. Nope. Double nope." He opened the cooler and took out another beer. "Big fucking mistake sticking up for this one, Fresko. Best thing we could've done is left her to take the fall, like Lightgate wanted. Big fucking mistake."

"Let Letty take the fall," Fresko replied with aggravation, "then this lummox? We end up taking the fall too, eventually. You saw those fucking FTC reports about us. You wanna be called Rogue Fae all your life?"

"If it means living longer," Mix said.

"Guys," Pax said, "this is on me. You don't put your necks on the line. Reach out to her, arrange a meeting, put me in a room with her. Convince her I'm on your side, that's all I want. I'll handle the rest."

"How? Jump down another sewer hole?" Mix said.

"I'll think of something."

"Without help, you'll die," Palleday weighed in. He gave the others a disapproving look. "Letty always deserved better than you two ingrates; look what happens when she finally finds someone useful. You're no-good cowards, you know that?"

"We're survivors," Fresko said, coldly. "Nothing more. You

want to duel with Lightgate, you go ahead."

"Maybe I bloody will," the architect snapped. "Seems someone has to, before she tears the whole city down. Now, did you thick-skulled morons, or did you not, just see what I saw when this behemoth took a sip of our beer?"

They hesitated. Mix mumbled, "Saw her waste a good brew."

"I've got dust," Palleday said. "Plenty enough for a human to huff. And Lightgate's been banging on doors around town, I'm due a visit. You give her the message I wanna talk and she'll come, won't she? The human can nab her as she waltzes in."

Though appreciating the vote of confidence (other than being labelled a behemoth), Pax didn't jump at the idea herself. Huffing Fae dust sounded like an unreliable plan.

Mix swung his bottle around. "We set Lightgate up like that, you know what happens? She rapes *her* face with a knife, then *yours*, then *yours.*" He pointed at them each in turn. "Then she skins yours truly alive."

"Go hide under a rock, then, like you're good at," Palleday answered, looking at Fresko instead. "Only takes one of you to give her the nod."

"Anyone gets through to her via any of us," Mix said, angering, "it's on *all* of us. You know what happened at the fucking Grit Plateau? That wasn't just a couple of bumbling goons, she killed like forty elite soldiers. On both sides, because they *pissed her off.*"

"Hold up," Pax said. "She wanted to see me, didn't she? She wanted to meet with Palleday, too? You'd be doing as she asked."

"Until you fuck up," Mix said, "and the trap becomes obvious."

"Then we make sure I don't fuck up, don't we?" Pax said. So she was accepting the really bad idea. "If that beer was something to go on . . . I just need to take a *lot* of your dust."

6

Letty grouped her hostages around the right side of the main table, she and Flynt covering them from up the sloped floor opposite. The guards' guns were piled on a table, and the corridor outside was empty. Letty perched on a desk, pistol loosely aimed at the crowd. It was time to face the music and she had no fucking idea what came next. Flynt's face mirrored what she felt. His adrenaline was shifting back to doubt.

Valoria, at the front of the crowd, got them started. "You know there's no way out, Letty. Whatever you do, my Stabilisers will hunt you to the ends of the earth."

"We'll see," Letty said. "Might be they're not so loyal when they understand how screwy you are."

"You have the faith of the deranged," Val said, blandly. "There is nothing you can say that will shake the foundations we've built. The FTC has thrived without your sort here. Haven't you seen it? Edwing" – she addressed Flynt – "he understood. This behaviour might have worked ten years ago, but not today."

"Ten years ago," Letty echoed. "The coup – that was bloody work, wasn't it? You had no problem with the rule of the gun back then."

"As a means to an end. I do not deny the origins of this peace, but –"

"*But*," Letty hissed, "it was more than a Fae uprising. Ten years ago, you didn't just take control – the humans stopped chasing us. The FTC got cemented. You made human friends – who royally fucked you last week. Don't talk about that, do we? There goes Letty, screwing us by talking to humans, while everyone keeps quiet about Val's contacts."

Valoria shimmered with restrained hate. Hit a nerve. It wasn't going to surprise anyone, but it was still shameful. "None would begrudge my efforts to deliver peace. We had a whole decade –"

"*Had*, Val," Letty said, loudly. "Fucking *had* peace, until someone else called it quits. What kind of peace was it? No one even knows. How can we say what went wrong, make sure it doesn't happen again, when you kept it to yourself."

"What went wrong," Valoria snorted, "was that you gave the humans –"

"Stop. Stop talking. It's all you do. Talk and talk in circles so no one's right but you. Let's focus on what *I* know, shall we? Your contact in the Ministry? Some corrupt fucker, Lord Asquith?"

The governor said nothing.

"He was a goddamned *plant*. You want to know why the Ministry attacked us? The same reason *we* attacked them. Because *you*" – Letty pointed sharply – "made fucking pacts with the devils underground. The second we got a clue to their real nature – 'we' being me and a human – then your mates, the *monsters* in the Sunken City, they panicked. What they were doing was scorched fucking earth. And what you're doing now is no better. Threatening the humans, locking our doors, burying your head in the sand."

"What I'm doing," Valoria rumbled, "is securing what's best for our people."

"With a poison out of Rostov? Where'd you get that idea? You prats all know about this?" Letty's eyes ran over the crowd. Many refused to meet her gaze, some returned it stubbornly.

"You are delusional," Valoria said, "if you think these good people will be swayed by your insolence. They recognise the need for decisive action." She stood, pulling her overcoat closer around her shoulders. "Letty focuses on the means, instead of the end. Yes, we have a poison, delivered by the Rostov Fae. A carefully poised, highly targeted threat, which we hope not to use. But such a threat requires a willingness to use it. A steel resolve, which human-sympathisers, such as Letty, would undermine. I shoulder that burden so you don't have to."

"Oh you noble sack of blubber," Letty said. "Does your neck ache from carrying gold chains on your people's behalf?"

"Indeed, show your true colours, Letty," Valoria warned. "I expect no civilised discourse from you. You believe yourself a victim, forcibly cast out, lied to. What have you ever done to earn a place here?"

Letty stared fire across the room.

Val sighed, heavily, like this was beneath her. "Flynt, it

saddens me to see you keep her company. She set you up, can you not see that? The human Pax Kuranes, now working with the Ministry, is everything we stand against."

"She talked the Ministry round!" Letty replied hotly. "Unlike you, who took handouts until they decided to stop giving them."

"Quite," Valoria continued calmly. "I have, indeed, been betrayed by the humans. Regrettably, on the back of your disastrous involvement. But our new measures guarantee such a thing will not happen again. We will never again rely on human trust. They will ratify our demands. We will be recognised, and securely separated."

"You can't threaten your way into that kind of peace."

"Says the one holding our government at gunpoint!" Valoria laughed with haughty bass. It inspired some of her supporters to snickers. "Dear Letty, your head was always in the clouds. You criticise my methods while bringing violence to this very chamber. You talk of sowing ill-will when it was *you* who murdered human agents?"

"That was Lightgate!" Letty jumped off the table.

"At least I own my mistakes, while you lay the blame at the feet of ghosts."

"Half your fucking Council's heard from her! They won't admit it because it was your head she was after!"

Valoria gave her Council an amused look, not taking it seriously. Her sycophants shook their heads. "Convenient –"

"She's telling the truth," Flynt said, plucking up the nerve to speak. "I've seen her, too. Edwing confessed to meeting her, didn't he? I was there when he turned her down."

Valoria's face turned steely. "And you didn't report it."

"They discussed human support," Flynt said. "Edwing knew you'd disapprove."

Deidre, at the back, cleared her throat to speak above a rush of murmurs. "I had the same offer. I also feared punishment for even entertaining human interaction."

"Deidre?" Valoria turned a heavy stare to her.

"Aye she wasn't the only one." Smark found some spine, at last. "Fust and Nailer received messages from Lightgate, too." The two councilmen both vigorously shook their heads. "And no one would be foolish enough to *pretend* to be Lightgate, would they?" He held Valoria's stare, acknowledging that it was exactly what she was accusing Letty of.

Valoria huffed. "It's no matter. The Stabilisers have tracked half the exiles in Ordshaw; they'll find her too. *If* she's out there. And it hardly exonerates Letty if she associated with the Scourge."

"You accept Lightgate's out there," Letty snarled, "maybe you'd accept someone else might've been vile enough to murder Edwing, not a human I consider a friend."

"A friend?" Valoria answered through tight lips. "Heaven forbid it should be what it appears to be. The inevitability of history repeating itself."

"Meaning Apothel? A man whose crime, let's face it, was wanting to *use* the Dispenser? Killed so you can keep us from the Sunken City?"

"You choose to believe –"

"It's the fucking truth!" Letty shouted, making her audience jump. She walked through the room, pistol arm up, stiff. "You're keeping the Dispenser from us, you always have! I *know* it works – your people could've made a new one any time they wanted. I've been in your fucking vats."

Valoria had a tremor in her wings. Council members muttered concern, even some of Valoria's closest supporters. "To not pursue such a venture was –"

"For the sake of the FTC?" Letty said. "Or just for *your* sake? So nothing ever changes. You'd give up everything for this seat." Letty gestured to the podium, the throne-like chair behind it. "You'd risk completely alienating the humans for it."

"To defend the FTC?" Valoria said. "Absolutely! How dare you –"

"How dare *you* keep the Sunken City from us!" Letty yelled, now only a few paces away. The gun shook in her hand. "You let me search for that weapon for nine years! Nine fucking years grubbing about under human feet, believing I could make up for everything! You never wanted it back and Apothel was fucking well *right* to steal it! That was the only hope we ever had of using it!"

Her audience gasped in shock.

"You simpering moles! You seriously think this bitch wants what's best?"

"You have no idea!" Valoria said, hands balling into fists. "We have a civilisation to consider, the survival of a culture, our infrastructure! An untested weapon, monsters underground, humans that have betrayed us – why should we *choose* that!"

"The weapon *was* tested," Letty answered, slowing down. "Why hide it?"

Valoria paused. "Then, as now, I bore the burden of a question too difficult to share."

Letty glowered. The woman was clinging to her righteousness like it was a life preserver. She wanted to punch it out of her eyes. "Well, it's time to open it to everyone. We have a weapon that can threaten the monsters. It's time we went for the heart –"

"What *heart*?" Valoria demanded. "The berserker is not the problem, you ignorant fool! How could anyone truly believe it was that simple, with the humans bending over backwards to protect the monstrosities below? The humans can keep the Sunken City. We do not need it. The FTC survives alone, as it should be."

Letty lowered her gun. It was a confession; Valoria knew of and ceded to whatever force operated behind the berserker. She had given up the Sunken City without apology. Still, the councillors weren't stirring. They looked like they would have preferred never to have heard all this. Easier to leave it to the governor.

"Are you satisfied?" Valoria said, reading the reluctance from the room. "Do you understand the futility of all this? The *necessity* of what I have done?"

"No," Letty said, straining to keep equally calm. "I'm a long way from satisfied. You're going to recall your Stabilisers, rein in that fucking septjad. Tell the Ministry it was a mistake and we'll make up for it. We'll work with them on securing the Sunken City."

"I won't, Letty," Valoria said. "I have only done what is best."

Letty tried again, angrily, "Make the call. Tell your men to stand down."

"No."

"Make the fucking call!" Chairs scraped and short shrieks met Letty's movement, her gun suddenly against Val's head. The bulbous Fae glared with trembling indignation as Letty hissed, "Do it, or I'll do you."

Despite her fear, Valoria said, "You will not. Not if there's an ounce of truth in your belief in Fae society."

Braced there, wanting to do it, wishing it was as simple as pulling a trigger, Letty looked to Flynt. He had that same expression she'd seen on him a dozen times now: worried she might go too far. With an angry growl, Letty dropped her arm and addressed the Council. "None of you got a damn thing to say? Edwing the only one of you with any balls?"

Smark ventured, "This *has* moved very fast."

"Should our future be made to wait?" Valoria replied, emboldened. "Whatever you say, Letty, the FTC needs my leadership. They *want* it. I am willing to pay the cost of peace."

Letty's fingers rapped against her pistol handle. Smark and Deidre's backing wasn't going to make a difference. This was Val's domain. But there was a whole city of people that might disagree. Surely, would disagree. To reach them would mean signalling what was happening here. Val's soldiers would be all over them.

There was no running now, anyway.

"Flynt." Valoria tried again to appeal to the scout. "Surely you see this is *for* your brother. You are angry, and grieving, anyone would –"

"Piss on it, Val," Letty cut in, meeting Flynt's eye herself. "Edwing wouldn't ever have wanted it your way and Flynt knows it. This chamber might not be willing to stand up to you, but there's thousands outside that might." Letty waved to where the camera was hidden, somewhere up above. "Put it out there, Newbry! Now!"

7

"Height of goddamned sacrilege, this is," Palleday complained, despite his hand in the plan. If it was so offensive to him to rest a (human) bottle of beer here, perhaps he shouldn't have built these towers with conveniently spaced ledges, including the one around chest height that Pax was using.

Trying to keep her hand steady as she carefully tipped a little tub of fine white powder into the neck, Pax said, "These sculptures would be great in pubs, you know. Lot of surface area for storing drinks without taking up a ton of space."

Watching with Fresko from the next ledge up, the architect made a noise that said she was making it worse. Mix, sat by them, focused on his own beer.

"But I bet they looked more stunning in use," Pax tried again. "Teeming with Fae."

"Oh, like a dream," Palleday assured her.

"With about as much substance," Mix contributed. "Ain't no one seen Palleday's towers in use for decades. Even longer since we had a city of them. If you believe there ever was one."

"Course there was, you disrespectful punk," Palleday said. "How you gonna understand, you ever even sniffed those tunnels?"

"Only you," Fresko said, "are old enough to remember *that*."

"What'd it look like?" Pax prompted, the chatter helping distract her from spilling their precious powder. So far only a few grains outside the bottle; Mix winced at every one.

"The population bringing these beauties to life was one thing," Palleday reflected, "but the plants made it. If you'd seen the way they lit the place. Ah – the *colours* –"

"Like, glowing plants?" Pax frowned. "From the weird underground weeds?"

"The Magnus family harvested them," Palleday explained, "for medicinal uses and the like. This was before dust was so ubiquitous. They took a real blow when we were driven above ground. But Valoria's people weathered it better than most." His bitterness returned. "Found new interests, didn't they. Kicked the old ways to the dirt."

"We're working on that," Pax assured him. She stepped back from the fizzing beer, thoughtful. "You must've known the Sunken City well, back then. You ever come across caves that nothing went in? Older chambers, shaped like –"

Palleday scoffed. "What're you messing with Chasm Shrines for?"

"Chasm . . .? Okay, so that's a firm *yes*. Tell me what you know."

"What's to know? Rooms where things never worked proper? Difficult to fly, even. Religious types used them for meditation, superstitious Fae steered well clear. Rumour was some Fae held out in the Shrines, when the monsters came, but you couldn't get out again, could you? One entrance, one exit. Bloody open graveyards."

Did that negative energy keep the blue screens at bay, too? Something for later.

"You done already?" Mix interrupted Pax's chain of thought.

She indicated the beer. "You think that's enough?"

"Would've done about two dozen of our stubbies," Fresko commented.

"Should work about twenty times longer than what you gave me before, then," Pax decided. Then paused. "If I down the whole bottle."

"Yeah, better put more in," Mix said.

"Unless the effects are exponential," Fresko suggested.

"That amount could kill a Fae," Palleday said.

Pax stared at the cocktail. Equally likely to be too weak to give her time to complete their plan and too strong to survive. "This is really idiotic."

"And exactly why *are* you doing it?" a female voice asked from above, and Pax jumped back. Unannounced, there she was, the brightly-suited menace of a fairy, posing at the peak of a tower, just above Pax's head height. Lightgate's face was impassive as she watched, the opposite of the others' fearful concern. Mix uttered, "Ah, fuck."

"How long have you been following me?" Pax asked, scolding herself for thinking she'd ever been safe from the fairy. Besides senseless murder and holding her liquor, Lightgate's chief talent was sneaking up on people.

"You think I have time for that?" Lightgate sighed. She tilted her head, demonstratively, to show a smear. Blood, or a charred patch? "Fresh from Salt Wharf, where a spirited young lady was being harassed by Val's people. She went to join the others. Third one today. Makes fifteen, twenty total? I'm not sure."

"Twenty what?" Pax said. "You're rallying an army?" The suggestion had been there before, with Lightgate's continual disappearances. Rounding up the outcast Fae. "Where?"

"They're out working. But I got the ball moving and thought, hey, the old man's missing out." She pointed her index finger and thumb in a pistol at Palleday and winked.

"We were about to invite you," Fresko said, tense.

"I'm sure you were," Lightgate said. "What else would you be conspiring about?"

"Well. We might've hesitated after seeing what you did to that councilman."

"Ah, you were there?" Lightgate beamed. "That's how you got away, Pax? I should've stuck around, but I never quite trust that lunatic Valoria's swarm."

"You're calling *her* a lunatic?" Mix said. "Saints alive."

Lightgate laughed. "Yeah, well, she outdid me. Have you heard she took deliveries from the Rostov Fae?" She directed the question to Pax, who said nothing. "Poisons. Spread across Ordshaw. Though I wouldn't trust her to follow through."

"What are you doing here?" Palleday rumbled. "You could've guessed I want nothing to do with you."

Lightgate looked at him like he was talking a foreign language. "You've got two deadly klutzes and this volcanic mess of a human with you. You clearly need help."

"They're here because this place is neutral. Everyone knows that."

"Oh, no one's neutral," Lightgate said. "As to what I'm *doing* here, now, I'm discovering what on earth you guys are up to?"

"Trying to survive," Pax said. "At least long enough to see whatever insane plan you're going to throw up next."

"Mixing Fae dust in beer? You know what that does to a person?"

"You do?" Pax replied with concern.

"I've tried it. Twice. Not that they knew it. One went into this kind of" – Lightgate raised a hand, covering a wide yawn, like she was boring herself – "seizure. Shaking all over, eyes moving a mile a minute, then nothing. Second one, it was the opposite. Slowed. Right. Down." She spoke in an extra drawn-out drawl. "Like wading . . . through . . . mud. Sort of fell asleep and never woke up."

Pax stared wide-eyed. Of course Lightgate had experimented with this Fae taboo, spiking humans, and of course she had killed two people doing it. With wildly different results.

"It's not a good idea, Pax," Lightgate continued flippantly. "Feeling particularly adventurous today?"

"Yeah," Pax answered, fighting down her own uncertainty. The startled looks on the other Fae's faces said they were thinking the same thing. Had they just mixed her a death elixir? "Certain toxic people keep making my life more difficult. The more extreme relaxation the better, frankly. Don't think it's worth the risk?"

Lightgate glided down from her perch with a few wing-flaps, onto the lip of Pax's beer bottle. She looked into the liquid to assess its contents. Pax waited, watching her. There was no telling how much dust Lightgate had given her victims; it might've been a huge amount. And Pax had tried it once . . . If she could get a good swig of that bottle, she could make a grab for the fairy. That's all it would take. Right?

If the beer worked the same way as before, and didn't outright kill her.

If Lightgate wasn't too quick anyway.

"How are your Ministry friends?" Lightgate said, stepping around the bottle rim idly, amusing herself with her own steps.

Pax took her time. Did the fairy know about Monroe and her feigned escape from the MEE? Would she even care? "Hopefully they're working on stopping your governor from getting everyone killed, right now. But I thought it best to leave them to it, seeing as no one entirely trusts me."

Lightgate raised an eyebrow. "Aren't you their golden child?"

"Not quite," Pax said. The fairy hadn't kept abreast of the day's events at all. "They got suspicious of my associations this afternoon. After someone tipped off my less-desirable contacts with a way into the Sunken City."

The fairy's eyes lit up. "Why didn't I think of that?"

"Because you're second fiddle to the bigger threat in this town," Pax said. "You remember, the one I said latched onto your turnbold plan? *Used* you."

"Used me to get what I wanted," Lightgate replied. "Tragic."

"What's your endgame, Lightgate?" Pax demanded. "Where are we, now? Three attempts to spark a war? All you've done is helped the bastards below."

Lightgate shrugged with a lazy smile. "Fun's fun, isn't it? I got Val shaking things up, for a start. That's where Fae thrive, in the *shaking* of things."

"Not all Fae. Edwing wanted peace. The FTC want peace. Valoria even wants peace, in her way."

"Those aren't *Fae*. They've lost their way. Know where I was two months ago?"

"Timbuktu?" Pax shot back. "Atlantis? Surprise me."

"Varanasi." Lightgate waited for a response. Pax eyeballed her, *so?* The fairy gestured towards their host. "Tell her about Varanasi, Palleday. Bet you've got some stories."

"What's to tell?" Palleday grunted. "Another lowly Fae city. Practically every Fae colony outside Ordshaw's barbaric, them included."

"They play a game, it roughly translates to the Moon Cull. Every full moon, there's a prize to the Fae that pulls off the most public sacrifice. Without putting the Varanfae at risk. One of them cut the throat of Varanasi's mayor. Or whatever their equivalent is. Probably made the news here?" No one responded. "Anyway, *most* places, Fae still know what it means to be Fae. What's important."

"That sounds like the exact fucking opposite of what's important," Pax responded irritably. "You're saying the Ordshaw Fae are the only ones remotely close to being civilised, so you absolutely *had* to stop them?"

Lightgate sighed and turned on the bottle again, stepping over the gap, stepping back again. "For *my* turn, I took out a kid. Son of a tech millionaire, died in an unfortunate hiking accident. But they never found the body. Kind of . . . missed the point of the game?" Lightgate looked to Pax for sympathy. Pax was sure she just wanted to highlight her own cruel depths. Such a small thing, capable of such terror.

"I'm happy to see you," Lightgate moved on brightly, lifting up off the bottle and hovering before Pax. "All of you. You were discussing what to do about me, weren't you? Will we, won't we, where will we go . . . I've got good news. You don't have to *do* anything. I've got enough people to blow a hole in Valoria's world without you. Of course, I would consider it a personal favour if you *would* consider joining me. All of you."

"Bollocks," Mix said, loudly. "I've heard enough. We're screwed, they're screwed, what the fuck ever. You win, Lightgate. You're a bloody star and I'm sure by the time the week's out you'll have ruined everything for everyone, big fucking deal. Can we drink already?" He raised his own beer bottle, and gave Pax a look. "If you're gonna burn the city down, I at least wanna see this human lose her shit on dust, first."

Lightgate grinned. She floated higher up, giving Pax space, and took her hip flask from a jacket pocket. As she undid the cap, she said, "You're really game, Pax? I think we can do big things. If you survive."

"Now you've painted me as a deranged killer?" Pax asked, pointing loosely at her beer bottle, asking permission. Lightgate tipped the flask towards it, go ahead.

"True Fae respect deranged killers," Lightgate said, as Pax lifted the bottle. This was the moment of truth, then. Liquid hope. Or disaster. "You think I'm mad – imagine, Edwing thought we might talk our way to happiness." Lightgate laughed. Pax felt the others' eyes on her, tensely waiting.

Pax took a breath and said, "Fuck it."

She threw back the beer bottle, gulping it down. The dust made it taste of earthy mushroom, and she gagged but kept going. She scarcely heard Mix's impressed cursing. She put the bottle back down and breathed deeply, checking her body – not dead yet.

"I like this girl," Lightgate told the others. "She doesn't do things by haaallllf –"

Her words stretched out, long, low, and as Pax looked up from the tower to Lightgate hanging in the air, the dust had an instant effect. The towers shimmered a ruddy brown; the three Fae on the ledge lit up, and Lightgate glowed brighter than all of them. A great, scarlet flare.

The fairy's wings beat in a smooth motion; the only object fast enough to counter Pax's slowed-down time. Lightgate's mouth pursed, impossibly slowly, and Pax narrowed her eyes. Yes. It was working – she was focused, she had time. And she was glowing, too. Pax raised her hands, gently, in wonder at the colour bursting from them. Bright enough to show through her sleeves. It wasn't the same as glo: there was the blue, but not only in her veins. It was all over her. Blurry, dazzling.

Something to explore later, Pax told herself, with an aside that she was calmer than she should be. With the world slowed down, she found serenity. She half-smiled at Lightgate. Zen Pax. Ready to seize the day with perfect clarity. Ready to seize the Fae. She laughed, a sound that bounced back as dull booms. The opposite of huffing helium, oh –

Pax shook herself out of it. She was giddy. Focus, *focus*, she picked out Lightgate again, and the Fae was slightly further back. Her face now fixed with concentration. Shit; she was moving away. Pax raised a hand, but it came slower than her thoughts, dragging through the air. Each passing moment, Lightgate flew further back, crazily slow but dangerously high. Her good arm drifted towards her hip-holster. Pax's hand lifted, marginally faster than the fairy. She stretched her fingers, pushing, hard, towards the Fae. She glanced at the others: Mix's mouth opening in a shout, Palleday and Fresko watching fearfully. She had to do it, for all of them.

Pax's arm was fully outstretched above her head when she closed her fingers. Snatching them shut. Time shifted gears again, catching up with accelerated speed, and Pax stumbled amid shouts from the trio of Fae at her side. Clarity was replaced by a painful, thrumming throb that made her vision blur, as her shoulder smacked into one of Palleday's columns. She lost her footing as the tower cracked. The walls shattered around her like a breaking vase, and she fell heavily onto her back. A rain of building shards crashed onto her as she looked up, willing her eyes to focus, bracing herself against the floor to stop the whole world rolling.

Way above, near the shadows of the ceiling, Lightgate floated free, a white silhouette in the dark. She called down, "Have a nice trip?"

8

Sam watched one of Obrington's hatchet-faced agents heft something large and dangerous-looking against his hip. Something near its centre hissed and gave the agent the smile of a child with a magnifying glass on a sunny day. Casaria jumped up and adjusted the man's gun strap with some judging comment.

Unlike when the Operations team had geared up to take on the Fae, Sam was eager to see these preparations. She had half a dozen men taking up arms and a dozen more hunkered over computers, all to help Pax. To help *the city*. And Obrington was arguing with the London office, trying to establish back channels to the Fae. He genuinely seemed to be preparing her to take over, which might leave Ordshaw in *her* care at last. As long as her agents didn't march into another slaughter.

"Reservations?" Obrington asked as he joined her in surveying the office. She shook her head, but he wasn't interested anyway, continuing, "I've got a few okays from London, things I might offer the buggers. Creating a no-go zone around the FTC actually works well for us. It'd help if they'd talk to us, though."

"We definitely can't give them Pax."

"Cross that bridge when we reach it. Talk to me about the purge."

Sam did so, grateful for a sounding board. Protocol 38 was, as she might've expected, a half-baked idea. The more they recalibrated their weapons according to what they were learning from the Duvcorp scanners, the less effective they appeared. The main gun they assumed would neutralise the *praelucente* was a glorified taser, which Dr Galler freely admitted had only a 60% chance of damaging it. Pushed, he also admitted that percentage was a guess. From the little time he'd had studying the Fae weapon, he was confident the Dispenser was a much better option.

The other complication was that Protocol 38's strategy assumed they would track the *praelucente* and its horde, advancing on it from the rear, whereas the new plan assumed it would be coming to them, lured by Fae bait. Support were plotting the best tunnels to defend, to channel the horde down a particular route. Darren Barton was advising them on predicting monster movement by sight, while Holly, comparing her own findings to the papers Sam had given her, had concluded there was no evidence, anecdotal or otherwise, that the black spots were harmful. The horde's aversion to these areas might make them ideal pockets for defending their bait until they could strike a finishing blow.

"And you've assigned the man responsible for that?" Obrington asked, once Sam was done explaining. He said it lightly, like the suggestion was harmless, while looking across the room to Barton. "Would be bloody good to use one of them, save us risking a better-trained, more trustworthy asset."

"Sir?" Sam replied with shock. "We're here to *protect* the people of –"

"*Would be*, I said," Obrington told her. "Obviously we can't rely on a civilian for something that important. It was a rhetorical question, Ward, we both know the answer."

Sam paused. Her first thought was: does the captain go down with the ship? She'd already proved herself against those criminals and Duvalier, now she might have to shoulder the ultimate responsibility – but, no. That philosophy would put *his* role in question. The obvious choice, in risking losing someone, was the man they didn't quite know what to do with. Too competent to discard, too unstable to embrace.

"Casaria shouldn't even be here," Sam said, quietly, watching him explain some detail of a pistol to another agent. "He lost a toe."

"He could've lost a lot more and you know it."

"But we don't know what will happen, with the weapons discharged, with the *praelucente* hurt –"

"Someone's got to do it. Perfect combination of skilled enough to do it and not too skilled to replace, should something go wrong." Obrington paused. "Not that it will, Ward. Keep that in mind. We might pull it off. And either way, he gets to be a hero. You gonna tell me he'd want anything less?"

Sam frowned. Given the choice, Casaria would surely volunteer. He'd been fearless going up against the grugulochs and in rescuing Pax before. But it was still a cold, dark responsibility. "Let me consider it."

"With what other options in mind?" Obrington said. She said nothing. "Heavy weighs the crown, Ward. But you'll do fine. Just make it sound like he's doing a good thing."

He lumbered away. Apparently the Fae weren't the only ones capable of dropping bombshells without negotiation. Sam wondered again if this would actually last, or if this illusion of control had been to force her to take on this responsibility. Once the smoke cleared, even if Obrington left, might someone else like him step back into the fold for the easy days?

Across the office, Casaria caught her watching him, and offered a light, gentle smile. She gave him a noncommittal wave back. What other options *did* she have?

Above the centre of the FTC, the news screen replayed choice clips from Letty's summit, Letty and Val's voices booming over the buildings: "We'll work with them on securing the Sunken City." "The humans can keep the Sunken City." Traders, manufacturers and skilled professionals hovered out into the airways between buildings, gathering to exchange concerns, slowly gravitating towards the Council tower. While the citizens hung in growing swarms, Stabilisers collected in the sky, near and far. The building was surrounded; there was no slipping away, no hiding, so why not embrace it.

Letty shoved Valoria, pistol at the small of her back, out onto the grandiose roof terrace. Flynt held back, watching the rest of the Council and the guards. The idea that Valoria could shield Letty, vast as she was, was ridiculous. Fae watched from all angles. No point even pretending she had cover now. Letty lowered her gun and strode away from Valoria, readying herself for the worst. Valoria's eyes were aflame as she waited for the salvo of unprovoked gunshots Letty half-expected.

"Tell these people exactly why you're keeping the Dispenser from us!" Letty's voice demanded from the giant screen in the sky. Newbry had done a good job rushing together the footage.

Valoria watched Hearlon and the other Stabilisers following Flynt out, armed again. None of them dared make the first move, though all looked ready to gun the rebels down. Val addressed Flynt loudly enough to reach the very back of the crowd.

"Your friends are being hunted, right now. Spreading lies, manipulating our communications channels, bringing such equipment into the Council chambers – you cannot get away with this."

Flynt stared coldly back and said nothing. Letty loved him for it. Valoria reddened, forced to continue. "Your brother was an insolent fool!" She turned to the Stabilisers. "What are you waiting for, arrest them!"

Hearlon's crew were hesitating for the same reason as the Stabilisers in the sky. The same reason Flynt had the gall to follow them out here. The whole damn city had questions, a thousand people or more around them, now. Letty squinted at the floating soldiers. She made out one of Smark's friends, and he was saying something to another. Indicating they see how this played out. The hesitation was infectious.

Their openness, being out here, made all the difference. This wasn't a fight, it was an unfinished conversation. Letty approached the edge of the building. Comments rose up:

"It's her!"

"What's going on?"

"What now?" Valoria shouted. "You have driven the city to confusion, congratulations – what *now*?"

"Why don't we ask them?" Letty shouted back, likewise making sure the crowd could hear. "If they're all happy for you to use fear and poison to seal off this city for good, you can fucking put one right here." She tapped a finger to her temple and turned to the citizens. "Or would you rather work with the humans to take back the Sunken City? Something we'll never do by suggesting we *kill* them."

Valoria set her jaw stubbornly. "Yes, I threatened the humans! I wished to avoid making our entire society complicit in it, and I wished – yes – to keep the Sunken City *out* of it. This is our home now. This is where we belong."

It didn't hit everyone the same way, or at the same time, but disagreement swept through the gathering crowd. Valoria had always known better than to make this a public discourse. Letty watched the governor as they soaked up the rising responses.

"There's a chance of getting the Sunken City back?"

"What *have* they negotiated?"

"Didn't Letty threaten the humans?"

"They butchered our councilman!"

"Did they fuck!" Letty railed at that comment. "I can *talk* with the humans! Get to the bottom of all of this! Follow *her*, and all you'll ever have is what she gives you!"

"Oh yes, talk with the humans." Valoria had a ready response. "Shall we befriend the female human who killed Edwing? Letty's new Apothel."

"Apothel was a maniac!" a woman cried out from within the hovering swarm. A score of angry comments, boos and demands followed.

The big screen went black for a moment, drawing everyone's attention up. It blinked and came back with the Fae media's usual logos. Valoria's people had regained control of the network, showing footage of where they were now. The crowds in the FTC centre, headlines scrolling: *TERRORISTS STRIKE COUNCIL.*

"I'm a terrorist?" Letty shouted. "According to people spreading chemical warfare through Ordshaw! You believe in making everyone safe, withdraw your fucking threats!"

"I will not –"

"We can talk to the humans!" Flynt shouted with an excited edge. "Edwing showed us that! I met Pax with him, she wouldn't hurt him!"

"We *have* to question this." Smark added his voice, stepping out from amongst the Stabilisers and other Council members. "If there are chemical weapons –"

"Waste Chief Smark, know your place," Valoria said viciously.

"My place is not knowing why in hell you're sullying our chances to spread our wings! We need *public* accountability, to give the humans a chance. At long last."

It silenced her, and he turned on the other Council members, all eyeing the growing public swarm with great caution. Mullon said, "Perhaps, Governor Magnus, it might be prudent to slow down."

"This . . . " Valoria's voice shook with anger. "This is precisely why I took the lead. We cannot establish autonomy with half measures."

"Nor if we drive the humans to destruction!" Smark replied. "We barely survived last time." Shouts of agreement and complaint swept through the crowd.

"We took their weapons – we better understand them now –"

"Stand down your men, Valoria," Mullon suggested, quietly. "We need a recess."

Valoria's gaze could have melted iron, but she was not fool

enough to resist the entire city's demands. Letty said nothing, letting the momentum of the FTC carry her. Shaking her head bitterly at Letty, Valoria raised a hand to her lapel, activating her radio, and the gathered audience quietened hurriedly. She spoke softly, but the rabble were so intent on hearing that her voice still carried. "Fang, this is Valoria. I have orders."

Letty looked to Flynt with swelling pride. This was working. The bastard governor was backing down, the people seeing sense –

"Fang, answer me," Valoria snapped, and the stiff silence was broken by mutterings of uncertainty. "Fang, now is no time for tardiness!"

She went quiet. No response was coming.

"Madam Governor . . ." Mullon ventured.

"There is a problem," Valoria said. She tried one last time, adjusting the radio. "Fang? Hooper? *Anyone* from Team 14?"

Still silence.

Valoria narrowed her eyes. She was as confused as everyone else, but Letty noted a calculating look as the governor saw an opportunity. Not knowing what was coming, Letty stepped towards her, about to shout *stop*, anything, but Valoria yelled, "This is a distraction! Letty's people have struck, they mean to take control of the very weapons she claims to fear!"

"What the fuck are –"

"Stabiliser Team 14 is compromised, Letty's people have them! Seize her, seize them all!" Valoria roared, taking quick steps away from Letty. The soldiers moved quickly – they didn't need to know what was going on, in the face of such firm orders. Rifles were raised, two men were suddenly on Flynt, Smark too, and guns were aimed at one or two dissenting soldiers in the sky. Letty, with her pistol half-raised, had three men around her, rifles pointed at her head. People shouted and panicked – Letty's complaints were lost in it – Valoria alone seemed to have a handle on the situation. "The rebels would spark a war under a white flag! Make true the threat against the humans! Send them to the cages!"

Letty bared her teeth but didn't take another step, more guns on her than she could count. In the mounting chaos, all reason was lost. She tossed her gun aside.

9

The world came back into focus as columns of Fae architecture loomed above like tree trunks, the ceiling a distant, grimy smear. Pax's head throbbed like she'd been hit with a bat. When she moved, a blanket of ceramic chips shifted over her with a clatter. She craned her neck to get a better idea of her situation. Fragments of a Fae tower covered her torso and legs. Worse than that, a tiny woman was standing on her chest with a silver pistol in her hand.

"I *really* like you," Lightgate told her, amiably. "I guess humans *can* take dust."

The gun pivoted idly as Lightgate swayed on the spot. Seeing the fairy rise and fall with her chest, Pax slowed her breathing, barely daring to move. It was fair to say this had gone badly wrong, and any sudden movement now might inspire an execution.

"Betraying *me* isn't really what I'd hoped for," Lightgate continued, "but the willingness to do so, I value that. Most Fae wouldn't stand up to me, so for a human to have a go . . ." Lightgate whistled with satisfaction. "Don't try it again, though."

"Seeing that it worked out so well the first time," Pax said.

Lightgate smiled. "You're too late, anyway. Whatever you thought you could do, there's war coming. For your courage, I'm still willing to deal. I could use you, yet."

"No, thanks."

"Pax. I'm a patient person, but I will take offence eventually."

"You framed me for murder."

"And you made some friends out of it!" Lightgate exclaimed, like she'd done Pax a favour. She gestured upwards to the towers where the others must've been lurking. They took it as a cue. A red dot appeared on her chest.

"I wouldn't call us friends," Fresko called from up high, "but yeah. We'd prefer you left her be."

"You'd prefer?" Lightgate replied with what sounded like genuine confusion.

"We've got you covered," Mix added, making her snap her head to the other direction. He was lower down, much closer, speaking from inside a tower. "Don't care how fast you are, we've got you fucking covered."

"You should care," Lightgate said. "You'll shoot her tits off. Not a good result considering how soft you've all gone for the humans. By the spirits, I should've come back to Ordshaw a long time ago. Where's the *spine* in this place?"

"Standing up to you, right fucking now!" Mix said.

"And don't overestimate," Fresko added, more calmly, "how much we care about this bitch's tits."

Pax kept as still as she possibly could, eyes flitting from Lightgate to the sides, where she couldn't pick out either of her apparent protectors. She'd gone from the champion of resolution to the scenery of a potential gunfight, and from the way Lightgate's posture was tightening, there was no question it was going to get ugly.

"Well, Pax," Lightgate said. "Any advice for your irresponsible saviours?"

"Honestly," Pax said, bracing herself, speaking clearly so Letty's men would understand, "I'm hoping they'll hit you between the eyes."

Lightgate gave her a withering look. "That's not very nice."

Fresko fired first, a crack of a shot that Pax felt rush past. Mix fired a split second later, two weapons at almost the same time. Pax flinched, throwing her body up and creating a rain of shattered debris, which Lightgate spiralled through. The fairy bent back in the air with the grace of a gymnast, pirouetting past the bullets. Arm outstretched, she fired back. Pax rolled, as quick as she could, shoulder rising past where Lightgate had hovered, and the Fae whizzed by her head. Another shot whooshed over Pax's hair, barely missing. Christ – they really didn't care about hitting her.

Pax darted forward at a crouch, picking out the scant space between the towers, head low, hands up. The firing continued, quick and loud, cracks rising from all angles; Mix roared as he flew from one side of the room to another, small flashes of light appearing where he went.

"I thought Letty might've trained you better," Lightgate goaded from the forest of pillars. "Come on boys, don't be shy."

To answer her, the other Fae guns barked back. Again, again.

Pax crabbed from side to side, trying to find a way out. The gunfire and her own panicked breathing almost blocked out another approaching noise; whirring and creaking. Heavy machinery coming to life, getting closer. She turned to it as Lightgate shot back into view. The miniature woman darted before her eyes, tossing an empty magazine from her gun and reloading by hammering her pistol into her gun belt. She slowed to face Pax: a mistake.

The towers exploded around them, cracking and shattering, falling in walls of ceramic. Pax cried out, hands over her head, and tried to dive clear but only fell deeper into the chaotic crumble, the weight of a dozen pots bringing her down. In the collapse, she saw flashes of white as Lightgate tried to dodge debris, but there were too many chunks to avoid and she disappeared beneath the mess, alongside Pax. A tower came down on Pax's side like a log, slamming her into the floor. Another crashed down in front of her, missing her forehead by an inch and shattering on impact.

When everything was still, Pax checked her body. Buried by Fae ruins, partially trapped, but alive. Definitely Not Dead. She twisted, knocking chunks of building off her, and coughed on the dust. Through the scattered remains she picked out a patch of white. Not moving.

Pax stretched under the weight of the tower that pinned her. She tossed chunks of building away, revealing Lightgate sprawled at the bottom. Her white suit was ripped and stained by terracotta dust and her hair was a disaster. Wings bent. But she moved, a hand reaching to the side, towards something tiny, a speck in the rubble. Her flask, bent savagely out of shape, torn and wet with a tiny puddle of spilt liquid. Lightgate took it, and titled it, one way and another, the flask empty. The fairy suddenly pushed herself up onto her elbows. Eyes picking out Pax, wings rapidly lifting her up, she bared her teeth in a snarl. Not so fast, having taken a heavy blow. Pax grabbed forward, but Lightgate evaded her closing fingers. She spun in the air and changed direction, down towards the floor. Pax saw the glinting metal of a gun, and forced her way desperately out from under the debris. Lightgate swept down to the pistol, plucking it up from the mess, and rolled, turning back as Pax's hand came down again. The gun went off with a crack and pain cut into Pax's palm as she slammed her hand through broken shards of tower.

She froze, then, wincing not just from her stabbed hand but with the realisation of what she'd done.

For a moment the room was completely still, Lightgate gone, under her hand.

"You got her?" Palleday called down, and Pax pulled her gaze up to him. His pulley device stood over her, with the fairy operating it at the top, like the pilot of a crane. It rocked on its wheels, hooks and chains swaying as they hung from the high arms; rams he'd used to smash through his works of art to bring Lightgate down.

"Yeah," Pax said, voice hoarse with the dust caught in her mouth. She spat aside, to speak more clearly. "I got her." She slowly lifted her hand from the floor, and cringed as Lightgate peeled off it, broken and sticky with blood. Pax sat back on her haunches with a resigned sigh, holding up her bloodstained hand and observing the body. There was little white left on the maniac Fae's suit. Her booted feet were twisted at odd angles to her body and her face, thankfully, was hidden by a mess of tangled hair.

"Better have," Fresko said, swooping down onto the machine next to Palleday. Something was wrong with his posture. "Because she fucking well got us."

Mix was dead before they got him clear of the carnage of Palleday's ghost town. Pax laid him gingerly down by the edge of the room, and Palleday landed next to him, supporting Fresko under an arm. It was hard to see where Mix had taken the bullet – he might have taken many – but his eyes were open and glassy, his face fixed in an angry death grimace. Pax knelt over them as Fresko slumped at his friend's side. The sniper was clutching his gut, shirt soaked red.

"Hold up, I've got stuff that'll help," Palleday said, and flew out of the room. Fresko made a pained, wheezing noise as he bent over Mix, then muttered what sounded like a string of curses, scolding his friend for dying.

"I'm so sorry," Pax said quietly.

"She dead?" Fresko asked, looking up. Pax held up her closed hand, Lightgate's legs hanging out of it. Shit, she didn't want to look at what she'd done. She placed Lightgate down a respectable distance from the others.

"I didn't mean to," Pax said.

"You should've," Fresko replied angrily. His voice was choked with emotion: maybe the agony of his wound, maybe grief. He tried to stand, but his legs wouldn't carry him and he slumped back down. "Fucking . . . coming to our town . . ."

"We needed her," Pax said. Would it still work? Would a dead Fae lure the creatures of the Sunken City, the same as a live one?

"Needed her like cancer," Fresko spat, but with his words came a splatter of blood, and he slipped onto his back, legs twitching. He tried to continue in broken syllables, fading.

"Fresko!" Pax bent over him, raising her free hand. To do what? Poke him?

Palleday landed next to him, an armful of bandages and plastic-wrapped supplies, and muttered in irritation as he went to work, trying to tie the wound. "Don't be a baby, come on now. What's a gunshot, what's it to you?"

Fresko answered with some wicked whispered curse.

"I'm so sorry," Pax repeated. "I should've – or shouldn't have –"

"You did fine," Palleday huffed without looking up. "Don't flatter yourself thinking this was all over you." His voice got lower, masked in fast breaths as he worked to keep Fresko alive. "If there's anything can be done, I'll do it. You want to go. Make this worth it."

"Uh . . ." Pax looked at Lightgate's body. Not wanting to touch it again. "I don't know that I can. This was – I mean – I wanted her *alive*."

Palleday paused to look up. "Well, the FTC should give you a bloody medal for finishing her, no fooling."

That was true. It might buy some favour, at last. And Letty – she needed help. How long had it been since that desperate phone call? Hell, hell. The Fae had the Dispenser, they had her friend, they had *poisons* hanging over the city, and what did Pax have? A dead criminal. "Can you get a message to them? The FTC leadership?"

"What?" The old Fae scowled. "You're serious? I didn't mean –"

"Please."

"Craziest darned human I ever encountered." He shook his head, then took his phone out. "Maybe Edwing's people still –" He froze, something on his phone chilling him.

"What is it?"

"Not good. Not good at all." He turned the phone towards her, as if there were any way she could make it out. He said, simply, "It's Letty."

10

Only after going through the arsenal thoroughly was Casaria truly satisfied that they stood a chance. His input clearly was needed. The revised plans that Support were feeding them, with choke points for fast-moving, dangerous creatures, suggested this was going to be messy. A battle bound for death or glory. And half the men hadn't handled MEE energy guns before. A rough guy out of London, Agent Marks, even commented, "It's usually *people* we need to stop." Obrington's hires appeared up for a fight, at least, but that wasn't enough. Good thing they had Casaria to instruct them.

No sign of Pax to see his results, but she'd be here. And Ward had offered more than a few encouraging looks. When she approached at last, a little shy, Casaria could see she wanted to make up. She said, "You're ready?"

"As we can be," Casaria said. "These guys are green, but they'll do."

Ward glanced across at the other agents nearby, ugly guys with scars and cold eyes. She looked unsure, so Casaria offered an encouraging smile.

"Can I have a word alone?" She indicated a side door. Casaria jumped up, quicker than he intended, and slowed himself down. Ward took him to the new medical bay. A brick chamber with a cot and some supplies, far from sanitary. Ward started, "We've had our differences, Cano, and you know my doubts well enough. This past week in particular. But I want to say we value you here. A lot. You're one of the most effective field agents we have in Ordshaw."

Casaria found he couldn't look at her, fearing he might smile. Didn't want to make it more awkward, knowing this must be difficult. He mumbled nonsense she'd hear as thanks, probably.

"You know our plan is to lure the *praelucente* to a trap. To strike it once we're sure it's all there. If there's . . . you know."

"The screens," Casaria said. "I know."

"Then you'll know someone has to – well – spring the trap. It's not a decision I take lightly."

It took him a moment to appreciate her point, and even then it was only because she was staring at him so earnestly. So worried. He frowned. Was she letting him down? Saying *she* would fire the killing blow? Or one of these vicious newcomers? He said, "Moving up in the ranks doesn't mean you're the best for everything, Sammy. This is mine to do, it's what I'm *good* at."

Ward was motionless, taken by surprise. He pushed the advantage.

"Obviously," he sneered, "it's *your* decision. But it'd be a big mistake to let anyone else do it. Most of all you."

"That wasn't my –" Ward started, but whatever feeble excuse she was going to make, Obrington cut it off with a shouted command.

"In here, Ward! Where the bloody hell is she?"

She gave Casaria a look, not wanting to leave this unfinished, but raced out into the office. He followed as Obrington said, "Kuranes is stirring trouble again."

Everyone was listening. The Bartons were up, Darren ready to hit something, Holly rigid with concern. Rufaizu bounced nervously on his feet.

"Where is she? What happened?" Ward demanded.

"Got an alert," Obrington answered, "saying she's taking herself right to the FTC. No word from her. Sound like our plan to you?"

"She'll have her reasons!" Ward protested, taking out her own phone. She cursed, no doubt missed a call on this. "I need to talk to her."

"Think we haven't tried? And I'm *still* not getting through to the FTC."

Casaria was already halfway across the office, nearing the exit.

"Where the hell are you going?" Obrington demanded.

"Where do you think?" Casaria replied hotly, and saw the warning on Ward's face. After he'd finally started making a good impression. He collected himself and tried again. "Permission to bring her back, sir. Before she gets herself killed."

"Denied," Obrington said. "She's practically there already, and *your* place is here." He looked to Ward. "You're aware of the responsibility resting on your shoulders, Casaria?"

Casaria met Ward's eyes instead of his. Her face was

crestfallen. What? She hadn't intended to pull the trigger on the *praelucente* herself. The woman was reluctant to ask him to do it. She didn't think he was up to it? Or . . . she thought it was too dangerous? She did care, she –

"Sir, there's something else," a plump analyst called from across the room, face in a computer. The man started to panic. "Uh. Sir! I'm getting alerts –"

Amid the office's flurry of concerned movement, Casaria himself was at the analyst's computer in a flash, at Ward's side. Shoulder brushing her shoulder.

"The creatures are moving." The analyst pointed at a map. "Spreading out – going in – this isn't good – that's a glogockle moving into Westlane Station –"

"Bleeding hell," Obrington said. "Something's tipped them off. We need to get down there *now*."

"They're not just scrambling," Casaria observed, eyes wide at what he was seeing. "That one's leaving the Sunken City."

The Trial Cages hung from a crane arm that protruded from one of the FTC's taller central towers, over a wide gap between buildings, fifteen storeys high or more. Six square lattices of rusty metal, each dangling from a chain with nothing but a drop beneath them. Letty, escorted by three Stabilisers, sent frequent looks to Flynt to draw strength from his quiet resolve. The bastards had taken her pistol and knife, and another soldier approached from the other direction with a couple of steel wing clips: pin two wings together so a Fae can't fly. But all they had to do was remove Letty's Clear Glider.

A great swathe of the population followed them between the buildings, a lot of bustle between them, dozens of soldiers brandishing guns one way and another, some shouting for justice against Letty, others that she should be set free – no one completely understanding what was going on.

Shoved into a cage, Flynt shouted, "It wasn't us, dammit! They're lying –"

"Hang fast, Flynt," Letty called out. A Stabiliser pushed her towards her own cage, and she spun to him but held off at the sight of a crackling baton.

"Your wing." Hearlon pointed at the hump on Letty's back. "Get in, toss it out."

"They'll stand trial, under all our watch!" Valoria boomed from high up, with a smattering of councilmen around her. Smark was there, flanked by a soldier. "Until we have confirmation that the septjad is secure – and of our men's safety!"

Glaring at Hearlon, Letty drifted back into the cage. She landed on the bars and growled, "I'm gonna tear your ribs out, you little bitch."

"Speak up, Letty," Valoria said. "Your trial's begun – let everyone hear your threats."

"Spin on it," Letty spat back.

The governor regarded her with a triumphant smile, twisting towards the onlookers. Over her shoulder, the edge of the big screen was just visible between the buildings. The anchor's voice drifted over with snippets about the disappearance of the Stabiliser elite, and fears that Letty and "her people" had plotted a citywide uprising.

"Is this not proof?" Valoria demanded, caught up in her own raving. "The threat of the exiles! The inability to hold civilised negotiations, with them *hijacking* our weapons! But the criminal Letty is caged! Her plot foiled!"

"You brought the septjad here, you delusional –" Letty shouted.

There was a crack of lightning as a Stabiliser hit his electric baton against the cage. The bars lit up with bright sparks and Letty was jolted into the air before landing, juddering all over, barely able to swear.

"Terrorist scum!" the soldier shouted, to a volley of agreement.

"Confess, Letty," Valoria said. "You invaded the Council at this sensitive time. You commanded your exile friends to assault our finest soldiers. You intended only to –"

"Look!" someone gasped.

People were turning away. Something was happening. Letty pushed herself up, regaining her breath. Her guards turned away, following the general sway. Up towards the big screen. It had changed from the news channel again, to a shot outside the warehouse. Newbry must have regained the network. An image of a desolate street, an empty landscape of ruin. A sole figure walked down the middle. "The fuck . . ."

A human at the perimeter. A human getting closer.

Not just any human.

The camera angle changed, closer.

"Pax . . ."

Letty gave Flynt a look; from his angle he probably couldn't see the screen, but his face was hopeful. Letty wasn't so sure. Pax had to be out of her mind, coming here.

Valoria regained her composure quicker than anyone. "Part of her plan, no doubt – but the human does not know we have thwarted Letty's coup. Activate the defences –"

"She's on our side!" Letty roared. "Would any human risk coming otherwise?"

A ripple of questions ran through the crowd, many pointing to the screen – text rolled across the bottom, like with the news stories. Impossible to see from here. Valoria began another order, but Smark cut her off. "We need to see what she wants."

"She's one human," Deidre agreed, "who must understand the danger of coming here. We should hear her out."

"Should we?" Valoria rumbled. "Are we not all aware of the threat that giving humans the *slightest* opportunity offers? Need I –"

"What's she holding?" the councillor in a toupee asked. Watching the footage rather than listening. "What's that *say*?"

"'Kuranes requests an audience'," someone closer to the screen read. "Via Palleday. The architect?"

"Palleday –" Valoria started derisively, but the cameras picked out the jar in Pax's hands. Half-finished questions swept through the crowd.

"Is that –"

"How did she –"

"Why would –"

"Are we to consider," Valoria started, unevenly, "that a human who could capture a Fae is someone to *listen* to? She may be carrying a weapon – a –"

"A peace offering?" Letty snapped. "You can fucking *see* what she's carrying. Proof of what I've been saying."

"She's close to the defences," a Stabiliser warned.

Before Val could say another word, Mullon shouted, "Deactivate them, for heaven's sake, she's caught *Lightgate*!"

11

In the orange light of dusk, Pax was walking down an avenue of derelict warehouses, towards the one she believed to contain the Fae Transitional City, when she finally answered a call. She'd ignored half a dozen from Ward, Casaria, and another number she assumed to be the MEE, on Letty's warning that the FTC were watching. If she wanted to get close, she needed to assure the fairies she wasn't an enemy. She ignored calls from Holly too, for good measure. But now that she saw the building, an imposing brick structure with black-iron-framed windows, she baulked at doing this alone. It was a call from Holly she picked up, but Ward spoke.

"Thank God, Pax – stop, please stop. What are you doing?"

"Helping a friend," Pax said. "Seeing as I've screwed everyone else." Ahead, the huge metal doors looked rusted shut, not opened in decades, and the street in front had the dusty, debris-littered sweep of a post-apocalyptic plain.

"The Sunken City's stirring," Ward said. "The creatures, they're breaking their patterns, moving away from the centre – with our sensor resets, we can see exactly where they're moving – something spooked them and you *shouldn't* be there."

"I can't help that, can I?" Pax said, not wanting to hear more. "But I can do something here."

"You'll get hurt – there are traps – no one's gone that close to the Fae in years!"

Pax tried to breathe calmly. One step at a time. "They know I'm coming."

Another step, and nothing exploded or harpooned her.

"Pax, we're moving into the tunnels – this is happening – did you find Lightgate?"

"Yeah," Pax said. "She's dead."

A brief pause from Ward. "Do you have a body? Bring it here – we've got our own negotiations going on with the Fae. They could kill you and we need you *here*."

"Yeah." Another step, and it looked safe to continue. They probably wanted her to walk right on in. It'd be neater to kill her indoors. "They must've seen me by now." She held the jar aloft, turning it from side to side, trying not to look at the bloody corpse inside.

"The first agents are already going in," Ward continued urgently. "You don't understand, the creatures might *surface*."

Pax stopped. That was bad. Their fears coming true, of what the screens might be capable of under threat. But why now? She frowned, studying her feelings. There was something. Far away, subtle, but movement, nonetheless. The screens sending signals. Were they still in the Ministry offices? Reading the computers? Aware of their plans? But they'd had half the day, why now . . .

"Fuck – they know I'm here," she whispered. They had felt her. The same way she felt them. If they didn't know exactly where she was, they knew she'd had a spike of her own energy, she'd tried Fae dust – they knew she was interacting with the Fae. Quickly, she told Ward, "I have to be here. It's *why* they're panicking."

Ward was quiet, not liking it.

"They're scared, Sam," Pax told her. "That's a good thing."

"But . . ."

"I'll call you when I'm done."

With a quiet voice, Ward conceded, "If you – *when* you get out, I'll have a car waiting."

"Thanks." Pax forced a smile and hung up. Never mind that she had Obrington's car back there, the promise of company was nice. She looked up at the door, tall and wide enough for two lorries to roll through. She expected Fae guards, warning shots, anything. There was no movement. In both directions, the road stretched away along the front of the warehouse, a fortress of a building, utterly abandoned. All this real estate, left to ruin . . .

Pax knocked on the metal door. The rap twanged up and down the adjoining streets. She hit it again, the sound strangely satisfying, then called out, "Hello? Anyone home?"

She paced to the side of the doors. The nearest windows, though huge, were a good ten feet off the ground, no way she was climbing in. "You know who I am? I've got a peace offering."

With no response, she continued searching for another way in. After the buildup, from what Letty had told her of the FTC, and what the MEE reported, she'd expected a minefield, snipers, barbed wire, *something*. This was just a dead building at the end of a dead street.

"Human," a small voice called out. She looked up the wall to a gap in the window. On the ledge stood a fairy in black armour, like the ones she'd run into at the lido. He had a rifle aimed down at her, and spoke with deep uncertainty. "You . . . stop."

Pax showed her free palm, indicating she was no threat.

The guard shifted position uncomfortably, clearly uneasy under the gaze of a human; he must've drawn a short straw for this.

"You know who Lightgate is?" Pax asked.

He made an unhappy noise, then said, "State your business."

"I'm selling jam, what do you think?" Pax said. "I want to talk to someone in charge."

The guard ducked back, conferring quietly. He pushed his cohort, neither of them wanting to get any closer. When his companion didn't budge, he reluctantly flew off the ledge. "I'm to search you. Do not move."

"You're . . ." Pax started, but gave in. Better let it play out.

The guard swept down to her, and stalled about two feet away. He hovered, looking her up and down fearfully. He muttered again, "Do not move." Then came closer. Pax followed him with her eyes as he flew around her. Up, down, between her legs, over her head. Finally, he hovered back in front of her face, an uncertain expression on his own. They shared a mutual understanding that it was an ineffective search.

He looked back to the window, swallowed his uncertainty and called out, "I can't see any weapons." No one replied. He gestured to the side with his gun. "Down there."

Pax looked along the wall, to a shaded area. There was a hatch, a drop-box for deliveries. She walked up to it, a two-foot square panel. The guard was gone. She pulled on the handle and the hatch opened with a heavy, rusty creak, pivoting down. The chute inside was barely wider than her, and dropped into darkness.

"Fucking seriously?" Pax muttered to herself.

She tucked the jar into her coat pocket and climbed into the hatch. It took a bit of manoeuvring, the panel rocking back as she tried to get her second leg in, and once in position she slipped on the chute, down, quickly, into the shadow. Pax yelped as she rolled out, and the jar flew free of her pocket, clunking on the floor. She grimaced, expecting a crack, for Lightgate to burst free, alive again. But it merely rolled clear of her, the fairy inside flopping about. Pax snatched it up and scrambled to her feet. She dusted off her knees and stood up straight, looking across the expanse of the warehouse. The chute had deposited her at the edge of a huge open space, big as a football field, enclosed by four bare brick walls, high metal beams crossing a dark ceiling broken up by grimy skylights.

At the centre, lit with a cascade of tiny electric lights, with a good twenty metres of space around it, sat the Fae Transitional City. The towers stood taller than Palleday's sculptures, glowing blocks of metal and glass, a modern city in miniature, with neon-lit bar signs, iron balconies, torn adverts plastering walls, pipes in complex networks snaking one way and another. There were dozens of towers, in all sizes and colours, stretching as far back as the city was wide.

And rising from the gaps between the buildings were the residents, a thousand fluttering winged people, all looking Pax's way. She stared in awe and slowly raised her free hand. With a small, insufficient wave, she said, "I'm Pax. Please don't kill me."

12

With no one coming closer, Pax took a step forward herself. The entire population of Ordshaw's fairy community were hanging there, countless eyes analysing her. They could speak loud enough to be heard by humans; there must be a hell of a din in here when they all got talking. Wrong time to wonder. She took another step forward and handfuls of Fae moved for the edges of buildings, ducking behind cover. The more stubborn ones, the vast majority, held their ground – their *air*. Pax spoke in what she hoped was a calm voice, "You see who I've got here? I know you know her."

"We know *you*," an aggressive male snapped, and a dozen or more agreed.

"I . . ." Pax stopped. It was an audience like she'd never imagined, like being on a stage at a great concert hall. And they hated her, didn't they? What was she thinking? Her skin tingled with the attention. What could she say that wouldn't get her killed?

The stirrings of a commotion drew her focus to one of the taller towers at the perimeter, where hovering fairies parted with noises of disapproval. A bulky fairy emerged from the crowd, her fine regal clothing out of time and place. She flew weightlessly, despite her round, bee-like proportions, and behind her came a trail of black-armoured soldier fairies, armed with batons and rifles. The governor and her retinue. She commanded, boldly, "Into the light, woman."

Pax did as she was told, approaching the outer glow of the Fae city. Drawing nearer, she saw the floating fairies were as varied as a cross-section of society anywhere in the world, from labouring overalls to suits, through to casual jeans and shirts, flat-caps – one in what looked like medical scrubs. Fat and slim, round and jagged, long flowing hair, unfortunate bald spots, moustaches, everything. Their skin colours, too, were as cosmopolitan as Ordshaw's more ethnic neighbourhoods: the darkest-skinned Fae were almost black, the lightest definitely anaemic. The only uniform thing was their ages: almost all young adults; no children, very few over forty or so. Did they not age?

And this vast crowd showed equal wonder for Pax. Questioning, curious looks, and fearful, disgusted stares. Of them all, their leader looked least impressed.

"Pax Kuranes," Valoria snorted. "Devourer of fairies. Murderer of men."

"Sixty-eighth best poker player in the world," Pax added for herself.

The responses were too quiet to hear, but were likely shocked remarks: *did you hear her speak?!* The memory of her first meeting with Lightgate came to mind, an unimpressed comment: *why is she talking about cards?* Cautiously, Pax held the jar a little higher. "I've brought Lightgate."

It chilled the crowd into silence, and Pax doubted her strategy. What if they didn't hate Lightgate as much as she'd been led to believe? Then she was just a human with a bloody Fae body in a jar. "Palleday messaged ahead. To let you know I was coming?"

That helped, murmurs of recognition for Palleday's name. But he hadn't done much to pave the way. Pax came another step closer, now barely two metres from the edge of the city, and the wall of fairies darted back an inch in fear, focused on the jar. It was Lightgate, more than her, that they were scared of.

"Stop," Valoria commanded. "Place the jar on the floor." To her guards, she added, "Keep her in your sights at all times."

"Got her," her closest bodyguard replied, for the purposes of the crowd. He had a rifle aimed at Pax's face. The handful of men around him aimed variously at her and at the jar in her hands.

"She's dead," Pax said, slowly crouching to put the jar down. She kept her hands on it, as though the body might yet break free and kill them all. "It was an accident, kind of. She tried to kill me. And everyone else." Pax stood back from the jar, carefully, as two soldiers swooped down to inspect it. "You know she was planning an uprising?"

A further flurry of concerned noises, but Valoria said, "And you kept her company."

"You call stopping a maniac keeping company?" Pax replied. The indignity of being addressed by an unreasonable woman trumped the anxiety of being watched. "More than *you* managed to do, wasn't it?"

Valoria replied curtly, "And we should be pleased, not concerned, to see one of our most notorious criminals dead at the hands of a human?"

"With Fae help," Pax said. "One of your own gave his life for it, another's clinging to his. And we trashed half a dozen of Palleday's best towers to trap her. I'm not some Fae-hunter extraordinaire, if that's what you're getting at."

Again, Palleday's name impressed a few people, a detail Valoria was quick to move on from. "Then what are you? You, aligned with Letty, a criminal no different to the one you have brought us."

"Yeah? Did Letty scourge any gritty plateaus?"

That impressed the crowd, too; another point for knowing something of their culture. Over their surprised comments, Valoria said, "Letty killed *humans* –"

"The ones Lightgate shot, you mean?" Pax lifted a foot to prod the jar, making the two nearby soldiers fly nervously back.

"And she's rallied exiles," Valoria went on, undeterred. "Disrupted our –"

"Again," Pax interrupted, "Lightgate's right here. Is there anything you're laying on Letty that wasn't *her* doing?"

Valoria went quiet. Despite her demeanour of intense distrust, the crowd was siding with Pax:

"Just like Letty said!"

"The Scourge *was* behind this!"

They were finally questioning the reality that their council had presented.

Pax rocked the jar under her shoe, demonstratively, and said, "She thought you should all be fighting. Against us, against each other. Letty tried to stop her before. I'm hoping, now, I actually *did* stop whatever army she's been mustering. I don't know where they are, but they'll disband without her, won't they?"

Valoria's closest guard leant in to confer with her. She flapped him away irritably, a *you think I don't know that!* dismissal.

Pax continued, "Edwing, God rest him – Lightgate killed him because he believed in peace. And obviously she didn't want you to trust me or Letty, hence how it all looks. But I just want to see Ordshaw safe. For all of us. Thanks to the Fae that talked to me, we've got some idea of the real source of all our problems."

"Whatever you bring," Valoria said, "Letty has shown her true colours today." For the crowd's sake, she added, "Forcing her way into the Council. Holding us at gunpoint."

Pax turned to the closest fairies, gathered around head height. A woman in a pantsuit, not dissimilar to a Ministry worker; a man in a checked shirt, with a beard. "You know all she wanted was to take back your home? She got desperate. Where is she?"

"Awaiting trial," checked shirt responded. "For . . . them things you said Lightgate did."

"For everything!" Valoria corrected. "For the –"

"Great, so I can help clear the air. Is she in your cages? Take me to her." Pax stood taller than she felt. With so many people watching, there were a lot of guns out there, but they needed to see her confidence. "If we co-operate, talk to one another, I know we can reach an understanding. Not just here, with my government, too." She gave Valoria a look, to make her point clear. "You want that, don't you?"

Valoria's face was a picture of malice.

"Would you rather bring Letty out here? I can wait."

"Once sealed," Valoria's gruff bodyguard answered, "the cages may not be opened until judgement is passed."

"That sounds dogmatic as shit," Pax told him.

"It is the way of our people," Valoria snarled. "You know nothing, and are –"

"Willing to learn," Pax said. "If you're finally willing to talk."

Valoria didn't respond at once, bubbling with resistance. But it was clear the crowd wanted answers. She said, "Very well. We will try these criminals together. To the cages."

Pax gave her a sweet smile. "You got one big enough for me?"

The fire alarm was screaming as Casaria leapt down the steps of Westlane Station, the arse end of the K&S Underground. Probably wouldn't have been anyone here anyway. But it had been cleared out, giving him a clear run at the monster lumbering in. Landon huffed along behind him, calling for Casaria to slow down. Fuck him. Casaria skidded around a corner and along the final tunnel, breaking out onto the platform.

There it was. The stocky humanoid beast, lines glowing between the panels of its carapace, pincer limb twitching over its shoulder. Right there on the platform, where on another day there might be twenty people waiting for a train into town. Its clawed feet crunched against the tile floor.

Casaria fired, catching its stomach and dropping the creature to a knee. It reared a horrific face towards him, glowing eyes screwing narrower in fury, and it coiled to charge. He fired again, one shot, between the eyes, flinging it back to the tiles.

Landon came panting to his side, pistol ready. As Casaria steadied himself, checking the rest of the platform and the shadows beyond, the overweight agent frowned at the body. "On the platform? If there'd been people –"

"Get on your bloody radio already," Casaria said. "Where's the next one?"

"Westlane's secure," the Support tech announced, to the relief of the office. "And Agents Vinton and Bolton have arrived at Lyle Park."

"Tell them to move faster," Obrington said, readjusting a gun holster. He was the last agent not already out in the field. Not including Sam. She had training, she should be down there. Reading her look, he told her, "You're staying put. Someone's got to co-ordinate this shitshow."

The readings were clear. Though still vaguely encircling a central point where the *praelucente* was, the creatures were spread across as much as a mile's radius now. It was questionable that their small group of Operations agents could contain it. Arming the civilians and support technicians would be futile and reckless, but with every passing minute their targets moved further apart. Casaria and Landon were under Ripton, another team outside Central, one more moving down from Ten Gardens; no one covering Nothicker or Farling, yet. The *praelucente* itself had reached the outskirts of New Thornton.

As Obrington prepared to join the fray, Sam helped him into something like a bulletproof vest, which likely defended against more than bullets. He gave her sharp instructions: "You've got charges set up in some of these tunnels; if it looks to be going south, blow them. And it might be barmy to send any of the rest of you down there, but better we swing bad punches than none at all."

He indicated the civilians as he said that, and stalked off towards their rear door. So it wasn't just her thinking it. Barton and Rufaizu were watching, one grimly ready and the other itching to join the fight. Holly, behind them, looked horrified. Sam hurried to them, to offer reassurances. Barton spoke first: "This is everything I expected from your Ministry. Heavy-handed goons fumbling over distractions, while the screens go to ground. The years they spent hidden, you think they haven't got out already?"

Sam gave him a stern look. She wasn't sure it was fair to call her agents heavy-handed, nor the monsters distractions. It would be hell for Ordshaw if just one of those creatures broke free, and so far they'd prevented that. She said, "We're doing all we can. And if they could disappear that easily, would they need a distraction?"

"It'll take days before you cull even part of the horde," Barton replied. "A good portion of them will have reproduced by then, you know? Assuming the screens don't generate more themselves. In that time –"

"In that time, Pax will come back," Sam said, firmly. "And we'll be ready." Except there was no one in the office not fully occupied. She fixed on Holly. "I hate to ask, but –"

"I'll go wherever I'm needed," Holly said, giving her husband a look that said yes, he would join her. Rufaizu sprang up, too, ready for action.

"I need someone at the FTC," Sam told them. "Not within their perimeter, but close enough that if Pax gets out, if she can get the Dispenser, then . . ." She hesitated, looking across the room to the table of guns. Half-empty now, and none of it proven to hurt the *praelucente*. "We're spread thin. We need all the help we can get."

"I'll take care of her," Barton said.

"We all will," Holly corrected.

13

Pax tried to focus on the positives, such as witnessing a marvel of a society that no other human had set eyes on, rather than the creeping sense of disquiet at being the centre of attention for an entire city. *Bloody Gulliver, I am.* An explorer, admiring a miniature apartment, chrome-framed windows, modern furniture a fraction of the expected size. Tiny steps on metal fire escapes. Tiny posters advertising . . . toothpaste? Faces of Fae celebrities? And delicate little pipes and lights; even the amenities a marvel. The thousands of faces following her weren't creepy, they were . . . well, not cute, but *interesting*. Surely?

The guards led her around the side of the city, instructing her to follow slowly, no sudden movements, and she trod carefully, the Fae population floating with the single-mindedness of a school of fish. She rounded the corner of the city to see it stretching back with the variety of any metropolis. A glowing vertical sign read *CINEXPRESS*. A tiny cinema? An architectural feat even stranger stood to the left, separate from the main city and enclosed in fencing so fine it looked like a net. Four buildings the size and shape of upturned bathtubs. No prizes for guessing that was where the Fae magic happened. Pax's fingers tingled as she focused on the buildings. Was there a blue screen in there? That would be a satisfying reveal – toss back a building and announce, "Ah ha!"

She edged along the city, glancing at the vats, trying to unravel exactly what she felt. A disquiet, blurring her senses the same way the dust itself had.

"Pax!" Letty's voice drew her attention away, and she almost hit one of the Fae towers as she turned. Shouts of anger met her, a dozen Fae flying near her head, guns out. Pax threw up her hands, taking a step back, and got more shouts. Her shoe had almost hit the vats' fencing. Letty yelled from between the buildings, deep in the maze of towers, "You great bloody loon! Out of your mind coming here!"

Despite the insults, Letty sounded absolutely delighted, and as

Pax peered through the crowd to see her suspended cage, her heart lifted too. "I couldn't leave you hanging."

"You've got answers, right?" Letty shouted. "You gaggle of pricks, she's gonna change everything!"

As the Fae between them parted, creating a channel, Pax carefully repositioned herself, getting as close as she could without touching anything. More wary now than ever that *everyone* was watching her. "Thanks, Letty, no pressure . . ."

"So what is it? The Ministry figured out these monsters? Agreed to clear out the tunnels and let us down there? How are we going to fuck that Blue Angel?"

The crowd was quiet, with confused exchanges being shushed by those eager to know how, indeed, Pax was going to change their world. Valoria settled on a rooftop close to Pax's head, with her entourage of suited Fae and soldiers. Beyond them, back over the centre of the city, a pair of Fae carried Lightgate's jar. They placed it on another rooftop, near the cages, and quickly retreated.

"I had a solution," Pax said, deliberating, "but it's a little complicated." Suddenly, the suggestion that she use one of these people as bait for a monster seemed dangerous. "It involved keeping Lightgate alive, so . . ."

"We're not here to brainstorm your plans," Valoria said. "You are being given the opportunity to defend your actions. Shall we start with the most recent? Why did you kill Edwing, one of our dearest and *kindest* statesmen?"

Pax gave her a vicious look. "Why *would* I? Edwing and I were meeting to discuss how *you* wouldn't let anyone talk with us humans."

Valoria scoffed, "You plot to destroy us –"

"Never," Pax said. "The Ministry didn't, either. There was corruption within their management. The blue screens of the Sunken City, the ones that created the monsters, were responsible. Now we know, the Ministry want to settle things peacefully. But again, *you* won't talk to them."

"Because the word of a human –"

"They could've killed you, in return for the attack on Greek Street," Pax said. "You took their weapons, you know what they could've done. But they withdrew. *I* persuaded them we might need each other. Only to have you insist we have nothing more to do with each other."

Silence followed. The majority of eyes were on Valoria instead of Pax.

"All this is," Valoria said, "is confirmation of how unstable and unreliable the Ministry is. We are right to demand boundaries."

"Boundaries, sure." Pax glanced at the dust vats, concentrating on the feeling for what was in there. She wondered what she'd see, through the eyes of glo, or dust, looking into this city. Lightgate had lit up like a star; would this whole city sparkle? Would the blue of a screen show somewhere? No. She would sense that presence, for sure. That wasn't it; this governor's resistance wasn't as simple as following the screen's lies. And it was something more than vying to cement her power here. Pax thought out loud, "Obviously staying hidden from humans, and away from the Sunken City is important to you."

"Quite," Valoria agreed, like she'd scored a point.

"But it's not like we couldn't find ways to agree on it. You're avoiding us for another reason. Are you that scared of the minotaur's horde? Knowing how they go after your energy? Because I get the idea they're scared of *you*."

"Trivial questions we discarded long ago," Valoria sneered. "Our society is established, here, and that is not in question. You stand accused of murder, of the highest –"

"No – stop," Pax cut in. "I brought you Lightgate. I've told you she's responsible. If you want everyone to believe I'm your enemy then you *have* to justify why. I want the screens gone – you have the means to defeat them. You want me to be your enemy – because if you avoid humans, you avoid the Sunken City – why?"

Valoria's fuming silence confirmed Pax was on the right track. Some of the governor's suits had drifted a little away from her. The countless onlookers were raptly watching, not sure what to believe. The governor said, "We do not have to justify ourselves to *humans*."

"Okay, but can you justify yourself to them?" Pax jerked a thumb to their audience. "Do they all know your real reasons for avoiding this discussion? Your dust manufacture is done behind closed doors; how many people actually understand your connection to the Sunken City?"

"Our dust is –"

"I know," Pax said. "Specialised, unique, your own recipe. Also closely connected, somehow, to whatever the minotaur –

excuse me, what you call the *berserker* – feeds off. The energy that its masters manipulate."

"Nonsense!" Valoria erupted. "More diversions, while our septjad is unaccounted for! The monster before us is –"

"Not sure exactly what you're talking about," Pax said. "You lost control of your weapon? If that was Lightgate's ploy, then whoever she forced into helping her is unlikely to keep going with her dead. And I heard you were trying to suppress Fae across the city, so dealing with rebel Fae sure sounds like a mess *you* created."

Valoria was speechless, at last, whatever paranoia she'd been sowing undermined.

Pax continued, "It's you that's looking for a diversion. Soon as I talk about your dust?" She twisted, looming over the vats, arms out to her side, trying to take in that feeling. It wasn't much, but she got it. A little piece of the Sunken City in there, for sure. Whatever energy pervaded those tunnels was here, too. Hadn't Palleday said Valoria's family, the Magnus clan, had adapted outside the tunnels?

"That's it!" Pax turned back to the governor, eyes wide.

"Hearlon," Valoria said, "this has gone far enough. Prepare the System of True –"

"The Fae thrived in the Sunken City," Pax said, quickly. "Or at least they could have. It wasn't just the freedom of Ordshaw it offered, it was something in the tunnels, too. You farmed weird crap down there, and the blue screens were drawn to some similar opportunity. They ousted you – but if you returned, if we got rid of them, you'd have options again. You wouldn't need . . . this." She pointed at the vats.

The Fae uneasily shifted on roofs and tilted in the air. Glaring wickedly, Valoria said, "Enough!"

Pax moved closer, ignoring the fairies scattering around her. "Letty's crime wasn't talking to me or wanting a space you could all call your own – it was raising the question of the Sunken City at all. Down there, you couldn't limit dust, could you?"

"What –"

"Whatever's in there" – Pax raised her voice, pointing at the vats – "is the reason you don't want to work with humans. You're not scared of conflict; you just don't want to reclaim the Sunken City because that would expose what you use to control everyone.

What is it? The means for Fae to grow their *own* dust?"

"Utterly ludicrous!" Valoria gave a bellowing laugh to prove it. "In the generations that the Fae lived underground, you think such a truth would've eluded everyone?"

"Yeah," Pax said. "Between the bickering, and the running, and the fighting for survival. And a coup that cost the lives of those that held onto that truth. You built this city on the blood of people that wanted something better."

Pax rested a hand against the wall of a Fae tower as she drew as close to eye-level with Valoria as the city would let her. The governor stared defiantly back, big torso heaving with angry breaths. She said, "Each word you say draws you closer to sealing your fate, human. Tie your own noose."

"If it's not true then what have you got to lose? Give me the Dispenser and we'll clear out the Sunken City. You can go back –"

"We're not giving butchering humans the slightest advantage! *Enough* – execution is too kind –"

"Stop," a bald, rotund Fae with many earrings said from close to her. He regarded the governor with suspicious eyes, and he wasn't the only one. Many of her companions were distancing themselves, even some of the soldiers. The civilians watched uneasily. "These claims require due consideration."

"This human wishes to divide us," Valoria hissed. "Her words are poison – it's time our Stabilisers did their job." She raised her voice to the barrelling tone of one passing judgement. "Pax Kuranes, the human, stands accused of devouring a Fae. Further, of conspiring with the Ministry to harm our people. Of murdering Councilman Edwing, and plotting our destruction by scheming to subvert the septjad!" Many shouts of disagreement rose in protest, but Valoria continued, "Further, she admits to the murder of Lightgate!"

As the voices of discontent rose, with Letty joining in, Valoria built towards a final instruction with her soldiers readying guns. It didn't matter if all these Fae saw reason; even with a clear majority, it'd only take one of Valoria's zealous supporters to shoot Pax. Her eyes flitted back to the vats. If they could feel what she felt, if they understood –

"Escort her to the wall!" Valoria commanded. "She will be –"

Pax took a step back and drove her shoe through the roof of the closest vat. The fencing tangled around her leg, scratching where it caught above her ankle, but offered little resistance. The roof and curved walls cracked like an egg, with an eruption of dust and debris. Cringing, hoping there was no one inside, Pax drew her foot slowly back out and wafted the air clear to reveal one of the vats. It was open-topped, the substance inside slowly revolving. Glowing, faintly, a murky green-blue. A miniature conveyor channelled something mossy into the mix.

A moment of confused shock passed before Valoria screamed, "Shoot her!"

"No! She'd crush the rest of it!" another Fae roared, spreading rapid dissent as Pax crouched and grabbed moss from the wrecked building. A figure darted between shards of the crumbling building – there *was* someone in there – apparently unharmed. Half a dozen soldiers fluttered into Pax's face, guns up, as she stood, amid the yelled arguments of the Fae councillors calling for her to be shot or spared – a contest joined by the crowd. Civilians were drawing guns, and Letty yelled at Pax to get down. One soldier shouted above the others, "Hold your fire! I'm ordering you, hold your fire!"

"There's heaps of this shit in the Sunken City!" Pax said, her raised voice shaking the towers and causing Fae to stumble. She held the glowing moss up, and as the Fae grew still she realised it was affecting her. Her vision was changing, energy pulsing into her through contact alone. The Fae glowed. She put it on the roof in front of the Fae Council, taking deep breaths and blinking away the effects. Trying to ignore that sensation, she said to Valoria, "This grows down there, doesn't it? You already know that?"

The room was deathly quiet.

Valoria glared at the moss, exposed for everyone to see. The pale horror on her face confirmed Pax's hunch. Her councillors and soldiers alike looked from the moss to her, no one quite sure what to do. Valoria's bodyguard, a pistol held firmly in two hands, took a defensive step in front of her. Across the city, Letty rattled her hanging cage and shouted, "I fucking love you, Pax! Give her a fucking medal!"

Pax fought the urge to smile, or even look Letty's way, standing firm, serious, waiting for the reality to settle in. It was on Valoria now, and the governor knew it. The large Fae didn't look up from the moss. She swallowed and said, "Everything I have done has been to protect our community. What would we have, if our systems broke down. What chaos, if everyone had access –"

"Just say it's not true," a thin, sallow-faced councilman demanded. "The Fae fungus was cultured in France. There are no means to harvest it here, in Ordshaw."

From the way Valoria winced, it was clear his disapproval carried a particular sting, and even clearer that she wasn't going to deny it. "I kept peace –"

"When it suited you!" Letty shouted. "Aiding the monsters you should've resisted!"

Valoria went quiet again. Other Fae were finding their voices, muttering disbelief.

"It's a lot," Pax said, trying to speak softly. "It's complicated, but – I have a way forward. Your Dispenser was designed to destroy what you call the berserker. I want to use it –"

"It won't work," Valoria said, sounding more defeated by the second. "It'll come back. The Sunken City was never worth –"

"Upsetting your seat of power for?" Pax cut in. "Yeah, I got that. Only, I think *I* can stop it coming back. The berserker's not the boss down there, it's the blue screens. And if I can draw them together, your weapon might wipe them out. Then we can talk about recognising your people, officially. Restoring your home."

"We have our place . . ." Valoria said.

"This is too much to process now," the sallow-faced Fae decided. "You will leave –"

"We're all out of time," Pax said. "The Sunken City is unstable. It needs to be now. Seriously. What have you got to lose?"

"Our technology –"

"For heaven's sake, get on with it," the bald councillor commanded. "Let the humans fight the fight we should've fought ourselves." To Pax, he said, "You truly have the means to stop these monsters?"

Pax paused. Of course, there was still *that* problem. The maniac Fae that deserved the fate of the horde bearing down on her was dead. She needed Fae energy to drive the entire horde to one target. An invalid Fae, not long for this world? A criminal up for capital punishment? There might be brave-hearted volunteers, even. Letty, shaking her cage, ready for release. She would do it, for sure. If she only knew.

But how could Pax ask that of any of them?

And then she understood, looking at that lightly glowing moss on the roof, that there was another option. She wouldn't just draw the creatures together, she could also confirm they were there to strike. Could confirm whether or not the weapon worked. Pax had felt it, time and again, the pulse of the screens. The glow in her veins. The feeling when her mind buzzed on dust, the tingle when she picked up that moss.

She gave the suited Fae a weak smile. "I *will* have the means. With your help."

14

Outside the Fae warehouse, Pax rolled the Dispenser over in her hands. About the size of a big water bottle, all glass and brass, and as esoteric now as it had been when she'd first set eyes on it in Rufaizu's slum apartment. She said, "Hard to believe I had this in my cupboard all that time. For all the trouble it's caused."

"Probably the least hard thing to believe about you," Letty replied, sitting on her shoulder, eyeing the road ahead as they left the FTC behind. There was a car waiting, lights on, people inside. "I cannot believe you just did that."

"You and me both," Pax said.

"Put Val in her place. Stomped on a building. I thought you might go full Godzilla for a minute. Not that you didn't do enough damage. Unbalanced our whole fucking society."

Pax smiled uncomfortably.

The car doors opened, revealing the familiar bulk of Darren Barton and Holly's angular shoulders. Waving her over, Holly called out, "Thank heavens, you're alive!"

"I got it!" Pax held up the Dispenser.

"Then you might want to hurry up!" Barton said.

Taking a breath, Pax picked up her pace, trotting towards them. Another Fae flew down, announcing, "Wait!"

She recognised the voice: Edwing's protector. He kept a careful distance as he hovered near Pax, holding a plastic canister about the size of a D battery. Letty stood, saying, "Pax, meet Flynt. The only person in that whole city I could count on. Had my back. And I broke his nose."

"It's not broke," Flynt replied with a nervous smile. "And don't forget Newbry." He flew closer, holding out the canister. "This should be enough, right?"

As the Bartons approached, and Flynt backed off, Pax gently took the canister and peeled back the lid. Full of white powder.

"If that's all for you," Letty said, "it could be lethal, Pax."

"Yeah," Pax said. It was a king's ransom in Fae dust, and

reportedly higher grade than what she'd got from Palleday. Hopefully that'd make it more effective, rather than more likely to kill her. She explained for the Bartons, "If my theory's right, this'll draw those creatures. And help me stop them."

"Draw them where?" Barton frowned. "To *you*?"

"I'll explain on the way," Pax said. She looked over to Flynt. "You coming?" The tiny man looked moderately terrified, so she held out a hand to him. "I can give you a ride."

"We can't go down there . . ." Flynt said.

"Not all the danger's below ground," Letty said. "You want some adventure, don't you?" Flynt took a bracing breath and nodded. He didn't go near Pax's hand, but flew closer.

Moving towards the car, Barton said, "They're already securing a position. One of those dark spots. They'll have at least a few tunnels cordoned off by the time we catch up. You really think it'll work?"

"Hey," Pax said, "I've just overturned the Fae seat of power. I did the same for the Ministry, so I'm quietly confident I can achieve a hat-trick?"

It was a five-minute drive to the closest Sunken City entrance. Holly kept sneaking glances at Pax and the fairies in the mirrors as she drove, trying and failing to ask questions, too many to know where to begin. Rufaizu, in the back, with Barton, was less restrained. "Great to see you again, Letty, little Letty, told you we'd do big things!"

"Less of the little, you bloody idiot," Letty said, not without affection.

"I'll take the weapon," Barton said, developing his own strategy. "I might not be able to run fast, but I take a lot of knocking over. Once you've got that dust in position, or however you want to do it, I'll be ready."

"I've got a better idea," Pax said. "How about you guard the least likely tunnel for the monsters to use? I'm not going through all this only to have Holly bite my head off for letting you die."

"It was my fight long before it was yours. Before it was any of yours." Barton leant forward in his seat, a hand on Holly's shoulder. "You know I'm the best person for this. Our whole city's at risk. For Grace, I can do it."

Conflicted, Holly refused to answer.

"It's not up for discussion." Pax saved her the trouble. "Near as I'm aware, you never developed a sixth sense for what these things are, or tested how fucked up you get on Fae dust, or had the universe basically shouting at you from all directions that this is, like, your shitty fate."

It was said partly in jest but definitely not taken that way. They all realised, as one, the gravity of her own strategy. Letty glared from the dashboard and said, "You planning on facing this thing alone or something?"

"Doing what I have to," Pax said.

"I thought the Fae –" Barton started. She quickly interrupted.

"The energy that draws the creatures, it's connected to this dust, and it's something the screens sense in me. They want me dead, they've made that clear. I'm pretty sure when I'm down there, tanked up on this shit, they won't see me much different to the Fae. They won't be able to resist, whether they like it or not."

"You barely survived being touched by the minotaur the first time," Holly reminded her. "We didn't come this far to –"

"Yeah," Pax sighed. "Yeah, we did."

"What's this *pretty sure* bullshit?" Letty asked, quietly. "You're talking about pissing them off to the highest degree. You want bait, fuck it, I'm right here – anyone gets to screw them, it should be me."

Pax shook her head. "Like Holly said, I survived the minotaur before. And a human needs to set off this weapon. I can do both jobs."

"Pax, you're out of your mind if you think I'd let you do that alone," Letty told her.

"And you're out of your mind if –" Pax began, but the fairy raised an angry fist.

"We need to be sure to get all those things together. I'm not banking on you being *pretty sure* they'll come for you. They'll definitely come for me."

Pax was quiet. Exactly what she'd hoped to avoid. But she knew how stubborn Letty could be. She conceded, carefully, "Let me get in position, first. Then come down after me?"

There might still be a way, if she was quick with the dust. She could keep Letty out of this. The steely look on Letty's face said it would be difficult.

They pulled into a parking bay for a low-rise complex, near a row of garages. Obrington was waiting, jacket and shirt crumpled, slick hair out of place, flecks of dark liquid across his face. With the barest squint at the Fae on Pax's shoulder, he waved a big hand to invite them all over and opened the end garage. "Hope you've got something good for us, Kuranes. Called me away from an important meeting."

Humouring him with a weary smile, Pax held up the Dispenser. He nodded, satisfied, and stepped back to reveal a trapdoor inside the garage. They all entered and he pulled the door shut behind them. "We've got men converging on here from all directions. It's messy but we'll have you secure." He handed Pax a radio, opened the trapdoor onto a set of descending stairs, and asked, "Who's first?" When no one moved, he said, "Kidding, of course. Follow me. Not you lot." He waved a hand generally, unclear who he meant. He took a few steps down before turning back. "Come on, Kuranes. The rest of you watch this space while we handle the beasts below. Ward's on her way, with medics."

"I'm coming too," Barton said.

"And me –" Rufaizu chimed, but Holly caught his elbow, shaking her head.

Obrington looked to Pax, deferring to her the same way he did to Ward. Christ, Pax wanted them all to come, just to surround her and keep the rest of the world at bay. But it'd be madness. She said, "You've all already done enough – Darren –"

"I'm coming." As impossible as Letty. And no sign that Holly was going to stop him. Pax accepted it and Obrington gave them all a broad smile.

"Right you are," he said. He drew a second pistol from the back of his belt, chunky like a nail-gun, and offered it to Barton. "Take this. Little recoil and barely needs to be aimed in the right direction." Without further explanation, he continued into the tunnel.

Pax raised her eyebrows to Letty as a cue, expecting the fairy to insist on coming right away. But Letty jumped off Pax's shoulder and flew to land on Holly's instead. "Holler when you're ready."

Pax nodded. Sure. As if. Barton embraced Holly with a whisper of love, before they continued after Obrington.

"I should –" Rufaizu whispered, but again Holly held him back.

"You should live a full life," she told him, plainly.

He cheered them on instead. "Kill a few for me, Citizen!"

Back in the Sunken City, they entered the older variety of tunnels; wet brickwork, greening at the edges, dimly lit. Arched doorways branched off every hundred metres or so. Obrington led a winding route, constantly referring to his phone.

Their advance was interrupted by the patter of feet ahead, and the breathless arrival of an unfamiliar agent. Also splattered with blood, his tie almost undone. He saluted Obrington like a soldier, not out of habit but from being caught up in a situation he didn't fully understand. "We're clear to the black spot; Agent Vinton's up the east tunnel."

He rattled off a series of other names, agents coming as quick as they could. Casaria was a way off yet, with Landon, engaged with a tuckle. It might be five minutes or fifteen minutes before they got here. Not good enough, Obrington said; the longer they waited, the more chance a monster might break loose. Report given, the agent mumbled something encouraging to Pax then broke away to cover another passage. The trio moved forward to a hefty metal door. Obrington opened it, took a look in then stepped back.

"Bleeding weird, but it's all yours. Give me a minute to take up position myself."

Pax let him go, staring into the abyss of the empty chamber. This one was formed of four walls sloping towards each other, meeting in a sharp point, designed to house a toppled pyramid. Pax mouthed, "Why . . ."

But the why didn't matter. It was a refuge, that was all. Somewhere the monsters didn't go, making it as good a place as any for them to make a stand. If it could help her get the minotaur alone, that was all she needed. Stepping inside, she was hit by the same emptiness that had struck her in the chamber they'd visited that morning. Hell, was it only that morning, when she'd woken up secure in her poker winnings, determined to help put her city to rights, unaware she'd be a human sacrifice by nightfall. It felt like a lifetime ago.

Barton followed and voiced a shudder. The slope was shallow enough that they could go in a few paces before it started to become uncomfortable, so they stopped before the centre of the room.

"I can still take it, at least pull the trigger..." Barton held out a hand to Pax, but she only handed him the radio Obrington gave her. He frowned, seeing she had no intention of calling Letty, but he said nothing. She drew the Dispenser closer to her. Fully fuelled with moss, cranks turned and ready. She adjusted her grip, finding the button that would set it off. Resting it against her hip, she popped open the canister of dust with her other hand.

"Get out of here," Pax told Barton. "Stay safe. I'll scream if I need you." Pax forced a smile. Fairly sure she'd be screaming anyway.

As he dutifully left the room, she tossed a heap of dust into her mouth.

15

Sam hauled the garage door up and ducked into the light of the tight space. Holly and Rufaizu stood either side of the gaping trapdoor, startled to see her. She said, "You should wait in the car – I'll keep an –"

She froze, seeing the tiny woman sat on Holly's shoulder. One wing, a pistol hanging over a knee.

"Yeah, we've got it covered," the fairy said, like it was nothing. Letty, wasn't it? Sam had heard her voice before, on the phone. She couldn't close her mouth for surprise. They were here, just like that. Sitting on a civilian's shoulder – armed – "I do autographs for a tenner."

"I – just –" Sam tried to shake herself out of the surprise. This wasn't the time. She dragged her eyes away from the fairy and drew a pistol. "I'll take watch here, you can all go."

"You ever fired that thing before?" Letty said.

"I think between being here and in the car," Holly offered, more reasonably, "it's not going to make a difference where we wait. So we'll wait together, shall we?"

"All pray on the bar fly," Rufaizu said, determinedly.

Taking in their companionable looks, Sam lowered her gun, hoping she wouldn't have to shoot again today. It was more likely a fleeing human would come up these stairs than a monster, surely? A distant, horrible moan rolled out on cue, the sound of immense pipes heaving, but belonging to something far less ordinary. Beyond that, something chattered rapidly, like a bird's sinister laughter. Mercifully a long way off. A bang followed, a short, sharp gunshot. The tunnels carried sound well.

"They're converging," someone said through Sam's radio. Letty snapped around with alarm.

"What the fuck's that mean? No one –"

Sam's radio crackled again: another agent. "I've got sickles."

The thrums of energy weapons followed. From another far-off location, the same agent's voice bounced up the hall. "Two down.

Two. I'm seeing movement!"

The escalating sounds of discharging weapons blocked out his further shouts, as Holly whispered quietly, "God save them . . ."

"Oh hell no, Pax, you bitch!" Letty jumped off Holly's shoulder, readying her gun. Another Fae rose from the shadows, making Sam's eyes widen further. Letty instructed, "Guard these fools, Flynt. I'll be back soon."

"You don't –" the second Fae protested, but Letty shot down into the tunnel like a bullet. As if responding to her approach, a series of pained groans echoed up the hall.

"I can go, should go too," Rufaizu insisted, but Holly's disciplined look told him *no*.

Sam stared blankly at the stairs. Should she go herself? There were countless threats, a horde that they'd always made it their business to avoid.

"Get some!" Letty's voice rose from the tunnel with the barest crack of miniature gunfire. Flynt flew by Sam's face, making her jump, as a screeching trill came up. The fairy steadied himself in front of the tunnel, silently waiting, not so eager to be here himself. She had to do the same: they were the last line of defence, here.

The horde moved quickly.

Only minutes after the radios had announced that Pax was in the tunnel system, another message reported, "It's working."

Casaria was running, ruing the fact he had entered so far across town. He hadn't expected Pax down here. Didn't even know if Ward had intended for *her* to draw the beasts all along – surely not, she'd come to *him*. Raging, he fired into the face of a screeching creature as it launched at him from the shadows. Not even stopping to check it was dead, not caring what it was. A terror goose?

It didn't matter. He'd carve a hole in the horde all the way back to Pax, to the centre of the chaos. He'd find Pax and protect her, as he had before. Pluck her from the clutches of the *praelucente*. Protect the city, as he –

More fiends came with the clicks of bone on brick. Tapping hurriedly down the halls, racing towards him. Casaria skidded to a halt and spread his legs, aiming ahead. The clicks got louder, moving fast, and were joined by a great groan far behind them.

Come on you bastards, come to me.

With a fierce clicking cry, a bunch spider scuttled into view. Behind it, a dozen more.

Barton stood with his back to the wall, watching the corridor past the doorway to Pax's chamber, unable to keep his hand still as he clutched the Ministry gun. A weighty, impersonal device. He'd never shot anything before. He hoped he wouldn't have to now. Better that Pax's plan not work; that the horde not come, and they give this up. He could track the minotaur the way he used to, quietly, with minimal conflict.

When the sounds started he knew that wasn't going to happen. They were advancing with the wretched shrieks and scratching claws of unholy beasts. Ones that would kill Holly and Grace, given the chance.

The Ministry men were firing, far off. One man was shouting, somewhere. The creatures roared closer before going quiet as they were cut down.

They were definitely aiming for Pax, with a speed and fury Barton had never encountered before, funnelled between gaps in the Ministry's defences. The men firing on the monsters would be making way for the light of the approaching minotaur. Let that one pass, as they culled everything else.

The clucking of a glogockle sounded in an adjacent tunnel.

His old friends, it had to be one of them.

But an electric discharge silenced that. Then came the rapid patter of something else, scraping on the floor. Barton aimed down the corridor and called to Pax, "Get ready!"

A sickle raced into view, a slick-skinned centaur with pincer arms stretching ahead of its gnashing zip-jawed mouth. Barton roared a challenge and pulled the trigger. The gun emitted a dazzling ball of blue light that startled him into throwing his arm, the projectile hitting the ceiling with a snap. He blinked to refocus. The sickle was halfway to him, about to pass Pax's door. He fired again and the second shot burst over its shoulder. The sickle kept going, ignoring Pax's chamber. Barton threw the gun down and hopped from one foot to another. The other being his bad ankle, which flamed with pain and made him trip.

Just in time – the sickle leapt the last few metres and its great pincers narrowly missed his head, slashing his shoulder. He rolled under it, down onto his rear, its bulk taking up most of the tunnel above. He threw his fists and knees up as the sickle fought its own momentum to twist back at him, mouth snapping. He caught it with a good strike to its gut, but barely slowed the thing down. It slashed at him, a blade-like limb slicing his face, and he cried out. Pax shouted, "Darren!"

"Stay there!" he yelled, blocking the monster with his forearm. It was heavier, stronger than him, and its jagged teeth bit close to his nose. He yelled at it and with a last effort drove his forehead into its jaws. It shook off the blow, regrouping, and screeched into his face. But the screech was abruptly cut off as the lower part of its jaw shattered, struck from the side. As it turned it was struck again, in the centre of its head, with a little snap of gunfire.

Barton winced as the creature collapsed beside him. Letty sped down the hall, firing two more shots into it for good measure, shouting, "Pax you motherfucker, you –"

A great cascade of noise made her turn back. Barton struggled to push himself up as a sea of shadows followed the fairy into the tunnel; at floor level, three-feet armoured bugs, giant roaches. Above them, a flock of leathery-winged, skeletal-faced birds. Flying to Pax's doorway, Letty shot at the mass expertly, dropping a handful of birds, but her bullets chimed off the roaches' shells. One scuttled up a wall near her, feelers probing ahead.

Barton grabbed it before the thing could reach the fairy, twisting it away from the wall and pounding it with his fist, the shell cracking. Letty fluttered by his head, reloading, and fired again into the approaching swarm. A screech drew Barton's attention back the other way; some other horror coming from the opposite direction. The tunnel was alive with movement, everything the Ministry hadn't held back descending on them – and as he shouted, punching, kicking, surrounded by clawing limbs, something serpentine slipped past, into Pax's chamber.

"Missed one!" he yelled, and Letty zipped past him, firing away.

Twisting to try and keep track, Barton was caught from somewhere below and dragged down, smacking a knee into the floor. Something tore at his upper arm, pushing him further down, and more roaches scuttled in – overwhelming him. He roared again, thrusting back at them with all he had –

A brilliant blue light burst through, and the shadowy mass of advancing creatures subsided with the speed of retreating spiders. Roaches rounded the far corner as ethereal tendrils of electric blue snaked into the hallway, the first hints of the Sunken City's vilest monster. It came in tentacles of light, exactly as Pax described, and Barton stared with wonder. Without the goggles glo had given him, he saw it now, in all its blinding glory. Definitely not a minotaur.

Time had not stood still for Pax, not like before; not once she realised that with the intense power of the dust high, she could *control* this feeling. Once she latched onto that, after the initial stretched-out sounds of advancing creatures and devastating weapons, she sped it up, the screeches and scratches reaching helium pitches. Then slowed it down to something like normal. She could feel the activity better than ever: every creature moving, even the people. The vocal agent, nervous and firing his weapon too soon. Obrington, businesslike, just doing a job. Landon, dispatching one creature after another with dogged determination – be good to get home again. Good to get home. Then Casaria, his aura unmistakable, tightening like a spring, wrapped in something that blurred excitement with deep, unspeakable fear. And Barton. Pure. More afraid of failing than dying.

Her feelings stretched to Sam Ward at the top of the stairs. Hopeful, quietly dreaming of success. Keeping a silent tally of possible deaths. Worried for her. Everyone worried for her. Them watching, waiting, and the others fighting, overwhelmed by the pressing monsters, all of one thought. *She's counting on me.*

Then Letty. A furious little ball of lightning rapidly approaching.

Hell, she should've stayed out of here. But she was in the thick of the fight, gunning down creatures fearlessly, and Pax sensed, with relief, that the horde wasn't going after her. They felt Pax, as she felt them; the dust worked, she was their target.

It was coming closer by the second, her nemesis. The beast, minotaur, berserker, *praelucente*. She felt its true heart – and knew it to be none of those things. There was nothing conscious in it at all, it wasn't a malevolent force, it was pure hunger. An unthinking, unfeeling parasite that would drain the world if it wasn't trapped here. If it didn't have the limitations the Sunken City held over it.

And with it came the screens.

All the screens, she felt each of them as individuals, racing through the city as fast as the beast itself, gliding over surfaces. Drawn impossibly along, some against their will, unable to resist her promise: combining the Fae dust and whatever part of the Bright Veins' magic ran through her, Pax was a magnet to them. And as they flooded towards her, she started to understand them. Their fears, their wants, their burning, arrogant scorn for humanity. Pax crouched, hands on the floor, feeling the whole system of the Sunken City, like the tunnels were a part of her. She started to get it. Even this room – this black spot, dark in her mind, fit a necessary part of the whole. She couldn't put it in words, but it made sense, she *felt* it.

Various energies competed for dominance, some with truly ancient roots. The screens, connected to the walls, locked it in place, preying, simply preying. The screens behaved according to their nature – aggressive, devious. They formed patterns of unthinking deception, manipulation that came as naturally to them as the design of a hive came to a bee. Even now, unhinged by their surge, ideas formed: *blame the Young One for theft – release the criminals from prison – poison her family –*

Then came the sickle, charging down the hall. Past her doorway.

Barton shouted. The fight going badly.

Pax couldn't move to help, caught as she was in the grip of the entire energy of the Sunken City. She cried out, but was fused to the spot, her own stubborn mission holding her as much as the conflicting sea of life energies.

Worse followed the sickle, a flood of creatures rolling over each other to fill the tunnel and claim her. Shapes passed the doorway in rapid, ferocious flurries, Letty out there now, firing without remorse, Barton doing all he could to keep from drowning. And then one shape slid in, a jagged-spined snake of a creature, red eyes fixing on her. It shuddered on the threshold, pained to enter, but pressed on, revealing a mouth of crooked, spiky teeth. Behind it, another monster crept around the entrance, a dozen limbs venturing in.

Pax stared, transfixed, unable to move as the world's energy held her.

The snake's head popped like a tomato and it dropped lifeless.

A second later the other monster was thrown back into the tunnel, shot off the doorframe. Letty hung in the air between them, a ball of light in Pax's warped vision. The fairy gave her an angry look, but Pax smiled back as time stood still.

Then something changed. Letty darted over and landed on Pax's head. She could feel her crouched, reloading, as the shapes outside hurriedly retreated.

A gentle glow suffused the doorway, a beautiful wash of blue. Gradually the minotaur stretched into view, intensifying to its full blinding self as it slid inwards, bright as a star. Pax slowed time again, one arm covering her eyes and the other closing over Letty, like her fist might protect the fairy. She knew the beast, what it wanted, what it would take. And they came with it, the blue screens swarming in, surrounding her. It hurt them, entering this chamber, but they couldn't resist. They called to the minotaur and its limbs stretched into them, anchoring into a score of locations around Pax with terrific lightning cracks. They didn't think in language but she understood: *her, her, of the human of the Fae, suck her dry*. Fear and hatred mixed with hunger. A tentacle quested towards Pax at tremendous speed, and she let it come, as she took the Dispenser in her hands.

Her senses slowed it right down. Almost to stillness.

Letty shouted something, low, too slow and muffled against Pax's hand to be heard.

Were they all here? Pax couldn't tell, their power boxing her in. Dozens, at least, had joined the feast. It had to be enough. She could wait no longer. With a defiant cry, the minotaur's grasp inches from her, Pax pulled the trigger and the Dispenser exploded forward. She felt that energy, too. Understood the raw power of the weapon, and exactly what it would do.

Cancel them out with a fearsome short-circuit.

The screens pulsed in realisation as the charge hit the minotaur's foremost limb and rolled through it. None of them was fast enough to detach from its suckling position, as the room was filled with devastating white light. Time accelerated again, faster than before, playing catch-up, and the terrific energy that burst through the room hit Pax full force as she screamed.

Abandoning an approaching host of scuttling creatures, Casaria ran towards the sound. The walls shook around him, dust tumbling from the ceiling and cracks spreading like it might all come down. He ran, and ran, vaulting a hound that crossed his path. Around a corner, striking out as he passed a veering sickle, the thing moving in the opposite direction, afraid. Finally he skidded into a hallway filled with a deadly scent. It bit at his eyes, a wall of smell he had to fight his way through, the tunnels quaking about him. Barton on the floor, bleeding, wheezing. Casaria ran past to reach Pax in darkness.

Pax, lying on her back, one arm out to the side with the discarded Fae weapon. The other on her stomach, fingers twitching – not with life, but being pushed, a fairy trapped within fighting her way out. Letty squirmed her way free of Pax's hand to look up at Casaria. She snarled, "Stop gawking and save her while I finish the rest of those fuckers."

16

The ground quaked, rattling Sam off her perch on a step. It shook for a full minute as Sam and Holly moved away from the stairs, garage door rattling. As the world rumbled gradually to a standstill, the sounds of the Sunken City were quietened. The remaining shrieks and groans came with a questing quality.

Then a horrific smell burst out from the tunnel, making Sam gag and cover her face. Somewhere between rotting meat and burnt hair. She coughed on the fumes. A monster screeched with murderous rage.

Flynt shuddered as though he could shake off the smell, and said, "That's it. That's got to be it."

The radio crackled. Obrington: "Did you do it, Pax?"

The answer came from Casaria. "It's gone – Pax –"

"I – I need to go," Flynt said, drawing a miniature pistol. Despite his frightened tone, he flew into the tunnels. Sam watched as Rufaizu ran after the fairy, whooping like a jester, "With you, I'm with you!"

A moment later, the sound of a firecracker cut short a horrible groan.

Somewhere further away, Letty's voice screamed insults.

Holly met Sam's eyes with quiet, frightened wonder. "What now?"

Sam had no answer.

One by one, as the sounds died away, the agents exited via the tunnel, and the garage became increasingly tight. Three of the new agents left with little to say for themselves, consummate professionals even as they were plastered with burn marks and blood. One came out shaking, wide eyes filled with fear as he collapsed against the rear wall. Landon arrived and went to comfort him, after checking Sam was okay. The agent who'd been making all the noise came next, erratically recounting all they'd been through. "Should've seen them – worst I've seen – just kept coming –"

Obrington calmed him down with a few brotherly pats on the back, his presence carrying an air of steadiness. He leant against a wall himself, though, and exhaled tremendous relief. His left hand was covered in blood, dripping at a terrible rate. When Sam approached him he dismissed her. "The girl comes first."

Casaria and Barton carried Pax up, each under an arm.

Her skin was dark, marred all over by something like ash, her clothes singed. Her head rolled forwards, no support from her neck, her feet dragging along the floor. Sam and Holly leapt towards her together, taking her from the men, lowering her.

"She's breathing," Barton assured. "It's okay, she's breathing."

Nothing about her looked okay.

Sam crouched to check her face, lifted her head from behind, tried to open an eye. It rolled in the socket, away from her, then back.

"We got a medic?" Casaria demanded. "Where's our fucking medic?"

"Outside," Obrington said, listing towards the garage door. He grumbled, betraying anxiety, as he opened the door. "The fuck did she do? I thought she had this covered."

"Fuck you, why wasn't someone with her?" Casaria frantically answered. "You all went down – didn't even consult me, left her with a fucking civilian!"

Obrington's eyes warned him off, but he said nothing.

"Easy," Barton said, a hand on Casaria's arm. Telling him it was done, over. Obrington waved to an ambulance outside and two paramedics hurried forwards.

Casaria watched, quiet for a moment, tears on his cheeks. As they passed him, his eyes were drawn to Sam. He hissed, "You let her do this. Her? I could've handled it, you *knew* –"

"This was *her* plan," Obrington said, as the paramedics crouched. "Kuranes chose this. But everyone – you did a fantastic job."

Sam stared, not so sure how fantastic any job could be that left a young woman in a state like that. The paramedics were fast at work, checking her vitals, getting her in the right position, reporting to one another.

"Should've been me," Casaria said, almost in a whimper, circling them. Sam regarded him uncertainly, no idea what to do, what to say, until she caught the eye of one of Obrington's grim agents over Casaria's shoulder. She nodded to him, *do something*, and the man obliged.

Marks nudged Casaria, and he flinched from the touch but calmed when he regarded the scarred man with some kind of recognition. The agent whispered something Sam didn't catch, but the gist was clear. We've done our bit, time to let them do theirs. The fellow agent's assurance somehow settled Casaria, as he looked beyond Marks to the rest of them, blackened with blood and burns, a host of people who'd given their all.

"You did great," Sam whispered her own summary. "You all did."

Barton tightened his grip around Holly as they watched Pax.

"She's alive," the lead paramedic said. Big bushy ginger beard, Scottish accent – Sam recognised him. But his face was not reassuring. "Got a strong pulse, responsive. Superficial burns."

"But . . ." Sam prompted.

"But, you tell me." He pulled up Pax's top, around her midriff. Lines snaked over her gut with the clawlike spread of varicose veins. Gently glowing, under the skin. A string of curses went through the garage as the medic said, "I don't know what that is – what to do about it –" Even as he spoke, the glowing faded. The light dimmed as though being absorbed back into her body. An illusion that was never there. "What the hell happened to her?"

"We won," Pax rasped, with effort.

Everyone surged towards her as one, to embrace her, thank her, touch her, anything, but Obrington forced them all back with a quick, sharp command: "Give her space, for pity's sake! Pax. You're still with us. You sure it's done?"

Pax considered it, barely opening her eyes, then nodded.

"How do you feel?" Sam asked.

"Probably worse than I look," she answered wearily. She drooped back into the ground. "I'd like to go home."

Casaria tried to approach again, but Marks stayed him with a hand. Not now.

"I've done for them," Letty shouted, speeding breathless up the tunnel. "You'd better have fucking done for her."

The crowd parted around her as she flew into its centre, face and clothes awash with blood. She ignored the startled medics and agents to hover down to Pax, chest heaving, shaking with violent energy. "Fuck – they did a number on you."

Pax raised a creaking hand, offering a thumbs-up, and said quietly, "I'm fine."

Letty stared, a furious moment. Then her gory face stretched to a smile. "Fine, she says. Someone take a photo. Call the press. Pax: gets fried, pretends she's okay with it."

Pax turned her hand and raised her middle finger instead.

EPILOGUE

From the notes of Holly Barton:

In the two months since Rufaizu first walked into Pax's life, everything had changed, and yet Ordshaw remained mostly the same. With a final set of tremors to complement the series that had already shaken the city, the MEE, under Sam Ward's guidance, came clean. Under the guise of a proxy gas company. They explained that an old, disused system of tunnels and pipelines had been breached during routine explorations. Once blame had been duly assigned, the big story became the City Council's talks to sell a small section of the tunnel system to a nightclub owner, to enliven Ordshaw's South Bank and bolster the city's coffers. With those promises, people lost interest in exactly where these tunnels came from, generally assuming they formed part of an abandoned third metro line.

Sam Ward managed a meticulous cleansing of the tunnel system, ensuring all the vicious phenomena were removed. The task was smaller than anyone imagined, thanks to the help of bands of roaming Fae and the unexpected widespread decline in the health of the creatures underground, once the *praelucente* (minotaur / berserker) was gone.

And it was, assuredly, gone. The Ministry's scans showed no further "novisan" surges. With that settled, Acting Deputy Director Obrington passed his position back to Sam. Deservedly so, he said, though he hoped to see her in London one day, where she could be put "to real use". She was happy to stay in Ordshaw for the time being, now the Fae were talking to her, and it appeared that the city was due some exciting changes. She became the Ministry's youngest ever (and *only* female) regional director.

Communication with the Fae remained limited, but even the slightest trickles were milestones. They entered into quiet negotiations about which parts of the Sunken City the Ministry were willing to trade off, and made agreements as to the Fae's behaviour in society at large. Generally, the status quo of *we leave each other alone* was properly ratified through MEE Management and Parliament. Things moved slowly due to the Fae having their own issues to resolve: it was understood that a new voting system was established to bring in a more democratic leadership. The MEE's Raleigh Commission, meanwhile, was decommissioned, and the director, Lord Tarrington, established a new governing body with better vetting. The first point of order was to decide a title and structure for this group, which was to be workshopped by the following spring.

That suited Sam Ward and Ordshaw just fine. She was left with general command of the Ordshaw Ministry, which was more than occupied with unravelling the complex background of the Sunken City. She kept the Barton family involved in this, as they had all proved themselves to be potential Ministry material – even the daughter might be considered once she came of age (should her mother allow it). Darren was happy to convalesce for a time, returning to his ordinary life, but Holly proved less passive. She valiantly took charge of documenting and analysing Apothel's book in her spare time, and became a frequent visitor to both the Ministry office and botanist Dr Mandy Rimes' renovated telegraph station. Between these visits and extensive research, with guidance from the eternally grateful Ministry, Holly began drafting accounts of events that would prove both entertaining and educational. She insisted that, given time, her husband would be happy to offer his full input, too. He was just being bull-headed as usual.

Rufaizu also accepted a Ministry offer, once it was made clear no one wanted to kill him. He came to their offices to receive general tuition and guidance in applying for a job, but despite Holly's best efforts to civilise the boy, his old habits resurfaced after things quietened down. One evening, he didn't return to the Bartons' house, and a rumour emerged that he had stolen from someone in West Quay. A letter arrived quashing everyone's worst fears, written in his familiar scrawl; he thanked the Bartons for their hospitality and informed them that he had "found ghouls behind Iceland". It was postmarked from York.

Agent Landon, the man Ward credited with the most world-weary knowledge amongst her staff, and an infrequent contributor to Holly's tireless accounts, claimed the Ministry had no interests in Iceland. However, he did reveal a general knowledge of more widespread activities that Sam Ward suspected existed beyond Ordshaw. He couldn't say exactly what was going on around the world, only *where* it was happening. Many international hotspots, including known Fae locations, have drawn MEE attention, but to our knowledge a bigger, clearer picture is yet to be drawn.

Against such concerns, Sam Ward began her own investigations (with specialist support from Holly, experienced in such matters after years toiling in offices) into the Ministry's wider interests. A chief question was how the big corporations were encroaching on their work. Ward had had only the smallest glimpse of Duvcorp's capabilities, but it was enough to worry her, and Obrington's parting advice was that she steer well clear of them in future. So, she made attempts to touch base with the company, but they pleaded ignorance regarding all concerns she raised and insisted that she had never had a meeting with their COO. When she raised this with Management, they echoed the attitudes she'd previously encountered surrounding the Fae and the Sunken City. It was above her pay grade. Ward vented frustrations about this to Cano Casaria, and he suggested they break into the Duvcorp offices and see for themselves what was going on.

Casaria had many such suggestions, which for the most part were, as Ward had come to understand, his way of saying he was up for whatever tasks might be thrown at him. Eager to prove himself, he had the enthusiasm of a loyal dog. Yes, he was still awkward, and mostly antisocial, and no, Ward had not encouraged his clear infatuation with her; but something in him had changed, leaving him somehow more desperate to please. Perhaps he regretted that his more unruly behaviour had cost him a chance to actually be a hero. Or perhaps he simply, finally, understood his place in the grand scheme of things. On one occasion, Ward told him he'd done good work and he was later heard crying quietly in the toilets. Much as Ward wanted to better understand what he was going through, she didn't want it quite enough to get closer to him. It would come with time, she imagined.

Or it wouldn't.

There were bigger, more important enigmas for her to unravel.

Chief amongst them was how to handle our dear Pax.

*

Pax huffed as she dropped onto the bench, finally. Sweat ran down her back and her face had to be red as a beet. It didn't help to hear Letty laughing at her discomfort. "You bloody walk it, instead of flying, see how you feel."

"I could walk it a thousand times over, the time it takes you," Letty answered, landing on Pax's knee. She pointed at Sam Ward. "You've got a long way to go before reaching this robot's standards."

Ward smiled guiltily back, standing off to the side, pretending to admire the view.

The view *was* impressive: Black Crest offered an incredible vista of the Drumdon Hills and Ordshaw combined. The climb was a hundred times worse than Pax's little hill in Weirway Park, which she now appreciated barely constituted exercise. She would never motivate herself to come here alone. But in this company, she was exposed to a new perspective: sweeping greens and oranges and a city as contained at this distance as the FTC had been up close. Still, out of breath and irritated that the others weren't, Pax preferred not to admit it was worth it. "I could see this on the internet."

"It's not the same," Ward replied. She always bit at such comments, and Letty always shared a knowing smirk with Pax when she did. Obvious enough for the Ministry lady to notice, otherwise where would be the fun? Ward caught them smiling and said, "Well you're getting much better, anyway. We only stopped once this time."

"When I get all the way up in one," Pax said, "do we get to never do it again?"

"Grow a pair," Letty said. "Hark at Ordshaw's champion, eats fireballs for breakfast but runs scared at gentle inclines."

Pax went to poke her and Letty hopped out of the way, staying close enough to punch playfully back at her finger. The fairy floated up in front of her face.

"In all honesty," Ward said, "I hope you'll stick at it. You're doing so well. You know how much potential you have?"

Pax eyed her warily. Another veiled suggestion that she delve back into the life that had left her twice burnt to a crisp. Made her a murderer of monsters and fairies and a deposer of corrupt regimes. Given her some kind of psychic gift, now dormant, and a modest drip of disability pay that was close to dry. As if being able to climb a hill would make her more likely to survive any easier in future.

"I'm thinking about it," Pax said. And it was true. She was considering that she definitely did not want a boss, nor to wear a suit to work, nor to write reports for anyone or do any work for people who would knowingly withhold information from her. Nor did she want to stick to work hours, or be expected to be somewhere at certain times, or talk in a certain way or anything like that. But the problem was, she also found it hard to sit at the card table, day in and day out, without her mind wandering. Like, maybe making a living wasn't enough. And Ward assured her of compensations: leeway with certain workplace demands, and a steady pay she could shove in Dad's face. But much more than that. Answers. More excitement than hitting a Royal Flush. People cheering her name, desperate for her to save them?

Part of that made her cringe, but then it also gave some queer warm feeling.

She'd saved this city from something no one understood. She'd visited a city of Fae. Where did you go from that?

Letty's visits to her apartment frequently reminded her of that conundrum. Letty had responsibilities of her own, what with the Fae expanding underground, with new towers going up and new enterprises emerging. That kept her from having too much time to spend goading Pax, but it also peppered their drinking sessions with weighted comments like, *Making a difference feels orgasmic, doesn't it?*

"What you want to do," Letty told Ward, "is not to keep asking what she wants. It's to just give it to her. She doesn't know what the fuck she wants."

"I know what I don't want," Pax countered.

"Bullshit, you don't even know that."

Ward looked thoughtful, warming to Letty's idea. "Well. There's a few cases that might interest you, Pax. I know you've got questions."

"That's why we're out here." Pax flapped a hand to dismiss the surrounding beauty of nature. "I always get you to spill fresh gossip to tide my curiosity over."

"But that only works when *I* have the answers. I need *you* to figure out some for us. *If* you'd grace us."

"Hey," Letty said. "I think we're exposing the snark in this square."

"Thanks." Ward took it as a compliment. "Pax, the blue screens are gone, as far as we know, but we still have explaining to do. We don't know that they were confined to Ordshaw. We haven't explained the apparitions that Apothel and Barton reported, things we've never seen or understood. The drummer horse and the invisible proclaimer?"

"What happened to Rik Greivous?" Pax brought up a bugbear, lightly.

"Exactly!" Ward said. "And we don't know how you came to sense novisan, or what really affects that. Your reactions to Fae dust . . ."

"Those experiments are on our to-do list, trust me," Letty said, and Pax smiled. She did not intend to try dust again any time soon. Eventually, maybe . . .

Ward turned to take more inspiration from the view. "And Duvcorp's experiments really trouble me. Their technology intersects closely with ours, and we're on their radar as much as they're on ours, now. And they're not the only ones. Mogami Industries, Warlowe, Raystaten – they all have projects we're not privy to, and Management insists I leave them alone."

"I'm not going to war with multinationals," Pax said. "That's *much* scarier than what we've been through."

"You wouldn't be alone," Ward said. "And it brings its own rewards, I'm sure. An international agent just yesterday requested permission to visit Ordshaw regarding Mogami. He's been to Detroit, Tokyo, Berlin, and now he sees an angle to pursue here."

"Sounds like he's bullshitting you to get a round-the-world ticket," Pax said. Ward didn't look amused, so she added, "That's my thinking at work, Sam. You want me on board, you'd better believe I'll hold your jet-setting international agents to account."

"I would like that," Ward insisted, seriously. "And if you'd put joking aside I think you'd see you want it, too."

"But if we put joking aside," Pax groaned loudly, "what have we got left?"

Ward went quiet. Letty gave Pax a mock sad look. The fairy drifted down onto Pax's shoulder and whispered, "You're a cruel, hard person, Pax. How much longer are you gonna keep her waiting?"

Pax stared at the back of Ward's head. Letty knew it as well as her, of course. She couldn't walk away. Had no intention of walking away. She said, "Until I can run a bit faster and further, at least. If we're gonna take on the world, it's not going to be with me bent double vomiting."

Letty gave her an assaying look. "You poor, deluded fool. It's going to be so much worse than that."

A Note from the Author

Thanks for sticking with me through the Sunken City Trilogy, and I hope you've enjoyed the ride. As you might have guessed, there's more to come – and you can return to the world of Ordshaw right now with the next book in the series, *The City Screams*.

I love to hear from my readers and do my best to keep everyone informed on my progress; you can find me on various platforms below. For special offers, and to be the first to hear about Ordshaw and related news, join my mailing list via my website.

And fresh from reading *The Violent Fae*, please take a moment to leave a review online (even if it's short – to be concise is a virtue, after all). As an independent author, a few positive words from fans like you make all the difference in spreading the word!

www.phil-williams.co.uk

You can connect with me through:
Facebook: **www.facebook.com/philwilliamsauthor**
Twitter: **www.twitter.com/fantasticphil**
Email: **phil@phil-williams.co.uk**

About the Author

Phil Williams is the author of the Ordshaw, Estalia and Faergrowe series. Living in Sussex, UK with his wife, he also writes educational books and spends a great deal of time walking his impossibly fluffy dog, Herbert.

ACKNOWLEDGEMENTS

The Violent Fae is the culmination of a project that started long before *Under Ordshaw*, and I must repeat the thanks that were due in the first two books. Once more, this book has been perfected through the careful attention of my editor Carrie O'Grady, and without her you would've had a much more meandering opening to this novel. (Though if you'd have liked to have seen Pax wandering around empty tunnels and having pointless chats over dinner with the Bartons, sorry!)

Massive thanks also to the readers, reviewers and fellow writers who have inspired me to continue through their warm reception of and support for my work. My advance readers throughout these books deserve great praise, Brian Busby, Eric Crawford, Lea Pert, Stephen Fielding, Ami Agner, Jan Drake, Yvonne Evans, Adawia Asad and Heathyr Fields. Bloggers who have been excellent supporters include Maddelana from *Space and Sorcery*, Steph from *Bookshine and Readbows* and Hayley Hart of *Paperplanes Reviews*. And extra special thanks to Lynn Williams from *Lynn's Books* who first gave Under Ordshaw a chance under the SPFBO contest. All these blogs are well worth checking out, give them your patronage!

In the course of writing the Sunken City trilogy I've also developed an excellent network of supportive authors who've helped me along the way, including Phil Parker, Jon Auerbach, Dave Woolliscroft, Carol Park, Josh Erikson, Travis Riddle, Kayleigh Nichol, Devin Madson and Scott McKinnon.

If I'm missing anyone you have my massive apologies and I'll include you in the next one; there'll certainly be plenty more.

Finally, repeated thanks to my brothers Nick and Alex who diligently read my most pointless nonsense, and above all my wife, Marta, who every day keeps me from receding into the despairing depths of the fantasy mind.

ALSO BY PHIL WILLIAMS

ORDSHAW SERIES
UNDER ORDSHAW
BLUE ANGEL

THE CITY SCREAMS
Tova's getting her hearing back. She's going to wish she wasn't. Alone in Tokyo for experimental ear surgery, she discovers a voice in her head telling her it's where she comes from that makes her special. Can she survive long enough to find out why?

ESTALIA SERIES
WIXON'S DAY
Marquos drifts through the cloud-concealed Empire of Estalia, searching for hope of a better future. In the Deadland of the North, they say the sky is clear, and the stars shine. But Marquos is about to find out how dark the world can be.

BALFAIR'S CONFINEMENT
Deni dreams of escaping her arduous life. When her master drags something from the swamp and excludes her from his secretive project, she finally sees her chance. She will do whatever it takes to break free – even if it means trusting in the warmongering Guard.

AFTAN WHISPERS
When Tyler meets a girl with enemies in the highest places, his life gets complicated fast. Deni isn't afraid to kill, and she's got a secret that could tear open the sky. Tyler soon discovers that the Empire's guardians are their most dangerous foe.

www.ingramcontent.com/pod-product-compliance
Lightning Source LLC
Chambersburg PA
CBHW021643110726
47902CB00007B/1801